The Mercy Rule

Books by Perri Klass

FICTION

Recombinations

I Am Having an Adventure: Stories

Other Women's Children

Love and Modern Medicine: Stories

The Mystery of Breathing

The Mercy Rule

NONFICTION

Treatment Kind and Fair: Letters to a Young Doctor
(Art of Mentoring)

*Every Mother Is a Daughter: The Neverending Quest for
Success, Inner Peace, and a Really Clean Kitchen*
(Recipes and Knitting Patterns Included)

Two Sweaters for My Father: Writing About Knitting

*Quirky Kids: Understanding and Helping Your Child Who
Doesn't Fit In—When to Worry and When Not to Worry*

*A Not Entirely Benign Procedure:
Four Years as a Medical Student*

Baby Doctor: A Pediatrician's Training

The Mercy Rule

PERRI KLASS

HOUGHTON MIFFLIN COMPANY

BOSTON • NEW YORK

2008

For information about permission to reproduce
selections from this book, write to Permissions,
Houghton Mifflin Company, 215 Park Avenue South,
New York, New York 10003.

www.houghtonmifflinbooks.com

Library of Congress Cataloging-in-Publication Data
Klass, Perri, date.
The mercy rule / Perri Klass.
p. cm.
ISBN 978-0-618-55596-3
1. Women pediatricians—Fiction. 2. Adult children of
dysfunctional families—Fiction. 3. Problem families—
Evaluation—Fiction. 4. Parenting—Fiction. I. Title.
PS3561.L248M47 2008
813'.54—dc22   2008007271

Book design by Melissa Lotfy

Printed in the United States of America

MP 10 9 8 7 6 5 4 3 2 1

Excerpt from *One Fish Two Fish Red Fish Blue Fish* by Dr. Seuss®
& copyright © by Dr. Seuss Enterprises, L.P. 1960, renewed
1988. Used by permission of Random House Children's Books,
a division of Random House, and by permission of Dr. Seuss Enterprises, L.P.

For my remarkable daughter,
Josephine Charlotte Paulina Wolff, with love

THOMASINA: If you could stop every atom in its position and direction, and if your mind could comprehend all the actions thus suspended, then if you were really, *really* good at algebra you could write the formula for all the future; and although nobody can be so clever as to do it, the formula must exist just as if one could.

SEPTIMUS: (*Pause*) Yes. (*Pause.*) Yes, as far as I know, you are the first person to have thought of this.

— TOM STOPPARD, *Arcadia*

The Mercy Rule

1

Silent Auction

Item 37: Three bottles ('91, '92, & '94) Von Heifetz Cabernet
Sauvignon. As true connoisseurs know, Franz and Leonora Von
Heifetz have for a decade been making astonishing Cabernet
Sauvignon from their small family vineyard hidden in a secret
lush section of the Napa Valley. You have to taste this to believe it. Their wines are not sold in stores but are available only
through their longstanding mailing list. Donated by: Henry
and Rifka Blackmountain. Estimated value: $330. Opening
bid: $90.

"Look, please, I'm serious," says Greg. "I'll do anything. I'll clean
out the refrigerator. I'll take your car in to be serviced—how's that?
Your inspection sticker runs out next month—I'll get you a new
one. Deal?"

Lucy would never be able to tell him this without feeling silly,
but it is one of those mornings, increasingly rare, when she feels
beautiful and graceful in all she does. All her adult life, these mornings have come to her unexpectedly, maybe in the heartburn-rid-
den seventh month of pregnancy, maybe halfway through a dreary
business trip to Philadelphia, and now today. She woke this morn-

ing to the sweet, slightly chilly air of a Saturday in late October, of fall in New England at its lightest and loveliest, full of change and possibility, and she rose from her bed, L.L. Bean ski pajamas and all, like the swan queen, like Princess Aurora, like the sugar plum freaking fairy. In another time and place and life, she would have gone after Greg, who tends to wake early, even on weekends, and she would have dragged him away from whatever stage of coffee preparation, since he is one of those buy-special-beans-and-keep-them-in-the-freezer-and-store-them-only-in-glass-and-grind-them-right-before-you-turn-on-your-two-hundred-dollar-machine fanatics. She would have hauled him back to bed, coffee-smelling fingers and all, and it would not be the first time in their marriage that she would have remarked on the similarities between that coffee smell and certain aromas that at certain moments can be inhaled in the general vicinity of his crotch. But that, among many other things, is absolutely and completely out of the question when the ten-year-old is already up and searching loudly for her shin guards and her cleats and demanding of the world whether anyone, anyone, *anyone*, has thought to wash her soccer team T-shirt. And the six-year-old, who has already poured muesli over most of the kitchen table, heaping it into hills and valleys according to some topological map in his mind, is aware that today is a birthday party day—although, to be honest, almost every Saturday is a goddamn birthday party day.

So here is Lucy, washed and brushed and dressed, mopping up the muesli with a paper towel and still feeling beautiful and graceful. She grabs the cereal box and holds it open at the side of the kitchen table, nudges the muesli over the edge and back into the waiting box. Why not?—tomorrow Freddy can pour it all out again. Why spend $4.79 on a new box, she thinks, folding the top flaps closed and noting the price, and why can't we buy him Rice Krispies if he's just going to pour it out on the table and play with it?

"Net wt four hundred grams," Freddy reads off the same box, pronouncing it to sound like "nitwit." It's one of his favorite terms. "That's not quite one point two cents per gram."

Greg is standing at the refrigerator, holding it open, surveying the mess. "How about this one?" he asks. "Four half-used bottles of ketchup, all vintage within the last three years—we think. For the last several decades, the Heinz Company has been making a remarkably consistent tomato product at their secret hydroponic family tomato patch. Hold your own ketchup races! Decorate your French fries! You have to taste it to believe it! No longer sold in stores because this vintage is past its expiration date. Opening bid: thirty-five cents."

"I thought we said I'm doing soccer," Lucy says. "And if I'm doing soccer, you're doing the party."

"I'll do soccer," Greg promises. "I tell you, I'll do anything."

"You can't do soccer," Lucy starts to say, but is preempted by her daughter, Isabel, who comes dramatically into the kitchen dressed in soccer shorts, shin guards, athletic socks, cleats, and the wrong T-shirt. Or rather, the right T-shirt in the wrong size; this is Isabel's last year on Fuchsia, and she has on the now much-too-small T-shirt that she wore her first year, when she was only eight, and it does nothing for her, most particularly for her chest, about which she is increasingly self-conscious anyway.

"You can't do soccer!" she says, sharply, to her father, and then to her mother, accusingly, "You didn't wash my shirt!"

"Yes I did," Lucy says. "I bet it's still in the dryer." And she ducks into the laundry room, as Isabel says reproachfully to Greg, "You can't ever do soccer again, and you better not try. Not ever."

"Honey, I'm sorry," Greg is saying, as Lucy leans into the dryer and disentangles the newer, brighter, bigger Fuchsia team shirt from the railroad train sheets and pillowcase that had to be washed after Freddy's last birthday party and the subsequent nighttime stomach upset. Okay, one small thing done right: Isabel has her shirt. Lucy returns to the kitchen in maternal triumph; Isabel snatches the shirt and hurries off to lock herself in her room, pull down her shade, draw her curtains, and make the switch.

Greg shrugs apologetically at Lucy. "You really think I'm banned for good?"

3

"I don't know, honey. But I think we better give it a few weeks at least. Joe Winnicutt takes this kind of thing pretty seriously."

"Asshole. Ripe, flaming, self-congratulatory investment banking asshole." Greg takes a jar of ginger marmalade from the refrigerator and stands it on the kitchen counter, pushing aside last night's unwashed glasses. He has an open bag of pretzel sticks, and he begins dipping them, one by one, into the cold, pale yellow jam, then crunching them in his mouth.

Last Saturday, Greg was asked to leave the girls' soccer game. He had violated the no-bad-language-on-the-sidelines law, or perhaps the parents-may-not-say-negative-things-about-the-other-team law, or so ruled Fuchsia's head coach, Joe Winnicutt, father of Vanessa and Adriana, the platonic ideal, blond, high-scoring fifth-grade offense star, who has been known to burst into perfectionist tears if she misses a shot, and the platonic ideal, blond, up-and-coming third-grade defense stalwart, who has single-footedly protected some of the team's most incompetent goalies. It is devoutly hoped by some, by Greg at least, and therefore loyally by Lucy, that any day now Joe Winnicutt is going to be indicted for securities fraud, but at this point it looks as if he may at least make it through the soccer season. Anyway, Greg did point out in his own defense that he had used no obscenities at all and had not actually said anything bad about the other team—Teal, it happened to be last week. Greg said—and has said it too many times—that it was meant to be funny, that he just got carried away with all those flowery, old-fashioned girls' names. From *Give it to them, Georgina,* and *Get in there and fight, Vanessa,* he had, he admitted, progressed to *Smash 'em good, Cecilia,* and *That's right, Adriana, kill! kill! kill!* Girls' soccer, he pleaded to Lucy in private, will do that to you.

So no, he can't do soccer. Isabel, as she has made abundantly clear, is already quite embarrassed enough—only a little less so because the week before last, Celeste's mother, the chiropractor, was told by the referee that she could come to future games only if she kept her mouth shut, not to mention that back at the very first game of the season, Georgina's father, a reasonably promi-

4

nent modern composer, got into a fistfight with the father of a girl on Jade, and both dads were banned for the rest of the season. But now Greg is trapped: not allowed to go with Isabel to soccer, and he still wants to get out of the Freddy-birthday-party as well, and he's pleading his usual excuse about a graduate student dissertation to read and an article of his own to be edited and checked over— but really, Lucy knows, it's because he hadn't looked closely at the invitation till now—he didn't know what particular kind of awful this day had in store.

"Please," Greg says again. He offers her a pretzel dipped in ginger marmalade, and she opens her mouth, accepting this particular mix of crunch and salt and spice and sweet in place of all she would have liked from him this morning.

> Item 58. Mrs. Coventry, our very own Resource Room specialist, will reveal her hidden talents by cooking a gourmet dinner for four and delivering it to your home, complete with antique china, crystal, and a beautiful linen tablecloth. Sample menus might include vichyssoise with caviar garnish, roast pork loin with juniper berries, fresh fruit sorbet, and a chocolate torte. Donated by: Mrs. Coventry. Estimated value: $400. Opening bid: $75. Please note: date must be mutually agreed upon; china and crystal and tablecloth must be returned.

Remarkably, Lucy is still feeling beautiful at the goddamn birthday party. She did it, of course, for Greg, though she made him go out and get the present and wrap it and stand over Freddy while he lettered the requisite card, all of which Greg was happy to do, anything but drive out to the western suburbs for a pool party hosted by the most awful parents in the entire first grade, the almost legendary Danny and Denny.

> Item 72. Enjoy a wonderful fairy-tale weekend next summer at a Nantucket beach cottage covered with old-fashioned climbing roses. Excellent bicycling, swimming, fishing, boating, golf, tennis. Four bedrooms will give you room for your whole fam-

ily and maybe even a child's best friend—sleeps eight, easily
—while Wendy, our faithful housekeeper, will cook the fish you
catch and help make this a weekend you will always remember. Donated by: Danny and Denny Dietrich. Estimated value:
$2,000. Opening bid: $500. Please note: weekend to take place
between June and September; certain summer weekends are
not available.

Danny and Denny have three boys, all extremely athletic. The
youngest of the three is in Freddy's class, and he and Freddy are
not particularly friends, but every boy in the class is invited to the
party, because that is how it is done. The three Dietrich boys are
named, if you can believe it, Dash, Donnie, and Davey, and Greg
and Lucy have often renamed them, "Doofus, Dreidel, and Dippy"
being the current favorites, though Freddy is getting to the point
where you have to be careful he doesn't hear and understand, especially if you are making jokes that include a word like *Doodoo-
head,* which would normally attract his full and immediate attention. Davey and Freddy are not friends, particularly, since Freddy
is so distinctly not an athletic boy, is in fact a child with strikingly
poor coordination and a slightly disturbing nerdy talent for math-
ematics, the kind of talent that you just know would never turn up
to trouble the Dietrich family, who will do just fine in the stock
market without it, thank you very much. So no, not friends, but
on the other hand, they're first-grade boys, Davey and Freddy, and
they were kindergarten boys together before that, so they get along
okay; either would rather play with or talk to the other than to anyone of a different age or gender. Lucy's first experience of mother-
hood did involve that other gender, in the socially acute person of
Isabel, who was an unerring guide to the at least six tension-filled
social levels of the little girls in her first-grade classroom, way back
when. For Isabel, there was no such thing as a simple category: a
first-grade-girl-like-me. Girl birthday parties, girl play dates, girl
seating at the lunch tables—all complex, highly fraught, and miles
beyond Lucy's well-intentioned understanding. Lucy, who still
bears some of the scars of first-grade-according-to-Isabel, is now

tense with waiting for the social pressures to hit with Freddy. Instead, Lucy is, as she has been before, a little amazed by the happy puppylike jumble that little boys seem to generate. Here in the locker room at the country club, they bump up against one another and giggle and put on their trunks, or their mothers help them, and they never look in the mirrors, not even once.

Don't even ask what some of the things are that Greg has suggested that Wendy our faithful housekeeper will do to keep you happy; Lucy smiles as she follows her son out the door leading to the pool, inappropriately remembering the fellatio-on-demand joke. But there, presiding, is Danny himself, in a bathing suit that is tight enough to bring the joke to mind. Lucy herself, needless to say, has not suited up. She accepts the curse of the birthday party parent; she knows she will have to stay for the party and observe and maybe even help, but surely there are limits. Let Danny Dietrich, patriarch, provider of the special D sperm, strut his stuff in this navy blue jock sock with white racing stripes—and to be honest, though he has good enough abs and no love handles at all, the basket itself is not so terribly impressive. Lucy will take refuge on the poolside bench, along with the other guest mothers, who are, surprise surprise, also fully—and snazzily—dressed. All of them are significantly thinner than Lucy, but none has risked a bathing suit, perhaps because Denny herself, the pool party hostess, has such famous muscle tone, which must surely be on display somewhere.

Greetings and enthusiasms are exchanged. What a great idea, a pool party. Just the perfect thing for the fall, when all the kids can show off how much progress they made last summer. And the pool here at the club is so great. Yes, other moms had to rush to get here from soccer, too. Your daughter's on Fuchsia, right? Oh, they're having a great year. That Joe Winnicutt is just the best coach. Yes, Lucy allows, they won again today. Against Saffron. Freddy will not play soccer on Saturdays, Lucy thinks with relief. He has no interest and he's so uncoordinated, and while girls' soccer is absolutely no-appeal obligatory, so that our daughters can learn teamwork and develop strong, self-confident, though of course soigné bodies, surely we can let the little boys out of it. Surely. Oh, hi, Denny. What a great idea, a pool party. The boys will just love it.

But Freddy is not loving it. Denny, in her hot-pink tank suit cut insanely high on the thighs, has come over to point out what Lucy might perhaps have noticed on her own, if she had been paying attention: Freddy is standing on the second step at the shallow end, not loving it. In fact, crying. And every time he is splashed by the spray of some swims-like-a-fish boy leaping off the side of the pool with his swimming-lessons-every-summer-well-you-know-he's-just-so-eager-to-be-allowed-to-take-the-boat-out form, Freddy gives a little yelp and cries even harder.

Lucy does her best. Cajoles Freddy—well, hauls him—out of the pool. Draws him over to the side, away from stray splashes and helpful mommies—here comes Claire Mancini bearing down with an enormous bright blue Styrofoam snake. Lucy keeps a friendly, calm smile on her face, kneels down on the tiles and hugs her shivering skinny boy, wipes the tears and snot off his face, which is otherwise, of course, completely dry. We'll get you a life jacket if you'd like, darling, or some water wings—oh, thank you, Claire! What a good idea! I think the water is a little colder and a little deeper than poor Freddy realized at first—we're just going to wait till he feels like going in, right, darling? Freddy looks at her, very dubiously. Looks at the bright blue Styrofoam snake even more dubiously. Claire—(*you officious interfering bizzom, you*)—do you think you could possibly look around for a life jacket—I think if he knew he would float, this would be easier for Freddy. Yes, Claire, I *know* the snake will help him float, too, if he holds it—(*why no, you patronizing, emotion-sucking ghoul, I thought it was just your favorite sex toy*)—but I think he might like a jacket, too, if they have one his size. Thanks so much.

What she would like to whisper in her dear, clumsy son's beautiful, beloved ear is this: Let's just go home, okay? You and me? We don't belong here, do we—I'm fat and lewd, you're skinny and scared, we don't either of us want to be here, do we? But that would mean no pizza and no watching to see which Lego sets Davey got and above all no party bag.

Lucy enfolds him in a hug. You'll really like the water once you get wet, she lies. It will seem nice and warm once you're wet all over. And we'll put a life jacket on you and then it will be just like you can swim! Either that or it will be like that scene in *Titanic*, but never mind that now. The family honor is at stake. Oh, thank you, Claire, that's just perfect. Wonderful—look, darling, Jason's mommy found a jacket exactly the right size for you.

Grimly, she buckles her son in and draws the straps tight. If she knew the tune to "Nearer, My God, to Thee," she would hum it. Freddy looks into her eyes, and she thinks she sees a certain brave gallantry in his: *Back into the pool I must go.* Ten-year-old girls, all of them, including her daughter, Isabel, act like they are mature, responsible adults who have been forced by an oppressive society to play subordinate roles, which they do with varying degrees of good grace and condescension. Freddy, on the other hand, has all these moments when his mother can see that he is spiritually swallowing hard and gamely agreeing to go on with the business of pretending he feels the things that children ought to feel.

But thank God for little boys—the mommies are all watching as she comforts Freddy, overgrown, cliquish ten-year-olds that they are, organized no doubt into levels and levels of mutually disapproving social order, all without reference to Lucy, but the little boys are not at all interested as Lucy leads Freddy back to the pool. The little boys, most of them, have been organized by the invaluable Danny into a long chain and are being swirled through the water in some slow-motion version of Crack the Whip. There's a pimply adolescent lifeguard out at the deep end, sitting in a white plastic deck chair and looking bored. Several of the weaker swimmers are not playing, and a couple of them are even wearing life jackets, Lucy sees with relief. She gets Freddy down to the third step and sloshes a little pool water up over his belly, his life jacket, his shoulders. He stands as tight and tense as he can—he hates this, she can tell. But he doesn't cry, thank God, and finally, damp all over, he takes another step down, and finally, finally, consents to inch his way out along the pool wall, away from the stairs, his toes securely on the pool floor, his hands clinging to the edge, and the life jacket, in a supernumerary sort of way, bobbing along on the surface. She would give him the bright blue snake, too, but he's obviously not going to let go of the wall.

However. He is definitely in the pool. He is in the pool and he is not crying. In some certain circles, that is victory enough, and she tells him what a wonderful, brave boy he is, what a good good swimmer—he is clutching the wall so tightly his knuckles are white—and she tells him how much fun he's going to have now that he's swimming in the pool—and thank God, along the wall comes Peter, a friend and another nonathlete, also in an orange life jacket, though he seems to be able to walk along in the shallow end without holding on. And as soon as Freddy and Peter greet one another, amazed beyond belief to find each other out here in these shark-infested, unplumbed depths, Lucy can get to her feet, her jeans wet through from the knees down, and scuttle back to the mommy bench to accept the kindly congratulations.

Item 123: Special behind-the-scenes tour of the Cumberland Museum of Modern Art. Your unique opportunity to see and share with your children the fascinating details of how a well-known museum puts together its exhibits. A modern art curator will take you through the collections on display and then back "behind-the-scenes" to look at the paintings and sculptures that are stored for future exhibitions and at the work of curating and cataloguing and preserving. A special lunch for four in the museum's famous "Sculpture Garden Café" will round out a day you will never forget. Donated by: Cumberland Museum. Estimated value: Priceless. Opening bid: $50. Note: Must take place in November; no children under 5, please. Subject to availability.

A grim and evil destiny hangs over this particular birthday party, but Lucy, sitting on the bench, thinks that she has won the day. And she is so grateful to see her son, for the moment at least, undeniably submerged up to his neck and undeniably social, that she does not react as strongly as she otherwise might when Peter's father, Bill the perpetual graduate student, sits down beside her on the bench, on her unprotected flank. All that Lucy thinks at first, in a burst of generosity of spirit, is that she's glad Greg didn't come, that this would just be one thing too many. And with some small remnant of her morning sense of beauty, she smiles at the poor schlumpf, as if she is well and truly glad to see a self-important trust-fund baby with a perennially unfinished doctoral dissertation and a perennial need to talk about it.

He asks after *her* work first, with only poorly concealed lack of interest—so poorly concealed that he can't quite remember what she does; he knows it's medicine and he knows it's do-good, but he couldn't care less. And anyway, what he really wants to do is get onto the subject of Greg's work—of Greg's tenured professor status in English literature. Of course, it's a long way from Victorian novels to Bill's own very special field of contemporary short stories by men affected by the women's movement and the men's movement, but still, they're colleagues of a sort. What a cozy coincidence, two first-grade boys who like each other, two fathers with so much in common, Bill has often remarked. Greg, for his part, has often remarked that if anyone ever suckers him into playground duty with Bill again, there will be blood on the sandbox. One would not have predicted Bill here at this pool party, because on weekends he is usually so tired from not writing his dissertation all week that he leaves weekend parental responsibilities to his wife, who has been working at her admittedly part-time architect job all week—trust funds will do that for you. But here is Bill, and there is never any getting away from Bill, once he gloms on.

And yes, Greg's department is searching in modern American literature next year, though Lucy allows herself to plead ignorance: I just don't keep up on the details. So Bill kindly enlightens her, tracing back the history of the department's inadequate attempts, over the last two decades, to grapple with the new and fascinating writing being produced in America today—particularly by male writers who have been, remarkably enough, strongly influenced by —guess what?—the women's movement and the men's movement! He'll have to talk to Greg soon about this search, about this job, Bill says, and Lucy nods. What else can she do? Well, she can warn Greg that this is coming, and warn him as well to be discreet: the world is small and news travels fast; don't say anything bad publicly in your department about Bill—surely you don't have to torpedo him, surely his CV all by itself will do that.

"So how is your work coming?" she asks, weakly. Weakly, because Greg would surely say, *Making any progress on the dissertation, Bill?* Or, *Well, Bill, if you're serious about applying for the job, you definitely need to hand in your dissertation immediately—are you even close?*

"Oh, you know how it is—especially with kids," says Bill, who has *one* fucking kid, who is away at school for six hours every weekday. "It's hard to get much done—and somehow the more you care about something, the more you want it to be perfect, the harder it is."

No, thinks Lucy, the more you care about something, the easier it is. And she thinks with real and true affection of Greg, who is home editing his article. Poor Greg: it is going to be a long siege from now until his department definitively hires somebody else. Here is Bill leaning in too close, confiding how perfect this job would be for him because, guess what? They wouldn't have to move! He could get a job as a professor and his family could stay right there in their perfect Queen Anne house with the turret he uses as his study—and after all, who knows whether they could ever find a school in some other city where Peter would be this happy—or where Bill himself could find such a wonderful turret-shaped study so conducive to not writing anything. Lucy nods sensitively, responding to Bill's conscientious fatherhood.

As she stares past him, thinking nasty thoughts, there is a sudden cry from the mother behind her, and then Bill himself shouts, "Oh, Christ!" He leaps to his feet and takes two steps and goes hurtling, fully clothed, into the pool, sending up a splash so large that for a second or two Lucy cannot see what is happening at all.

Item 57: Handloomed Tapestry Created by Craftswoman (and fourth-grade parent) Marguerite Davenport Cooke. This striking, one-of-a-kind, three-dimensional wall hanging incorporates many different natural fibers and textures, expressing in fiber art form the essential nurturing quality of family life. It will instantly transform your room into a warmer, richer place, adding a new dimension to your décor. Marguerite Davenport Cooke's work has been exhibited at several galleries and has won prizes at craft fairs throughout the state. Donated by: Marguerite Davenport Cooke. Estimated value: $700. Opening bid: $80.

"You have to get him the job if you can, Greg. I'm sorry, I know it's a bitter pill. But if you can, you get him the job."

They are eating pizza, and it isn't even upscale thin-crust pizza, suitable for adult professionals on a Saturday night. Greg just didn't have it in him to drive the extra four blocks; this is pizza from the place around the corner. Saturday night. Isabel is out at a slumber party, which will no doubt have to be reciprocated some day, if she decides that her parents are up to hosting at an acceptable level. Poor Freddy has been put to bed, though Lucy is alert for any sounds from upstairs. The pizza, therefore, is just for the two of them, and there is no need to worry that any slice will go uneaten. Extra cheese and pepperoni.

"I can't get him the job. He hasn't got his goddamn degree—he's never going to finish that awful dissertation."

"You have to do what you can."

Greg takes his fourth and last piece, so Lucy matches him. The empty cardboard round, liberally stained with oil, lies between them on the kitchen table.

"Look," she says, trying to make a joke of it, one of their jokes, "why don't we just agree that from now on you're going to do all the birthday parties with Freddy. That way I'll never get you into this kind of situation again." She puts down her pizza and she starts to cry. She wipes her eyes with the napkin that the pizzeria thoughtfully included with the order. Greg puts his own slice down as well, regards her for a sob and a sniff or two, then reaches over to pat her shoulder. Lucy shakes her head. "You didn't see him," she gets out. "You didn't see what he looked like when Bill pulled him out of that pool. Oh, Greg, he looked so little and white and . . ." But the only word to put at the end of that particular sentence would seem to be *dead*, so she just honks again into her napkin.

He wasn't dead, of course. Just wriggled out of his jacket somehow, and somehow submerged in water just an inch or two too deep for him—what unsuspected reserves of courage and adventure had he found, their sweet six-year-old, in those moments when she was looking away, talking to his friend's stupid, self-aggrandizing father, the finest man on earth, a hero and a saint. Who pulled Freddy out of the water and whacked the water out of his lungs—pulled Freddy out, Lucy thinks dizzily, before he could be more than dazed and groggy, before anything could happen to his beautiful strange brain or his precious beating heart.

Oddly enough, that had actually gone through her mind in the first terrified second she watched Bill kneel beside Freddy—she had thought crazily, Okay, we'll give up the math, it's okay if he loses that, as long as we get him back. And then she fell to her knees, and Freddy, abruptly, turned his head away from her and vomited. Right into the pool.

"Listen," Greg says, as gently as he can. "This is truly not something I can do—it's not something I have in my power."

"But you'll try? You'll do what you can?"

There is a faint sound from upstairs and they both freeze, then Lucy starts to get up, but Greg puts a hand on her shoulder, pressing her back in her seat, and he goes himself. She can hear his footsteps change in tone as he starts up the stairs; the house is old and creaky and each piece of flooring has its characteristic note. Greg goes all the way up to the second floor, and then a few seconds later she hears his footsteps coming down, and she can tell from their cadence that nothing is wrong. Lucy closes her eyes and sees not Freddy's wet white face that afternoon but randomly selected children from one time or another in the emergency room. Near-drownings, children pulled alive, but only just, from cold water to be gradually rewarmed to see whether their hearts would start again, whether their brains had been preserved. A three-year-old found floating in a Wellesley neighbor's decorative garden lily pond. A high school student from Pennsylvania on a class trip to Lexington and Concord, who got dared to dive into the deep end of the motel pool and couldn't swim. If Freddy hadn't revived, she would have done something—she would have started CPR. She doesn't even try to think about doing CPR on Freddy, she just opens her eyes and smiles at Greg as he comes back into the kitchen.

And so we are in debt forever to Bill, Lucy thinks. I will never look at Bill without remembering him pulling our boy from the pool. Long live Bill. Bill for president.

Lucy offers her uneaten last slice to Greg and watches him chew. She shakes her head.

"You didn't see him," she says.

You didn't see him when he suddenly sat up and looked around and saw us all kneeling and standing there and looking at him —when I could see him wonder, *Should I start to cry?* But instead he smiled at me, ignoring the other kids who were climbing out of the pool as fast as they could, making noises of disgust, and the parents with their clucking and their suggestions and even the fucking useless lifeguard who was holding, of all things, a cell phone, the better to call 911—Freddy smiled at me, first a little smile, then a bigger smile. "Hi, Mom," he said, like an opening bid. "I went in the water. Three feet is the same as one yard, which is thirty-six inches. But it comes out to more than ninety-one centimeters, so it's less than a meter. Did you know that?"

2

Open Case

YOU WOULD THINK that in doing the work I do, I would come to be forgiving of parents who can't quite manage. I mean, here I've done this clunkily obvious yet heartwarming thing—I've taken the lemons of my own life and made public lemonade, and I work day in and day out with the families that just can't keep it together. They are *undergoing extreme life stresses*, they urgently *need more supports in place*, they would *profit from additional services*, and all the other phrases you can safely say of just about anyone, which is why all reports sound exactly alike. And sometimes I get so furious at these parents that I have to go lock myself in the ugly clinic bathroom and make a furious little speech to the mirror. And then I splash water on my face, take my ten deep breaths, and head back out again.

No one removed me from my birth parents for my own protection. I came into the foster care system because my mother died and my father could not care for me on his own, and he knew it. And in my second foster home, the only bad one, the only one that had some of the Dickensian awfulness that people expect when they hear how I grew up, there was an older brother—a biological son of the foster mother—who was having sex with the other foster child. I didn't quite know it at the time, because I was only five and new to the risks of this particular world. I was relatively recently out of my original home, my birth parents' home, as we say—that home I wish so much that I could really remember, beyond those tiny dreamlike images of a staircase with a very steep spiral and flowered carpeting that wasn't perfectly fixed in place by the brass rods, so that you had to hold like grim death to the banister, especially coming down. A very high and very big bed with a ridged salmon-pink chenille cover—I remember standing next to such a big high bed, and I choose to believe that it was indeed my mother's bed—her deathbed eventually, speaking of Dickensian—and I choose to believe that when I remember standing close to that bed, I am remembering standing close to my mother.

And I have some other pieces of that home in my mind, some of them real memories, some of them articles of faith. But the home was gone and my mother was gone, though when I was in my first foster home, which was completely blurred in my memory by the new and terrible awareness of my mother's death, and then in that second foster home, my father was still alive. Still alive, still coming to see me every week—or every two weeks, or every month—returning from a business trip, with an apology for not having sent a postcard, with an inappropriate present picked up in a hotel gift shop. And you must remember, please, that all this did not seem quite so very strange four decades ago. A sorrowing widower (and I choose to believe that he was greatly sorrowing) with a job that kept him on the road at all times, no family nearby on either side to take the child—at times I have made my father over, in my mind, as every possible tragic and wandering American salesman, from Willy Loman to the father in *The Glass Menagerie*, who fell in love with long distances. Well, try to picture one of those guys on his own with a five-year-old girl. Doesn't fit, right? It certainly didn't fit back then. If you didn't have relatives to help out, then I guess you left the kid with a foster mom, and you came to visit, and you brought presents, and you promised that one day soon you'd stop traveling and there would be a real home. He did his best, I think. I choose to think. And then, he got drunk one night in Dayton and a truck ran him over. Or maybe, one night in Dayton he drank enough to get up the nerve and stepped in front of a truck. I don't know; nobody told me. Nobody told me much of anything.

So I had found my way into the foster care system because my mother had died from something that could be named only in a whisper; remember how people used to hush their voices over the word *cancer*? I was everyone's idea of a sad-case almost-orphan. No one had "removed" me; the evil agency whose name could not be spoken aloud had removed my mother. And when I lived in that second foster home, I was just beginning to understand that other foster children were in a different situation, that yes, it was possible to have a mother alive and well somewhere and still spend your life shuttled from one foster mom to another. No one explained that very clearly either, which I suppose was a good thing; how much should a five-year-old have to know?

But where is it written, tell me, that we must coddle the clueless? Clothe the naked, okay, feed the hungry, you got it. But where is it written that a mother who cannot do what every stray cat can do—lick 'em clean, feed 'em till they're full, keep 'em in a safe place, and snarl at intruders—needs a therapist and a residential substance-abuse program and some respite babysitting when she comes out? As far as I'm concerned, if you need regular supervised urine tests to show that you aren't too bombed out of your mind to hold the baby, you lose the baby. You're a loser and you lose. Two strikes and you are out of the goddamn game.

Naturally, I do not go around saying this. To tell the truth, I do not always go around even thinking this; I have my tolerant and liberal days. But there are times, as I listen to stories of children switched back and forth—now back with bio-mom, who is really getting it together, finally, and then back into foster care because mom was turning tricks again to buy crystal meth, with the kids huddled in the closet out of the way—well, there are times I just wonder who the hell we are all kidding.

That being so, I absolutely cannot explain why I like Athena Harris as much as I do. Why I don't think she's a loser on her tenth strike, which she definitely is, no question. Why I am always glad to see her and greet each new Athena Harris disaster with an almost comic sense of *Oh, no, here we go again*, as if we were talking lovable slapstick. I cannot explain it. But there are plenty of bio-moms—and bio-dads, for that matter—who evoke in me a desire to slap or shake or scream, and then there is the occasional likable Athena, and there you have it. Personality is all in this world, I guess. Well, not all. Not all.

The older brother in my second foster home was a real piece of work. You are probably imagining a hulking bully, but he wasn't like that at all. He was handsome, blond, and open-faced, a tenth-grade star, an emissary from the world of children with carefully straightened teeth and new pairs of ice skates every year. Oh yes, he could skate, and I remember watching him, one day that winter, playing ice hockey on the little frozen-over pond that was not too far from his mother's house. I could not skate—I still can't skate—and in any case, I had no skates. I was standing with the other foster child, Lauralee was her name. So many children who end up in the foster care system, still today, have such elegant or elaborate names, as if their parents had expended all the attention they were ever going to give in coming up with that single idea and offering it as life-long proof that, all other evidence to the contrary, somebody once did really care, somebody marked and celebrated this birth. Lauralee. She was thirteen years old, with astonishing breasts. I was astonished by them, too, although I don't think it ever occurred to me that they had anything to do with my own future development, and I suppose you could say that in some ways they didn't. I mean, I never did wake up one morning, as I later hoped and feared that I might, to find two perfect, pointed Snocones rising from my chest. Lauralee was otherwise a fairly unremarkable-looking child, slightly dumpy, dull, dirty blond hair worn below her shoulders with scraggly bangs that needed trimming more often than they got it. Regarding her breasts, my theory now is that when they first sprouted, she was left, of course, to keep wearing the clothes she already had, to squeeze herself into T-shirts or button her blouses and leave them to gape and pull. By the time someone finally faced the inevitable and bought her a bra and a few shirts engineered for someone with a bosom, it was too late.

Mary Ann, the head nurse at the clinic, understands that I am fond of Athena Harris. She even understands why—or at least she understands that over time, individual doctors and nurses find themselves drawn into particular long-standing follies with patients who somehow get past the guard, past the posted set of rules, and settle in for a nice long dance, comfortable as can be. I'm not saying she necessarily understands why Athena, why me, but Mary Ann is wise enough to understand, absolutely and truly, that first, there are many people out there who do things in a different way than she would, and that second, there's lots in the world that she can't alter. These are concepts, if you ask me, that doctors are not any too good at grasping. But now that I think about it, maybe every good nurse everywhere is brought by life and training—and maybe by working with doctors—to a deep and full appreciation of the Alcoholics Anonymous serenity prayer. Mary Ann truly has the serenity to accept the things she can't change, the courage to change the things she can, and the wisdom to know the difference. Or do I just say this because I suspect the secret at the center of her long but totally offstage marriage is that her husband has been in AA for years? She never talks much about him, except occasionally to announce some plan in the plural: *We'd like to drive up to Maine if the weather's good this weekend. We're talking about maybe going on a cruise in February, but they're all kind of expensive.* Meantime, I babble on constantly about Greg and Freddy and Isabel, spilling my life all over the clinic, boasting and complaining and just using them as my everyday chatter, and even sometimes bringing a child to work when school and childcare arrangements fall through. Mary Ann and her husband have no children.

She comes in to tell me that the patient in the next room is Athena Harris. It's not really Mary Ann's job to tell me this; it's my job to grab the next chart and walk into the next room and deal with whomever. But Mary Ann is announcing Athena, our old friend, and warning me that whatever's going on in there, it's likely to take me a while. Mary Ann makes a baby-cradling gesture across her chest and rocks her arms back and forth.

"You're kidding! Don't tell me!" I say in shock and horror, but we can both hear that I am also saying, *Good old Athena, here she goes again.*

And sure enough, there is a tiny, brand-new baby in Athena's arms when I walk into the room, and she smiles at me with proud possession, the way a new mother not on her first baby might smile at the doctor, an experienced mom who wasn't overwhelmed with fear, because she'd been this route before, but who wanted some acknowledgment that each new baby is a miracle and a joy.

Except maybe when all your other children have been removed from your care and custody, of course.

"'Lo there, Dr. Lucy," she says. "Look what I got."

"I didn't know you were even pregnant, Athena," I say, and she smiles again, as if she has once more pulled off a special trick.

Athena is not from Boston. She's from somewhere south, she originally said Kentucky, but I think she was lying or stretching the truth a bit, because the aunt who long ago showed up and rather grudgingly took the two oldest kids back with her was from South Carolina. Why she might lie about a thing like that I'm not sure, but I can perfectly well imagine that she left some trouble behind and didn't want it tracking her down. In any case, because she is southern and white, a category that is not particularly well-represented in our Boston clinic, any number of people have described Athena's social category as "trash." We allow ourselves, I suppose, to be a little freer with the slurs when a person is white.

"It's a little girl again this time. Popped right out. One more week and she could have been a Thanksgiving baby and you get a special turkey dinner. Over to the Brigham to have her, and they treated me nice. Except the room wasn't so big as at the Beth Israel, the room they had me staying in. Nurses were real nice, though."

Oh yes, I want to say, *and how were the social workers?* I also want to ask, *I don't suppose you consented to a tubal ligation this time around, did you?* but I'm sure I know the answer and besides, whatever the history may be, there are certain things one says first off to the mother of a new baby, and that isn't one of them.

There is a much-too-big snowsuit lying discarded on the exam table—but at least there is a snowsuit. I peel back the edge of the receiving blanket, which I note without surprise is hospital issue, one of those that Athena received from the real nice nurses at the Brigham, and stare down at the round, pale pink face. Eyes closed, eyelids even paler than the rest of her, papery crescents that tremble slightly as she sleeps, as if the blood pulsing through her small body was almost too much for her, as if every pump of her heart was fluttering her and shaking her and making her tremble. The baby has a halo of bushy brown newborn hair.

"She's beautiful, Athena." I tuck the blanket back around her and take my own seat across the little desk. I cannot bring myself to say congratulations, but she looks congratulated. "How many is this now?" I ask, trying to keep my voice light.

"This here's number ten," Athena says proudly, drawing out the word *number* into two drum-roll syllables, as if she were announcing a record broken, a winning lottery combination, a grand prize. As if numbers one through nine were not in the various stages of temporary placement, long-term foster care, termination of parental rights, and adoption.

"Number ten," I repeat, without special emphasis, I hope, and we sit there and look at each other while the baby sleeps.

Athena was probably beautiful once, though since I have known her, which is a good seven years, she has always had that used-up look. She's tall and she was intended by design to be thin but a little bit rawboned, and though ten pregnancies have left her more padded, she's a big woman rather than a fat one. Periodically she diets down, in between children, and takes on a hungry, rangy look, all

22

tight jeans and wifebeater tank tops that show the tattoos on both upper arms: one a cobra, for some long-gone guy in the Marine Corps, and one a wreath of deep red roses.

Today, postpartum, she is soft-edged again and wearing black stretch pants and clunky snow boots and a faded long-sleeved cotton shirt, printed on the front with a picture of a swan boat. It's the kind of shirt she might well have gotten from the clothes pantry downstairs, since surely Athena's children have never been taken on a swan boat ride, at least not by Athena. Although as I sit here in this fluorescent-lit room on this dark November day, suddenly I can picture it: summer in the city a couple of years ago, one of those heavily funded family preservation programs, some very well-meaning social worker, new to the job and full of idealism, leading Athena and any three or four of her children through the Public Garden, eager to give them this strong positive family experience. They wait in line, and the social worker buys them all bags of peanuts to feed the ducks. Athena stands slightly off to one side, her face smooth and accepting and without any curiosity. By the time they get to the front of the line, she has eaten all her own peanuts, and when the children point this out to her, she shrugs. If the social worker wasn't there, she would have had theirs as well.

The children are wild with excitement on the ride—let's give them that. Pointing out the ducks coming to follow the great white swan boats, tossing peanuts wildly, and squealing as the ducks dive or snap or chase each other off. Blinking and looking around at the green banks of the Public Garden, the blue sky and clouds above, the couples and families sitting under the trees and waving to them. And the quick looks you get at the city around you in all its glory, the Ritz-Carlton over there, and Newbury Street, the pleasantly distant mutters and putts of traffic on Beacon Street. *What city is this, what place is this?* the children are wondering. *Who made this magic? Can this be Boston?*

Athena is sitting one row behind her children and the social worker. By the time the boat comes back to the dock to let them off and pick up the next group of passengers, she is sitting farther over, quite close to a fellow in a T-shirt with rolled-up sleeves, out of which he is taking a box of Marlboros, and he is offering her one, even though smoking on the swan boats is forbidden. Athena meets his eyes and helps herself to four, tucking them into her purse for later, her blond straight hair blowing around both their faces.

I did not, of course, understand exactly what was going on between Lauralee and that boy, whose name I think I have deliberately forgotten. I mean, it must be deliberate, to forget his name when I can remember every detail of that room that Lauralee and I slept in together, the pink dust ruffles on our twin beds, the vanity table with the matching pink skirts sewed to two little curved arms that could be folded back out to the side, so that the skirts spread wide and you could open the drawers. The vanity table had no matching stool, but Lauralee had set it up at the foot of her bed, so she could sit on the bed and arrange her cosmetics on top of the vanity. The walls of that room had particularly interesting pictures on them: two different paintings of dogs playing cards. I don't remember the details, but I remember I had given all the dogs in the picture nearer my bed special names, and that I used to put myself to sleep imagining the details of their card game, which had rules that I had invented myself, combining my two favorite card games, War and Spit.

Spit was that boy's favorite game, the biological son, the one whose name I have forgotten. We played it almost every evening, after our statutory hour of television. I was too young to have homework, and Lauralee, on her way to flunking everything, always denied having any as well. The son of the house was older, and the idea was that he would do his homework, his more weighty high school homework, after we younger children, we foster children, were sent up to bed. I wish that I could remember his mother clearly—well, of course I wish that I could remember *my* mother clearly. His mother was actually a kind woman, I think, because I seem to remember her sewing me an angel costume for a school play—unless that was the next foster mother, but I don't think so. But what I do remember is what a crazy fool she was for her own golden son, how one evening she drove back to the shoe store three times until she returned with the exact pair of sneakers that he wanted, while he and Lauralee and I played game after game of Spit, until finally, with his mother just gone out again for one last trip to the shoe store, the son told me to go put myself to sleep. It's too late for little kids to be up, he said. I wanted to protest, because generally, to simplify things, Lauralee and I were put to bed at the same hour, but I was already learning to be very careful about defying orders. I was jealous, of course, of the way his mother prized him, the way he was loved. Lauralee, I would guess, was jealous, too, in her more complicated, more grown-up way. I left them together and obediently went to bed. I had the notion, I guess, as many younger children do in foster care, that there might be good-conduct prizes to be won, chief and most unimaginable among them, of course, the resurrection of my mother, and the reestablishment of our own house, my mother, my father, and me.

I examine Athena's new baby. Perfect in every way. Perfect except for being born into a situation you wouldn't wish on a jellyfish or a dung beetle. I refasten the diaper, rewrap the blanket, and hand the infant back to Athena, who receives her with a faint air of surprise, as if she is more accustomed to having babies taken away than to having them handed back, which I suppose she is.

"What does DSS say?"

"Oh, they filed right away when she was born." Athena is long past any hostility or embarrassment about the Department of Social Services' involvement in her life. She speaks of them factually and with a certain resignation, as if she is describing some naturally occurring phenomenon, occasionally inconvenient in its eruptions, like an attack of cold sores. Which is not an idle comparison, since Athena has in the past suffered from genital herpes, along with pretty much every other sexually transmitted disease there is, with the exception, so far, of HIV. I can already see by the baby's hospital discharge sheets, which are surely here now with

Athena only because some social worker made her bring them, that she had highly inadequate prenatal care, missed most of her appointments, and that she came to the hospital in active labor, her membranes already burst, and that all they could do was deliver the baby; no chance to take it out by cesarean, as you might in some cases consider doing when the mother has a history of herpes. The record shows a careful exam of Athena: no active lesions, although that doesn't absolutely mean the mother can't be shedding virus.

"When's the last time you had an episode of herpes, Athena?" I ask, distracted by my chain of associations.

"Lord, Dr. Lucy, I haven't had those nasty things in years. Maybe two, three years ago?"

I can see that she is making an effort to recall, throwing her mind back, counting off however Athena marks the years.

"Good," I say, as if this shows some evidence of cleaning up her act. "So after they filed, what's the situation? I mean, they let you take the baby home."

"They got an open case on me," she says, as if her case had ever been closed. "Say I can keep her if I get my urine checks every two days and I go to my appointments and you say she's okay. Got a visiting nurse coming every day to weigh her on one of them portable scales, and got a home visitor comes and passes the time of day. And my caseworker, of course. She's the one brought me here today. She's out in the waiting room."

And what are the odds, Athena, that you're going to keep her past her first birthday? Even with the visiting nurse, and the home visitor, and the caseworker? Will you two even make it through the winter together?

When I was ten years old, I read *Oliver Twist*. I was a ten-year-old foster child, and actually, I was given the book by the woman who would first take me in and then adopt me, the woman who would determine the course of my life. I was a good reader, but it seemed to me *Oliver Twist* was the first real book I had ever read. I read over and over the opening chapters—the poorhouse, the gruel, the beatings! And yet I was well-fed and unbeaten, in the care of respectable New Jersey housewives. When I have looked at the book over the past few years (and I do look at it, though I also know large excerpts from it by heart), I have been struck by how excellently Dickens makes the case for the contradiction that is at the heart of my own life and work. There has to be a system, and he knows it; there has to be a place to catch the people who go tumbling or drifting out of safe society. A net, we would call it today. The net can be made of a system that is essentially kind and good, or it can be like the poorhouse where Oliver's mother died, leaving her son to be starved and abused—but there has to be a system. But here's the contradiction: the system is not enough; the net does not represent real safety. Institutions and official involvement are not sufficient—but they are necessary.

We look at each other, Athena and I. I am trying to think of something to say. She doesn't get up to go, and I give no signal that the interview is over. We both know, I suppose, that I could send it either way. I could tell her the baby is healthy, which she seems to be, review a few quick and standard rules for caring for a brand-new baby—while acknowledging that Athena has to be considered an experienced mother, a mother who has been through the newborn phase many many times. I could tell her I'll see her in a week; to the list of Athena's check-ins and rituals, we will now add a weekly schlep into my clinic for me to weigh the baby yet again and check for any evidence of neglect. Athena will have to feed her so that she gains weight, and change her regularly so that she doesn't develop terrible diaper rashes, and zip her into warm clothing appropriate for the season, and keep track of what day it is and mark her appointments on the calendar—and the caseworker, I hope, will continue to bring the two of them to and fro. Because if not, Athena will start missing appointments, and then I will have to make the call that sooner or later someone is going to make.

Still, that hasn't happened yet, and here she is with her new baby, and I could end the visit now like any standard newborn visit: *Congratulations, your new baby is perfect, get some rest, enjoy her, see you next time.* Or alternatively, I suppose, I could conscientiously go back over as much of Athena's history as we are able to resurrect, review her every false step and risk factor, emphasize to her the importance of keeping strictly to all the standards that have been set, and remind her, as if a woman on her tenth child needs to be reminded, of the danger that hangs over her.

We sit quietly in the exam room, two women, one baby. I am not sure whether she is waiting for me to say something or whether I am waiting for her.

"Athena," I say, finally, "do you want to keep this baby?"

"Sure I do, Dr. Lucy," she says, in a slightly too-eager voice, as if, I cannot help feeling, she is reassuring me, gentling me, letting me down easy.

I am looking at her face, trying to see a sign of that rapturous, overpowering love that makes new mothers offer up anxious promises of care and attention and protection, and I don't see it, but I maybe see something better, or more convincing, or more touching: a kind of businesslike, experienced-mom acceptance of this new assignment.

"They'll take her away, you know, if you do a single thing wrong, with your record. Any bad urine test. Any urine test you fake or switch." Yup, that was Athena, a couple of years ago. Brought a bottle of someone else's pee with her to her doctor, tucked inside the baby's diaper bag.

I'm launched now, and I can't seem to stop myself. "If you miss bringing her in to see me, Athena, I'll have to let them know. Or if she doesn't gain weight. You have to watch your every step, you have to do this perfectly. I'm not kidding."

My voice has started to sound shrill in my own ears, and I stop, abruptly. What am I doing? Athena knows these things as well as I do. She is not my friend; I have helped remove at least three other children from her care, joining forces with the social workers to agree that they are not thriving, that they are not being cared for appropriately, that they show evidence of medical neglect or nutritional neglect or just plain ignore-them-all-day-long neglect.

And now I am sitting here with Athena telling her essentially all the reasons that she is going to lose this brand-new tiny girl somewhere along the way. She stares at me steadily, and I cannot begin to imagine what she is thinking.

"Get some rest," I say at last. "The baby is perfect. I want to see her in a week."

Athena nods. "In a week," she says. "Thank you, Dr. Lucy."

She stands up, folding the hospital blanket more closely around her baby, and then zips the whole bundle, baby and blanket and all, into that too-large snowsuit. She gathers up her purse and the Healthy Happy Families bag that I know the home visitor brought her.

"What's her name?" I ask, standing aside to let her through the doorway, baby and bags and all.

"Cassiopeia," she answers. "Like in the stars."

I watch them go out the door, and I think of Athena and her children on that swan boat ride I invented for them. They do not live in that friendly, picture-book city, not Athena, not the children who are already gone from her care, not the new baby. Athena walks a different road, with different lures and dangers. I will never say it to her, obviously, but I offer up a paragraph from *Oliver Twist*: "London!—that great place!—nobody—not even Mr. Bumble—could ever find him there! He had often heard the old men in the workhouse, too, say that no lad of spirit need want in London; and that there were ways of living in that vast city, which those who had been bred up in country parts had no idea of. It was the very place for a homeless boy, who must die in the streets unless someone helped him. As these things passed through his thoughts, he jumped upon his feet, and again walked forward."

I lay awake in that pink-decorated room in the foster home and wondered where Lauralee was. I was not used to going to sleep alone, and there were too many bad thoughts that could come. Lauralee had a bedside lamp, and she used to lie in bed and read Archie comics as I fell asleep. Little Lulu, Richie Rich—they were the first things I would read myself, later that year, and I remember realizing one day in the spring that I was reading them faster than Lauralee could, and that she had started asking me about hard words. But the night that the boy sent me to bed, I could not yet really read, and in any case, I did not want to lie there alone reading. I wanted to close my eyes and go to sleep with Lauralee right across the way, moving her lips very slightly, keeping me company into the night. Eventually, then, I got back out of bed, intending to go down the hall to the bathroom for a drink of water. Perhaps Lauralee, whom I imagined still playing Spit downstairs, would hear my footsteps going along the hall and would be reminded of the pleasures of our room, and the call of the comic books.

But she was not downstairs. And someone did in fact hear my footsteps. That boy, the one I keep referring to as the biological son, came out of his room, moving fast and looking scared. He must have thought it was his mom, come home too quickly with the shoes. His face was very red and his shirt was unbuttoned and pulled out of his pants and he was trying to do up the snap at the front of his blue jeans, and I noted with interest that I could see his underpants. When he saw it was me, he seemed both relieved and angry, and he demanded to know what I was doing, up out of bed. You're supposed to be asleep, he said, and I offered, rather frightened, the classic I-needed-a-drink-of-water excuse. He said I had been spying on him, hadn't I, and that if I didn't admit it, he would shut me in the vacuum cleaner closet and let the mice eat me. This closet was, in fact, used for punishment purposes at rare angry moments by this particular foster mother, and I had conceived a rather exaggerated fear of it. It was a perfectly ordinary closet, right off the upstairs hallway, that made a good jail cell just because it was so big, with lots of room even though a big upright vacuum cleaner lived there, and a folded ironing board, and a whole troop of mops and brooms and dry mops, and even a dim little light bulb with a pull chain. In fact, my younger child now sleeps in a bedroom not so much bigger than that closet. The foster mother very occasionally shut Lauralee or me—never her own son, of course—in there as her all-purpose punishment for the sin of "always getting under my feet." It was thus a practical penalty, since it got us out of her way, and not, as these things go, a particularly cruel one. My own fear of the closet started, I would guess, as a kind of standard good-child's fear of crossing the line into the bad-child zone, of losing all my good-conduct points and with them the possibility of any kind of special, not-to-be-named grand prize. But the biological son had whispered to me of mice, hordes of mice that came out when the door was shut and locked, and ran up and down the walls and across the floor and nibbled at everything they encountered. And somehow this had gotten mixed in my mind with something that my father had said to me at some point about my mother's body, now two years buried in the cemetery, which I had never visited. I had been asking questions about death and burial, technical questions about coffins and burial and what would have happened underground, and my father, never at all sure how to talk to a child, had reassured me at great length that the body was of course well-protected, that worms and bugs could not get to it. I had turned that reassurance inside out, as children will, and built my nightmares out of images of bodies being nibbled away underground in the dark, and these mythical hordes of mice running around a dark closet fit nicely with my terrors. Actually, from what I remember, this foster mother was a meticulous housewife, and I suspect now that evidence of even one solitary mouse would have resulted in traps and poison and a visit from the exterminator.

She was a meticulous housewife, and she was not a bad woman. I think about it now, and I am pretty sure that she was the one who sewed me that angel costume. She was a single mother back when divorce was less common, a woman who probably had no way of earning a living, trying to eke out a little extra income by taking in foster kids, so that, for example, she could buy her son the pair of sneakers he so craved. She kept us clean and properly fed and decently clothed; she never hit us, even when we drove her crazy. In the evenings, we did our homework and watched a carefully regulated amount of television on her black-and-white set and then played card games with her son. Where on earth, I could ask you, with the retrospective wisdom of my professional career, was she supposed to get the expertise to deal with Lauralee's learning disabilities—there probably weren't even words at the time for them—or Lauralee's new breasts? Let alone for the combination of the two, and the effect of it all mixed together on a high school boy? And by now, I no longer know whether I am talking about my foster mother, the mothers of my patients, or my own confusions with my own children.

I talk for a few minutes with Athena Harris's caseworker, out in the emergency room. She's a rather officious woman, not young, probably on her way to being a supervisor. Trim, African American, with impressive muscle tone visible in her arms as she sits there in a sleek, sleeveless white blouse, and a jeweled American flag on the lapel of the blue suit jacket she puts on while we speak. She clearly doesn't expect Athena to make it with this baby, but then again, she strikes me as fair-minded and ready to play it by the book; if Athena follows the rules, so will she. Athena could do much worse.

She brings Athena back the next week, and the baby is obligingly gaining weight and beginning to lose, just a little, that fragile newborn look. Athena says she's a good baby, doesn't cry much and sleeps four or five hours already at a stretch at night, and I warn her that she can't let the baby go more than four hours now without a feeding. I can remember when she had children removed from her care, two of them, because they cried all night with hunger while their mother slept—or rather slept it off—and finally the neighbors couldn't stand it anymore and called the Department of Social Services and demanded to know what the fucking hell they were thinking of.

"She's gaining that weight, isn't she, Dr. Lucy?" Athena asks, and I have to admit that yes, she is gaining that weight.

And she goes on gaining it for several months. We turn the corner into the new year, and the days start to get longer, and the baby grows, and I cut back the visits to every two weeks. The caseworker is still bringing them, but I don't know how long that can last; by anybody's standards, a mother is supposed to be able to get her child to a doctor's appointment without having to be brought by an official government employee. I find myself hoping, though, that maybe she can get Athena through the winter, so that she won't have to contend with bad weather. In spite of myself, in spite of what I know will happen, I am still cheering for Athena.

At Cassiopeia's four-month checkup, I smell trouble. I have never actually stopped expecting it, but I see this baby so often that I have come to know her and wish her well. She is a lively, dancing-eyed infant, a grabber and a chewer, and if you hold her just a little bit away from you, you can watch her plotting her next snatch and grab. In my more sentimental moments, which I try to repress, I wonder whether in this baby I am seeing some of the liveliness and the curiosity and the readiness to be surprised by all the delights of the world that were possibly there in Athena herself as a baby, as a small child, before the world did to her whatever it did.

In my even more sentimental moments, which I rigidly repress and absolutely do not allow, I dream, of course, of taking Athena's baby home, of concluding our long-standing folie à deux with this so obvious exchange. My younger child is six years old; there has been no baby in my house for a long time. I will take this lovely little girl, whose arms reach out to grab my glasses, my stethoscope, the beads of my necklace, and I will bring her back to a house where there will be milk in the refrigerator and graham crackers spread on the tray of her high chair when she gets old enough and a mobile over her crib and piles of inherited picture books, and Cassiopeia will grow up knowing only that when you reach out for the world, you usually grab something good. Yes, indeed, she will grow up to be everything that Athena maybe could have been, loved and tended and cherished from such an early age that she will remember nothing else.

And when this feeling comes over me, I whisper to myself the lines I memorized thirty-five years ago, from *Oliver Twist:* "'You will make me happier than I can tell you,' replied the young lady.

'To think that my dear good aunt should have been the means of rescuing any one from such sad misery as you have described to us, would be an unspeakable pleasure to me; but to know that the object of her goodness and compassion was sincerely grateful and attached, in consequence, would delight me, more than you can well imagine.'" The system is not enough. People need rescuing even with systems in place.

Well, in my job these are the kind of thoughts that you absolutely and completely must learn to turn off. What I need to do is send Cassiopeia back out into the home into which she was born, with the mother to whom she belongs—as long as it's safe and as long as I ethically can. And then, I know, when things start to fall apart, I will have to watch her slip into the system, watched over perhaps by that rather severe caseworker, whose maturity and no-nonsense air will, I hope, make things work as well as they can for this baby. And surely the caseworker has also imagined, and also quickly suppressed, how easy it would be to take this baby home, just take her home. We all have these little moments; they go with the job.

But the four-month visit, as I said, triggers my alarms. For one thing, Athena herself is clearly getting back into fighting trim. She bulges a little out of her jeans and her stretchy pink shirt, dressed much too lightly for the weather; her eye makeup is back, and the jeans are new, very dark, unwashed denim blue, with metal studs up the sides. And then there's her behavior: she isn't jumpy, exactly, not twitchy and nervous as I have sometimes seen her in the past and known she was using, but she's somehow more distracted. Twice during the visit, a cell phone goes off in her pocketbook and she grabs it out, listens for a moment, and says exactly the same thing: *I can't talk now, I'm at the doctor's. Uh-huh, I'll call you back.*

Cassiopeia at her four-month visit. Unlike her mother, she's dressed warmly, and I strip her down. Athena regards me, but doesn't help. She does tell me that the baby is now rolling over from her front to her back and from her back to her front. We watch together as Cassiopeia lies on her stomach, naked, on my examining table and does pushups, arching her back and holding her head up proudly. I hold her just under her arms and she squats on the table, then presses her body upward into a stand. She feels dense and solid and full of muscle, and she has indeed gained weight since the last visit.

"She gets four shots again today," I tell Athena. "How'd she do after she got the two-month shots?"

"She did fine. She didn't have no problems, no fever, nothing."

Yes, I want to say, in a mean mood, and I once filed on you for bringing in a ten-month-old for his regular checkup with a temp of 105, so dehydrated it took four days in the hospital to get his fluids and electrolytes back where they should be—and all the time you insisting that he'd been perfectly fine at home. That was one you nearly killed, Athena, and when you say this baby didn't have any fever after she got her two-month shots, you're probably right, but I suspect you mean that you never once touched her to find out.

"She's doing well," I say. "She's looking good. Let's go ahead and give her the shots, and then—do you have a bottle to give her afterward so she can calm down?"

Another little test. Athena must get tired of them; anybody would. But she is chronically undersupplied, always asking if she can have a diaper, or a few extra diapers for the rest of the day, or an extra blanket, or a clean onesie if the baby spat up. She has long ago stopped carrying that Healthy Happy Families bag; her pocketbook today, the one with the busy cell phone in it, is fake ponyskin with a long fringe.

But Athena has a bottle. Even in this unlikely pocketbook, she has a bottle, and she produces it triumphantly to show me.

I keep my voice neutral. "What are you giving her? What's that stuff in the bottle?"

She looks at it with a faint air of distraction, as if she can't for the life of her imagine who filled that bottle, and with what, and what does it have to do with *her,* in the end?

"Kool-Aid," she says, and we both look at the bright blue liquid. "She really really likes her Kool-Aid. And it's good for when you're going out, Dr. Lucy, because, you know, it don't go bad if you leave it out like milk can do."

And we both know, or at least I know and Athena must suspect, that she is now in for a firm lecture by me on infant nutrition, and that I will be documenting this in the baby's medical record and reporting it to the caseworker, and that in this, as in everything else, she is being watched and judged and most appropriately found wanting. And we also know, I think, both of us, that eventually the judgment will go against Athena. Whoever is on the other end of those phone calls is not going to be good news. Or else it will be someone else or something else, in the unfathomable equation of Athena's life, and Cassiopeia will be, so to speak, factored out. Taken away. Gone. Yes, mother and daughter have made it through the winter, but I don't believe they will see another one in together. When the state finally does take this baby, we'll hope she won't have been hurt or neglected so badly that permanent damage has been done. Except that permanent damage is always done; that much I know.

Don't get me wrong, Athena doesn't hurt her kids. Oh, she probably whacks them now and again, when they're two or three or four years old, but she doesn't beat or torture; she doesn't lose it when a child cries too much or won't go to sleep, probably, the cynic in me wants to add, because she isn't home or isn't in any state to notice. She's had a boyfriend or two along the way who hurt her kids, but if she was present and conscious at the time, I don't think she would let it happen. For that matter, she's had a boyfriend or two along the way who hurt *her*, and I don't think she puts up with that for very long either. Maybe that's why I like her; because even after all she's been through, Athena doesn't seem to see herself as any kind of victim. She has, in fact, something of her daughter's air of watching, with interest, to see what will come along next, what life will deal.

So yes, the biological son. He opened the vacuum closet door, and dragged me down the hallway, and I started to scream so loudly I think I startled us both. He got me as far as the closet and pushed me inside, but I pushed the vacuum cleaner out, blocking the door so he couldn't close it, and I pulled down the ironing board, and I managed to get them wedged in place, so that in order to get the door closed, he had to open it all the way again and rearrange me and the vacuum cleaner and the ironing board. And as soon as he had the door open and was folding the ironing board, I pushed past him, still screaming, and headed back down the hall toward my own bedroom. And then I saw Lauralee, standing in the doorway not of our bedroom, but of the boy's bedroom, so carefully stocked with his sports trophies, and Lauralee was completely naked. Just standing there in the hallway, pink and sleek and beautiful out of her clothes, as she had never looked to me in anything I had seen her wear. She was looking at me, as I came running toward her, screaming my head off, and looking past me to the biological son, who was still trying to get everything shoved securely back in the closet. And I was suddenly sure, and it turned out to be true, that when he looked around and saw her standing there he would forget about disciplining me, that *he* would be somehow scared and know himself in danger, even though I didn't quite know why. But I don't think Lauralee was predicting how things would go, the way I was, even in my distress. Or that she was assessing the shifting balance of power, her naked, him expecting his mother home, as she stood there in his doorway. I think she was just looking, playing her part, using what she had. And on her face was that same expression I see on Athena's face now, that expression of waiting and watching, of knowing things will happen to you, and waiting to see what they will be.

3

Unaccompanied Minors

I. Heading West: Business Class

Like probably just about any doctor, Lucy cherishes a long airplane flight as a beeper-free, cell phone–free interlude, a moment, no matter even if she is jammed into a middle seat eating a little bag of some stupid party mix, when the world will just have to get by without her, when she cannot be reached and therefore cannot be responsible. She has a full-fare, middle of the week economy-class ticket, and an upgrade certificate from the travel agency, and the flight is pretty empty, so they bump Lucy up to business class on the flight to San Diego, off to give a lecture to a bunch of West Coast doctors and thereby improve the lives of children everywhere. It's a tough job, but someone's gotta do it. Saving the world is pretty hard work, you know.

Up here in business class, as a flight attendant respectfully relieves her of her old black cardigan and hangs it carefully on a hanger, and then hurries to bring her a club soda with lime to sip as the rest of the passengers board, Lucy feels ridiculously elated: *Let the games begin!* She tries to stare balefully at the proletariat, shuffling back past her with their oversize carry-ons that won't quite fit, their duffels and their laptops, their wheeled suitcases and their shopping bags. Her own wheeled suitcase is stowed up in that capacious first-class bin, her laptop is way out of sight under the big seat so far in front of her. The game is not to grin like an idiot at finding herself up here; what kind of forty-five-year-old professional woman thinks six hours up at the front of an airplane is a trip to the amusement park? All around her, most likely, are real business types who take this completely for granted, who routinely fly business class wherever they go. She shouldn't be sipping her club soda with such disbelieving gratitude; she should be looking disgruntled because it isn't Perrier, or really, she should be busy on her cell phone closing one last million-dollar deal before the plane takes off.

Well, actually, if it comes to that, she does have a little trailing business to take care of before takeoff. Lucy reaches into the bag stowed under the seat in front of her and digs out her cell phone.

"Hi, Mary Ann? I'm on the plane!" And it's after five, it's almost six, and Mary Ann shouldn't still be in her office, but of course she is. Behind her, she can hear a business tycoon starting his cell phone conversation with the same announcement: I'm on the plane! Oh, the miracle of technology! Oh, we're all so important, everyone better be keeping track of our coordinates!

"What about Athena," Lucy asks, "did she ever call in about missing the appointment this morning?"

"No, she didn't." Mary Ann knows that Lucy is not surprised by this—just as Lucy knows that Mary Ann is not surprised. Athena is missing appointments with her baby. They document this, notify her social worker, and begin—or continue—the process of establishing that yet one more time around, Athena is not capable of caring for yet one more baby. "I've already let her DSS worker know," Mary Ann says.

"Look," Lucy continues, because there is nothing more to say about Athena, "about the new family—you know the one I mean?" Lucy is pretty cautious about confidentiality, but sure enough Mary

Ann can identify them right away, Anthony and Joey DelBanco, a brand-new pair of kids, coming into foster care, as usual, without any medical records—without even explanations for the medicines they take. "I had a couple of thoughts about the older boy on my way to the airport," she continues. "First of all, I think in addition to the psych eval, he should have a full speech and language. There's just something—I'm not sure what it is, but I think we're missing some big piece of whatever's going on with that kid."

"Got it." Mary Ann's voice has that competent consider-it-done ring that makes you love a good nurse: the IV line is in, the med is given, the vital signs are charted. Next?

"And along the same lines, if you don't mind, I want him to get set up with neurology. And we should tell the foster mom to bring that mysterious bottle of pills along when he comes for his next visit in two weeks."

"You think they're anticonvulsants? Because she really needs to know if he has seizures—they shouldn't put a kid in her home and not tell her that."

"I hope to hell they aren't anticonvulsants. I hope they're multivitamins, or leftover antibiotics, or antihistamines—it makes me really nervous to have kids on meds and not know what they are or what they're for." Lucy thinks about children arriving out of the night, on the wings of social services, with their oddly assorted garments, their blankets, their fragments of whatever crumbling lives they've been leading up to now, before the crisis point was reached. Their bottles of mysterious medication. There is a silent invisible army of these children in every single city, moved from place to place, from placement to placement.

"The DSS worker is supposed to call me today and read the label to me, if there's a label—if not, she'll describe the pills and I'll see if I can identify them—and if I can't, I'll just have her make an extra trip and bring them in, okay?"

"Thank you, Mary Ann. You're wonderful." Lucy is not a bit surprised that Mary Ann already has a plan to solve the problem.

"Have a good trip to California." Mary Ann is not teasing; Mary

Ann is not trying to make her feel bad. Mary Ann simply has things under control.

She tries a token goodbye call to home, but gets only the answering machine; Greg must have taken the kids out for dinner, and maybe a movie.

Lucy has pretty strict rules for herself about flying; she doesn't usually end up jammed into that middle seat. And she always gets her bag up overhead, no matter how crowded the flight is, which means she's one of those aggressive passengers, hanging out in front of the ticket counter and pushing ahead right when she calculates her row is about to be called, and sometimes putting the bag up over someone else's seat, way forward of where she's sitting, if it's clear that there's no room farther back. She takes a window seat, thank you very much, and on the rare occasions that she can't book one in advance and they give her something else, she has a whole repertoire of techniques designed to get it switched at the last minute at the check-in counter. She likes to sit down, ideally the first person in her row, occupy her middle armrest immediately, take off her shoes, and cross her legs. It is her theory that if she is there first, whoever comes next cannot in any way make her feel self-conscious about her foot in its sock or even her bare foot sticking out in his direction. And most important, she does not speak to her seatmates. Ever. Well, of course she makes a little technical conversation: *Could you pass this to the flight attendant, excuse me, I want to go use the restroom, sorry to disturb you, thank you so much.* But any overtures—even a casual "so are you going or coming?"—or any comments on her reading materials or even any chitchat about the flight are to be responded to with at most a one-word answer ("Going") or, if possible, a wordless *mmm*.

Lucy has a whole crackpot theory, in fact, about how women tend, as travelers, to subsume their interests, hesitating to take up space (grab the overhead bin, stake out the armrest, recline the seat back all the way), letting themselves be made uncomfortable. On a recent trip to Minneapolis, she was asked if she would mind occupying an aisle seat a little farther forward, so a family could sit together, and Lucy, that tireless worker for distressed families everywhere, said firmly that she was so sorry, she preferred her window seat, and the family made somebody else move, and Lucy sat triumphantly, arm on her armrest, laptop tucked under the empty middle seat beside her, which also meant a tray-table she could lower for her Diet Coke and still keep the space in front of her free, and felt not a pang. Well, actually she felt rather self-congratulatory, which might have to be considered a kind of reverse pang.

But should those rules apply up here in business class? Lucy leans back into the softer, bigger seat and allows herself a tiny fantasy: kind of your standard-issue handsome man sits down beside you in an airplane fantasy. I mean, after all, here she is off for two nights in what is supposed to be a very nice hotel in San Diego —why not imagine a ripening friendship over the complimentary cocktails that ends with the two of them, on a terrace overlooking the Pacific, gazing at each other in the kind of wordless mutual understanding that can only lead them to take those few steps into the bedroom and consummate all that must be consummated—on the luxury king-size bed with the ultra-high-thread-count sheets.

"Excuse me, I think this is my seat." It's a kid, of course; after that fantasy, it would have to be either a kid or maybe a nun—except surely nuns don't fly business class. Not that you necessarily expect a kid to be flying business class either. He's wiry and small, but Lucy has a fifth-grade daughter, and he could easily be in Isabel's class; that's what a lot of the boys look like, even in the sixth grade. He's just young—what's called in the trade "pre-pubertal"; he's young and skinny and he has a pointy little intelligent face.

He is checking his boarding pass again, and then the seat numbers up above. The flight attendant comes bustling over, but he shakes his head. "Thank you very much for your concern, but I can manage."

In fact, he holds up the line of boarding passengers while he opens his backpack, takes out a number of electronic toys, a couple of books, carefully closes the backpack, thinks of something else and opens it again, takes out a small metal object the size of a paperback book, closes the backpack, puts it up above, and then finally sits down in his seat, opening the pocket in front of him to deposit his various electronic toys, his books, his flat metal object, and what looks to Lucy like a tiny television set.

To Lucy he says, "I am not flying as an unaccompanied minor this time. I used to have to fly as an unaccompanied minor, when I was younger, and then up through last year my father always insisted on paying the fee, but now I'm too old, and I don't need their help. And also, I always hated flying as an unaccompanied minor because they make you wait and be the last person off the plane so the flight attendant can walk you out and sign you over. So now I have my father book this airline in part because it has better policies. With regard to unaccompanied minors, I mean."

This is maybe four times the total conversation that Lucy has had with a seatmate in the past two years of busy travel. But she has a reason for being interested: Freddy. In a couple of years, Freddy could be this boy, with his gadgets and his contained energy and his, well, weirdness.

"How old do you have to be to be too old to fly as an unaccompanied minor?" This is a test. If he is really like Freddy, he will be very precise.

"With this airline, it's twelve. I'm twelve. By the way, I'm in the sixth grade, not that that matters for the airlines. They only care about your age and not about your grade level, which doesn't really make sense, but that's the way it is. But don't get me wrong—with certain airlines, you can choose to have your child fly unaccompanied but not pay the extra charge and then it's just that no one meets him and takes him off the plane—but my father would always rather pay extra if it's possible. It's something that I have noticed about my father, that if you give him a choice, he will always choose the extra services and pay more, but that isn't true of many people, because many people would rather save money, but it is true of my father."

"Well, maybe he loves you and he worries about you," Lucy says, gamely trying to hold up the adult end, but also wondering, *How did we get so personal so fast? Is that what Freddy would do, open up his family to any casual seatmate?*

"My mother says it's part of not having any common sense."

So Lucy will find herself remembering this exchange the next morning: as she launches into the carefully calibrated personal note at the beginning of her standard academic lecture, she will find herself reflecting briefly on the politics and strategies of personal revelation.

> Thank you so much, Dr. Berkowitz—Joe—for that very generous introduction. I am honored to be here. I would like to start this lecture by giving you some personal history. I am a foster-child success story; when I was four years old, my mother died and my father was unable to care for me, and in fact died himself two years later, and I was put into foster care and lived with several foster mothers in succession. This was not actually so unusual, way back when; a widower without relatives to help him could turn to the foster care system without feeling disgraced; no one expected him to be able to care for a small child on his own. My father died as well, and I stayed in the foster care system; eventually, I was adopted by one of my foster mothers, who sent me through college, and whom I still regard as my family. So that's why I am a success story; the system was there for me when I needed a safety net. It caught me and it held me, until I was ready to go out on my own.

The strategies of personal revelation. Lucy considers her new business-class seatmate and takes a guess. "Do you fly so much because your parents live in different cities?"

"Yes," says the boy, "you're very clever to see that right away. Many people don't. My father lives in San Diego and my mother lives in Boston. I'm going out to spend my spring break with my father because mostly I live with my mother. But that does mean that I fly a lot." When Lucy is silent he adds, after a moment, "Most people say something about my frequent flyer miles."

Something in Lucy is tsk-tsk-tsking about parents who can't manage to stay in the same city for the sake of the kid—and something else in Lucy is reminding herself that actually, she has a lot of work she wants to do on the flight and will perhaps have to extricate herself from all this chat after they take off.

But after takeoff, the kid immediately pulls out a book and says to Lucy, "Excuse me, but I will be reading now for the next little while," which oddly leaves her feeling mildly snubbed.

As soon as the pilot announces that it's okay, Lucy takes out her laptop, but the flight attendant is already there with the offer of a drink, a little glass bowl of mixed salted nuts. With that sleek and darkly promising businessman next to her, Lucy knows just what she would have asked for: a bloody mary, and she would have sipped it with the pleasure of someone who never in all her life has a serious drink before dinner on a weekday.

"What brand of apple juice do you have?" asks the boy, sounding worried. The flight attendant, who up here at the front of the plane is trained to show no surprise or irritation, goes away and comes back with the carton, and the boy inspects it with evident relief. "That's fine," he says. "I would like half apple juice, half sparkling water with no ice, and two pieces of lemon in it. Thank you very much."

"I'll have a bloody mary," Lucy says. After all, what the hell kind of virtue is it to have a life so goddamn predictable that you would never have a drink before dinner on a weekday?

"That has vodka in it," says her seatmate, informatively. Lucy nods. "And a sidecar has brandy, and a manhattan has bourbon or whiskey," he continues. "A martini can have vodka or gin, and a whiskey sour has whiskey, of course."

Lucy, who is feeling more and more dipsomaniacal by the second, looks over at his book—the cocktail handbook, no doubt, which he is no doubt studying to understand the things that mean the most to his father, or something like that. It's a thick book from a series on Civil War battles—*Antietam: The Bloodiest Day*.

"And a margarita has tequila, and a dayk—how do you pronounce it?"

"A daiquiri?" Lucy's voice is a little louder than she had intended, since she has to call it up out of her throat very deliberately, and the flight attendant, who is reaching forward to hand her her glass, filled to the brim with thick red stuff and topped with a large and plumelike celery stalk, pulls back, looking surprised.

"I'm so sorry, ma'am, I thought you ordered a bloody mary."

"I did." Lucy reaches up and grasps the cold glass, firmly.

"She did," the boy reassures the flight attendant, who has also brought his glass, another serious, heavy, pebble-bottomed cocktail glass, filled with a thin, pale amber liquid and a couple of prominent lemon wedges. "I was just saying that a daiquiri is made with whiskey."

"Sometimes with rum, actually," says the flight attendant, and winks at him. She is a cheerful woman, about Lucy's age but much better tended. Her eyebrows are neatly plucked, her makeup is skillful and flattering, and her hair curves obediently around her head like a shining brown helmet. Her uniform is neat and serious; her nametag says she is Andrea.

The boy is looking at her very seriously. Actually, Lucy has not seen him look anything but serious since he came down the aisle.

"How come some drinks tell you in the name what they are, like gin and tonic, or whiskey sour, or rum and Coke, or brandy alexander?"

"Vodka and tonic," suggests Andrea. "Tequila sunrise."

"Tequila sunrise?" The boy looks interested. A new one!

"They were really popular when I was young," Lucy says. "I don't think I've heard of anyone having one in years and years."

"We used to go out for them when I was in college," Andrea says. "Back when the drinking age was eighteen, and I think that might be the first drink I ordered legally."

"But other drinks you have to just know," the boy continues. "Like a daiquiri." He gets the pronunciation right. "Or a rusty nail. Or a white russian."

"Mmm, white russians," says Andrea. "I used to love those." Then she looks rather severely down at the boy and asks, "So how come you're so interested in these things? You don't look over twenty-one to me!"

Lucy smiles, but the boy does not. Nor does he look offended or patronized. He just launches into his explanation in the same flat, slightly pedantic tone.

"Of course I'm not over twenty-one. And I hope you notice that I did not order a drink with any alcohol in it when you asked me."

Andrea nods, taking him seriously.

"I'm just very interested at this point in what forms of alcohol are used in what mixed drinks. It's one of my interests, that's all, so I'm trying to pursue it. That's what you do when you're interested in a subject—you master it. I have a book at home—actually it's my mother's book, but she never uses it. I think it might have been a wedding present when she and my father got married, because I don't think either of them would be likely to have bought it. They don't drink very much except for wine sometimes. When they were married, I don't remember them ever having any of those drinks at all, and even though that was not one of my interests at the time, I think I would remember. Actually, now that he lives in California, my father has become quite interested in wine, but that is not one of my interests. Not at this point."

Andrea nods, accepting this information with a kind of professional efficiency, and then has already moved on to bring drinks to the people in the row behind. Lucy sips her bloody mary, tasting tomato and spice and the thin chemical sense of the alcohol beyond. She closes her eyes for just a second. You know how you have these flashes sometimes where everything about modern life seems frankly unbelievable, precarious, absurd? Here she is, miles up in the atmosphere, protected from a freezing, airless death by this thin skin of metal and plastic, protected from crashing way down to earth only by the thousand little maintenance steps that keep these engines functioning, leaning back against a leather cushion and drinking vodka mixed with spiced tomato juice. The sheer energy of human beings seems quite improbable and almost touching—to build such a machine! To fill it full of liquors and juices! To fly it back and forth!

"Cocktails are not actually one of my main interests," says the boy's voice beside her. "I just found this book—the one that belongs to my mother now even though I think it was probably a wedding present to both my parents—and I thought it would be good to know about different drinks, so it's kind of like a hobby of mine. A minor interest. But even a minor interest is something you can master."

Lucy opens her eyes. "Is the Civil War one of your main interests?"

"Actually it is," he says, "but how did you know? Oh, of course, you saw my book."

"I did," Lucy agrees. "Is it good?"

"I find this whole series to be excellent in giving both points of view on a battle. I have the whole set. I've read this one before, but I like to read things over and over again."

I'll bet you do, Lucy thinks. Is this what Freddy is going to be like in a few years, her peculiar son, who has to learn his way around people so carefully, step by step, but who lives his life in a brightly lit mind full of lists and categories and fascinations? So which way did this kid's parents go, she wonders, have they had him assessed and diagnosed—what about that father, after all, who would always rather pay more and get extra services—or do they just think he's smart and he's a little on the weird side?

Thinking of her own son, she says, "My name is Lucy," and the boy immediately sticks his right hand across the wide business-class armrest between them.

Lucy hastily puts her drink down on her other armrest and extends her own right hand. Only when their hands are clasped does the boy say, "My name is Theodore. I don't like to be called Ted or Teddy. I'm happy to meet you."

"I'm happy to meet you, too, Theodore," Lucy says, and her hand is released.

Lucy thinks of her laptop and of the work she could be doing. She thinks again of Freddy, and she says, "What's so interesting about that particular battle, Theodore?" After all, here she is, flying all the way across the United States of America in order to pontificate—doesn't Theodore deserve a few minutes at the microphone?

Today's talk will focus on the medical needs of children in foster care, on the ways in which those needs often go unmet, and on some modifications we can make that offer real benefits in health outcomes for these children. But first, let me take you through some quick history. The foster care system in this country can trace its origins back to the end of the nineteenth century. It may not surprise you to learn that from the very beginning, the system has been a mix of good and charitable intentions and horrendous missteps, often founded in a patronizing readiness to meddle in the lives of the poor, and often resulting in the destruction of families rather than in their preservation. In the middle of the nineteenth century, Charles Loring Brace, who was secretary of the New York Children's Aid Society, originated a policy of taking children out of the cruel unwholesome city and sending them out West to live and work on farms, and, it was hoped, acquire good work habits, strong bodies, and honest heartland values. Starting in 1854 and continuing right up to 1929, there were more than 100,000 children sent out by train. Who were these children? Some were orphans, some were abandoned—but some were just the children of the poor, especially the children of immigrants, whose parents, new to New York City, new to America, couldn't take care of them properly, and those children got sent off into the unknown. There wasn't much supervision of the homes these children went to, and there certainly wasn't any system of support for the families who took them in. Some of them had their religions changed—made over from Catholics into Protestants, which didn't please the Catholic Church at all. Some were essentially adopted into their new families, even though they had parents back in New York who hoped to see them again someday when times were better. And for some, it was a chance at a new and better life, a family, an opportunity, an education, that would otherwise have been out of the question. As always, when you start taking children out of their homes, it was complicated. And you can see that some of the most controversial and persistent issues were with us right from the beginning: *are children being taken away from their parents just because those parents are poor? What kind of support and supervision do foster families need? What happens to a child who is put in foster place-ment with people of a different race or religion? And finally, are you ever going to be able to put these families back together, and is that really the goal?*

Theodore has been discussing the Battle of Antietam for per-haps fifteen minutes flat when back comes Andrea to start serv-ing their lunch. Filet mignon or shrimp scampi, she asks, and Lucy goes, unhesitatingly, for the filet mignon. Theodore says shrimp.

"I don't usually get to fly business class," Lucy confides. "It's kind of a thrill."

Theodore looks at her, confused. Then, to Lucy's surprise, he blushes. He looks truly embarrassed and uncomfortable, and she wonders whether he has never before in his life met a person who doesn't fly business class.

"I should have asked you something about yourself," Theodore says, almost in a whisper.

"What do you mean?"

Andrea descends again, opening their trays for them and spread-ing out napkins and silver, but no food. Theodore waits until she moves away.

"I just talked and talked about my own interests without ask-ing you anything about yourself. Didn't I? I'm not supposed to do that."

"Hey," Lucy says, distressed by his look of genuine misery, as if he has definitively and publicly failed at something important. "Hey, Theodore. You were doing just fine. Really you were, you were doing a great job of talking to a grownup and a stranger on an airplane flight."

He looks at her balefully, so she charges forward. "The truth is, Theodore, I don't usually talk to the person next to me on an air-plane—I always have work to do and I never want to listen to the stories of their lives—so the only reason I'm talking to you is be-cause you're so nice and polite and pleasant to talk to. Because you were so *interesting.*"

He is still watching her, so what the hell, she keeps going. "Really, I never talk to people on airplanes. In fact, sometimes I have to be pretty rude. The nice little old lady next to me says, *And where are you going, dear?* and I just growl at her. Grr! Back, back I say! Don't talk to me, don't tell me about your grandchildren!"

Theodore smiles. He does have a most lovely smile, a smile so much like Freddy's smile, back home, that Lucy can't help it, she says, "Tell me some more about Antietam."

"Well," says Theodore, looking worried, "just to recapitulate, because I know it's hard to keep the chronology straight, as I mentioned before, the battle was fought on September 17, 1862, along Antietam Creek in Maryland, which, as I told you, is quite near Sharpsburg. And as I said, just to remind you, the creek is where the battle gets its name. Should I review the casualty figures, just so you keep them in mind?"

"Yes," Lucy says, in order to hear him recite his numbers again: for the Union, 2,108 killed, 9,540 wounded, 753 captured or missing; for the Confederacy, 1,546 killed, 7,752 wounded, 1,018 wounded or missing. The bloodiest single day of battle in American history, as Theodore has already informed her.

"And remember," he tells her anxiously, "in those days, many of the wounds were much more serious and more likely to lead eventually to death or at least to a permanent handicap. Surgery was very primitive and the battlefield conditions were terrible, and no one knew about germs and about keeping things sterile and there was no anesthesia."

There is simply no end to his information. How McClellan lost the chance to really smash Lee. How Lee chose his position stupidly because his soldiers' retreat was blocked by a river. Hooker. Hood. Mansfield. Jackson. Lucy figures, What the hell, you can't work on your laptop when you have food on your table, and it's hard to read and cut your steak all at the same time. I'll pay good attention to Theodore here and listen to all his battlefield statistics, and in return could you make sure that if Freddy ever has to travel alone, he gets a nice lady doctor to sit next to who enjoys his eccentricities and engages him in conversation about one of his pet subjects? Thanks.

And by God, she is going to eat every single morsel of this food. She suspects that the casual of-course-I-fly-up-here-at-the-front-of-the-plane-all-the-time thing to do would be to leave it, or to demand something not on the menu—*Could I just have a plain green salad, please?*

Oh, but here comes the salad, rolling down the center aisle on a little cart, Andrea tossing it for each passenger with a big wooden spoon and fork, sprinkling it with pecans, dressing it as requested. Lucy says yes to salad, yes to pecans, yes to more pecans, yes to blue cheese dressing. Theodore says no, thank you.

"I don't care to eat much salad. I'm just like my father in that way. He doesn't eat much salad either. My mother does eat a lot of salad. In fact, she has salad every day for lunch, just about, and even when she goes to a restaurant that's all she orders, a salad." Theodore is examining one of his shrimp, carefully and critically.

Somewhat guiltily, Lucy digs into her steak. And you know what —it's a perfectly okay little steak, tastes fine sprinkled with salt from her tiny glass shaker, eaten off a real china plate, up here in midair. Lucy will tuck the menu card into her laptop case and take it home for Isabel, who will enjoy the notion of filet mignon and shrimp scampi and salad tossed in the aisle—and most of all she will enjoy knowing that regular passengers pay a couple of thousand dollars extra just for that steak, or just for that shrimp. That's Isabel's kind of information, a little factoid that proves to her that there's a sucker born every minute. Lucy can just imagine Isabel, returning to the joke over and over again: *So, Mom, is your hamburger as good as that thousand-dollar filet mignon?*

She takes a few careful, surreptitious looks at Theodore's table manners, since table manners are not Freddy's strong point, but Theodore is eating his shrimp quite competently. He sometimes talks with his mouth full, but that is because there is just so much to say about the Battle of Antietam.

His narrative gathers strength as he proceeds—or perhaps it would be fairer to say that the accumulation of facts and figures and stories, all offered in this intense, absorbed way by this skinny, serious kid, gathers strength and becomes a narrative.

"So the thing about Antietam, the reason I find it so interesting, is who really won? You can argue it so many ways. Lee retreated—he pulled his troops off the battlefield first—so that makes it seem like the Union won. But Lee was much better than McClellan—McClellan had him outnumbered, he had his secret plans—he should have smashed him, and he didn't. In fact, President Lincoln thought McClellan was so bad, he relieved him of command—so you couldn't really call him a winner. And lots of people would say everybody lost, since after all it was the single day in history on which the most Americans died—did I mention that already?"

Lucy nods.

The plates and silverware and glasses have been cleared. The cart has come down the aisle again, this time offering ice cream and your choice of topping. Lucy has chocolate ice cream with butterscotch sauce. Theodore doesn't want the ice cream. "I don't like anything that's too cold in my mouth," he says, and Lucy thinks, Oh right, no ice in his apple juice.

"On the other hand," Theodore says, as Lucy fills her own mouth with cold, "Antietam may not have been much of a military victory for the North, but Lincoln used it as an excuse to issue the Emancipation Proclamation—you know what that is, don't you?" He waits again for Lucy's nod. "And it marked the end of Lee's campaign to take the war North, and to raise support for the Confederacy in Maryland. So it was a real turning point in the war from that point of view."

He pauses and takes a deep breath, and Lucy is nerving herself to say, *You know, I really need to do a little work now.* Because she really does—she needs, if nothing else, to go over the talk she's going to give—and besides, she's feeling a little bit exhausted after the single bloodiest day in American history; who knows how many more Civil War battles there may be to fight?

But instead Theodore leans forward, pulls a disc player out of the seat pocket.

"Please excuse me," he says, very politely, to Lucy.

"Of course," she says.

"I can't talk to you now for a while," he says. He snaps a disc into the player. "I have to go over my bar mitzvah lessons."

Partly because of some of the objections that were raised to these rather drastic early attempts at foster placement, officials began to formalize the standards and the procedures for keeping children in foster care. And what was also formalized, and I'm referring now to the White House Conference on Children of 1909, was the goal: *foster care exists as a temporary measure in order to restore children, ultimately, to their biological families.*

II. Out West: Excellent Questions

Lucy stands at the podium in one of those high-tech medical lecture hall wombs, which they seem to grow out here on the West Coast. The console in front of her bears no buttons or switches at all—it's a computer screen where you select commands with a mouse, illuminating the hall with any perfect combination of dim and bright lighting, making screens roll up and down, videotape projectors snake down out of the ceiling, perhaps activating a trap door or the ejector seat. In any case, Lucy has been forbidden to touch any of these controls by TJ, a big, fat, brown-bearded AV guy in ragged denim cut-offs and a T-shirt that says "Harvard, the UC Irvine of the East." TJ was waiting when she arrived at 7:30 A.M., took over her laptop for her and hooked it up, rapidly ran a bunch of tests, told her he'd be back in the glass AV booth and he would take care of everything, and that the only thing she should touch is the little forward arrow that advances her slides. And, of course, the little backward arrow if she wants to reverse. He didn't actually say, *Think you can handle that, Doc?* but it was clear in his every gesture.

And he is back there now, taking care of everything. The lights dim a little for her word slides, dim further for her photos, come up full if she addresses the audience more directly. Lucy imagines that what TJ would really like would be a bunch of new variables—with this finger, he makes the music swell, with that one he brings down a haze of blue mysterious lighting. He moves his mouse, and the podium starts to grow, like the Christmas tree in the *Nutcracker*.

Yes, TJ, you are a pro, but Lucy is a pro, too, in her tiny little way, and she can see by the digital clock on the console that she has exactly seven minutes left before the hour as she moves toward her conclusion. Two minutes for her peroration, then five for questions, and a thank-you from the chairman of the department. Lucy hates speakers who crowd the end of the hour; she doesn't like that whole posturing strut—*I have so much more to say because I know everything and you don't, but they're hooking me off the platform here.* If you know so much, pick the most important things to say in fifty minutes.

She winds up neatly, if not particularly originally, with a recap of the challenges and problems, an expression of hope for the future, and a somewhat emotional charge to her audience that together, committed to the welfare of children everywhere, we can make things better. The applause is more than token. Her final slide is a photo of a group of smiling children, three siblings she took care of maybe five years ago, great foster mom took the kids in, adorable children successfully reunited with their biological family after four months, bio-mom stayed clean, bio-dad came back to stay with bio-mom after she cleaned up her act, everyone did okay. One of the good stories. Which is why she has permission to use this photo, not that anyone would be likely to recognize the children. The oldest, Maurice, must be fifteen by now. Lucy remembers very clearly his furious paternal determination to protect his younger brother and sister; his great fear had been that they would be separated, and he had tensed up—and sometimes acted up—whenever the foster mother suggested a separate outing, even to buy the school clothes his little sister needed. Lucy wondered at the time, and she still wonders, whether Maurice could possibly grow up to be the kind of protective, gentle father that he tried to be at the age of ten. Could that happen? Could you spend the first ten years of your life watching your own awful parents demonstrate how *not* to do it, how to let things slide and ignore their kids and trade away anything they had for the right spoonful of something, and could you then turn it all around and become vigilant on behalf of order and safety and protection?

Oh, shit, someone has asked a question, and Lucy wasn't listening. She blinks; TJ has turned the lights up all the way to show that it's question time and to wake up any sleepers. The amphitheater is big, but it's pretty densely populated, just a couple of really empty rows here up front. The photo of Maurice and his siblings fades to pale, blurry shadows as the lights come up, and then clicks off as TJ tidies up. But a pleasant-looking woman in the center section, white coat, short brown curls, has asked a question, Lucy can hear the echo of her voice in the air.

TJ to the rescue. He comes clomping down the stairway from the AV booth, moving pretty fast, gesturing to Lucy not to answer, and hands a little microphone, the size of a cylindrical automobile cigarette lighter, to the woman who asked the question. "We're broadcasting this," he tells her, "so you have to speak into the mike."

So she repeats her question, and Lucy listens this time. Then there is a certain amount of good-natured laughter as the department chairman, who is moderating the questions, gallops around the amphitheater with the mike, handing it to every new questioner and retrieving it immediately after the question is asked. The department chairman, whom Lucy has met before, is a pretty good guy, well-meaning, not too desperately pompous, but more than a little stiff and formal, despite all his efforts to go California, and probably he relishes this chance to loosen up a little in public.

That's an important question, and thank you for asking it. As I said earlier on, even basic health care, regular health supervision, for foster children *without* any medical risks is very complicated, and they often don't get the standard of care, and I think we all know that. And then, when you look at children with complex health care needs, the picture gets even worse.

And these may be some of the kids who end up in foster care in the first place because their medical needs just overwhelm their biological parents. If you find yourself taking care of a child like this, I think you have to make sure the foster parents are getting all the help and education and financial support they need. And the financial piece is very important. Some foster parents end up spending way beyond what they're reimbursed—I took care of one child with bigtime grand mal seizures, poorly controlled. His foster mom was afraid he would hurt himself, so she went and got a carpet and pads for his room—actually, I think she turned it into something like a padded cell! But my point is, she did her best to modify the home environment and make it safer, but she did it without any help or guidance or reimbursement from social services until we intervened and we said, Look, this mother needs teaching, and she needs more money, and she shouldn't be spending her food money on bottles and bottles of Tylenol and Motrin because she's so afraid he's going to get a fever and start to seize.

TJ, as he is disconnecting her computer and packing it away for her after the talk, has a quick comment. "Nice talk. I actually listened." Praise from the AV guy is praise indeed, but Lucy has an expert flash of what's coming next. "I saw the title on the schedule, and I was interested. Actually, I was a foster kid, for a while."

"I think there are a lot of us out there," Lucy says. The chairman is waiting, as is the woman with the curly brown hair, and a few other people, but she suspects TJ is too important in the department for anyone to mind his getting in first. This is part of the job, as Lucy knows: someone, likely or unlikely, will come up at the end of the talk to say, *I was in foster care.* Sometimes it's a terrible, unbelievable story, and sometimes they want to tell it. Lucy once had a rather distinguished middle-aged pediatric immunologist get distinctly teary, right in front of several members of his department. She is prepared for anything; part of the job. But she would put money on TJ to keep it light, all things considered.

And he does. "My mom had five of us and it just got to be too

much. After my dad left, I mean. She said it was five against one and she was losing." He chuckles, enjoying the joke all over again. "She put the older three in foster care—well, I don't know if she put us, or if someone from the welfare office decided it, but we always thought of it that way—she put us. Always came and visited us though. And it wasn't a bad deal. I was out on this artichoke farm—pretty good place, and the food was a lot better."

The chairman, who is standing nearby awaiting Lucy's attention, is plainly listening and is plainly a little bit surprised. "I didn't know that, TJ," he contributes, and TJ looks over, as if noticing his existence on the planet for the first time. Cute contrast, Lucy thinks, the chairman with his trim little silver-gray academic beard, his gleaming white coat, his snappy little red bow tie, and his aggressively glossy wingtips, and TJ with his fraying denim cutoffs and his wild mountain-man brown beard.

"Did you end up going back with your mother?" Lucy asks.

"Oh, sure." TJ seems to take that totally for granted. "She married again—they bought a pretty big place, and she took us back in age order, youngest first, so I was last. Actually, I was kinda bummed because I thought I was going to go to the high school out near the farm and I was going to run track—I had it all planned. You might not believe it to look at me now, but I was a pretty skinny kid—I looked like a runner. Then I end up going to high school in the city after all, and instead of going out running along these little roads out in the farm country, if you ran track there you practically had to practice in the bus station. So I was kind of bummed —but I guess also kind of glad to be back with the whole crew of them."

"Do you still keep in touch with your foster family?" Lucy asks. She has had versions of this conversation many many times, and she can predict the answer. But she's still interested.

"I usually go out there the day after Christmas. Boxing Day, she calls it, my foster mom. Her family was from England, and it's a big deal there. So I do Christmas with my mom and my brothers and my sister and their kids, then I go out the next day and see the other guys." He smiles. "How about you, Doctor?"

"My foster mom died when I was in medical school," Lucy says. "She was a little older when she adopted me—she didn't have kids of her own. And she died kind of young."

"That's tough," TJ says.

Okay, now, the chairman is beginning to look impatient. He needs to be deferred to, and Lucy, who has had versions of *that* conversation even more than she has had the foster child memories, knows her responsibilities.

"TJ, thank you so much for making everything go so smoothly with my talk—I'm totally intimidated by these high-tech places. You were great."

"That's my job, Doctor. Dr. Weiss. Hey, which name do you use?"

Great question, TJ. There's one that nobody ever thinks to ask. "It's my foster mother's name. I didn't take it right away, because I wasn't adopted till I was already in elementary school, and they wanted me to keep the same name, but when I was in medical school and she got sick, I changed it legally. It meant a lot to her." And to me. But enough. Lucy turns to include the chairman. "It's a pretty amazing facility you have here, I have to say. We don't have anything like this back in Boston. State of the art." There, that ought to make both of them puff up a little and feel good, TJ *and* the chairman of the department.

You know, the same way you can suddenly realize you are miles up in the air in a metal tube, drinking vodka and some spiced tomato mix, and wonder, *What am I doing, how can this have come to pass,* you can sometimes find yourself politely gasping at the wonderful art installation in the hospital lobby, this huge mobile hanging by multiple wires from the ceiling, set just far enough off the floor that no real children can hang on it, and you can ask yourself, *What is the meaning of this system of academic lectures? Why did I fly across the country to give your 8 A.M. weekly lecture, why am I admiring one more hospital when I've seen so many, when I could be home in my own doing my work?*

But this, of course, is merely the passing existential angst of the slightly jet-lagged professional circuit rider, and Lucy snaps herself out of it. She's perfectly happy to let him walk her through his hospital, to compliment the lobby sculpture, the department of pediatrics, the hotel where they're putting her up. She tells him that she enjoyed giving the talk, and it's perfectly true: lovely auditorium, interested audience, good questions.

They stand waiting for an elevator, Lucy and the chairman, and they're joined by a pair of parents pushing a little girl in a long wooden cart painted to look like a fire truck. Well, a fire truck with an IV pole attached. The child is perhaps four years old and completely bald; you can tell she's a girl mostly because instead of a hospital johnny, she is wearing a Disney costume outfit that Lucy recognizes as the dress from *Beauty and the Beast*. The mother pushes the cart while the father fusses with the IV pole, which has three different bags hanging on it and way too much tubing. The elevator comes and Lucy steps in and presses the button, holding the door open, while the chairman helps the father steady the IV pole across the threshold. Lucy looks down into the child's solemn face and wants to ask her name, and maybe more. Instead, she releases the door open button and asks the parents which floor they're going to. "Five," they say in unison. Lucy presses five, and says, quietly, to the child, "Cool dress."

They ride up to the fifth floor, where Lucy again holds the elevator door open, and the chairman again helps the family maneuver themselves out of the elevator. "Need help getting back to the unit?" the chairman asks, and they assure him that they're all set. He and Lucy stand together in the hallway and watch the two parents steer the fire truck cart through a set of automatic doors and out of sight.

"We need to go up two more floors to get to the primary care offices. Shall we take the stairs?"

"By all means," says Lucy.

They clop professionally up the hospital staircase from five to seven, like health-conscious doctors who are taking their own advice, Lucy thinks, like healthy people who are leaving the elevators for the sick.

"Dr. Pearson wanted to meet with you—Liz Pearson, our director of primary care—she was there at the end of your talk, but she couldn't wait—she had to meet with someone right at nine. She's the one who asked the first question—about families that aren't going to be able to be put back together."

"It was a good question. They were all good questions." Although the best question of all, Lucy thinks, was really TJ's: what name do you use, what do you think of as your family, where do you really belong?

That's another interesting question, and of course it's highly controversial. As I said in my talk, the initial reason for being, the underlying assumption behind foster care, has always had to be this presumption that this is a temporary option and you're trying to reunite families. But there has always been this pull in the other direction, and as you'll remember, I mentioned the Adoption Assistance and Child Welfare Act of 1980, which was specifically designed to make sure that children didn't stay in the foster care system forever—that at a certain point, if the biological family wasn't getting it together, parental rights would be terminated and the child would be eligible for adoption. But I think you're asking something slightly different, if I understand you, and what you're expressing is a frustration and even an anger that everyone who works with these kids comes to feel, and I've certainly felt it myself. It's this sense that some of these parents clearly aren't going to make it as parents, they're just, well, hopeless, and we all put in so much effort and so many services when it's perfectly clear that you're never going to reunite this family, or if you did it would be a total disaster for the child. And I think that's a very very real part of doing this job, and I wish I could tell you how to deal with those feelings—or deal with those parents. But I also think you have to keep in mind that when you look at the big picture—more than 450,000 kids in foster placements in this country—well, there aren't adoptive homes waiting for all those kids. And the foster homes aren't always great. And the truth is that for many of them, their best bet is to put the biological family back together and prop it up, because that way at least they have a place in the world. It's not totally satisfactory, but it may be the best we can do.

"I liked what you said about the hopeless parents," says Elizabeth Pearson, making Lucy welcome in her crowded office. Lots of low-maintenance plants, spider plants and pothos and wandering jew and rubber plants. Lots of books, lots of journals, lots of framed diplomas and certificates, and a wall of family artifacts, photos of kids—at least two of them, maybe a third, if the cute little blond boy naked on the beach isn't the same as the darker, older boy in the next picture over, dressed in a jacket and tie. Lucy makes an automatic resolution about her own office at the medical center back home, which is pretty bare and functional. She does have one picture of Isabel and Freddy, though it's already kind of old, but you would never sit down in her office and get this feeling of exuberant greenness and happy childhoods.

"Thanks," Lucy says, "I thought I was kind of running on a little there with the questions. I think it's jet lag—it kind of disrupts your sense of timing."

She leans back in Elizabeth Pearson's guest chair and accepts a cup of tea that smells of cinnamon. This is her first time meeting Elizabeth, though they've corresponded about Lucy coming to give this lecture, but they have already managed some kind of quick-and-dirty female-doctor bonding, which, without ever mentioning the chairman, allows them both to drop the manner they automatically assume around him and talk to each other like normal people.

Which is a relief. The male doctors are all very well, but they can wear you down. Lucy thinks of her husband, Greg, far away, and his set of favorite doctor jokes: a guy goes up to heaven, and as he's waiting at the pearly gates, he sees a mysterious figure go by, wrapped in a white coat, and he asks, *Who's that?* and Saint Peter says, *Oh, that's God, he likes to play doctor sometimes.*

"Do you want a tour of the clinic?" asks Elizabeth. "I mean, we can if you want, but it's just a clinic. You've probably seen them before."

"Actually, I would love a tour, later on, after I drink this." The schedule says that Lucy will meet with the residents at noon for a teaching session, and then after that, she thinks, perhaps she can get someone to give her a ride back to her hotel, which is, amazingly, right on the beach, and she can put on normal clothes and go for a walk along the ocean, and sit somewhere gazing out at the blue and reading the novel she brought along but has not yet opened. An afternoon on the beach, before it's time to go back to her room and dress up again and be picked up and taken out to dinner.

Elizabeth's beeper goes off, and Lucy sips her tea, makes the universal routine gesture of go-ahead-and-answer, and then finds herself listening in to something that it is in no way routine: Elizabeth, suddenly sharp and furious, telling someone off fiercely.

"The pediatric intern did everything she was supposed to do. She assessed the patient correctly and she called for help. And the pediatric resident responded promptly and supported her assessment, and what is absolutely inexcusable is that it took surgery over two hours to respond!" Elizabeth sets down her mug with such an emphatic bang that tea splashes out onto the papers on her desk. She rises to her feet and her voice gets louder; she is clearly interrupting the person on the other end of the phone.

"No, I am *not* saying to you that this delay was the critical factor, and I do *not* appreciate being misinterpreted *or* misquoted. But I am warning you not to try and explain this by accusing the pediatric intern—"

And now, Lucy thinks, the person—the guy—the surgeon on the other end of the phone has raised his voice and cut her off.

"Listen," Elizabeth says, almost yelling. "This is completely pointless. Clearly, this is a signal event, and there will have to be a full investigation, and everyone involved is going to feel really bad. And I don't know enough at this point to tell you whether you ought to be feeling bad in surgery *because* your residents are overworked and overwhelmed, or *because* they don't get enough support, or just *because* they're too arrogant to come when a nonsurgeon tells them it's urgent. But it's really your job to figure that out, not mine." She hangs up the phone and turns to face Lucy, flushed and furious.

"I'm sorry," she says. "We just had—just the other night—we had a total disaster. Never should have happened. Near-death experience, and I don't just mean for the patient. And I'm left picking up the pieces with a totally devastated intern and a resident who thinks he almost killed a kid because the fucking surgeons are just being unbelievable!"

She tells Lucy a terrible story: a kid who was being watched in the hospital for an array of peculiar symptoms, including some abdominal pain, who turned out to have a walled-off abdominal abscess and suddenly got much sicker, with horrible peritonitis—and basically almost died on the operating table. Still not out of the woods, still in intensive care, we don't know yet if his brain took a hit when his pressure bottomed out. And it should never have happened. And the surgeons are saying the pediatric residents didn't do this or didn't do that, when the truth is, Elizabeth says, getting up and beginning to pace, "The truth is that the surgeons knew about this kid all along, and they didn't think he had anything surgical, and I'm not really blaming them, because to be honest, neither did we."

"But then when he got sick, they didn't come right away?"

"Oh, you know, it was the usual surgical crap about how we're in the OR, we're so busy saving lives. They didn't take the call seriously enough and they know it and they missed a surgical diagnosis and they know it and a kid nearly died—and I have an intern who is feeling suicidal, because they've made her think she personally almost murdered this child!" She takes an audible deep breath, then shakes her head vigorously. Takes a gulp of her tea and starts a new subject. "You said you were adopted out of foster care?"

"Yes," Lucy says. "Actually, I was adopted by one of my teachers. You know, I think in lots of ways it was a different world back then—people weren't so shocked that my own father put me in foster care, and then after he died, it kind of made sense to everyone that my teacher adopted me. It was like, oh, she gets good grades in school, naturally a teacher would adopt her."

"I assume it was a lot more than that, actually."

"Actually, it was everything," Lucy finds herself saying, in a sudden rush of instant intimacy, the kind you feel with someone you know slightly but recognize more fully. "It was like—well, the word I always use to myself is *rescue*, and you know how we always think about the possibility of rescue, and the responsibility to rescue."

"And the ones who don't get rescued."

"Not that my life was so awful, you understand. The women who took care of me were mostly kind enough and conscientious enough—again, it was a different era, they were middle-class housewives trying to earn a little extra money. I don't have a lot of atrocity stories. I look at the kids I take care of and I know how lucky I was."

"And then someone rescued you." Elizabeth smiles at her. "So, you want that clinic tour?"

Lucy takes the clinic tour, and she lectures to the residents at their noon conference, while they munch on caesar salad. She looks them over, wondering whether the guilt-ridden intern is among them. They look young and fresh-faced and they eat all the oatmeal cookies.

And within half an hour of lecturing to the residents, Lucy is back in a cool, dim hotel room, draped in forest green, with a window that looks right out over the Pacific.

Another simple travel rule: have your comfortable clothing ready. And look how it pays off, as she strips down, hangs her coffee-colored linen suit and her white blouse in the closet, and eagerly puts on her elastic-waist slacks and worn cotton turtleneck and sneakers. She takes off gold earrings, necklace of gold and pearl beads, and wristwatch and makes a little clinking pile on the hotel dresser. She lets her hair down out of the professional knot and braids it back over her shoulders into one somewhat wispy braid, and pulls a cloth-covered elastic band off the handle of her hairbrush to secure it. She has an out-of-school feeling, a sense of having been dropped by her life unexpectedly into a secret sunny patch, and she slides the little computer card room key into her pocket and practically runs down the flight of stairs to the lobby.

And she is still almost running as she moves along the paved walk that takes you way down the beach, to where the land swings out again to a point. Lucy is a veteran of many medical center hotels, many Marriotts and Holiday Inn Crowne Plazas and Radissons, and she well knows how rare it is that at the end of your flight, as you clutch your laptop and your handouts, you find yourself walking into a luxury resort set along a curve of white sand beach and blue water. It's a little chilly for swimming, but there are windsurfers out, wearing wetsuits, and there are plenty of people sitting on the beach, some fully clothed, some sun-worshipping in bathing suits. Maybe people on vacation, but probably people whose lives can easily happen to include a few hours on the beach in the afternoon, and Lucy is one of them, just for today. She feels a flash of travel serendipity, which comes every now and then even to the professional journeying lecturer who thinks that everything is predictable and functional and prides herself on her fussy little habits of preparation and her trivial tactics of travel one-upmanship: look what can suddenly unfold!

Lucy veers off the path and walks across the sand toward the water. Plops down, pulls off her sneakers and her socks, grinds her feet into the sand. Leans her head all the way back in the sun, closes her eyes, and lets her mind go a little bit blank. Ocean sounds, traffic sounds, voices, a breeze playing over her face with a definite feeling of salt. *Here I am. Here I am. Saving the world, one luxury resort at a time.*

No one really gives very much thought to the sexuality of the forty-five-year-old woman with a couple of kids and a perfectly fine husband and a good busy job. Lucy has considered this unexamined subject before, usually while traveling, and she considers it again now, sitting on the beach. The potentially ravenous but highly unembarrassed sexuality of someone who does not even have to pretend to be surprised by the strange compulsions of bodies. Who has done the reproductive thing, been and gone and knows it all, from birth canals to breasts, and is left, once again, *unembarrassed.* What do they dream about, these women, as they wheel their rolling suitcases along? What do I dream about, Lucy thinks, beyond a hotel room to myself and an unexpected hour on the beach? Do I dream of something unpredictable, the faint crunch of some new body settling down on the sand next to mine and I open my eyes to see—what? A nineteen-year-old in a naval uniform? A researcher from the oceanographic institute, here at the beach to take readings of something or other? A body-beautiful, works-out-every-day millionaire just my age, looking for a cause to endow? A leftover sixties California pothead potter, mellow and sun-browned with extraordinarily strong fingers? Perhaps I dream of Dr. Elizabeth Pearson, unpredictable in another way, but very attractive as she stood there in her office. If she sat here with me now, would she think, even a quick bewildered thought, of kissing me?

Lucy lets herself drop backward onto her elbows, then, what the hell, flat down on the sand. So she'll get a little sand in her hair; the hotel bathroom is full of tiny richly colored bottles, and she will shower and shampoo and condition before she goes out to dinner. How drowsy she is now, in the sun. So no one really gives much thought to the sexuality of the forty-five-year-old woman with a couple of kids and a good busy job. And put her down on the beach, and maybe she enjoys a few raunchy thoughts, but then off to sleep she drifts, the light, delightful seize-the-moment sleep of the forty-five-year-old woman in the sun.

III. Returning East: Rapid Onset

In the obviously ill-omened crowd at the check-in desk that afternoon, Lucy sees a face she knows.

"Theodore!" she calls, and the boy turns, searches the crowd with his anxious eyes, finally sights her, smiles, waves. He tugs the arm of the man next to him in the much shorter first-class line, points to Lucy, explaining excitedly. Then he waves Lucy over to join them, but she shakes her head; she belongs right where she is. And by her side is Elizabeth Pearson, who was the person Lucy called when she returned to the hotel, when she got the urgent message from home, when she returned the call, when she finally tracked down her daughter, Isabel, and figured out what was going on.

"My husband's been admitted," Lucy said, grateful for another doctor. "Sudden onset, severe right-sided abdominal pain. They think it's an appy." *And I don't want to think about that kid with peritonitis who almost died.*

"So you've got to get back," said Elizabeth. "Do you know if there's a flight still tonight?"

"There's one at five-thirty," Lucy said. "I already talked to them, and they'll let me use my ticket."

"Perfect," said Elizabeth. "I'll pick you up outside the hotel in fifteen minutes."

Only on the drive to the airport did she ask any questions, and most of those were exactly the same questions that Lucy herself had asked when she finally got hold of Isabel at someone else's house, after finally deciphering the phone number on the crumpled pink hotel message slip. *Yes, it moved really fast, this morning he thought he had a little upset stomach from something he ate the night before, then he started vomiting, and by this afternoon when it was time to pick Freddy up at school, he could barely drive. That's when he got scared, and he got the kids home and then called his friend Michael, who came over, took one look at him, and said, You're going to the hospital, something's wrong. I talked to Michael; he says that Greg really looked terrible.*

And so the kids are over at Michael's house; they're old friends, Michael and his wife, Leora. Good old friends, the kids know them very well. But still.

"You need to be there," said Elizabeth, switching them smoothly into an exit lane and off the freeway. "Did you reach your husband?"

"I called the hospital twice. The first time they said he wasn't formally an in-patient yet—he must have still been being evaluated in the ER. The second time they said he was in a room, not in the operating room—but when they rang the room, no one answered. And I was in such a hurry to get packed, I just didn't have time to keep calling and waiting around on hold."

"Go ahead, call again. You've got time."

So Lucy punches redial on her cell phone once again and gets the hospital operator once again, and gives a slightly haughty speech about being Dr. Lucy Weiss and needing to get in touch with a patient, and having been switched to a phone that no one would answer last time. And the operator spends a few heavy-breathing seconds looking for the name, and then the music again, but then the phone rings and Lucy hears Greg's voice.

"Hello?"

"Hi, Greg, it's me. I'm on my way to the airport. I'm going to fly back tonight."

"This is the weirdest thing," he says, but he doesn't sound like he's in agony. Or like he's expiring. So she takes a deep breath and puts the lid on the wilder feelings that have been bubbling up ever since she got this message.

"How are you?" she asks.

"Well, I'm a little better than I was. Michael brought me in to the emergency room, did he tell you?"

"Yes. It sounds like he was great."

"Well, I was feeling really terrible there for a while, I had these unbelievable stomach cramps and I was throwing up but I didn't have anything more left in me so I was just having the dry heaves. And Michael just packed me up in his car, and he dropped the kids off with Leora and brought me in. And he's still sitting right here—ooh." Greg's voice breaks off for a few seconds.

"Greg? Greg? Are you still there, honey?" Oh, goddamn these cell phones, who knows if the hospital operator will ever be able to find him again.

"I'm here. I just had a bad twinge of—of whatever this is."

"What do they think it is?"

"I think they thought for sure it was appendicitis, and they did x-rays, and they were talking about doing surgery right away, but then it got a little bit better and they decided to keep watching me overnight. So here I am." Once again his voice changes, and she can tell he is suddenly in pain at the end of the sentence.

"I love you," she says. "I wish I were there. I'm on my way home."

"Good," Greg says, but his voice is washed out and without energy.

"I'll call you later. If anything—happens—if you go to the OR, I mean, would you have Michael leave a message on my cell phone, so I can know what's happening? I'll be on the plane as soon as I can—but I'll check for messages—I'll call you, maybe I'll call from one of those sky-phones they have."

"Sure. Lucy, do you want to talk to the doctor? Is there anything you should ask the surgeon?"

He means, she supposes, that he would like her to make sure she approves of whatever surgeon may decide to operate—and maybe make sure that the surgeon knows that Greg is married to a doctor, and an academic doctor at that. And maybe he also wants her to find out the privileged inside information, the kind that many people rightly believe that doctors only tell other doctors.

"What's his name?"

"Her name. Well, the resident at least. Her name is Suzanne Preval. And she has an attending coming in to check me out, but I don't know the name."

"I'll call Suzanne Preval from the airport. But in all honesty, deciding whether someone does or doesn't have appendicitis is a really basic surgical call. They make it all the time. And there's no way I can tell them anything from three thousand miles away. But I'll call her." And I'll let her know I'm watching. No question this is a really basic surgical call, but people do get it wrong. But this is not the time to think about the kid who almost died. "I'll call her," Lucy says again, thinking about the kid. Peritonitis.

"Thanks," he says. "I think I'm going to stop talking now. It's starting to hurt again pretty badly."

"Goodbye, my dear," she says. "I'll be there soon, I hope."

She hangs up. She relays the medical details to Elizabeth, who by this point is parking in the airport lot, and who insists on going with her to make sure she can get on the flight. Lucy appreciates the gesture, and as they hike through the terminal, the two of them agree that it is almost certainly appendicitis, that Greg will probably be in surgery by morning, and that it's great that Lucy called and arranged to get on the afternoon flight.

But they get to the counter and it's not so great. Because clearly everything is fucked up somehow; there is no departure time listed on the screen at the airport for this five-thirty flight, just the one word, DELAYED. And there is this angry crush here at the check-in counter, all these other people who have been disarranged and inconvenienced trying to find out what the hell is happening. And Lucy veering back and forth between a kind of rueful calm—if it's appendicitis then they'll operate and he'll be fine—and a crazed desperate desire to scream and cry, to bellow out her despair at being those three thousand miles away from where she needs to be: *I have to get home!* Elizabeth volunteers to go look for someone with information, while Lucy holds her place. So she stands restlessly in this line that doesn't move, and the day is a jumble in her mind: Greg's voice, Greg's pain, the sun on the beach, the bald child in the hospital elevator, and way back at the beginning, her lecture, her moment of imparting information and answering questions. And now, please, at the end of the day, she has to get home. Does everyone understand how important that is? She has a home and it's far away, and she needs to be there.

What is the significance of home in children's lives? Thank you for asking that very important question. You might as well have said, of home in all our lives. Of belonging somewhere. Major medical studies have shown that when we are far from home, we cease to exist in any real sense. We are all made up of lies and improbable molecular collisions, like what is on the inside of a helium balloon. Our only chance to exist is to get home again, where we are real.

"Excuse me, I think you are the lady my son was pointing out." This man is clearly Theodore's father, thin and dark and serious-faced, appearing now beside Lucy in the economy-class line.

"I sat next to him on the flight out. I didn't realize he was going back so soon."

"Unexpected events," says Theodore's father. "Plans have had to change."

"Mine, too," says Lucy. "I thought I was going back tomorrow, but I actually really need to get back to Boston as soon as possible."

He doesn't say, *I hope everything is okay.* But then, come to think of it, neither did she. What he does say is "Would you come join us in our line? It's much shorter."

"I'm not in first class," Lucy says. "They upgraded me on the flight out, so I ended up next to Theodore, that's all."

"I see what you are saying. I understand." He speaks almost as if English were not his first language, as if he had learned to talk from memorizing sentences in a phrase book, though he has no accent. Lucy thinks about the careful, slightly off way that Theodore spoke, about how you could look at his face and see his thoughts working hard within him as he struggled for the right phrases in this some-what strange human language. Same with his father. "I wonder if I could persuade you to join us on our line nonetheless. Even so. I have a suggestion I would like to make to you—something that would help me out very much in a difficult situation and might be at least a little bit to your advantage as well. I think I can make it successful for us both."

"Sure," Lucy says. What the hell. It would be better to be closer to the front of some line than way back here at the hopeless end of this one.

Just then Elizabeth Pearson rejoins her, looking annoyed. "No luck," she says. "I couldn't find anyone who knows anything."

"Actually," Lucy says, "I'm going to switch lines. There's someone here who may be able to help me." She gestures rather helplessly toward Theodore's father, whose name she still doesn't know. He makes no gesture of acknowledgment or introduction. "Elizabeth, thank you for everything, but I shouldn't keep you waiting here. You have your own family to get home to."

Elizabeth looks around her, dubiously: the angry people, the line that doesn't move, the noise and the crowd, and now this weird guy. "What if you can't get back?" she asks.

"I am going to ensure that she gets on the flight, in any case," puts in Theodore's father, earning another dubious look from Elizabeth. But her kids *are* waiting for this unexpected evening that Lucy's departure has abruptly freed up from the chairman and the visiting professor dinner, and so Elizabeth and Lucy say goodbye, Elizabeth wishes her luck, Lucy says we'll hope for the best, Elizabeth says call me or e-mail me, let me know how it worked out, and Lucy says you bet, and thanks again for everything. A beat, and then they hug.

And then, after Elizabeth has gone off, Lucy obediently wheels her suitcase over to the first-class line, where Theodore is holding a place at the very front.

It's all quite straightforward, really. All families have their little crises. Theodore's father is required to depart this very evening for Seoul, a business-related emergency. Not possible to postpone. So he arranged to send Theodore home, because Theodore's mother doesn't want him staying with anyone other than his father out here, and now they get to the airport and the flight is delayed indefinitely.

"Indefinitely?" Lucy can hear the squeak in her own voice.

"There are thunderstorms in the Midwest, apparently, and everything is disrupted." Now, under normal circumstances, Theodore's father—"I'm so sorry, I failed to introduce myself, call me Eric, and I am, of course, Theodore's father"—under normal circumstances, he would simply take Theodore home and try again tomorrow, but here he is holding this ticket on a flight to Seoul that leaves in a mere two hours, and he absolutely must be on that flight. And he begins to explain to Lucy—or is he actually explaining to Theodore? And does Theodore understand?

"You have to understand, it's a relatively new company, just at the follow-on round of our financing, and we're off our projections a little. Actually by almost ten percent, but that isn't really surprising in this kind of a start-up."

"My father is starting a new company," Theodore says, anxiously, to Lucy. "When a new company starts, right at the beginning, you have to take good care of it. Companies can even die, did you know that?"

Lucy tries to smile at Theodore, tries to look past him to see whether there is any action at the counter.

"The thing is," Eric says to her, "we aren't off our projections by that much, but our lead investor—this Asian investor—is getting nervous, and he's threatening to pull the funding."

Shut up, Lucy wants to say, *shut up and let me worry about my own worries.* She doesn't say it, obviously.

"The last time, you didn't even let me come to California," Theodore says, miserably. "There was an emergency with the circuit board shipment and he had to go to Asia and I was already all packed and I couldn't come."

"I really don't have much latitude here, because this particular investor is our primary source of cash," says Theodore's father, now looking very intently into Lucy's eyes, as if he expects a click, a nod, a sudden comprehension: *Oh, well, of course, in that case . . .* But in that case, what? "In fact," continues Eric, "we are possibly looking at a complete disaster."

Fortunately, at that moment, something in his shirt pocket beeps loudly, and he takes out a very advanced cell phone, turns his back on Lucy and Theodore, takes a few steps, and begins to talk, hunching over the phone just a little, as if to keep his conversation secret.

Theodore watches his father. "He has to go to Korea," he tells Lucy, sounding mournful. "He has to go tonight. And there isn't anyone here to take care of me."

Theodore's father straightens up, slipping the phone into his pocket. He swings back around and says angrily to Lucy, in a totally different tone, in a rush of words, "My general manager in Korea, completely useless! In fact, he may be the one who has made my lead investor so anxious. Before I finish this trip, I'm going to fire his ass."

Theodore repeats it, a little bit louder. "He's going to Korea. He has the ticket and he's leaving and there isn't anyone here to take care of me. I could stay in his house all by myself perfectly well, but they won't let me. Even though there's a maid and everything."

"You can't stay there alone," his father says, somewhat irritably. "Your mother would call out the police and the fire department and the army and the navy and the air force." He takes the cell phone out of his pocket and inspects the screen carefully, perhaps hoping for another call.

Well, good for her, thinks Lucy, who is suddenly sure that his father would happily leave Theodore alone in the house and go off to Korea. Would maybe leave him standing in this endless check-in line for this flight that may never take off, and go board his own plane, if he didn't have to worry that Mom would hear about it.

"So you see, when Theodore pointed you out and told me that the two of you had made excellent friends on the ride out, I had a brainstorm, and I thought maybe you would be willing to take charge of him going back."

"Take charge of him?"

"Make sure that he gets on whatever flight is offered. That he gets back to Boston okay—easy since you're going there yourself. In return, I would be very happy to buy you a first-class ticket as well, so that you would again be able to sit with him."

"What if the flight gets canceled? What if it just never goes?"

"What would you do yourself if the flight gets canceled?"

"I've got to get back to Boston," Lucy says. "I'd probably fly somewhere else and connect—I'd work something out."

"Exactly!" says Theodore's father, Eric, with relief and enthusiasm.

· · ·

Which explains why Lucy is dragging her suitcase through the Dallas/Fort Worth Airport at nine o'clock at night, with Theodore, wearing his backpack, right beside her. The flight back to Boston was canceled, and the airline started booking people onto morning flights almost immediately after Theodore's father, his relief quite obvious, finished paying for Lucy's ticket, provided her with all the Boston addresses and contact numbers she insisted on, and took off at a run for Seoul, carrying his little blue nylon garment bag. Only after he was out of sight, moving fast, did Lucy realize that he had not asked for *her* name, or for any other information about her. What a fucking idiot, she thought, in that none-too-charitable mood that airport delays induce in the kindest and best. What a criminally careless schmuck.

Some people should not have children, Lucy thought. And in fact, it was a somewhat familiar thought; her work has her thoroughly accustomed to parents who should not have children because they are too crazy or too disorganized or too addicted or too distracted. But to be distracted by your business trip to Asia does not usually buy you a social worker investigation. All the same, some people should not be allowed to have children. And after all, when the people who should not have children nevertheless go ahead and reproduce, then you have to hope the children will be lucky enough to find other relatives or teachers or friends to give them some of what they need, Lucy thought. So let me be Theodore's little piece of luck, in the middle of this disastrous trip, which has once again shown him exactly where he ranks on his father's to-do list. I'll be his little piece of luck and bring him safely back to Boston, and he can be my piece of luck, and together we'll all get through the night, even Greg, and we'll all end up home and safe and sound.

The Boston flight, fortunately enough, was canceled right when she and Theodore were still standing at the first-class check-in desk, and the woman who had just sold Lucy's new ticket was clearly specially trained for the high-end customers, because she responded instantly to Lucy's distress, to Lucy's almost tearful explanation about needing to get back to Boston, or to somewhere near Boston, and she had them booked on the 4 P.M. flight to Dallas, which they could just make if they ran, which would give them just enough time to connect to the last flight to Boston. Yes, Lucy said, we'll do it, thinking of herself, walking in late but there, truly there, to Greg's hospital room: *I made it, I'm home.*

She called the hospital again, after they had boarded the plane. And amazingly enough, she got through to Dr. Suzanne Preval, who turned out to be the chief resident in general surgery, and who told Lucy in clipped tones that her attending had arrived and examined Greg and they were going to get an abdominal CT and then probably take him to the operating room. The x-rays were inconclusive, she said, and the ultrasound as well. Nothing clearly there. But his pain is worsening and his white count is elevated. And she doesn't think he's perfed, but the CT will help with that. Lucy asked who the attending was, and Dr. Preval named a name she did not know. But if you go to the emergency room with appendicitis, you take who's covering, and Lucy knows that perfectly well. And all your wife sitting on an airplane in California can do, Lucy thought, is rub it in a little that she's a doctor and will be judging the care you receive through educated eyes. So she did that. And then hung up and worried about peritonitis and missed abdominal diagnoses and people who almost die—or really die—on the table in what should be routine surgical situations.

Lucy and Theodore flew first class to Dallas/Fort Worth. Had a nice dinner on the flight, at least Theodore did. Lucy couldn't eat. She had become possessed by the ridiculous, far-fetched, statistically highly improbable notion that off in Boston, Greg was dying. Or dead.

Healthy men in their forties don't die from routine appendectomies at good academic hospitals in the middle of Boston. And it is in some sense, therefore, ridiculous for a healthy woman in her forties, her mind trained extensively in all that is most medical and statistical, to sit on an airplane and worry that the one person in the world who needs to be waiting for her at the other end of this journey may not be there.

What if Greg stopped existing? What would home be? What

would I be? What if I got off the plane in Boston and he wasn't any more, as if I had dreamed my whole life and dreamed finding him? Dreamed meeting him and knowing him and loving him and living with him and having children with him? Can all of someone's jokes and memories and ideas and thoughts just stop? asks Lucy of herself, Lucy who has attended professionally at more than a few deathbeds in her time. No, it does not seem possible. Or perhaps it seems all too possible.

"Theodore," she said firmly, the mommy, the doctor in charge. "Tell me about your time in San Diego."

He had opened up that flat metal box that she noticed on the flight out yesterday, and he was playing some kind of game on the screen. But he put it down in his lap and turned to her, his face as pinched and unhappy and anxious as her own son Freddy's might be if you told him he had to sled down a steep hill.

"I was supposed to stay for six nights, but I only stayed for one," he said.

"Yes, I know. Your father had the business emergency—he was telling us in the airport," Lucy said, cursing herself for bumbling into what might very well be a sore subject.

"I think his company is going under," said Theodore, miserably. "A lot of the new companies do go under, you know. Do you know about the dot-com boom? People thought that they would all be millionaires, and instead their companies just stopped existing, and the people lose their jobs, and the offices are all empty. Even very big offices."

"Yes," Lucy said. "I'm sorry. That must be very hard on your father."

"He's trying to save it. A lot of people don't understand that trying to save a company can be just like trying to save a person's life. That's what he told me about this trip. The emergency trip, the one he had to go on. That's why I didn't stay out there the way I had planned to, because he had to go on this trip, and it was a real emergency, like it would be if a person was dying. If my father said, Oh, I'll go to Korea, but not till next week, that could be like say-

78

ing, Oh, this man needs this drug but I'll give it to him the day after tomorrow. You know what I mean."

Lucy nodded. For a moment she did not trust her voice. But she called up doctor mommy again, and said as much to Theodore. "I do understand. As a matter of fact, I'm a doctor."

Theodore nodded. "And there isn't anyone else my father can send. It's his responsibility to save the company, and if he sent someone else and that person didn't do the right thing and the company went under, it would be my father's fault." He was crying, without making any noise. Not a sob. Tears were running out of his eyes and down his cheeks and soaking into his yellow polo shirt on either side of the little buttons.

Lucy wasn't sure whether you could hug a twelve-year-old you didn't know very well. But she was remembering Freddy last winter, when he got up to the top of the hill and refused to get on a sled at all, not with his father, not with Isabel. How he asked again and again to be taken down, and they told him again and again how much he would like it if he only tried, and how he finally sat down in the snow, holding on tight to a rather scraggly bush, and cried and cried, until Lucy pried him away from his bush and carried him down and home. So she reached out and put her arm around Theodore's shoulders, cradled his head against her, and pulled the cocktail napkin from under her glass of seltzer to dry his tears.

He didn't apologize. He didn't burst suddenly into the passionate denunciation that she is sure his father deserves (*He never keeps his promises! Something always comes up! Everything is more important to him than I am!*). But neither did he stop crying, as Lucy hugged him awkwardly, one first-class seat to another. He just sat there and cried and cried.

Well, that is the $64,000 question right there, isn't it? Give the guy a prize! Why the hell do people have kids and then not take care of them? Or, to put it another way, what is going on with these parents who look at their kids and don't see what they need? Spare me the rhetoric about poverty and multiple social stresses; the world is full of rich fucks who don't know how to take care of their children. Who push them away and push them away and stamp on any little light that flickers. You can take it from me, because I know: no one who has not been wanted and attended to as a child ever forgets the feeling of not being wanted and attended to. Ever. The feeling of looking around at all the other children who come first with someone, who stand at the center of their worlds. I sometimes think we go through our whole lives waiting to have everything taken away from us again, no matter how much we have, because we learned so early and so thoroughly the lesson that we were, somehow, wanting. That we didn't deserve what other people deserve, and what other people get, and what other people take for granted.

Very unfortunately, there was a little rough weather around the Dallas/Fort Worth Airport, too, and one runway was closed, and the flight from San Diego had to circle for half an hour. And that tight connection to the last Boston flight turns out to be just a little too tight for comfort, as Lucy and Theodore come panting up to the gate, only to find it closed, the attendants gone, the plane pulled back.

"We missed it," says Theodore. "I can't believe we missed it! We missed our airplane! It took off without us!" Lucy is afraid he may start to cry again, but he is dry-eyed and astonished, as if such a thing has never been known to happen in recorded human history. She herself could easily start bawling, but instead, Lucy rushes up to an agent at the next gate over. She gasps out the situation, her breath still short from the run up from the stupid goddamn little train that makes you miss your flight because this goddamn airport is just so goddamn big and you can't get from one gate to another just by running hell-bent with your wheeled suitcase zooming along behind you.

"A family emergency, I have to get home," she gasps to the agent. "My husband is sick, I have to get home and take care of my children. I have a first-class ticket! What can you do for me?"

"There is a flight to New York JFK boarding, just five gates over," says the agent. "Would that be of any use to you?"

New York. She could get to New York tonight. She could rent a car and drive to Boston in four and a half hours. She could feel she was close to home. Yes. New York. We'll take it. And then another, but much shorter, dash from gate to gate, and they are practically the last people to board the New York flight, and the doors are closed and the safety announcement comes on before Lucy even thinks of pulling out her cell phone.

It's okay. She'll be in New York soon. From New York, a person can get to Boston. Many many times a day. Lucy shivers in her seat; this seems to be an exceptionally air-conditioned plane. Don't let me start thinking of the things that can go wrong in surgery. The kid in San Diego with the abscess and the peritonitis. And then all the other bad possibilities. The anesthesiologist can intubate your esophagus instead of your airway, and just like that, no oxygen. Your body can react idiosyncratically to the anesthetic agents and your blood pressure can bottom out and you die, right there and then. They can open you up to take out your appendix and find a horrible cancer that no one suspected. The one-in-a-million stories that, of course, I've heard. Don't let me start picturing his body on the table, his mind put to sleep, his innards held apart with retractors. Just get me home.

"Are you worrying about your husband?" asks Theodore.

"Yes," Lucy says. "I'm very worried about him. I still feel very far away—I think I'll feel better when we get to New York."

"It's nice that you worry about him," Theodore says. "I worry about my dad when I'm far away from him. Like now he's going to be in Korea, and I'll be back in Boston. That's very far apart."

"We'll call your mother as soon as we get to New York and let her know what our plans are," Lucy says, trying and failing to imagine some scenario, any scenario, where Freddy might be flying through the air from city to city to city in the charge of a total stranger.

"Okay," says Theodore, and then, a little tentatively, "what *are* our plans?"

And Lucy shrugs, a little comically: search me!

And then they both begin laughing, and then Lucy asks him to tell her about Gettysburg, and that takes care of the rest of the flight to New York JFK.

In New York, though, Theodore starts to fall apart, to "decompensate," as Lucy would say. He doesn't like one bit the idea of an all-night train ride back to Boston, with no place to lie down and only a seat, a pillow, and a blanket. He's tired, he says, and he wants to get a hotel room and take a bath and go to sleep. And he really really hates Penn Station, he hates it, he hates it, he doesn't want to be here! Lucy looks around and sees the enormous underground echoing spaces and she can see Theodore cringe at the impossible-to-understand static-filled overhead announcements and she can see that he is frightened by the many street people, searching through garbage cans or sitting quietly with their shopping bags of stuff in the waiting areas and maybe also by the hordes and hordes of late-night Long Island kids, waiting for their commuter trains home, dressed and made-up for the city clubs, but drunk and tired and wasted, in ill-natured clumps everywhere you look. But it's a train station, and a station with a train leaving for home, and Lucy keeps hold of Theodore's arm and repeats, over and over, "We need to get on our train, we need to get back to Boston, your mother is going to be waiting for you at the train station in Boston."

Lucy has called Theodore's mother. It took everything Lucy had, but the woman is now relatively calm, or at least, Lucy thinks, she is reserving her fury appropriately enough for Theodore's father. Who, it turns out, did *not* call her to tell her about the delay before he got on his flight to Seoul, or to tell her about Lucy, so Theodore's mother was waiting for him at the airport in Boston; she had just come back from a trip all the way in to Logan Airport, to meet that original flight from San Diego that Theodore did not take, and that she did not know had been canceled until she got there, which left her feeling exactly as you would expect. But yes, she'll be on the platform at South Station at 6 A.M. to meet the train, and she, unlike her ex-husband, wrote down Lucy's name, cell phone number, home address, place of work, and pretty much everything but her identifying moles and birthmarks. So at least Theodore has one parent who wants to know something about the person who is banging around the continent with her twelve-year-old, by plane and now by train.

And it's not that bad, she tells him, the all-night train. She has bought business-class tickets for Theodore and herself, she tells him, hoping that will sound familiar and reassuring. In business class on the train, she tells him, the seats recline quite a bit, and they give you pillows and blankets, and there is a conductor there to look after the passengers and to shoo away anyone who has only a regular ticket. That would intrigue Isabel, perhaps, but it goes right by Theodore. Look, Lucy says, it will be so comfortable I bet you'll go right to sleep, once the train gets going.

But Theodore continues to be very agitated, as they wait in Penn Station, suggesting over and over and over that they give up, that they go to a hotel, that they call his mother and tell her they aren't coming.

"One o'clock in the morning is too late to get on a train," he tells Lucy, anxiously. And then, a few minutes later, when the big board flips its letters over to announce that their train is delayed fifteen minutes, he tugs Lucy's sleeve and begs once more, "See, it's delayed, everything is messed up tonight, please, please, can't we just go to a hotel and go to sleep? And then tomorrow we could go to Boston. You know what? Tomorrow we could even fly to Boston, and my mother could meet me at the airport!"

"Theodore." Lucy keeps her voice level and firm and kind. After all, it is one in the morning, and she herself feels she has been voyaging for weeks, and there is poor Theodore, with Lucy the one slightly familiar face in all Penn Station, and how familiar is she? "Theodore, I have to get home. I have to. Remember what I told you, my husband is in the hospital. My children are at a friend's house. I need to be there when everyone wakes up tomorrow and take care of them. That's just the way it has to be."

He turns away and won't look at her, but then, when they are settled into their seats and the train pulls out, only twenty minutes behind schedule, which on this particular journey feels pretty good, he watches with fascination out the window and then turns back to her, his face alight.

"I used to really really love trains!" he says. "They used to be something I was really interested in, back a long time ago!"

"Before the Civil War?" Lucy asks, and sees that he has misunderstood the question and looks perplexed. "I mean, before you got interested in the Civil War?"

"Oh, very long before that. After I was interested in trains, then I was very interested in astronomy for a while, and then for a long time I was interested in the Middle Ages."

"Did you ride on many trains?"

"Some. My parents would take me on trains whenever we were somewhere where there was some special train ride. That was when they lived together. And my dad helped me build a big model train set. He still has it in his house out in San Diego, but usually we don't play with it now when I go there. We didn't this time. Of course, I was only there for one night."

Lucy changes the subject back to trains. No more tears. "So does it make you happy to be on this train now to Boston, even though you weren't sure you wanted to come?"

And his face is dancing again. "I love being on this train!" he says. "I love how it goes all night and comes into South Station very early in the morning to get us home."

"And your mother will be there waiting," Lucy says, and he nods.

"I'm sorry I said I didn't want to go, Lucy. I'm sorry I said that about going to a hotel. I was just upset still from when we missed that other plane. Or maybe I was just upset because all my plans got changed and everything seemed to be going wrong. I'm sorry I said that. I know you have to get home."

"It was one in the morning, and you've been traveling for a very long time already," Lucy says. "You're doing very well, all things considered. And I'm very glad to have your company on this crazy trip. But now I think you should lean your seat back, wrap up in your blanket, look out the window for a while, and let the motion of the train just put you to sleep."

She herself, of course, makes a phone call. Greg is in recovery, and she talks to his nurse. Things went fine, and it *was* appendicitis, clear enough when they got in there, and in fact it looked like it was just starting to perf, but the operation went well and Greg did fine. The nurse writes down Lucy's cell phone number, and promises to call if there's any change at all, and for the first time since she got that original message, back in the hotel three thousand miles away, Lucy feels relatively in touch, relatively close by.

She has to conserve the phone battery, which is running low, so she lets herself call and check only once an hour on the rest of the ride to Boston. Otherwise she sits awake, her arm around Theodore, who has slumped way over to lean against her in his sound sound sleep. I am your little piece of luck tonight, she thinks. She holds him tight and looks out the window into the night, sometimes passing lights and cars and buildings, mostly just staring out at the blackness moving past. And the train goes all night and comes into South Station very early in the morning. If we're patient, it will get us home.

4

Double Whammy

LUCY CALLS GREG UP as soon as she gets to her office. She was the one who had to run, as soon as the teacher conference was over, who took off like a bat out of hell, heading for her car, leaving Greg to a more leisurely walk home, no doubt a stop on the way for a pricey cup of coffee. Greg is still taking it easy, three weeks after his appendectomy; he walks more slowly, he tries not to carry anything too heavy. And that's the academic life for you; he'll run into half of Cambridge out for a springtime stroll or sipping intently in the coffeehouse. Lucy herself drove—somewhat aggressively and even slightly dangerously—across town and then lucked into a perfect parking place at the hospital, the occasional bright benefit of coming late to work, when you get a spot right next to the building, a spot some nightshift nurse maybe occupied at 1 A.M. and has now vacated neatly in time for your tardy arrival.

A fast drive and a lucky parking spot mean that Lucy is right on time for her ten o'clock appointment, and then to further her sense that God is giving her the break she sorely needs, it turns out that the social worker has called and the Williams twins are not in fact coming in for their asthma compliance checks today, and she has an hour free. So she kicks her office door shut, sinks down in her chair, slips out of her shoes, and dials Greg at home.

"Howdy there, Paw," she says, and he starts to laugh.

"Gee, Maw," he says back. "Guess you 'n' me have done gotten our hillbilly asses mixed up with some mighty high-steppin' folks."

"Back on the farm, we thought folks was dressed nice if'n they didn't have their long johns on *outside* their overalls," Lucy says, but she knows the joke is over.

"What an unbelievable self-righteous, sugar-coated, poisonous bitch!"

"Jesus Christ," Lucy says, signaling agreement.

The first-grade teacher had sat across the little round table from them, all three of them too big for the first-grade chairs. She looked, as she always looks, as they have only ever seen her look, competent and patient. She wears slacks and a sweater, and she usually has on a piece of fun jewelry, a cow made out of beads and sequins, or a necklace that looks like painted Tinker Toys. Her name is Mrs. Gallow, and Lucy finds these pieces of jewelry remind her of the bright smocks and scrub jackets printed with cartoon characters that nurses sometimes wear to make children think they don't carry needles. Greg has been calling her "Old Gallows" all year, strictly in the privacy of his own home, of course.

Lucy has always liked elementary school teachers. School was her refuge and her hideout when she was a child; she belonged in her classroom as surely as any of the other children, as she never quite belonged in a foster home. She believes that she grew up with a real liking for institutions, which now translates over to hospitals: she likes structures that make sense and people who know their jobs and big buildings where you can feel safe and protected. And indeed, thirty-five years ago, it was an elementary school teacher who saved Lucy's life, more or less, or saved her from the life she was living, who recognized her and plucked her off the foster care merry-go-round and brought her into a home where she had full rights and citizenship. Miss Weiss. She thinks with almost overwhelming nostalgia about her own first days in sixth grade, when Miss Weiss was just Miss Weiss to her, and walking into Miss Weiss's classroom (6-W) every morning made Lucy feel unbelievably lucky. And she didn't even know yet how lucky she was going to be.

But walking into Mrs. Gallow's classroom just doesn't do it for Lucy. It's a perfectly nice classroom, with bright colors and lots of stimulating materials wherever you look, and perfectly orderly. But Lucy doesn't like Mrs. Gallow and she doesn't trust her, fun jewelry or no fun jewelry. And this is the woman to whom they send their sweet, strange Freddy each and every weekday morning. Actually, their sweet, strange Freddy likes her fine, as much as he ever likes—or notices—an adult female other than his mother or his grandmother, which is to say, if you ask him how he likes the class, he'll politely tell you fine, and if you ask him if he has a nice teacher, he'll politely tell you yes, and if you ask him what her name is, he can now, in the months just before the end of the school year, usually remember it, and Lucy thinks he could probably pick her out of a police lineup. And surely, if the earth opened and swallowed up Mrs. Gallow, Freddy would put down his baseball cards long enough to ask anxiously who was going to be the teacher tomorrow, since change of any kind makes Freddy a little nervous. Well, maybe he wouldn't actually put *down* the cards, but he might pause in laying them out. The baseball cards are a relatively new thing—*baseball* is a relatively new thing in Freddy's life—but the season has begun and for whatever reason, Freddy, who has never wanted to hear about anything athletic, who has never wanted, God knows, to play any sport, is entranced. Any one of the Red Sox, Lucy knows, he could identify immediately, he could tell you what position he plays, he could probably tell you last year's OBP or ERA. His first-grade teacher, well, that's another story—she has no fascinating statistics to offer, and she doesn't appear on a baseball card. Greg and Lucy sat stiffly in their little chairs, and stiffly they smiled at her, hoping for the best.

It's not that Lucy and Greg were expecting a completely smooth parent-teacher conference. Those are what they have with their daughter Isabel's teachers, always and forever, as Greg says, as long as the sun shall shine and the grass shall grow, and the Great White Father rule in Washington. Freddy's kindergarten teacher last year, an almost insanely good-natured, guitar-playing young woman named Sandy Sullivan (Greg called *her* "Sister Bertrille") had folded up her habitual smile once or twice to tell them that some of Freddy's habits might seem, well, a little bit peculiar to some of the other kids, though of course everyone loved him and gosh, you could just tell he was *so* smart. But kindergarten was new and strange, and anything new and strange makes Freddy very anxious, and when Freddy is anxious he does things that indeed might seem a little bit peculiar to the other kids. So yes, last year he used to knock rhythmically on the wall whenever he got anxious, tapping out patterns that he swore were Morse code messages, but Sandy Sullivan, God bless her, worked out a system where he could go over into the block corner and knock quietly whenever he needed to. And she let him talk about Morse code at circle time. And yes, last year he used to hang out in the block corner, painstakingly sorting everything by shape and size, but the teacher chose to interpret that as helping her keep the room in order. And then he measured each of the different-sized blocks and worked out this whole way of measuring other things in the classroom using the blocks as units, and Sandy Sullivan called it a math project and let him spend his choice time doing that, while the other children dressed up in costumes and built towers and cooked plastic food on the little wooden stove.

This year he knows his way around the school and is much less anxious, and anyway there is much less free time in class; Freddy does not do so well with free time. And so, his parents hope, he is a little less strange and a little less scared, and in any case, here in first grade, surely the fact that he can read like a grownup and do math like at least a fourth-grader must count for something. First grade in private school, after all, is the year of the reading frenzy, the parents who want their money's worth. Everyone will read by the end of the year, everyone always does, Mrs. Gallow assured the parents over and over, way back at the fall Open Classroom Night, and Greg whispered in Lucy's ear, *You know how Old Gallows achieves those perfect results: a pack of slavering wild dogs to whom the nonreaders are thrown in the spring.*

And here we are in the spring, and yes, indeed, Mrs. Gallow had only kind words for Freddy's reading skills. Something about the woman, every time she says "Freddy," you imagine her putting a "Little" in front of it. She just has that kind of smarm in her voice.

"Clearly, Freddy has wonderful reading skills," she said, but with very lukewarm enthusiasm. "He's a very strong reader, and of course we try to encourage that and foster that in this classroom."

No you don't, thought Lucy. You have him reading *Frog and Toad* with the other good readers, you have no idea at all what he's interested in or what goes on in his brain. For which we should perhaps be thankful. Freddy's reading career is being shaped completely by his older sister; at school, he says, they mostly read baby books. Freddy likes baby books, mind you; he needs *One Fish Two Fish Red Fish Blue Fish* read aloud at least twice every night—once on the couch before he has his bath, and once when he is in his bed, with his blankets and his decks of cards all properly arranged—with the result that every member of the family knows it by heart. Before that it was *Madeline and the Bad Hat,* and before that it was *Horton Hears a Who.* Lucy is happiest with *One Fish Two Fish Red Fish Blue Fish,* which seems to her, as she reads the familiar rhymes night after night, to be full of great and pungent wisdom to be applied in daily life.

But Lucy could use some great and pungent wisdom right now, to soothe her husband and herself, to turn this phone call back into something they can take lightly, to send them off into their days a little better fortified.

"She doesn't get him at all, does she?" Greg asks. "She sees him every day and she hasn't got the faintest idea who he is. It's kind of sad, really."

"It's probably lucky for us," Lucy says. "She wouldn't like what she saw." In all their conferences and conversations with their son's teacher, in all the carefully punctilious teacher attentiveness that they are paying for by the pound, Mrs. Gallow has never betrayed the slightest understanding of Freddy's interest in numbers, in units of measurement, or the baseball that has now taken over his brain. All nonsense to be ignored, all cobwebs to be briskly swept aside. But that is probably all for the best, Lucy thinks; if Mrs. Gallow tried to figure out Freddy's brain, if she looked closely, she would want a diagnosis. She would not want to stay with the category that Lucy and Greg are both hoping they can maintain for their son: very-eccentric-and-very-bright. So let her put Freddy in the handy category of already-reading and turn her attention to diagnosing his classmates, the ones who are still struggling with the alphabet. It keeps Freddy safe, Lucy thinks, though she knows this is irrational, and though she knows that Freddy is not necessarily safe, and that there are real dangers out there, not just officious first-grade teachers.

Lucy feels safe right now, that's the funny thing. Safe and in place, exactly where she belongs, here in her tiny and not at all cozy office, which she has still never bothered to decorate in any way. Connected by phone to Greg, who is home in his office in their house.

> *This is no good.*
> *This is not right.*
> *My feet stick out*
> *of bed all night.*
>
> *And when I pull them in,*
> *Oh dear!*
> *My head sticks out of bed*
> *up here!*

In the picture, the sad-faced, fuzzy-edged beast sticks his legs out through two holes cut in the board at the bottom of this bed —then on the next page, his feet are in the bed, but his woebegone head protrudes through a hole in the headboard.

Oh, they tried with Mrs. Gallow. They told her what a wonderful year Freddy was having in her wonderful classroom. In fact, when they first came in, prompt to the minute, another matched set of parents ushered out into the hallway, Greg praised the classroom so lavishly that Lucy worried it might be too much. The murals! The Our Book Forest display of all the different books they've read! Those wonderful African bark paintings they've been making! They tried hard to make her like them, because they believe that if she doesn't like them, she will take it out on Freddy, who is pretty completely in her power. And of Freddy they are highly protective, always worrying that the world will fall in on him, and he will discover the terrible truth: that he sticks out in all directions.

Mrs. Gallow gave Freddy his due: Reads well. Good at math. Much better now about not interrupting at circle time. She pointed to a large sign: "Our Classroom Rules—Help Make 1-G a Great Place to Learn and Share." And Greg and Lucy sat there and nodded appreciatively at her bland and all-purpose remarks about their child and admired the math quiz sheet she showed them on which Freddy's awkward, wavering penciled numerals expressed the exact correct answer fifteen times out of fifteen.

She saved it for a kicker. They were winding up, thanking her for her time and for giving Freddy such a wonderful year. They thought they were safe and free: no big problems, no concerns, no questions. There *is* one thing, she said.

Lucy braced. She can remember bracing, physically, her feet flat against the classroom floor, her shoulders suddenly tight. She did not look directly at Greg.

"Freddy comes to school, well . . ." Mrs. Gallow paused, as if it was almost too awful to be said. Then she made herself do her duty. "Freddy comes to school looking as if he has slept in his clothes. I mean, it's one thing to wear sweatpants, I know some of the boys *do* wear sweatpants to school—but surely not every day—and when they do wear them, they should be neat, and there shouldn't be any holes. And the shirts are just always so wrinkled, and sometimes there are stains, or spilled food."

Lucy, almost holding her breath, cut her eyes sideways quickly at Greg. He was carefully not looking at her. Greg, she noticed, had done Mrs. Gallow the courtesy of putting on a jacket. Actually, it was the most dressed-up she had seen him since his surgery, which he seemed to have taken as permission to spend a few weeks in his pajamas, even though he wasn't in bed. Usually, he wore a jacket and a button-down shirt on Tuesdays and Thursdays to teach his classes, for example, but the day before Lucy had seen him go off to work in baggy army pants and a navy blue sweatshirt. So this had to count as dressed-up today. Under the jacket, though, he wore a brown cotton T-shirt that had definitely seen better days. In fact, Lucy could see clearly, the edge of the neck was fraying in a slightly moth-eaten scalloping, and there was a halo of tiny pinprick holes around the seam that joined the neckband to the shirt. Great. She straightened even more in her tiny, awkward chair. She thought about the fresh scar below and to the right of his bellybutton, with the little round holes left by the sutures, slowly healing. She felt, in her uncomfortable chair, overcome with love and gratitude.

"I'm not saying this to make him feel bad," Mrs. Gallow said, hoping in fact to make everyone feel as bad as possible. "But you know, sooner or later the other children will start to notice this, so we might as well start now to get Freddy looking right."

Thank you so much, Mrs. Gallow. We'll get on it right away. How good of you to clue us in. How helpful you are. What a great-looking classroom. They bobbed and nodded and bowed. *Thank you for your time.* And out the door they went, to be replaced, immediately, by the next parental dynamic duo, who were poised out in the hall, waiting for their moment.

Greg said two things as they hurried out of the building, Lucy moving fast to get to her car and get to the hospital in time for the Williams twins, first: "These fucking parent-teacher conferences, these fucking people, this fucking school!" He said it under his breath, but still, Lucy wanted to hush him—all Freddy needed was to have his parents expelled from the building for bad language. Then, as they were already outside and heading for the car, Greg swung on her and said, full voice, "For Christ's sake, he's a little boy! He has food on him because he's a messy eater! Don't we want them to play outside? If they play outside, they get dirty or their clothes get torn, and that's what it's like for little boys!"

"Goodbye, honey," Lucy said, and kissed him, and then, key already out and poised, she was inside her car. She leaned out the window and called to him, though she doesn't know if he heard it, "Check out that T-shirt you're wearing!"

What a great project for the whole family, she and Greg whisper back and forth that evening: first we'll iron Freddy's T-shirts. Then we'll fold them tenderly into perfect rectangles. Oh, and maybe one of us should run out and buy starch—needless to say, there is no starch in the house, except for the pasta on the kitchen table. Isabel has finished eating the one exact portion of rigatoni that she allows herself and is peeling a clementine with fastidious fingertips. Freddy himself has half a plateful left, but he has drifted dreamily away from eating, and instead he is arranging his rigatoni into careful furrows. A noodle shoots off his plate and onto his lap, and Isabel gives him a look of disgust. Yes, Isabel and Old Gallows might easily find some common ground.

And what about this business of not sending Freddy to school in sweatpants every day? What fun for everyone, looking for some pants that aren't sweatpants. Once there were some jeans, but Freddy hasn't worn them in months, and they are not easily findable. And anyway, for Christ's sake, Freddy has trouble with snaps and zippers. Hey, how about we just let him wear his sweatpants and leave him alone, okay?

After the kids are in bed, Lucy thinks, she and Greg will pursue the joke far enough to have clean and ironed and neatly folded clothes waiting for tomorrow. So okay, it's stupid, but it's doable and they'll do it and they'll be done.

But you can never draw a single safe breath when your name is out there on the fifth-grade phone tree. Oh, you can run, but you can't hide.

Jessie Baxter's mother, the terminally overinvolved Bianca Baxter, calls them to ask if they were aware there had been an incident in the fifth grade and the school was taking it very seriously and there would be a meeting for all fifth-grade parents the next day at three.

"An incident?" Lucy's brain ranges generously: a sexual molestation, a racial epithet written on the wall, a gun found in someone's backpack. And at the same time, a squeak of protest from her very bowels: *I went in late this morning because of the fucking parent-teacher conference, how can I take tomorrow afternoon off for a meeting?*

"The school is taking it very seriously," Bianca Baxter intones, yet a second time.

"What kind of incident?"

"I don't know all the details. I think Ms. Lederer is going to go over those at the meeting tomorrow. I really feel she's excellent in a crisis, don't you?"

Lucy tries to imagine Ms. Lederer in a crisis. What can Bianca be thinking of? The capital campaign falling short? Someone seeing a mouse in the woodworking studio? Ms. Lederer is a personage, all right, but who the hell has ever seen her in a crisis?

"What's the crisis, Bianca?" Lucy asks patiently. Then, craftily, "I'm going to have to call the next family on the phone tree, and I'm sure they're going to ask." Thinking: *Where the hell is the phone tree, or will Isabel possibly remember who came next after us, or should I just confess and ask this hellhound herself who I'm supposed to call?*

"Oh, don't worry about that, Lucy. I know you guys are awfully busy, so I just went ahead and called the Rogerses myself, earlier this afternoon. So that's all taken care of. I thought I'd wait and call you later because I know how busy your schedule is."

"One of us will try to make the meeting," Lucy says wearily. "But if you don't have any idea at all of what's going on, I should get off the phone and call Abby's mother, because she's pretty plugged in, and she might have some information." Take that, you bright-winged avatar of death and destruction!

"Well, I'll tell you what I know," Bianca says. "There was an incident where some girls were tormenting another girl."

"So?" Lucy can't help it. These girls have been happily torment-ing one another since pre-K. It gives them a reason to get up in the morning.

"Epithets were used," Bianca says, lowering her voice.

"Racial epithets?"

"No, not that," Bianca says with clear relief. "Not quite as bad as that, but almost. Ms. Lederer called them socioeconomic epithets. The school is taking this very seriously."

> *From there to here,*
> *from here to there,*
> *funny things*
> *are everywhere.*

Freddy hates the jeans, which Lucy has so triumphantly un-earthed from a pile of unclaimed laundry. Freddy cannot zip the zipper or snap the snap at the top of the zipper. He isn't strong enough, he says. The zipper keeps slipping out of his hands. The snap doesn't work right. He says he has never seen these pants be-fore, even though Lucy feels sure that he must have worn them. Freddy is so thin that he doesn't really outgrow his pants, they just gradually get too short, but the jeans have rolled cuffs and could go for years.

"No," Freddy says. "I want my sweatpants. I won't wear these awful, stupid pants to school."

"Other kids wear jeans," Lucy says, reduced to the lowest level.

"But *I* don't," says Freddy, in no doubt whatsoever. And then fi-nally, clearly, as she goes on suggesting that he just wear them for a day, Freddy says to her, "If I wear them, I won't be able to go to the bathroom. I won't be able to get them open. I'll pee on myself."

Well, yes, there's that. Lucy imagines Mrs. Gallow, her righ-teous, concerned phone call. Okay, Freddy. Game, set, and match. Sweatpants it is, elastic waists forever, thus saith the Lord, thus say we all.

So Greg will go to the meeting. He has to. He expresses him-self eloquently about losing the afternoon, one of his precious at-home afternoons, when he teaches in the morning and then zips back home, puts on one of those suspect T-shirts, and works on his book. He's way behind with his work, he says, he's just lost all that time when he was sick, when he was recovering. But Lucy has patients scheduled, and she did take the morning off for the parent-teacher conference. So Greg will complain but Greg will go; he can go without missing a class, and she can't go without canceling patients.

But what do they mean by socioeconomic epithets? That's what Greg really wants to know. They can't ask Isabel, Lucy warns him; Bianca Baxter said it was not to be discussed with the kids until tomorrow. Well, they might have bent that rule, but Isabel has taken the occasion of her parents' logistical discussion to get herself virtuously into bed and is sleeping what may be the fake but ostentatious sleep of those whose homework was done hours ago, whose trim, color-coordinated folders are already neatly packed into a backpack for tomorrow.

So by the time they go to bed, they're friends again, united in the face of what Greg calls the prep school double whammy: two compulsory school events in two days, one for each child.

As they turn off their reading lights, Lucy shows off a little: she offers up a paragraph of *Oliver Twist*. She knows that a few lines of Dickens put her Victorian literature–minded husband in a good mood—and also impress him; he does not memorize books. Actually, neither does she; *Oliver Twist* is a special case. "Mr. Bumble was fairly taken by surprise, and fairly beaten. He had a decided propensity for bullying: derived no inconsiderable pleasure from the exercise of petty cruelty; and, consequently, was (it is needless to say) a coward. This is by no means a disparagement to his character; for many official personages, who are held in high respect and admiration, are the victims of similar infirmities. The remark is made, indeed, rather in his favour than otherwise, and with a view of impressing the reader with a just sense of his qualifications for office."

"What do you think the girls said?" Greg asks. They are lying together in the middle of their bed, a good sign that the day is ending well. Greg's arm is splayed out across the bed, and Lucy pillows her neck on exactly the right comfortable part of his biceps. She lets herself think about starting to stroke his stomach, right around his bellybutton, where there is a soft tuft of hair. It's a weeknight, but it's not too late, and it's a full three weeks since his surgery, and don't people need a little reward in between ironing their six-year-old's T-shirts and trotting off to the compulsory parent meeting to discuss the fifth-grade socioeconomic epithet emergency?

"My dad's richer than your dad," Lucy sings softly, to that old teasing tune. Her hand finds the little tuft of hair.

"How come your parents take you to that cut-rate ski resort every winter? Why don't you own a condo in Vail like all the rest of us?" But his voice is shifting slightly, thickening, and he folds his arm back over her, pulling her close.

Lucy feels righteously glad that the next afternoon is, in fact, incredibly busy. She has sat through an interminable lunchtime meeting about ICD-9 billing codes and reimbursement and productivity, every doctor's least favorite subjects and easily the tenth such meeting this year, and the meeting ran over a little because one of her colleagues got very angry about how it was easily the tenth such meeting this year and started ranting at the new special billing codes consultant, who no doubt charged the hospital royally for the extra twenty minutes he spent listening to the rant. And that meant that all the afternoon patients got backed up, because by the time everyone got back to clinic and got down to work, they were almost forty minutes behind, and it turned out to be one of those afternoons when everyone who is scheduled shows up, and some of them bring their cousins.

So she spares a thought for poor old Greg, but it is a virtuous I-couldn't-possibly-have-gone thought, as she finishes removing the sutures from a well-healed laceration above Katika Lashore's right eye. Or maybe a slightly lewd thought, remembering Greg's own scar, the shadow of his sutures, the two of them together last night.

This is maybe Katika's sixth or seventh injury requiring stitches; she's three now, and the first four or five injuries were part of what got her taken out of her bio-mom's home and placed in foster care, although there were plenty of other issues as well, like the fact that she had never had any immunizations and she was fifteen months old. But whatever foster home you place her in, Katika will find something sharp to butt her forehead against, or a creative way to fall off a little tricycle and slice her leg on the edge of a chainlink fence.

Katika, who is sealed neatly into a papoose, a massive Velcro cocoon, toddler-sized, for holding small children down and still, is screaming like the proverbial banshee, but she stops the moment Lucy straightens up, her back aching slightly from the effort of holding her arms and hands so tightly tensed, snipping and pulling on those tiny electric-blue nylon sutures that contrast so effectively with Katika's dark skin. The nurse releases Katika from the papoose, and she is immediately upright on the exam table, standing on the open papoose, and no doubt contemplating a swan dive off onto the floor. Her foster mother, moving fast, gathers her up and provides her with a massive lollipop, ready to hand in her purse.

And how remarkable it is, when you stop and think about it, that you can stitch children's skin up and see it heal, close over and grow together, as if the broken glass or the table edge or the chainlink fence had been a minor disruption.

"It was completely insane," Greg tells her that night. "Lunatic."

"Retarded," contributes Isabel, and is immediately shushed by both her parents. Lucy says, "You can't use that word, not ever." Greg says, "Do you want me to have to sit through another compulsory parent meeting with a special consultant so I can learn that some people are slower mentally and some people are quicker mentally and both ways are good?" Greg and Isabel both crack up.

And after all that, Greg complains, nobody even knows exactly what was said and done. Isabel comes closest to knowing, of course, because the fifth grade has been buzzing. The actual culprits, Kate Dykstra and Michelle Blumenthal, are known and are walking around the school with red-rimmed eyes and a certain aura of drama-queen untouchable evil, having spent the last two days in multiple meetings and what Isabel calls "lamebrained therapy sessions" with teachers and counselors and with their victim, Vanessa Hubbell. Isabel can keep all this straight without any trouble at all, keeps much more complicated things straight all the time. It's her clueless parents who keep mixing it up and saying Michelle when they mean Vanessa.

But even Isabel does not know exactly what Kate and Michelle *said* to Vanessa, except that part of it was about her dad being a carpenter. In fact, George Hubbell is a very-much-in-demand cabinet-maker, who probably charges enough every time he redoes one of Vanessa's classmates' kitchens to pay her way through till twelfth grade quite comfortably, thank you very much. In fact, Lucy and Greg, who could never afford a renovation on his fine-woods-custom-built terms, have in the past joked that for George Hubbell, the school tuition is a business expense; it's how he meets his clients. But there is no question that he drives a van with his name written on it, and he doesn't wear a suit. And if it comes to that, neither does Greg wear a suit, though academic drag is so well-understood in these parts, including its high-prestige, low-rent implications, that perhaps even the slower fifth-grade girls get the picture.

Anyway, Kate and Michelle made Vanessa cry. Which is nothing very new or surprising, if you ask Isabel; last month Kate and Michelle made three other people cry, but no one else went running to Miss Rexall, the school counselor, who just happened to have recently returned from an independent school counselor retreat (bet that was a treat of a retreat, Greg commented) at which a whole afternoon session had focused on socioeconomic epithets, led by these wonderful consultants, who were the same ones she brought in today to lead one compulsory assembly for the fifth-graders, and one for their parents.

And having hushed Isabel for describing her assembly with a forbidden term, Greg uses another to describe his. "Un. Fucking. Believable. We had to sit through a fucking PowerPoint presentation about different ways that people can make other people feel bad. Personal epithets. Racial epithets. Ethnic epithets. Socioeconomic epithets."

"It's a rough world."

"And then this I-don't-even-know-what-to-call-her woman puts us through this completely insane discussion, calling on people left and right, about how we all *feel* about there being some socioeconomic discrepancies in the school, and how we're going to help our kids *handle* that."

"Just so you know, Isabel, *we* are the socioeconomic discrepancy in your school," Lucy announces to her daughter, who is happily perched on a kitchen chair watching them pull dinner together, happy to be part of their aristocracy of disgust on a brief break from her own. "You happen to go to a school that costs a great deal of money, and some of the families there are very very rich, and some are only very rich, and then there are people like us, and we're perfectly comfortable and highly privileged, and don't you ever forget it, but by the standards of your school, we are probably down at the bottom. So you, Isabel, are the socioeconomic discrepancy."

"It's like describing the black children as the diversity," Greg tells her, helpfully. "It's called euphemism."

"Oh," says Isabel, worldly-wise and weary, "it's just their usual PC stuff, that's all."

"This woman," Greg says, covering the tomato sauce and turning from the stove to face them. "I thought she was kidding, I honestly did at first. She had a fucking flip chart and she was writing down what people said about ways to help children think about socioeconomic discrepancy here at Master Race Academy. And people are saying things like, *Well, be honest,* so she writes down HONESTY. How much do you think she got paid for this performance?"

Lucy thinks of the hospital billing consultant; word is he's pulling in a cool ten thousand a week.

Automatically, she and Greg both turn toward Isabel and start, "You can't call it—"

"Master Race Academy, I know, I never do. How much *did* she get paid?"

"We're in the wrong businesses," Lucy says. "That's why we're the socioeconomic discrepancy."

"You think you guys had it bad?" Isabel asks. Without anyone suggesting it, she has started setting the table; she is on their side and part of their team. "*We* had to go around the room and say what we thought went with being part of different socioeconomic groups. And she wrote it all down on one of those flip charts, too."

"What do you mean?"

"Oh, you know." Dismissively. "Like there are blue-collar people who don't wear jackets and ties and they don't make much money and they drink beer."

Lucy and Greg regard their daughter. She is folding the paper napkins into swans, one for each place setting. When Isabel sets a table, she sets a table. She looks up to see them staring.

"Don't ask me. It was what we had to do. We wrote down what we thought were all the assumptions and prejudices about different socioeconomic groups, and then she led this discussion about how all of them were equally good in their different ways and we should never make anyone feel bad about which one they belong to."

"You mean," Lucy says cautiously, "never tease someone because her parents happen to be very wealthy?"

"That's what Andy Constantine said," says Isabel, who almost never mentions a boy, and who has mentioned this particular boy before. "He asked if she thought it was just as bad to make fun of people for being rich as for being poor, and she said yes, it was, because people couldn't help what they were and it was just as good to be one way as another."

"And what did you guys all think of that?" asks Lucy in a neutral tone, to head off the tirade she can see coming from Greg's direction. Yes indeed, is this why we pay these insane tuition bills. Just as good to be one way as another. The socialist millennium has come, and its name is Mason-Rickover Country Day.

"We all thought it was completely and totally re—I mean lame. Sorry. It was lame. It was just the way they always do this stuff, where you have to process it and process it, when all the time you know that Michelle and Kate were just being Michelle and Kate. I mean, they probably said that stuff because Vanessa is even skinnier than they are, because sometimes they go around asking people if they want their waists measured. Michelle has this little tape measure that she carries."

"You do understand that all of this is total crap?" Greg says. "All your stuff about blue-collar people drinking beer—those are stupid clichés. Social class in this country, and socioeconomic status, are much more complicated than that—and much more interesting." A little bit of his lecturing voice has crept in, and Isabel likes it. The table is beautifully laid, napkin swans and the good water glasses and four matching plates—the only four left, as it happens, from their old set, but Isabel dug through the dish closet and found them all.

"Like Vanessa's father," Lucy adds. "You can be a carpenter who is an extremely talented and highly paid worker, like he is—he's an artisan, I guess you would say, and incidentally, he's a person who makes lots of money and who doesn't have enough time to do the work for all the people that want him. That doesn't mean that it was okay for Michelle and Kate to say those things—it would have been wrong to say them if Vanessa's family was poor, and wrong to say them if Vanessa's family was rich. Michelle and Kate are rude and stupid and mean—but you already knew that."

Isabel grins at them both: indeed she did. "I bet," she says, "that Vanessa's family has more than four matching plates."

Greg nods. "In their inlaid teak and ebony cabinets," he says.

> *Look what we found*
> *in the park*
> *in the dark.*
> *We will take him home.*
> *We will call him Clark.*
>
> *He will live at our house.*
> *He will grow and grow.*
> *Will our mother like this?*
> *We don't know.*

Lucy's favorite page. A little boy and a little girl carry an enormous round flask filled with turquoise water, and floating happily in the water is a Dr. Seuss creature much bigger than either of the children. His flippers wave languidly in the water, the two horns at either side of his mouth turn upward in a friendly kind of way, and his topknot is downright perky. The children are clearly moving fast, hurrying to show him to their mother. It always makes Lucy smile, and when she turns to that page, Freddy always checks her face.

Lucy sits on the couch, with Freddy curled up beside her. His T-shirt, which really did start the day washed, ironed, and folded, now bears extensive evidence of the tomato sauce from dinner. Probably, buried under those stains there are stains from lunch, or dirt from recess, or paint from art class. Why shouldn't he accumulate a little road dust as he goes through his day, doing his best? Why can't the school get a consultant in to teach the teachers not to use appearance-related epithets?

She stopped on the way home and bought him a pair of elastic-waist chinos. They may be a little too short, but they're the biggest size she could find with an elastic waist. She had to cut the price tags off before Freddy would try them on, because he's scared of those little plastic loops that hold tags on to clothes. And then, since she'd already cut the price tags off, she went ahead and cut off the label, since labels always bother Freddy. Anything to encourage him to try the pants on and like them. Maybe elastic-waist chinos with the tag cut off could turn out to be the magic garment, the one that transforms Freddy.

And he did pull them on. And they looked, to be honest, terrible on him, silly high-water pants bunched around his too-skinny waist. Or maybe it was the way he stood in them, tense and miserable, wanting his sweatpants or his pajamas. Freddy does not take easily to any innovation. And then Lucy, looking at him in his misery—over what, after all, over nothing—had one of those bad moments of wondering just how strange Freddy really is, and just what life will hold for him. Mrs. Gallow, after all, must be only the beginning. Put your sweatpants back on, sweetie, Lucy told him. Let's read *One Fish Two Fish Red Fish Blue Fish*. Children heal over, she tells herself. Think of Katika Lashore, and the way she heals up after tearing her skin open.

But okay. She will get Freddy into bed, and then she will go iron a T-shirt for tomorrow. She will iron a T-shirt and the one pair of sweatpants that has no holes whatsoever, and put them on a hanger in the kitchen, and Greg will come in and see them and crack up. Poor boy, you're going to have to learn to struggle with those snaps and zippers. Can't stay a hillbilly forever, not at Master Race Academy. And maybe this means nothing, this stuff about the clothing, maybe it will fade to the small, idiosyncratic preference of a smart, idiosyncratic guy—look at Greg, after all, who can't wear anything that fits closely around his neck, who spends his days by preference in those worn T-shirts. Let's think of Freddy that way, let's not predict that every single day of his life there will be things that are easy for everyone else and impossible for him.

Isabel is still hovering close, very unusual. Sat with them in the kitchen before dinner, set the table, and now she is sitting right across the room in the big armchair, pretending to read the Cleopatra volume of a girls'-book series called The Royal Diaries (which Greg keeps saying he hopes will issue a volume on Isabella herself, and how she launched Columbus and did in the Jews; *Isabella and the Inquisition*, he has suggested it should be called). Is it possible that Isabel is actually somewhat shaken by what is going on in her school? Certainly they seem to be fomenting a kind of hysteria, processing and reprocessing and never ever leaving things alone, which is how they always do it. That school counselor is a notorious menace. Miss Rexall. She lives to make a small, private meanness into a large public trauma for all concerned.

"Come sit with us," Lucy says to her daughter, who closes her book and crosses to join them on the couch, sitting on Lucy's other side and actually leaning very slightly against her mother. Tense and tight and controlled she is, but she is leaning. Lucy turns a page of the book, moving slowly and gently so as not to frighten anyone.

Then she turns back a couple of pages and reads them her very favorite page once again. She is fond of the picture of the children bringing home the strange and large whiskered monster, Clark:

> *Look what we found*
> *in the park*
> *in the dark.*

They carry him in his big, round, balloonlike tank.

> *He will live at our house.*
> *He will grow and grow.*
> *Will our mother like this?*
> *We don't know.*

She loves it just for its trueness to the spirit of childish determination and trouble, for its sly, manic certainty about what Mother will actually think. But over time, reading this story again and again, she has come to wonder whether in fact Freddy himself is Clark, whether Isabel is Clark, whether in fact Clark is just the child who comes out of the dark to live at your house and grow and grow.

5

❦

About Me

I. I Cannot Stand to Watch My Daughter Eat

Graziella cannot stand to watch her daughter eat. Surely this is not a healthy thing and surely it does not say anything good about Graziella as a mother. But there it is: she sits at the table and she thinks, I cannot stand to watch my daughter eat. When she was very little, Cleopatra was one of those kids who divide up the food on their plates so nothing touches anything else. She built barricades. She didn't eat the edges of the mashed potatoes where the chicken gravy had contaminated them. Graziella thought it was kind of cute and bought her one of those plates with subdividers, like they used to give you with TV dinners. That was back when it was easy to solve problems and Graziella was a good mother. Put the mashed potatoes in one compartment and the chicken in another and the green beans in the third and there you go. And then, oh then, there was a golden period. Cleopatra got over the food-can't-touch fetish and they could take her anywhere and feed her anything; they were the proud parents of the six-year-old who begged for more raw oysters, or another round of spareribs with spicy salt, the seven-year-old who craved tekka maki and beef with hot basil and extra an-

chovies in her spaghetti puttanesca. But now Graziella sits at the table and she thinks, I cannot stand to watch my daughter eat. There sits Cleopatra, across the table, dissecting the food on her plate. All the little pieces of tomato go on this side in a red pile, all the little black shreds of olive go here, all the chunks of Canadian bacon there. The noodles, with their sauce dissected off them, sit forlornly in the center of the dish. Cleopatra's fork moves delicately, prying, separating, classifying. Only when everything is sorted to her satisfaction will Cleopatra risk a bite, and then she will eat her way through each pile completely before she starts on the next. And she will end with the pile of noodles and leave exactly half, like a half-dome, the way she leaves exactly half of every sandwich. She still eats almost any food, Cleopatra, but she eats it only after she has carefully sorted it out. In a restaurant, Graziella averts her eyes so as not to have to see the tofu cubes here, the ground pork there, the rice neatly mounded in its own corner of the plate. Nothing touching.

It is so unbelievably unfair. Mean and unfair and stupid and not even true. And not any of anybody's business. It makes Isabel want to cry. Or no, maybe not cry, but stamp her feet and shout at her mother. The problem is, she is not really supposed to be in her mother's study using her mother's computer without permission, and she is certainly not supposed to be reading private files on her mother's desktop, which makes it difficult to confront her mother with the evidence of how awful and stupid and mean and unfair she is. Isabel is actually crying now, and she's a little bit worried about whether her parents and her brother will be getting home soon, so she can't really read the rest of this stuff, even though there's a lot more. She will have to come back and read it the next time they go out. Thank God for a mother who is so clueless she will never realize that Isabel has been using her computer; Isabel doubts that her mother even knows that the History function exists. She doesn't know that every time Isabel sits down at her mother's computer—or her father's—she can check all the websites they've been to recently, all the documents they've been working on, just as she pleases. When they finally get Isabel a new computer of her own,

108

she will guard it carefully with passwords, and she will check it, every time she turns it on, to make sure that her dumb little brother, Freddy, who is actually not so dumb about computers, has not been messing with it. By then, with any luck, she will have a real lock on her bedroom door, the kind you can lock as you leave the room.

Isabel also knows that if she asked permission to research her Haiti project on the Internet or to look up some more poems about winter for that stupid poetry poster—for something educational like that, of course her mother or her father would let her use one of their computers. And she knows she should be asking this permission regularly, because that way they will be reminded that she really needs Internet access herself in her own room, even though it will mean replacing that antique piece of junk she uses now as a word processor.

Which she brings up with Abby, who telephones right as Isabel is shutting down her mother's computer. Isabel has the portable phone waiting right there on her mother's desk, and she grabs it up on the first beep.

"Have you done your list?"

"Just the way we said."

They made up their lists together during study period. You get to request eight girls you would like to have in your squad, and they promise to try and give you at least one. Or, of course, eight boys if you're a boy. Abby and Isabel were giggling over the idea that Jessie Baxter would *rather* list eight boys, and they came up with the list she would probably make, too. You aren't supposed to rank the girls you list, but Abby and Isabel have agreed to put each other's name first and circle it and underline it, and since in addition they are both going to list the same seven other girls, they calculate that they have a pretty good chance of ending up together.

"They really ought to let you make a list of the eight girls you most *don't* want to be put with," Abby says.

"Oh, we should do that! That would be great—not to hand in, of course! Imagine if you handed that in."

"Right, sure, to Ms. Lederer. I bet."

"Oh, my God!" Isabel is laughing, and she can hear Abby laughing at the other end. Her mother's computer has fully shut down. Almost immediately, she wants to turn it back on and read what her mother wrote one more time, but she doesn't let herself. She's good at not letting herself do things, and she tests herself all the time.

Instead, she gets up and looks over her mother's desk, checking to see that it appears undisturbed, which is to say, kind of disturbed and disorganized.

"I bet my list would be the same as yours, and I bet I know who numbers one, two, and three would be."

"Don't tell me," Isabel says. "I'm going to write down the list and you write down yours, and then we'll trade. If my parents would just get over it and buy me a computer, I could IM it to you."

"No, you couldn't. Mine got this stupid thing that lets them turn off my access whenever they want, and they say I can only go online for one hour every night. It's something my mother read in one of her how-to-be-a-good-parent books."

Isabel thinks of the line on her mother's computer, "That was back when Graziella was a good mother," or something like that. If her mother really wants to be a good mother, maybe she should try asking Isabel what to do.

The truth is, there are times it makes Isabel very happy to check up on her parents by looking at what they have been doing on their computers. Once they get her a new machine of her own, and set her up for Internet access, she will no longer have any excuse to sit in their studies, unsupervised, and roam around on their computer desktops. She likes to know what they are working on, even though she doesn't always understand what each project is or what the titles mean. *Incidence of complex medical disorders requiring multiple subspecialty referrals among school-age children in foster care.* Isabel can hear her mother's voice pronouncing these words; if this is what her mother is working on, then the world is as it should be —or at least, her mother is busy trying to make the world what it should be, in her old familiar way. Tomorrow, Isabel tells herself, she could go check out her father's computer. But she won't. Even as she artistically arranges the uncapped ballpoint pen and the pad of orange Post-its on her mother's desk to look as they looked before—not that her mother would notice—Isabel knows that the next chance she gets she will be back. *Cleopatra. Graziella.* Isabel thinks that Graziella is a ridiculous name.

So here's why Isabel was crying. She knows perfectly well—or at least, she suspects with the certainty that is the next thing over —that often her mother does not want to look at her. Yes, at the table, but also at other times. There is something about her, about Isabel, which Lucy just plain doesn't like, something about the way her glance catches on Isabel, as she sits, for example, smoothing down her hair in the car on the way to school. The way Lucy's glance catches quickly on Isabel, as if on some tiny invisible annoying snag. Shakes free and then moves on to smile fondly on stupid retarded Freddy. Freddy will be sitting there with his nose running or with food all over his face from breakfast. Freddy will be sorting through his stupid baseball cards or marking up the sports section of the morning paper with his red pen, and Lucy will look at him and smile with relief no longer to be looking at Isabel, with her clean face and her neatly clipped, clear-polished nails, carefully raking into place the last slightly straying hairs.

"You have to go to the Parent Information Session," Isabel said patiently, but with the capital letters clear in her voice. "It's obligatory."

Her father tried kidding around in his usual lame way. "I thought you didn't want to have to go on the trip—maybe if we skip the obligatory Parent Irritation Session, they won't let you go. See? That way everybody wins!"

Isabel concentrated on her mother; if Lucy wrote this on her calendar, she would come. "Mom. It's obligatory. You have to."

And sure enough, after the other parents are already assembled in neat rows on the folding chairs, with information packets on their laps, after Ms. Lederer has already begun to talk about bonding and class spirit, there is a little bustle in the back of the room, and Isabel looks up to see her mother pushing her way in through the knot of fathers with cell phones and beepers who always hang out back there, waiting for an excuse to step back into the hallway and maybe disappear for good. Lucy will stay back there with them, because, after all, whose beeper is most likely to go off? Somewhere recently, in some book, Isabel has seen the expression "most likely to succeed," and now for a minute she considers awards for parents at obligatory Parent Information Sessions. Most likely to have a beeper go off. Most likely to ask a really embarrassing question. Most likely to take notes.

She cracks a secret little smile, then realizes rather abruptly that that is her father's kind of joke. It was Greg who came home from her Open Classroom Night this year with a story about one of the moms—at first he wouldn't tell her which one, but after she teased for a while he admitted it was Jessie Baxter's—taking notes in every fifteen-minute session with every teacher. He even said he deliberately sat next to her in English class, and there she was, hunched over her pad and writing down every word the teacher uttered—it was Mr. DePaul, who never ever says anything worth writing down, in Isabel's opinion, not even in class. Greg did this really funny imitation of Mrs. Baxter hurrying to get it all down on paper, saying the words one by one in a slurred zombie voice while scribbling desperately in the air with his hand: the-students-will-concentrate-on-their-critical-reading-skills-that-will-allow-them-to-handle-more-difficult-material-as-the-year-proceeds.

No, her mom will not take notes back there. She won't disappear for good either, even if her beeper goes off; she'll just start to look kind of worried and keep checking the clock and then looking back down at the beeper, and finally she'll turn and push her way to the door, nervously pressing the little button on the side that makes the numbers blink into place on top—Isabel knows how to do it because a couple of times on weekends, her mother has gone out to make rounds at the hospital and accidentally left the beeper home, clipped to the front pocket of her ridiculously heavy week-day briefcase. When that happens, her mother calls home from her cell phone in the car, desperate to know whether she's being paged, and since her father insists that the workings of the beeper are completely beyond him, Isabel gets to clip it to her waistband and call Lucy on the cell phone if it beeps, press the button and read her the number.

But don't let Lucy's beeper go off now—someone's cell phone is certainly going to ring while Ms. Lederer is talking, someone is going to get paged, but don't let it be Lucy. She's already been last parent in, don't let her be first one out, and then have to come back in again looking a little lost and depending on Isabel to have listened carefully and found out everything important. They'll get in the car together and Lucy will say something like, *Well, honey, so is there anything I have to do to get ready for your trip to Wissacoho?*—like that wasn't the whole point of the obligatory Parent Information Session! At which point in her thoughts, anxiously poised, looking straight ahead at Ms. Lederer but still half-turned mentally, monitoring the parents standing in the back, Isabel realizes that in fact she is not listening and will not be able to supply her mother's deficiencies, so she focuses her attention and her memory back on the head of the school, taking mental notes for Lucy.

She doesn't wear a watch, Graziella. Nor Herbert, though he worries about the time. They are both of them skilled in locating the time on various devices: her cell phone, the VCR, the microwave—fortunately they have a son who can program all programmable devices, and who has the times on every clock and timer in the house coordinated to the minute. And they are both inveterate askers, Anybody know what time it is? And once again, fortunately, they are saved by their children, by Cleopatra in this case. Cleopatra, of course, always wears a watch. And I mean always, strapped tight round her wrist, always choosing the tighter hole, the closer pinch of skin. Graziella, who cannot stand the sense of anything tight around her anywhere, sometimes wants to reach out and loosen her daughter's watch strap, but would never dare to.

It's not that hard, really, to manage without wearing a watch. Especially, Graziella thinks, in this world of digital everything, especially,

Graziella would say, if you are an artist and less tied to a schedule of meetings and appointments. Especially, Cleopatra herself would say, if you're going to rely on other people to keep track of everything for you.

But you aren't an artist, Mom. You're a doctor. Doctors do wear watches. Abby's father is a doctor and he wears a Rolex and Abby says it cost thousands of dollars and her brothers aren't even allowed to touch it and once they hid it on April Fool's Day and left her youngest brother's broken Pokemon watch in the special place on her father's dresser where he always keeps it—and their father thought that was such a good one that he bought them all new Swatches, after he got his Rolex back, of course. Not that Isabel would actually ever tell this story to her parents, especially to her father, because it would probably bring on an attack of his Abby's-father-Daniel-is-the-Best-Dad-in-the-World routine, and who needs that? Clearly, she should never have told him, back three years ago when she and Abby were first becoming best friends, that Abby's father schedules special time every week with each one of his three children, and the times are marked in red on the big Sierra Club calendar that hangs in their kitchen. *Don't worry,* she would like to say to Greg now, when he goes into his shtick ("Kite-flying? Did someone say kite-flying? But I bet the Best Dad in the World wouldn't be content with any old store-bought kites! When you're the Best Dad in the World, you make your own!"), *don't worry, you guys aren't in the running. You don't even have a family calendar—just like you don't wear watches.*

Because that much is true, as far as it goes. Lucy and Greg don't wear watches, either of them. And Isabel does keep a watch strapped fairly tightly around her wrist, but it's a good thing somebody does.

And you aren't an artist, Mom. And you tell time by your beeper, which as it happens Isabel, and not her dumb little brother, knows how to adjust. And for that matter, Isabel knows how to set the time on the microwave and the VCR, though it's probably true that Freddy is getting to the point where he can do those things as well.

He's certainly very focused on having all the digital displays in the house show the exact same time, but actually Isabel is with him on that one, and if she ever checked, Lucy would find that her beeper is in perfect step with the music system in the living room and the clock on the stove, and even with her computer—Isabel allowed herself to adjust the time on that as well; Lucy hadn't even bothered to fix A.M. and P.M.

You aren't an artist, Mom. And for that matter, even though you certainly need to get yourself in shape and do something about your hair and the way you dress, you aren't actually really fat and all dressed up in totally weird clothes like you describe Graziella. Why would Lucy do that? She writes about Graziella, who is obviously supposed to be herself, the mom, the one who doesn't wear a watch, the one who can't stand to watch her daughter eat, and she makes her some kind of a freak. Graziella is so fat that she has to shop in the special fat lady's department, while Isabel knows for a fact that her mother is sometimes a size 12 and sometimes a size 14. In fact, Lucy jokes that if they manufacture the clothes so that the size 12 fits, it suckers her into buying something. Just think what they could sell me if they were willing to make the size 10s bigger, she said to Isabel when they went to the mall to buy school clothes and then just stopped for a minute to look for a suit with what Lucy would consider an appropriate-length skirt for herself, with pockets. And Lucy was giving her why-don't-they-make-real-pockets-in-women's-skirts speech when she shifted topics and said that if the clothes makers had the sense to run the suits a little large and she happened to fit into this one particular suit in a size 10, she would probably buy it, even though it cost four hundred dollars and didn't even have any pockets, but instead they had cut it so small that even the size 14 felt tight, so that made her feel fat and awful and no way would she think of buying it. And Isabel thought of saying, *You know, Mom, if you lost maybe twenty pounds you would probably BE a size 10 and no doubt about it,* but she didn't. The conversation made her uncomfortable, and that was way back before she even knew this stuff about Graziella, who can't watch her daughter eat, so instead she asked, "Can't you put your stuff in your pocketbook, Mom, isn't that why they don't put pockets in women's clothes?" On cue her mother returned to her familiar rant about how nobody expects a man to drag a pocketbook with him through his workday, and how she needs a place to clip her beeper and tuck a couple of dollars for the soda machine—her mother has a serious Diet Coke addiction—and a pen and maybe some index cards.

Graziella's clothes are the kind of outfits that would make you just plain commit suicide if your mother wore them to your school. She dresses like a gypsy, it says, she wears one long, brightly colored skirt on top of another, with an embroidered apron tied over the whole thing; she wears white peasant blouses that slip off her shoulders and let her bra straps show; she wears scarves around her neck and long, dangly earrings and lots of big necklaces with colored beads. And she's big and fat. Isabel can see her so clearly, coming into the classroom on Open Classroom Night, into Ms. Granger's advanced math class, where everything is so very neat and orderly, including Ms. Granger, who wears a perfectly pressed oxford-cloth shirt every single day, tucked into a chino skirt—and there is Graziella, too fat to sit comfortably in the student seat with the armrest, and joking about it—*joking* about it, while the other parents look at her in horror, probably wondering whether she is some kind of important diversity that they have to treat with a lot of cultural respect.

But, Mom, you don't look like that at all. You don't act like that at all. At the Wissacoho Parent Information Session, Lucy stood in the back and her beeper never did go off. She was there in plenty of time to hear Ms. Lederer give almost all of her rather long speech about how the boys and girls were growing up, and the ending of fifth grade was also the beginning of middle school, and the sacred school tradition, and the powerful bonds forged at Wissacoho that would carry them together through middle school, through high school, and through life. And when she and Isabel got in the car to drive home, Lucy didn't ask what she was supposed to do to get Isabel ready for this important tradition—she had listened carefully, and she knew. In fact, she and Isabel had a good time, driving home, laughing at the questions that some of the other parents had asked. The parents who were upset that the kids wouldn't be able to call home for the whole time they were out at Wissacoho—what did they think a camping trip was supposed to be, anyway? And how angry that father in the first row was that they wouldn't let his son take a cell phone along—and how he clearly didn't believe Ms. Lederer when she said that generally cell phones don't even work out at Wissacoho because of the coastline and the hills and no tower anywhere near. And that mother who kept asking what if her daughter got really homesick and really missed her?

"I mean, come on," Isabel said. "I mean, we are finishing up the fifth grade and all—I mean, next year we're in the middle school. Wouldn't you think pretty much everyone has been away from home for a couple of days before?"

"I guess some kids are just more sentimental than others," Lucy said. "They're not all as cold-blooded as you are, my sweet. There you'll be, in your sleeping bag, and all around you will be the girls crying out for home and mother. 'Oh, if only my wise and understanding mommy were here right now to give me her usual invaluable advice and wipe my——nose for me!' "

Isabel understood quite clearly that her mother had started to say *wipe my ass*, and she laughed as heartily as if her mother had said it. She felt so easy and happy with Lucy that she even risked a request.

"Mom, I know this is kind of silly, but could we please not tell Dad about that question Angela's mom asked?"

Her mother turned slightly to look at her. "Which question—oh, was that the one about what if one of them gets her period for the first time while you're there?"

"Yes."

There's a pause for a few seconds, as Isabel can sense her mother turning over the request and its implications. It was without any doubt the most excruciating moment of the assembly—right in front of all the teachers, she asked that—in front of the boys! The male teachers! And although Isabel doesn't completely understand why, she knows that her mother will think it's part of the joke, that she will tell it back to Greg when she describes the meeting, and somehow Isabel doesn't want her father to hear that part of the story. Doesn't want her parents to discuss it. "Could we just not tell Dad about that one?" Isabel repeats.

"Sure," Lucy says, and Isabel takes a deep breath and relaxes. When it comes to "most likely to ask the most embarrassing question," she thinks gratefully, her mother is not even in the running.

"But, honey?" Her mother has decided she must make a statement.

"Mom?"

"It wasn't a bad question to ask—or at least, it isn't a bad thing to think about and plan for. At some point, the girls in your class are going to start getting their periods."

"Mom, I know. We've been over that in health so many times."

"Yes, you have, and I think you got a hundred and five on the menstruation test."

"I got all the extra credit," Isabel cannot keep from saying, even though she knows her mother thinks the menstruation test was funny, too.

"But even though you have the information, it can still be pretty scary—or pretty embarrassing—or just overwhelming, when it actually happens to you. So you can see that if it happened to someone out in the woods—well, it's important to know the nurse is prepared, and it was probably good for you all to hear Ms. Lederer say that about just telling a female teacher . . ."

"Well, who does she *think* we're going to tell? Mr. DePaul?"

"And, honey, if it's any comfort to you, I don't think you're anywhere near getting your period yet."

"Really?" This would be wonderful news; Isabel does not even want to think about this happening, and then happening again and again, and on and on for years and years. What a terrible idea, she thought when she first heard about it. What a stupid unfair setup. And since, as far as she knows, it hasn't happened to anyone in her grade yet, it's still possible at certain moments to preserve the hope that it's not really true, or not really true for everyone, that the adults made it up or got it wrong, and it isn't really going to happen.

"Well, you can't ever predict this exactly." Her mother's work voice, where you know she is bringing in things she really *knows,* you can hear the sureness in her voice. Isabel loves this voice, the way she likes seeing those impossible sentences about foster children and multidisciplinary clinics and complex medical conditions on her mother's computer screen. "First of all, I was thirteen myself, and they say you can estimate by subtracting a year from the age that the mother was—so that would give you a little more time. And second of all, you're so slim—that usually means you won't be one of the earliest developers."

And Isabel, who is actually rather frightened of having to go to Wissacoho, who is worried of course about which other girls will be assigned to her squad, who has no desire at all to go sleep in the woods in a sleeping bag for three nights without even being able to wash properly, if you believe what the sixth-grade girls say, is suddenly filled with light, happy joy. *Second of all, you're so slim.* Is she really? Is that what she is? Slim? So slim? Well, her mother is a doctor, after all, and that is what her mother says. She must be slim. She must be so slim.

"Mom," Isabel says, "Mom, you really like what you do, don't you?" She means it as a compliment. Maybe even as an apology, and she knows that her parents think she has great trouble apologizing. The problem is, Isabel thinks, that feeling happy makes me want to apologize. Makes me happy to apologize. When she feels good, like right now, Isabel can be pleased that she was way wrong about her mother, who after all came to the meeting and listened and understood and asked no embarrassing questions and then afterward even let Isabel ask an embarrassing question and didn't make her feel bad. *I'm sorry, Mom, for the way I underestimate you all the time.*

"Mostly I love what I do," her mother says.

"Do you ever think about other things—really different things —you could do?"

"Like what? Like investment banking?"

"Like being an artist? Or a writer or something?" Isabel wonders if that is a dangerous question, if even the word *artist* will signal her mother to think of Graziella and Herbert.

"It isn't something I ever thought much about." Lucy is driving a little bit aggressively, the way she does, jumping on lights as they turn green, getting them home quickly.

"You mean you think about it now?"

"Sometimes," Lucy says. "Sometimes I think about it now, more than I used to—I think about the parts of my brain that I use and the parts of my brain that I don't use. Or about being someone else —when I watch you and imagine all the things you could be and all the ways you can live. With the kind of job I do and the kind of training I did, once you commit to it, you're totally sucked in. You never get ten minutes to think about the alternative lives you might have lived."

Isabel doesn't know what to say. She wants to ask, *Am I part of the alternative lives you might have lived? Any of them? All of them?*

II. Graziella Is No Fool

Cherries. Cleopatra is obsessed with cherries when spring comes around. Graziella buys the cherries, which are still pretty expensive this early, and Cleopatra eats them and begs for more. But it's another one of those weird food behaviors of Cleopatra's—she doesn't want anyone else to touch the cherries, which she keeps in a special bag in the refrigerator, and Graziella would almost swear she counts them. And she eats them in her patterned, obsessive way; she fills a certain specific little Chinese soup bowl with cherries, she takes a sheet of paper toweling for the pits, and she sits in the big red armchair in the living room, methodically biting each cherry in half, holding the half that contains the pit while she carefully chews the other half, then digging out the pit with thumb and forefinger and eating the other half. *The pits are arranged on the paper towel, which is spread carefully across the arm of the chair, arranged in tight little compulsive rows, military cherry-pit formation.* Graziella averts her eyes. She wants to ask, *If the pits fell down and got out of order, would you have to regurgitate everything and start again?* but she doesn't. She doesn't actually want to bring up anything about throwing up or other funny eating patterns with her daughter; she's afraid that Cleopatra may be headed in that direction. *Well, if you read certain stories in the newspaper, it seems like every young girl may be headed in that direction.* But still, Graziella knows enough to see that she and Cleopatra are a classic set-up: *Mother fat. Daughter very focused on exactly controlling everything she eats. Daughter obsessed with food but maybe not really enjoying it. And Cleopatra, for all her strange eating patterns, for all the vehemence with which she refuses food that does not perfectly fit her standards, for all the tortuous slowness with which she dissects her cooked dishes and eats them, component by component by component, is still distinctly plump.*

Oh, it is so unfair. Just because her stupid mother decided that instead of making Graziella plump, like Lucy is, stupid Graziella would be fat fat fat, so now the daughter has to be plump. Isabel knows perfectly well that she is the one and only member of her family who does not in any way have a weight problem. Her mother is, well, someone who only sometimes fits into size 12. Abby's mother, she happens to know, is a size 6. Isabel's father has that belly that you can certainly see when he wears a bathing suit, and he knows it, too, because he stands up straight and sucks it in, and then laughs and lets it out. And Freddy is too skinny, always has been, and sometimes he has to drink these really disgusting cans of stuff to make him gain weight—if you can really call that a weight problem. But Isabel can see perfectly well that Freddy's body does not look healthy. And for that matter, she, Isabel, is in no danger at all of having any kind of eating disorder, since she can also see perfectly well that Maya Winkler, the girl in the sixth grade who is famous for being anorexic, looks just horrible all the time, not to mention the way everybody jokes about her smelling of vomit because supposedly after she eats these lunches, which Abby says they made her sign a special contract, in writing, that she would eat, she just goes in the bathroom and pukes them up. Abby says that sometimes in the sixth-grade classes when Maya raises her hand—supposedly, she's very smart and she gets straight A's—the boys make puking noises.

Just because of the cherries, that's what made her mother write this. All Isabel did was ask her mother, Look, could you get lots of cherries, I really like them?—and then her mother bought only one plastic bag of them, and not very many at all, and then when Freddy started to help himself to an enormous bowlful, all Isabel said was, Look, are you really going to eat those? Because they're my favorite fruit, so if you're just going to play with them or something, could you take grapes instead? And Freddy didn't seem to care much, but her mom and dad got totally bent out of shape, probably because they always want stupid Freddy to eat, they always want to find things he'll like—if *he* had asked for lots of cherries, the refrigerator would be full of them and there would probably be a sign saying CHERRIES ARE FOR FREDDY ONLY.

So okay, she will never line up her cherry pits again, at least not where her mom can see. So okay, it wasn't nice to pick on Freddy about the cherries, even if he didn't care, and she knows her parents were looking at her, wanting her to say she was sorry. But when she's angry or when she's hurt, Isabel cannot say she's sorry, she just can't. It's like that part of her is all locked up at those moments, and just when her parents are expecting her to apologize, she is waiting for everyone else to apologize to *her* for making her feel so bad. But that does not make her plump, that does not make her a person who is going to have an eating disorder and go around making herself puke like a crazy idiot.

Isabel is taking a chance and she knows it. Her mother is only in the shower, not out of the house, and she has no particular business being here in her mother's study. It's a mess, as usual, with all those photocopied medical articles that never look like anyone has read them spilling all over the desk, even covering part of the keyboard.

But Freddy is in bed and Greg is out at some dinner for his college, and Lucy always takes at least twenty minutes in the shower, and Isabel has to check. She just has to. There is more stuff about Graziella all the time, and she doesn't have time to read it all. In fact, she doesn't want to read it all; most of it is about fat, artistic Graziella and her dumb husband, Herbert, and both of them are some kind of stupid artists and their house is full of stuff like blown glass sculptures or hanging things made of old shoes and spray-painted. Isabel knows how to use the Find function, and what she wants to read about is Cleopatra.

Cleopatra is hanging around the kitchen, watching Graziella cook. She makes Graziella self-conscious, which is hard to do. But as Graziella picks up her giant yellow can of olive oil to pour more into the pan where the pork chops are cooking, she can feel Cleopatra's eyes upon her, and she pours in only a drop, not the generous slug she knows the pork chops need. Graziella can easily imagine her daughter eating the pork chop, scraping off the mushrooms and onions and peppers, then sorting them into separate piles, then slicing off tiny perfect cubes of pork chop, one by one, to put into her mouth. The thought of it makes Graziella feel hot and irritated and unhappy, just at this moment when she should be enjoying the good smells in her kitchen, so she grabs the bottle of cheap Italian red wine that she was planning to use in finishing up the pork chops and pours herself a glass. It crosses her mind to offer a sip to her daughter—maybe a few drops of wine diluted in water, or maybe just a tiny drink of her own, and she can almost imagine the fellowship of the two of them together in the good-smelling kitchen—but she can more easily imagine the disgusted look on Cleopatra's face as she shakes her head, No, never, what a bad bad idea.

Isabel hears the bathroom door open and close, and she scrambles to shut down the computer, hoping to be on the couch reading a book by the time her mother comes downstairs. But the computer takes too long, and though she turns off the light and rushes out of the study, she's sure her mother could tell which room she was in.

• • •

The day that they get their squad assignments for Wissacoho, Isabel makes it all the way home before she starts to cry. Her mother finds her about two hours later, still crying, lying flat on her bed, face deep in her damp pillow.

"I didn't get *anyone*. I requested eight different girls and they didn't put me with anyone!"

"Who are you with?" asks Lucy.

"Awful people. People I just hate. Jessie and Alex and Sarah H. It's going to be so horrible. And they said they would put us with our friends! They said!"

"Did the other kids all get put with their friends?"

"Yes," Isabel cries, and her sobbing breaks out again, with new strength. Everyone has a friend or two, everyone but her.

"Honey, I could call the school," Lucy suggests, with appropriate hesitancy.

"And do what? Everybody's already assigned! There's nothing anyone can do!"

"Listen!" Lucy says, with a certain urgency. "That's ridiculous. Of course there are things to do."

"Like what? Call the school?"

"Well, I could call tomorrow and speak to Ms. Lederer and say that you're very disappointed . . ."

"Don't call the school, Mom!" Isabel wails.

"Or else, you know, you could just not go—if you think it's going to be a miserable trip. I could write you a medical excuse."

Isabel pulls herself to a sitting position and regards her mother with amazed and hostile incredulity. "Not go? Not go on the end of fifth-grade class trip to Wissacoho?" (This suggestion is quite possibly the stupidest thing she has ever heard. *Ever.*)

"Well, if you're feeling so bad about the trip and the girls you're going with—I mean, Isabel, your father and I don't care whether you go to Wissacoho and sleep in a tent, so don't do it for our sake."

Great. Isabel has the parents who don't care whether she goes or not. Other parents take notes and worry about their kids being able to make phone calls.

Her mother's hand lands gently on the back of Isabel's head. "Dinner in twenty minutes," Lucy says, which Isabel knows from long experience is unlikely to be true. Double it and add five minutes more to clear off the kitchen table and set it, is more like it. Call it forty-five. And then her mother can't stand to watch her eat. But right now her mother is touching the back of her head and looking right at her and not looking away.

"Okay, Mom," Isabel says. "Thanks."

Her mother pauses in the doorway, hand on the knob. "Are you sure you wouldn't like me to call up the school tomorrow, honey? It really doesn't seem fair to me if everyone else got someone they requested and you didn't, and I would be happy to say that to Ms. Lederer, really I would."

"It's okay, Mom. Don't call the school," says Isabel, and flops back down on her bed, and she knows in that moment that it will indeed be okay, and that she will get through the trip just fine, and all the teachers will be impressed with her resourcefulness and her good behavior, and no, she won't turn out to be friends with any of those idiotic girls they've put her with, but she'll get by. In fact, Isabel is lying on her bed now filled with a sudden and probably passing certainty that she will get through her whole life just fine, that everything will fall into place.

Her dad isn't home for dinner that night, and he gets back late, just as Isabel is getting ready for bed. Her dad comes up to her room to kiss her goodnight and tells her, "Mom and I are just going to take a walk around the block for a little while to clear the cobwebs out of our heads. She's carrying her cell phone, so call if you need us—I doubt you will, though. Freddy's fast asleep."

And so should Isabel be fast asleep; she is very careful to get to bed on time and her sleeping habits are excellent, according to the rate-yourself poll they did in health earlier this year. For example, she never reads scary or disturbing books late in the evening, or watches anything frightening on TV, and she always flosses before going to bed. But here is a very bad habit: she is sneaking back into her mother's study to turn on the computer, to search for Cleopatra.

The file opens, and there is a new first paragraph on the screen, all in capital letters.

CLEOPATRA KNOWS A LOT OF THINGS ABOUT GRAZIELLA THAT GRAZIELLA DOESN'T KNOW SHE KNOWS. BUT GRAZIELLA IS NO FOOL, YOU KNOW. SHE CAN TELL PERFECTLY WELL WHEN CLEOPATRA HAS BEEN SNEAKING AROUND HER ART STUDIO AND LOOKING AT THINGS THAT ARE MEANT TO BE PRIVATE. IT'S A FUNNY THING, BUT GRAZIELLA, EVEN THOUGH SHE IS A LITTLE BIT SLOVENLY AND SOMETIMES KIND OF LAZY, WOULD NEVER NEVER NEVER SNOOP AROUND IN CLEOPATRA'S ROOM, NEVER READ HER DIARY OR ANY OTHER KIND OF WRITING SHE LEFT LYING AROUND. THERE'S SOMETHING SO TERRIBLE ABOUT READING SOMEONE ELSE'S PRIVATE STUFF — GRAZI-ELLA WOULD BE AFRAID THAT IF CLEOPATRA FOUND OUT HER MOTHER HAD BEEN DOING IT, SHE MIGHT STOP TRUST-ING HER ALTOGETHER. AND IT'S VERY HARD TO LIVE WITH A PARENT — OR A CHILD — IF YOU'VE FOUND OUT YOU CAN'T TRUST THEM. AND GRAZIELLA ALSO KNOWS THAT IF SHE, FOR EXAMPLE, SNOOPED AROUND AND READ CLEOPATRA'S DIARY, WHY THEN THAT DIARY MIGHT LOSE ALL ITS APPEAL FOR THE POOR GIRL. AND THAT WOULD BE A TRULY TERRIBLE THING TO DO, BY GRAZIELLA'S STANDARDS AT LEAST, TO MAKE SOME-ONE, ANYONE, EVEN HER OWN DAUGHTER, FEEL THAT SOME-THING THAT HAD BEEN PART OF HER MOST SECRET SELF HAD NOW BEEN SPOILED. GRAZIELLA WOULD NEVER NEVER NEVER DO SUCH A THING, DO YOU HEAR ME, ISABEL? NEVER. YOU SHOULD BE ASHAMED OF YOURSELF.

Isabel turns the computer off without shutting it down prop-erly. She wants to curse, or to wait hunched up on the stairs until her parents come home and then say something, anything, to her mother. *I love you, thanks for a great dinner,* maybe even *I wish you would go ahead and call the school about the Wissacoho trip.* Well, no, she's not as upset as that—no calling the school. But the stairs are pretty dusty, and her nightgown is chilly, and her parents aren't out for any old twenty minutes, either. So Isabel goes up to bed.

Every day all week as her mother drives her to school, Isabel thinks about saying something. If she admits that she saw the paragraph in capital letters, then she's admitting everything. Just like her mother could write anything she wanted there, her mother could write *You are wicked and evil to look at my private things,* and Isabel would see it only if she deserves it. She wants to say she's sorry, and Isabel knows her parents think she has a lot of trouble saying she's sorry. She wants to say that no, she never thought about it exactly before, but she guesses that she does know that her mother would never go through her stuff or read her diary. Not that her mother would ever find her diary, of course, Isabel thinks, and then, with one of those grown-up flashes, she knows that her mother *could* find her diary if she wanted, anyone could, all she has is one little bedroom to hide all herself and all her secrets. And when she thinks about having secrets and hiding secrets, then she feels bad all over again.

But she just can't do it; she just can't say what she wants to say. Freddy is always there, and even though usually he doesn't listen when other people are talking, you can't really depend on that. And hearing his sister apologize would be just the kind of thing to make him look up and pay attention. What she really wants to ask her mother is *Did I spoil it? Do you still write about them, you know I'll never look again, Mom, so just tell me you still keep it going. Graziella in her colored skirts and Herbert who never wears a watch and makes shoe sculptures and Cleopatra dissecting her food. I didn't kill them, did I, Mom?* And then, maybe, after she apologized, she could ask about whether her mother really cannot stand to look at her, especially when she is eating.

Finally, on the morning her mother drives her in for the Wissacoho trip, Freddy is not there. His father took him so Lucy could devote her full attention to Isabel and the four-page what-to-take-to-Wissacoho checklist. Isabel, of course, has already been over the list twice, once with a red pen and once with a green pen, and everything is all set, but as they drive, Lucy makes her read the list aloud and confirm that she has everything, and it gives Isabel a very nice, secure feeling to tell her mother over and over that yes, she has a rain poncho, yes, she has three extra pairs of heavy wool socks, yes, she has two flashlights and four batteries.

"You're so well-organized," Lucy says. "I'm very impressed. You did it all. I should hire you to put my life in order."

And just like that, Isabel says it: "I'm really sorry I went in your office, Mom, and looked at your stuff. I'm really sorry."

"You won't ever do it again?"

"No. And I'm really sorry." Isabel wants to ask, *If I promise I'll never look again, will you promise you'll write more?* But she doesn't ask; she is filled with a kind of surprising joy at having apologized, and she wants to sit and taste it a little.

Instead, her mother says, "You know, I sit at that computer so much, but I've never in my whole life written anything that wasn't, you know, for school or for work. I've never kept a diary or written poetry, nothing like that."

Isabel wants to say that she keeps a diary, but she doesn't; if she said it, she knows she and her mother would both think about how her mother would never snoop and read it. Also, she wants her mother to go on talking; she is almost holding her breath waiting for her mother to go on talking.

Which she does. "And the stuff I write for work—it's all about describing things exactly as they are. You know, notes in patients' charts or research papers—and you can't change things, even when you want to. You can't change the data. It's kind of amazing how once you start making things up you can use real things but change them, too, and sometimes it seems closer to reality than all the real details."

They pull up beside the school, and there is a really big bus, not a school bus like for most class trips, but a big silver tour bus, and there are all the parents and the kids and the backpacks and the checklists and the teachers wearing jeans and Ms. Lederer, who is not actually going, and who is not in jeans but is still in charge, with a clipboard and the biggest list of all.

Lucy parks and offers to help carry stuff, but Isabel has arranged it so that she can manage it all and slings the backpack up with just a little help, and her mother trails her as they walk to the bus, and there is Abby, so she runs to catch up, because there's no reason they can't sit together on the bus even if they aren't in the same squad. After Isabel stows her backpack and sleeping bag in the bus luggage compartment, she turns to look for her mother, and sees Lucy standing there with a mother who Isabel doesn't even recognize, and the other mother is sobbing. Tears are running down her face. Lucy, who looks a little bit lost, is offering her a tissue, and as Isabel moves toward the two of them, she can see clearly the blotches of the other mother's mascara, black against the tissue, and what must be her eye shadow, a kind of smoky blue. Which explains why this other mother, whoever she is, is standing there with what look like two black eyes.

"Oh, there's my daughter," says Lucy, with very evident relief. She smiles at Isabel. She pats the other mother, who is maybe a perfect size 4 to Isabel's appraising eye, on the shoulder of her tight little suede jacket. "You'll be fine," she says. "The kids will be fine. Come now, dear, let me walk you to the bus." And she clasps Isabel's arm firmly and off they go, leaving the other mother standing there.

"What was that all about?" Isabel hisses, but Lucy shakes her head, still too close to the other mother to talk, and walks her around the front of the bus. As soon as the bus is between them and that other lady, Lucy gives a comic *whew* and shakes her head.

"Mom? What was that all about?"

"She's just upset because she doesn't feel her son is ready for this."

"Her *son*? She's a *boy's* mother? Who's her son?" No wonder Isabel didn't recognize her.

"I don't even know," says Lucy, which Isabel suspects is a lie. "But whoever he is, he's got his hands full, I'll tell you that. That woman had hold of my arm so tight I bet she left bruises, and she said to me, 'I just have to keep remembering, this isn't about me, this is about him.'"

"What? You're kidding!" Isabel is grateful not to know whose mother it was. She is grateful that her mother is her mother.

"Could I make up a thing like that? 'This isn't about me, this is about him.' She must have said it five times. 'This isn't about me, this is about him.'"

Solemnly, knowing it's the right thing to say, Isabel says to her mother, "Mom, this isn't about you, it's about me."

And it is the right thing to say, and her mother cracks a big, fond smile, as if she loves to look at Isabel and see her standing there, and she wraps her arms around her for a quick hug and murmurs in her ear, "Actually, this is about a compulsory three-day camping trip and a school tradition and a getting-ready-for-middle-school bonding experience, okay? Could we just get that straight? You're going to be away from home for three whole nights, with enough teachers there to sink a ship, stuck with a group of girls you don't even like, and I hope you have a very good time, okay?"

The hug is over and they smile at each other. "Okay," Isabel says. And she smiles at her mother one more time and then runs over and climbs onto the bus, where Abby is saving a good seat, way at the back. She looks out the window long enough to find her mother and wave, and then watches her mother heading back toward the parking lot. Some of the other parents are hanging around to watch the bus depart, and Isabel knows what her mother would say about them, the some-people-badly-need-a-life remark. Surely the boy's mother with the smudged eye makeup is among them, and she peers through the window trying to identify her, and thus gets to see Ms. Lederer, armed with her clipboard, march over to the group of parents and, unmistakably, tell them to go on home.

The sleeping bag, which her mother borrowed from this guy she works with whose older daughter is a professional trail guide or a forest ranger or something, is at least warm enough, because Wissacoho, just as everyone said, is amazingly cold at night. The teachers told them that some schools come here as early as April or even March, and that even in April, you can wake up and find the drinking water is frozen. In fact, that very first night at Wissacoho, Alex Airhead Brewster gets so cold in her own sleeping bag that she demands that the teachers get up and drive her home immediately. Which, of course, they don't do. They tell her to put on more layers. Isabel huddles down deeper into her warm, slightly funky-smelling bag, reasonably comfortable on the mattress pad that the park ranger daughter also passed along. Yes, Isabel is reasonably warm and reasonably comfortable.

In the morning, wouldn't you know, they pair her up with Airhead for the wildlife scavenger hunt. Isabel already has her suspicions about this; her father told her they probably put her in the group with all these dim-bulb, loser, boy-crazy types because they are depending on her to hold things together, and even though she told him that was the stupidest thing she had ever heard, she thinks there is a possibility that there is some truth to this. I mean, could the teachers really let Alex Airhead and Tight Jeans Jessie go wandering off together into the woods with a map and a compass? Isabel wishes she could say as much to Abby, but Abby is lost to her, just like all the other reasonable people in her grade. And instead here she is, linked to Alex, leading her down the path. Isabel, needless to say, has taken control of the compass and the map, and Alex is following along, as docile as a sheep, probably thinking about how she always used to beg to copy Isabel's math homework way back in third grade, before they separated out the math classes by ability, and Isabel got away.

Most of the scavenger hunt is pretty lame—*Find an object used as food by the Native Americans*—but actually, it's kind of nice out here in the woods, if you ignore the Airhead. The path is mostly pine needles, nice and soft to walk along, and it's gotten warm, and the sky is a bright, sharp blue up above the pine trees, and, well, it smells like spring.

Two things happen at once—Isabel hears the sound of voices off in the distance, and Alex runs forward, catches up with her, and grabs her arm. "Listen," she hisses, "that must be one of the boys' teams."

Isabel nods. Probably. The woods right now are full of scavenger-hunting pairs of fifth-graders. All part of the bonding.

"Let's go find them," Alex says, excitedly. "I think it might be

Troy and Matthew. Or maybe Burton!" She is pulling Isabel in the direction of the voices, pulling her off the path. Actually, Isabel is impressed—Alex Brewster may not be able to identify a scavenger-hunt pinecone if it falls on her head and hits her, but if she can really tell which fifth-grade boys those are off in the distance, then she does have certain skills—certain *wildlife* skills, Isabel imagines saying to Abby, when this stupid trip is over and she is released from all association with airheads.

"We're supposed to do this on our own," Isabel says patiently, offering Alex the list of scavenger-hunt directions. *Do not join up with any other teams or give any advice to anyone but your own partner.*

"Come on!" Alex says. "They're right over there." Again, she is pulling Isabel in the direction of the voices.

Isabel makes herself dense and solid. She holds out her hand, offering the map and the compass. "Here," she says, "if you're going to go off the path, you better take these." *Do not under any circumstances leave the marked Wissacoho Nature Association trails.*

Alex studies her. If Isabel were describing it to Abby, she would say, *You could see her trying to think. You could see her trying to figure it out.* "I won't tell anyone," Isabel says, encouragingly. "I'll just go ahead and finish the scavenger hunt." Alex is a little bit taller than Isabel, and she has this very limp blond hair, which today is pulled back into a limp little ponytail, and when she tries to think, she tugs on it.

Isabel realizes that she likes the idea of being alone on the path through the forest; she will walk along slowly and find the remaining five or six items on the list, she will hum to herself, quietly. She will be alone in the woods, and she will not be afraid—and meanwhile, Alex Airhead will be getting into trouble for joining another team—or all three of them will get into some kind of stupid mess—or she will be getting lost in the woods and not be able to use the map *or* the compass, so she will have to stand there and scream, probably in the middle of a patch of poison ivy, until Mr. DePaul comes to rescue her.

But Alex doesn't take the things. She doesn't plunge off the path alone. She shrugs and makes a face, and she says, "Oh, never mind," and then Isabel continues ahead down the path, and Alex shadows her. And though Isabel wouldn't know exactly how to put this into words, even for Abby, she does understand that Alex Airhead Brewster at this moment in her life is not capable of doing any single thing all by herself, while she, Isabel, had genuinely hoped to be left alone on the path, and she understands that this is a very very important difference, and that the advantage is all hers. And even though she is stuck with the Airhead glued to her, this makes Isabel a little bit kind, as they check off their last items, as she guides them very directly back to the Campfire Circle. Also, not that this is really a competition or anything, since the goal is to teach self-reliance and teamwork and cooperation, not to mention nature appreciation, but Isabel and Alex are the first team back with every single item on the list found and identified correctly, so in a certain sense, they win.

And for reasons that Isabel cannot quite understand, this whole experience leaves Alex following her everywhere. Alex sits with her all afternoon for the Wampanoag legends talk and the crafts demonstration. Alex roasts her hot dog right next to Isabel for dinner, sticks to her like melted marshmallow as they all sit around the campfire and share their feelings about moving on to the middle school. Isabel, needless to say, does not share any feelings, but Alex and Jessie and Sarah H. all have plenty to say. Abby is way across the campfire, with her own squad, but Isabel can look across and meet her eyes whenever Alex or Jessie or Sarah says anything particularly dumb.

And in the middle of the night, when Isabel is warm and snug in her sleeping bag and sound asleep, Alex starts hissing at her—Alex has positioned her sleeping bag so it's the next one over.

"Isabel! Isabel! Are you awake?"

"No," she whispers back. "I'm asleep. It's the middle of the night."

"Isabel, I have to tell you something. I can't sleep and I have to tell you."

"Tell me tomorrow," Isabel whispers. "Tomorrow you can tell me all about it."

"I think my father might die," Alex whispers. "What would you do if you thought your father might die, and they weren't telling you?"

"Why will he die?" Isabel asks. Actually, this is something she has sometimes worried about—that her mother or her father will get very sick, and they won't tell her anything about it.

"He has something wrong with his heart," Alex says. "Something bad. He had an operation. They said it would only take him a few days to get better, but then he was in the hospital for two weeks. And now he doesn't move around very much and his face is this funny color."

"Did you ask?" Here is Isabel, whispering in the middle of the night in the group shelter; any minute, someone will wake up and hush her. There are two teachers sleeping in this group. Isabel is breaking the rule, she's going to get caught, and she doesn't care.

"My mom just says he's getting better. She says, slow and steady. She says everything will be okay. But I think she's lying, you know how you can tell when they're lying. I think he might die." It is clear even from her whispering that Alex is crying. Isabel reaches a very tentative hand out of her sleeping bag and tries to pat Alex right about where she thinks her shoulder might be.

Right at that moment, there's a piercing shriek from the campsite closest to the shore, where several other squads are encamped. And whoever it is just goes on shrieking. Isabel sits up, still inside her sleeping bag. She watches as the teachers crawl out of their sleeping bags and let themselves out of the tent, and she hears their feet slapping on the path as they set off at a gallop to see what is going on. Maybe somebody got her period for the first time, Isabel thinks, but doesn't say aloud. Actually, she thinks it in her mother's voice.

But all eight girls in Isabel's tent are now awake and some are turning on their flashlights and chattering. And in the light of someone's flashlight, Isabel can see that Alex is sitting up, pulling on her ponytail, squealing and fussing right along with all the others. Isabel lies back down, snuggles down deeper into her sleeping bag, and closes her eyes.

It turns out the shriek was from Lauren Pasternack, who swears she felt some animal walk right across her face, though Isabel and her squad don't hear any details until the next morning. The teachers come back and get into their sleeping bags and tell everyone not to worry, it was just someone having a bad dream.

Isabel is drifting back to sleep herself now, in the unaccustomed cold, sweet air of the little wooden shelter hut. She is thinking about Alex, who was lying there, awake, thinking about her father. She thinks about her own parents, and what would happen if one of them got sick. About how inside Alex there are all these memories and these worries and these thoughts and these fears—and they still add up to someone who can't read a map or use a compass. But still, inside Alex there is all that stuff. Isabel is thinking about her own mother again—about all the stuff that's inside that people don't tell. She thinks about the moment, back on her own bed, when she knew so certainly that the trip would be just fine. And then Isabel thinks about Graziella and Herbert and of course about Cleopatra. Suddenly she can imagine her mother—maybe she is dreaming this—no, she's still just awake—but she's thinking about her mother, and her mother is looking right at her, looking at her with love.

Isabel hears the distant call of some night-hunting bird, probably a food source for the Native Americans, and the very distant rhythm that they have all agreed has to be the sea, and she presses her face into the comforting flannel lining of whoever's sleeping bag, and she whispers the names to herself. Graziella, however you pronounce it. Herbert. Cleopatra. Isabel thinks about the jokes that some of the boys were making at dinner while they waited for the hamburgers to cook. The postcards you could send from the Wissacoho gift shop, if only there was one. Having a wonderful time with the bugs, wish you were here. I froze my ass off at Wissacoho. I partied with the bears at Wissacoho.

Dear Graziella and Herbert. Dear Cleopatra. Having a wonderful time. Wish you were here.

6

How I Spent My Summer Vacation

FOSTER MOM KILLS SELF AND TWO CHILDREN, 4 AND 7.
The headline blooms slowly as Lucy watches the laptop
screen, late at night, in the small, square living room of a
tourist efficiency cabin near the beach in North Carolina. FOSTER
MOM KILLS SELF AND TWO CHILDREN, 4 AND 7. The Internet connection she has finally managed to establish here is slow and not
very reliable, and her initial idea was to sign on quickly and check
her e-mail, as she sits awake in her nightgown at 2 A.M. on what is
supposed to be a relaxed family vacation beach holiday with the
children. But tomorrow she can tell Greg, *I finally got us on*, and
once a day, after they have showered off the sand and the salt and
rinsed out the bathing suits, and before they have mixed their ceremonial gin and tonics, they can go ahead and log on, while the children revel in the tourist cabin television, which is understood by
vacation statute to be absolutely free of all the is-that-public-tele-
vision-you-have-on-there rules that apply at home, where, Isabel
has informed her parents, they were among the most extremely re-

136

strictive in the fifth grade, and where, according to Freddy, everyone else in first grade was allowed to watch cartoons for hours on weekends.

Well, he is watching cartoons as much as he can here, and the interesting thing is that Isabel the sophisticated watches right along with him, the two of them lulled into such temporary accord that it makes Lucy a little dizzy. But not at 2 A.M., of course; the children are asleep in their twin beds in the second bedroom; everyone in every other efficiency cabin is asleep, no doubt. Tired children with salt in their hair, miniature golf scorecards under their pillows. And sunburned or drunk, happy or irritated, post-sex or pre-divorce, all the vacationing parents are asleep as well. There is only one person in all these little cabins, Lucy imagines, who is awake and worrying about what goes on in the world. TWO CHILDREN, 4 AND 7. Foster children.

Anxiously, Lucy clicks again and again on that headline, now firm and black and unwavering on her screen. But the computer is still loading, or transmitting, or whatever it does, still humming at her electronically, talking to what she vaguely imagines as the great *Boston Globe* in the sky. Sometimes the strangest thing can save your life, she is thinking, incoherently. It is a familiar thought that comes back to her at moments of great emotion, especially when children get lost. Sometimes the littlest thing, the strangest thing. When Lucy starts one of her lectures on foster care with a little personal information, here is the thing she never says: *A poem saved me. I think a poem saved me, when I was in sixth grade.* It's not that she thinks, of course, that she would have ended up dead if Miss Weiss had not saved her. It's the rare disastrous exceptions who end up dead. But Lucy still knows she was saved, and Miss Weiss saved her, and all because of a poem.

Lucy's fists are clenched and there is a strange harsh taste in her mouth, as if she has been sucking on some metallic piece of industrial debris. Right there in the center of her palate—she tests it again and again with her tongue. TWO CHILDREN. Two foster children. She knows so many, and it could so easily have been Lucy who was the last doctor to see and evaluate these children, whoever they are, the last doctor to speak with their foster mother, whoever she is. She knows so many.

Finally finally here is the story. Lucy rubs hard at her eyes; everything is blurring. Oh, Jesus. What a story. In the middle of a record Boston heat wave. Police called to a home by the neighbors because of screaming and crashing. Entered to find two small children, a sister and a brother, with, Jesus Christ, their throats cut. Dead on the kitchen floor. And their foster mother waving a knife, ran from police into her bedroom, locked the door, and then, as they forced their way in, shot herself in the head with a gun that had apparently been there in her night table.

Lucy reads it. Reads it again. They don't give names. Names are withheld pending full notification of the children's biological family. The Department of Social Services is investigating. I'll fucking bet they're investigating! Lucy thinks. Who the hell put these little kids into this home with this foster mom? What the hell happened? The newspaper future unscrolls for her: the lurid stories on what will be discovered about this foster mother's past, her mental illnesses, her arrests, the incredulity that anyone could have considered trusting her with kids, the grief-stricken biological family, asking over and over—and most loudly through their outraged lawyer—how anyone could possibly call this "child protection," how is this "protective custody," when you take the children away from their real mother and father, from their loving aunts and cousins, and hand them over to a lunatic who murders them in cold blood?

Heads will roll over this, Lucy thinks, and then, Ouch, poor choice of metaphors. She is trying hard not to think about the way a cut throat must look; actually, she has never seen one in the course of her professional duties, thank God, but of course she knows what the great vessels in the neck look like, more or less. Seven years old and four years old. Jesus Christ.

There is absolutely no way she can not walk across the flimsy little living room, moving as quietly as she can, and open the creaky door to the second tiny bedroom. Twin beds, carefully symmetrical along the side walls, a narrow aisle in between, two pressboard dressers squeezed in right and left of the door, and that's it. Except for the books and clothes and stuff spilling out of dresser drawers and piled on the floor. Isabel's sacred school backpack is sticking out from under her bed; she has refused to carry it to the beach because she doesn't want it to get sandy. Freddy's baseball card collection, in several plastic Tupperware boxes, sits on top of his dresser. Well, not his entire card collection; just the minimum subset that he absolutely had to bring on vacation. And it is Freddy, of course, who Lucy most needs to see, Freddy, who is seven now, like the little boy who died. Which child died first, which died second, did one see the other's throat cut, did the boy try to defend his little sister, did he run screaming through the house?

Freddy sleeps, only and always, on the diagonal, with his head at the very far left edge of the bed and his feet almost hanging off on the right. The bigger the bed, the broader the sprawl, the longer the slope of Freddy's diagonal; on one ill-fated family trip a couple of years ago, they got stuck with a room with two double beds, and Lucy made the mistake of asking Isabel and Freddy to share, and Isabel woke up the whole motel screaming at him at one in the morning, because in an effort to stretch his small body across the big bed on his usual diagonal, he had squirmed himself into a completely horizontal position, lying flat across both pillows, reaching out with his toes for the far coast.

And there he is, safe and loved and asleep and breathing. Boy, seven. She listens to him breathe for a while. Lucy, of course, the foster children specialist, knows all about young children cast out on their own in the big, cruel world. Boy, seven, girl, four, that part is nothing new to her. But she also knows all about boys, seven, and how impossibly young they are, and how tenderly and anxiously you guide them along. She touches her son gently on his slightly wrinkled forehead; Freddy sleeps deeply and intently, and Lucy suspects he has vivid and even lurid dreams, but he cannot ever remember, or describe, or explain them. She adjusts the blanket over his shoulders; none of them are accustomed to sleeping in air-conditioning, and the little cabin is noisily air-conditioned; by the middle of the night it is always chilly. She steps across the tiny aisle and adjusts one over Isabel, but carefully, since Isabel is a much lighter sleeper. Isabel, who is being, all things considered, a reasonably good sport about sharing a room with Freddy. Isabel, who has maybe, dare we say it, her parents speculate, loosened up just a little tiny bit at finding herself far from home, far from anyone she knows who might possibly see her with her parents or her brother. Isabel, who spent at least three hours in the water today, boogie-boarding, and then gobbled crab cakes and begged for a round of miniature golf and a tin-roof sundae.

Lucy whispers the first few lines of the poem so softly that she doesn't make a sound. "It was many and many a year ago, / In a kingdom by the sea, / That a maiden there lived whom you may know / By the name of Annabel Lee." And then she shuts the door on her sleeping children, leaving them in their air-conditioned box, their kingdom by the sea. Appropriately sea-soaked, stuffed with vacation food. Isabel had won the miniature golf game, thanks to two very lucky holes-in-one. But she had won it fair and square, since mini golf brings out her father's competitive side, and there is no way Greg would ever take it easy on her. Winning gives Isabel a certain glow, like getting the bonus points on a test.

Police were called by neighbors to a home in Mattapan last night after several neighbors reported hearing screams and crashes.

Lucy needs to know those children's names, and the name of that foster mother. Needs to know who was involved. She is running over lists and lists in her mind, has been doing it since she first saw that headline. A brother and sister, a four-year-old girl and a seven-year-old boy? Mattapan? So far, she has not come up with a match, but that's no consolation. She sees so many, she knows of so many, she advises on so many. It's a little embarrassing, but it's true, of course, as it always is, her biggest most demanding question right now is *Was this somehow my fault?*

Here is what she is imagining—imagining that it happened,

imagining that it will be described in tomorrow's paper. A brother and a sister coming to her for their annual school physicals, coming to Lucy because she is, after all, the foster children doctor, the one who works so closely with DSS, the one who is always in the paper ranting about foster kids and the system and their health. So here they are, the brother and the sister and their foster mother, and Lucy is in a hurry, of course, more patients waiting, so she greets the foster mom hastily and asks her a quick how's it going, and the woman nods, or says, Okay, I guess, and Lucy leaves it at that and gets the kids up on the exam table, one after the other, moving fast. And they're neatly dressed and they look well-enough cared for, so she focuses her attention on getting their shots up-to-date so they won't have any trouble when they register for school, and maybe she shakes her head and clucks her tongue and says something to the foster mother about how hard it is to get complete immunization records on these kids in protective custody, and how she, kind Dr. Lucy, hates so much to give any child an extra, unnecessary shot—and maybe the foster mother nods her head, thinking her crazy throat-cutting thoughts, and all the while there is Lucy, babbling on about MMR vaccines and school forms, and she orders three shots for each child and leaves the kids waiting in the room, crying because the shots are coming, and never once did she ask them, that brother and that sister, if everything is okay.

What she should have done, obviously—in this visit that she can picture and imagine, without actually remembering it, because odds are, of course, it never happened—what she should have done is asked the foster mother to take the little girl out in the waiting room while she examined the boy, taking her time, getting to know him, building the proverbial doctor-patient rapport. She knows how to do it, and often it works fine, but in her imaginary, self-punishing scenario she didn't do that, she was rushed and not sufficiently interested and just needed to get these kids out the door with their school forms and move on to the next thing—and that's often enough the way it is, too. But if this visit *had* really happened, and if she *had* taken some time with the little boy and given him a chance to tell her whether anything was wrong in the foster home, well, then she would have saved his life. And all by following her very own guidelines—see, for example, "Special considerations in delivering primary care services to school-age children in foster care settings: age-specific protocols." Often cited, often photocopied and handed out to residents. Somewhere in there, Lucy remembers, she made a great point of the importance of asking a child, in private, about how the foster home was working out. And yes, sometimes she does that, really she does, but sometimes she doesn't. And what if she really did see these children and what if she really didn't ask? What if this is all her fault? What if this is something she could have prevented? What are these children's names? *Are they mine? Somebody saved me, and nobody saved them.*

This is silly. Why does she keep thinking of Miss Weiss? There is no real connection, is there, between this horror story and that moment in the sixth grade when Miss Weiss looked at Lucy and the two of them began to recognize each other. Except that it is a poem about being by the sea, and about death, of course, and Lucy's brain is tired and disordered. And she is wondering whether this terrible thing happened because no one looked carefully at these two children, no one recognized them and their situation. Foster children cannot save themselves. They need the system, and they need help.

Lucy is a long long way from sleep. The computer is still connected, and she scrolls through the story again, looking for clues.

The Department of Social Services, which had protective custody of both children, refused to identify the social worker responsible for the case, pending notification of the children's biological parents. "Obviously this is a terrible tragedy, and we're going to work as hard as we can to determine how this happened to these children," said Andrew Callahan, Deputy Director for Public Affairs.

I'll tell you how it happened, Mr. Callahan. You needed to place the kids, because odds are they come out of some hellacious family, and you had a lady who was willing to take two, and she's not great but she's okay and the kids aren't special-needs kids, and the social worker is probably twenty-two years old and she did her best, and the children ended up in the care of a fucking maniac. A fucking certifiable, homicidal maniac. And one night in the middle of a heat wave she snapped, or God told her what to do, or the little girl wet the bed, and she chased them through the house, and—and Lucy is sitting on the scratchy plaid efficiency cabin couch, knees drawn up under her summer nightgown, arms wrapped around her knees. And we all dropped these children, that's what. You, Mr. Callahan, and your workers, and me, if I was the one who did their physicals. And their parents, who did whatever they did in the first place, or didn't do whatever they didn't do in the first place. So the kids got taken away. And the neighbors who didn't call till the screaming started. We all got together and we dropped these children off the cliff, okay? And yes, now there will be endless stories asking how this could have happened, and Lucy knows that really, even if she *was* these children's pediatrician, it is highly unlikely that anyone would think to blame her—to dig up the story of that last checkup, even if it actually happened, even if it happened exactly the way she has imagined, and to blame her in any way.

But she has to know who they are. She has to know if they are in any way hers, and she already knows that yes, of course they are, in a certain sense. If she were home in Boston right now, she would have been quoted in that *Globe* article or been interviewed today for tomorrow's follow-up story—the doctor who does all that stuff with foster kids, who runs a special clinic to take care of them. And she would have been stuck saying something very much like what Mr. Callahan said: *A terrible tragedy, we have to investigate.* But she would have known much more, of course, she would have been on the phone to DSS, she would know the circumstances, the worker, the family story. She would know for sure whether the children had ever been to see her, and if so, had they come with this particular foster mother, and if by chance they had, she would have read and reread and reread her notes on the visit to see what she had noticed and imagine what she should have noticed.

Tomorrow I can call, she thinks, and then, looking at the newspaper page on her laptop screen, realizes that it is already tomorrow, 3 A.M. tomorrow, and that it is Sunday. There will be no way to reach the people she knows at DSS today, only the emergency covering people—back in her office in Boston she has a couple of home numbers, a couple of possibilities, but nothing here. She is going to have to wait through the day without knowing.

If Lucy were telling her own story in a lecture, here is what she would say: I was shunted from one foster home to another, and most of them were okay. Way back when, it was something that women left on their own could do for a little extra money. And I was a pretty neat and well-behaved child, and, you know, in some ways, I don't remember too much about those years. I think I closed down. I did my homework and I did my chores. Was I waiting? I was too old to think I was waiting for my own family to come get me—and after all, first my mother was dead and my father couldn't take care of me—and no one thought that was surprising, way back then—and then both my parents were dead. So was I waiting for anything at all?

Lucy was ten years old and starting the sixth grade, her second successive year in a small New Jersey elementary school. It was the fourth elementary school she had attended, including an awful fourth-grade year when she had had to switch schools in the middle of the year because her placement changed, so there was something wonderful about being a returning student who knew her way around in September. She was placed with a perfectly nice woman, a devoutly Catholic widow with a small, neat apartment that centered around a color TV. Lucy's room was small but private—no other foster kids—and a good place to do homework. Lucy's fourth-grade report cards had been all A's, and her foster mother had signed them with pride. And Lucy was feeling lucky; everyone in the school knew that Miss Weiss was the sixth-grade teacher you wanted to get, and Lucy had gotten her. Miss Weiss was big and round and dramatic, with suspiciously coal-black hair that she wore straight down her back. She dressed in bright colors, and she was famous for putting on a stupendous musical every year. She took her classes on legendary field trips—to the Statue of Liberty, of course, but also all the way to Philadelphia to see the Liberty Bell, to a real farm, to a stable where they got to ride horses. There were children who had been waiting since kindergarten for their chance at a year with Miss Weiss, and one girl had cried when the class lists were posted. And there was Lucy, unlucky, marginal Lucy, in the lucky class.

Then Miss Weiss assigned the sixth grade to go home and memorize a poem, and Lucy, sitting in her little room, paged through a treasury of American poetry and found "Annabel Lee" and memorized it. And she still knows it by heart; whatever the rhythm sang to her, thirty-five years ago, she hears it still. And her favorite lines are still "And neither the angels in heaven above, / Nor the demons down under the sea, / Can ever dissever my soul from the soul / Of the beautiful Annabel Lee."

There was one word in the poem that Lucy didn't know. She took the book out into the living room and showed the word to her foster mother. "Sepulchre," said her foster mother with assurance. "Like the Holy Sepulchre."

Lucy was good at memorizing. She already knew her memory was quick and reliable—that she never had any anxiety about spelling tests, that the fifty state capitals had been a piece of cake. But there was a feeling of power and control when she stood in front of 6-W and recited "Annabel Lee" that was like nothing she had ever felt. No one else had memorized anything longer than twelve lines, and several of the boys had tried to get away with limericks, but Lucy would have liked her poem to go on and on and on. It didn't seem to her that she had really memorized it, not the way that she memorized spelling words. It seemed to have entered into her brain so that she understood the poem perfectly, and she needed to tell the world about it.

And when she finished it, she looked away from the students and saw Miss Weiss looking at her, figuring her out, recognizing her, saving her.

· · ·

Another stunning blue-sky summer day. Greg is feeding the children cereal when Lucy comes trailing out of the bedroom, still wearing her nightgown—it feels like she has been wearing this nightgown forever.

"You didn't get much sleep, did you, Luce?" he asks.

"I was up for a while in the middle of the night," she says, and he nods; it's familiar enough. Isabel and Freddy ignore them—another boring parental conversation about sleep patterns or work or worry or logistics.

"Can we watch TV till we go out?" Freddy asks.

"Can they?" Greg asks, and Lucy wants to turn to Isabel in turn and ask, *Can they?*

"Sure," Lucy says, and Freddy grabs the remote and some battling robots cartoon rivets them both as they finish spooning up the cereal.

"You okay?" Greg asks her softly, under cover of the TV noise.

Lucy shrugs. "Bad night. I'll snooze on the beach. Don't worry."

He has made her a cup of tea, and he hands it to her, and as she takes it, he slides his hand over her shoulder, looking worried, and she smiles at him. "Wasn't Isabel great in the water yesterday?" she asks, and watches his face light. Greg loves the water, loves the beach, and has worked so patiently, year after year, to teach his children to enjoy it with him. And now Freddy, who at one point looked just absolutely out of the question, seems to be coming along a little, and there was Isabel, boogie board firmly tied to her wrist, in there with the bravest yesterday for hours.

"She was terrific. And Freddy could see how much fun she was having, and how she didn't want to stop."

They are talking about their children in that television-shielded undertone, faces close, barely moving their lips. Loud cartoon battle noises come from the TV, and the children have moved side by side to the scratchy couch and watch in intent synchrony.

Lucy knows she's already held them up, so she doesn't try to make a phone call before they leave for the beach. She tucks her cell phone into her beach bag along with a notebook. She puts on her dark green tank suit, and her oversize gray T-shirt dress and her straw sunhat, and she applies the first coat of sunscreen to Freddy, as he sits there, still staring at the TV. Silently she holds the bottle out to Isabel, who waves it away impatiently.

"Will you put it on at the beach?" Lucy asks, and Isabel nods, once, exactly, impatiently.

Actually, Lucy hates sunscreen herself, which is an awkward dislike for any kind of doctor, maybe especially for a pediatrician. She puts it conscientiously on her children, and yes, she puts it on herself, though less conscientiously, but she hates it. The feel on her skin, the smell—there she is at the sink washing her hands with soap and water after gooping up Freddy.

On the drive out to the beach, they stop at a grocery store and fill the cooler with sodas and bottled water. Lucy adds a box of Pepperidge Farm Goldfish, which are considered a virtuous snack, although, as Greg points out, a seagull magnet. "I mean, they're even shaped like fish." He himself, less virtuously, adds a box of Sara Lee chocolate doughnuts, to stay cool in the cooler. Isabel, without comment, throws in a copy of some teenage-girl magazine. Lucy wonders if she could get a chance now to make her phone call, here in the parking lot. She wonders whether there will be a signal out on the beach. But the moment passes and they are in the car driving on toward the beach, and her cell phone is still in her bag.

And in fact there is no signal on the beach. Total blank. Okay, she thinks, I'll sit here for a while and then I'll get up and stroll over to the ranger station. There might be a signal over there.

They have a large umbrella, family size. Lucy, who has not really applied adequate sunscreen, huddles under it on a beach chair, still in her big shirt. And she makes Freddy stay under it, too, since she is so terrified of him getting sunburned. Isabel, who carries her own beach bag to the beach, takes out a tube of a very particular upmarket sunscreen, and applies it somewhat languorously to her arms and her face, then comes and stands in front of Lucy and waits for her back to be anointed. Freddy, who is alternately terrified and excited by the waves, and who is in any case very eager to gain his father's total and full attention, demands to be taken in swimming. And so Greg takes him, and Isabel sinks down on her own beach chair—there is only one that she is willing to use—and opens her new magazine.

And Lucy thinks again about the children in Boston. Who are they? Who was their social worker? Who was their doctor? Was it me?

And she also thinks, This is crazy, here I am on a beautiful beach in North Carolina with my family, and what am I thinking about?

"Mom?" Isabel sounds slightly tentative.

"Yes?" How soon can she legitimately get away and try her phone over at the ranger station?

"Can I ask you something?"

"Ask away." And who will she call first? Mary Ann Glock, maybe; her home number is programmed into the cell phone and she usually knows what's going on. She's the head nurse at the foster kids' clinic, and she and Lucy have worked together for almost a decade. Good old Mary Ann will have figured it all out.

"What's a blow job?"

"So what magazine did you have us get you?" Lucy asks, cracking up. The tender mother-daughter moment—you have to laugh. "What the hell are you reading over there?"

"It's not from the magazine," Isabel says hastily, protectively closing it up. "I mean, I saw it here but I heard people talking about it before. In school."

"Well," says Lucy, "what do you think it is? From what you've heard, I mean."

An uncomfortable silence. Isabel does not like not knowing the answer. When Isabel puts her hand up in class, she does it because she *knows*. Finally she ventures, "It's something about sex?"

"It's slang for oral sex," Lucy says, firmly. She thinks to take a quick look around just to be sure there are no other families with young children, no doubt being reared according to strict North Carolina fundamentalist Christian principles, close enough to be within earshot. In fact there are no people at all very close to their umbrella, but then again, it's still early. "A blow job is when a woman—actually, or a man—takes a man's penis in their mouth. It's something people do for sexual pleasure—especially to give each other sexual pleasure." She looks at her daughter's grossed-out expression and adds, "It probably sounds sort of disgusting to you right now, but the thing about sex is, it really doesn't start to make sense to you until you're older. That magazine is really written for people older than you are."

Isabel looks dubious, and Lucy knows what that means: *Lots of people in my grade read this magazine.*

"Mom, do you mind my asking that?"

"You know I don't. I talk about stuff like this with kids all the time. It's part of my job. And I'd much rather you asked if you don't know something." The familiar pious parental reply; Isabel seems to find it reassuring, maybe because it is so familiar and so pious, and she goes back to her magazine.

Lucy struggles up to her feet, out of this low chair. "Honey? I'm going to take a little walk. Stretch my legs. Enjoy the beach." Protest too much.

Isabel doesn't even look up. "Have fun."

"I'm leaving you in charge of all the stuff, okay? Don't go off anywhere until your dad comes back."

And she claps her straw hat on and sets off for the ranger station, where they went two days ago with Freddy to hear a nature talk, which unfortunately involved a live crab that Freddy found completely terrifying, especially when the kindly ranger tried to pass it around the circle of children. Oh well, scratch the nature program. What's one more public disaster, with Lucy hauling ass out of there, poor Freddy clinging to her like a piece of wet seaweed, and howling, "It's going to pinch me, don't let it pinch me!" at the top of his lungs? They'll sure be glad to see Lucy back at the ranger station, yes siree. As she marches along the dunes, Lucy looks out for Greg and Freddy. There they are, directly in front of the lifeguard's chair, in the water up to Greg's knees and therefore Freddy's waist, holding hands and waiting for the next wave. And when it comes, Greg lifts Freddy up and over, and though they are too far away for Lucy to hear her son's voice over the sound of the waves and the seagulls, she can see that he is screaming with pleasure as he is successfully elevated up over the wave and then set down again on his feet. She thinks of how scared he was, only last fall, of the quiet, chemically treated water in a swimming pool—and then remembers how he almost drowned in that swimming pool, and shudders. No, Freddy has come a long long way, and so has she, that she can stand there on the sand and smile at him jumping waves.

Lucy smiles and claps, but they don't see her. Just amazing that Freddy should consent to be in the water at all. Either he's growing up and changing, even if you can't see it in most of the things he says and does, or else it's some kind of daddy magic. And just amazing, this beach full of people connected in families. Taking care of each other. Whatever it is, it makes Lucy's heart glad as she flips open the cell phone and clicks it on. Electronic beeps of frustration and a message on the screen to tell her that there is no possibility of making a call, so she hurries along. The ranger station is set back behind the dunes, and her theory is that there, farther from the water, the cell phone may work. Well, actually her theory is more half-baked than that: she believes, vaguely, that around real buildings containing electricity and computers and people with college degrees wearing shoes and socks, the cell phone vibrations, whatever they are, are more likely to congregate, and therefore the cell phone may work.

Which it does. It beeps in and out of reality, but it basically announces its willingness to make a call for her, and Lucy thinks resentfully, About fucking time. The low wooden building in front of her is familiar from having brought Freddy in and dragged him back out only the day before yesterday. She leans against the side of the building and dials Mary Ann Glock's number. Be home, she thinks, be home, answer my questions, fill me in, tell me it's no one I know, so I can go back and enjoy the beach, and educate my daughter as *Prepubescent Cosmo*, or whatever it is, requires, and admire my son's totally unexpected prowess in the ocean—Be home, Mary Ann, and get this off my mind for me!

"Hello?" says Mary Ann's familiar voice, and the phone immediately goes dead.

Lucy mutters invectives as she tries to get her signal back, but no use. Dead and gone and dead again. There is a pay phone just beyond the ranger station, and with a sigh, Lucy lifts the receiver, which is hot from the sun. She needs to connect to a special operator for her calling plan, but the first four times she tries, she gets a Southern Bell operator, which translates in her mind as a Southern Belle operator. But the Southern Belle operators can do nothing for her, they each explain; they cannot connect her to another carrier. She will have to use her access code and dial directly.

"But I *did* dial directly—and I got *you!*" Lucy protests, and the Southern Belle says it all over again.

The fourth operator is able to connect Lucy to some other credit card plan, not her own, where they are happy to let her charge the call on her credit card. But of course, she has no credit card on her at the moment, just her bathing suit, her T-shirt dress, her hat, and her cell phone.

Anyway, the whole thing just doesn't work. And the cell is still dead, and the pay phone receiver feels sweaty and unpleasant and smells of beer and maybe old sunscreen—or maybe the old sunscreen is just her own skin she is smelling. But the sun is hot and there is poor Isabel alone on the beach, no doubt wondering now why the number 69 is supposed to be funny, and back goes Lucy, foiled and roiled, and imagining again that fatal scene in her clinic, and also the newspaper story about that fatal scene in her clinic.

Although Dr. Weiss is a nationally recognized authority on the medical problems of children in foster care, and although her clinic is specifically designed to identify and address these problems, Dr. Weiss did not identify any problems or tensions in this home during her recent comprehensive general health supervision visit with these children.

Lucy is ashamed of herself, but in a rote, familiar sort of way. When she gets anxious, which she often enough does, especially on vacation, she always punishes herself this way, writing out impossible news stories about her impossible mistakes, stories in which the newspaper is the exact accusing voice of her conscience (*"Com-*

prehensive general health supervision visit!"). It's just good old magical thinking, what every conscientious, evidence-based, scientifically oriented specialist needs: if I write out this worst possible scenario, then it won't happen. I can prevent the bad things from happening if I describe them in sufficient detail. Right. For your information, Dr. Weiss, you nationally recognized authority on the medical problems of children in foster care, the bad thing has already happened.

If Lucy were telling her own story in a lecture, here is the context she would give: it was more common thirty years ago for children to be placed in foster care by a parent or parents—to be in foster care without having been formally removed by social services for parental abuse or neglect. A widower with a job that kept him on the road, like my father—since he didn't have family members to take me in, this made sense. Probably he thought someday he might remarry and take me back. I hope he thought so. As I remember it, foster care was kind of unremarkable back then. The ladies took you in, and then their nephew got out of the army and needed a place to stay or they decided to go visit their sister in Florida, and the placement changed. And I kept wondering, How is it that everyone else has all these connections, these nephews, these sisters, these people they want to visit and want to be visited by. What happened to my share?

And then Miss Weiss, the sixth-grade teacher that everyone wanted to have, took note of Lucy. Found out Lucy's situation. Gave Lucy a lead role in her production of *Oliver!* She had adapted the show for her sixth-grade cast, and she wanted someone to introduce each scene with a reading from the Dickens novel. Lucy was initially sorry not to have singing or dancing to do, but she read the novel through with amazed recognition, and Miss Weiss kept making her introductory readings longer. And then, like some ridiculous fantasy coming true, the sixth-grade teacher that everyone wanted to have offered to take Lucy in as a foster child. And Lucy, suddenly released into a dizzying everything-is-possible world compounded of Dickens, field trips, and show tunes, became the most envied child in the sixth grade.

If Lucy were giving a lecture, she might point out that nowadays you probably wouldn't let a teacher become a foster parent for a child in her class. While she was in the sixth grade, she called her foster mother "Miss Weiss." The next year, they changed it to "Ina," by mutual agreement. And by eighth grade, when the formal adoption proceedings began, Lucy was calling her "Mom"—though for her, all the time, the title "Miss Weiss" retained a certain magic, a certain overtone of winning the lottery. And when she took the surname herself, while she was in medical school, it was partly to honor and please the woman who had saved her, and partly because she thought, even then, that "Dr. Weiss" might be a title with some of that magic clinging to it.

If Lucy were giving a lecture, she would say, When I was in sixth grade, someone looked at me and recognized me and claimed me, a wonderful, kind woman with a restless mind and big appetites. She took me in and she saved me, once and for all. And now when I hear about kids who should have been saved somehow but weren't, I understand how it happens. You can go from month to month and year to year without anyone noticing you. You can be properly cared for and fed on schedule, you can show up in school every day in clean, appropriate clothing, you can visit the doctor punctually—but it can all happen without anyone really knowing that you're there. And when there's a disaster, when we see so little that we leave children in a very dangerous place, and the danger closes over them, I understand how that can happen. I know about the demon down under the sea.

Lucy walks more quickly back down the beach, which is already getting crowded. She will go back to Isabel, insist that she come under the umbrella and put on a little more lotion, and then talk her through the magazine; it will make Isabel feel attended to, and Lucy herself feel virtuous, since she is more than a little proud that her professional practice in handling adolescent and preadolescent bodies and bodily problems has left her cheerful and matter-of-fact in discussing pretty much any issue with pretty much any child, even her own.

But where could she go to make her call? She picks her way around a group of college students, boys and girls, with perhaps the world's largest cooler, you would need at least four beefy frat boys to carry it over the dunes, and there they are, all four of them, trying to get some reception on their boom box. And then sights her own home umbrella, with Isabel still parked outside the circle of shade, reading her magazine in the sun, but with Greg and Freddy back now, digging in the sand.

Greg doesn't ask where she was, because he probably assumes she had schlepped over to the bathhouse and the bathroom. Which is, in fact, where she is planning to try her phone next—maybe Freddy will need to use the bathroom, or request an ice cream pop. In some ways, she'd rather not drag Freddy along when she has to make a phone call, especially since this might turn into a series of phone calls, but she'll do the best she can.

"How was the water?" she asks Freddy, and Isabel looks up, a little competitively, to hear his answer.

"Great. I was jumping waves."

"You were terrific," Greg assures him.

Freddy has brought to the beach a shopping bag woven out of green and blue plastic strips that contains his collection—well, a small part of his collection—of measuring cups and measuring spoons, beakers and graduated cylinders. He loves anything marked off in measurement units, but most especially in volume, and at home he cherishes some European containers labeled only in metric increments, brought back by Lucy from a trip she made last year to Switzerland for a conference, and by Greg from a couple of different trips to England. Sand is one of his favorite things to measure, and he has already made a perfect row of small piles, each consisting of one perfectly leveled tablespoon, teaspoon, half teaspoon, quarter teaspoon—and now he is matching them with a row of piles, each of which is *two* tablespoons, and so on. And so on and on; unless he is interrupted, Freddy has been known to keep going until he is making piles of thirteen or fourteen spoonfuls.

"Freddy, put your T-shirt on," Lucy says. "And your baseball cap. And in a few minutes I'm going to put some more sunscreen on you."

"It's waterproof, Mom," says Freddy, who reads all parts of labels very carefully, though none are as interesting to him as the volume measures, of course.

"It *says* waterproof, but some comes off in the water and more comes off when you dry yourself. And tell me if you need to go to the bathroom."

Lucy sits down in the shade and reaches into her beach bag. She has a lurid novel all ready to hand, but she knows that right now, today, she isn't going to be able to concentrate. So instead she pulls out a medical journal, the special issue on physical abuse, and settles down to read a cozy little research article on color variation over time as different kinds of bruises heal. Greg pulls another beach chair over very close to her, sits down, leans back, and closes his eyes. Lucy can see his book: *The Corseted Other: Gender Inversion and the Myth of Victorian Sexual Dysfunction.*

"Well, here we are," she says softly to Greg. "The American family goes to the beach." He opens his eyes and looks at her blankly, and she gestures. Your book. The pictures in my journal, nicely reproduced color photos of healing bruises on abused children. Our son over there measuring out the sand. And don't even ask what our daughter is reading.

Greg smiles at her, very fondly. "Hey, Isabel," he says, "what are you reading about?"

Isabel regards him rather coolly, and Lucy knows she can hear the joke in his voice, and therefore guesses what is coming, so to speak. "Blow jobs, Dad," Isabel says clearly, though of course not loud enough for the college students to hear. She puts down her magazine, stands and stretches. "I think I'll go in the water for a while now."

Lucy and Greg watch her walk away, clutching her boogie board, picking her way carefully down to the water.

Lucy makes herself read the article, which is nothing new at all, amazing it even got published, all those expensive color reproductions. But what is happening in Boston is very much on her mind, and she wonders whether it's time to confess as much to Greg. *There was this terrible story in the newspaper I saw late last night. It's very much on my mind. I think I'll take a walk and try to call Mary Ann. I'm worried it might be some kids I know.*

Greg will understand, more or less, but he will also be a little annoyed; it won't be the first time that Lucy has gotten all anxious and wrapped up in some work thing back home when they are supposed to be on vacation, won't be the first time she has been slipping away again and again to check in or try to page someone or other through the maddening hospital system. What he will think, but probably not say, is that she is unable to leave home, afraid to go away on vacation and relax, and therefore she invents endless reasons why she is so important that all the other twenty million doctors and social workers and nurses in Boston can't keep things going without her for even a week. And he does have a point, and certainly she also can remember other vacations complicated by her own obsessing over some clinical thing back home—but on the other hand, this is real, isn't it? She really did turn on the computer last night and see a story about two foster kids being murdered. And if she tells Greg the story, throats cut, he will be shocked and horrified and outraged, just like everyone else reading the *Boston Globe* today, and he will understand if she says, *I have to find out who those children were.* Won't he?

"I'm a little antsy," Lucy says. "I feel like taking a walk. Maybe I'll wander over by the bathhouse—anybody want anything from the concession stand?"

"A Fourth-of-July rocket pop," says Freddy.

"What a surprise," says Greg, and Freddy looks confused. He has asked for a Fourth-of-July rocket pop every time ice cream is offered this summer; sometimes he eats three a day, and his parents, eager to find caloric substances that he will actually eat, not play with, are doing their best to foster the addiction. Rocket pops leave him with a peculiar bright blue around his mouth, and with both red and blue blotches on his T-shirt, and as far as Lucy can tell, they don't ever come out. Whatever chemicals they use to make those rocket pops, the dyes are serious.

"Ice cream sandwich," Greg says, looking down at his book again, and Lucy feels a sense of relief—she's done it, she's gotten away with it, she gets to make her trip and try her phone.

But Mary Ann doesn't know who the kids are. Were.

"Isn't it just the most terrible story?" Mary Ann's voice, familiar, slightly breathy, not at all a voice that would make you expect her total unshockable efficiency, her been-there-done-that years of nursing, comes only rather patchily through Lucy's cell phone. "I sure hope it isn't any of our kids—though it's so awfully tragic whether it's our kids or not."

"I really want to know who they are," Lucy says. "It's kind of on my mind." *Like I didn't sleep last night, and I'm sitting on a barrier island beach in North Carolina thinking about those kids with their throats cut. Like that.*

"Well, I certainly understand," says Mary Ann, who probably doesn't. It probably hasn't crossed Mary Ann's mind even once that maybe there's something the clinic or Lucy herself didn't do for these children—and that's because there's never any part of her job that Mary Ann doesn't do, and she thinks Lucy is similarly perfect. Well, no, not really. It's more that Mary Ann isn't nuts, Lucy thinks, she does her job well and she knows she's not responsible for every single thing that happens in the world. Mary Ann would probably say that this tragedy is the fault of the crazy woman who killed these children, and the clueless social workers who trusted her to care for them. And Lucy can see her point.

"Who could I call? Is there someone you could call? It's Sunday, I know—do you have any DSS big shot's home number?"

"Well, I don't think I have anything here at home," says Mary Ann, sounding a little confused now. "I guess you might call the police—or maybe the ER, if they brought the children in there."

A noisy family, the mother carrying an infant, the father hauling a toddler, and what seem to be maybe five boys a little younger than Isabel, are using the chain-pull showers in front of the bathhouse, not far from where Lucy is standing. She steps away to avoid getting her cell phone wet, and loud static interferes, and for a second she thinks she's lost Mary Ann. But no, here she is, at the end of a sentence, apparently offering to go into work and try to get a specific number, if Lucy can tell her where it would be.

"No, no, don't do that," Lucy says. "It's Sunday—and I hope it's beautiful there like it is here."

"Oh, yes, we've been having some very hot days you know, but today's not so humid."

"Well, you stay home and garden."

"That's just what I was planning to do—but I really could drive over and get you that number."

"Don't be silly," Lucy says. Like a sane person herself. "You go work in the garden, and tomorrow I'll call you at work and you'll know everything. It's not like it's going to change anything whether I know today or tomorrow."

After all, she says to herself grimly, after hanging up, they're already dead. Before getting in line at the concession window, she tries one more call, dialing the hospital page operator and asking to have Dr. Maddox paged while she stays on the line. Jack Maddox is the child abuse expert, head of the child protection team, and he has excellent contacts at DSS. The page operator switches her over to the endless loop of *Masterpiece Theatre* music, and then, of course, cuts her off. Not the cell phone this time, it's the fucking page operator, probably misconnecting her at the exact moment that Jack returned the page. Of course, it's also possible Jack isn't on call today, or isn't carrying his beeper, but Jack is on call a lot and he carries his beeper even when he isn't. Lucy knows the feeling.

She has to walk a little bit closer to the bathhouse to get her signal back. Her battery isn't too well-charged, she notices—another call or two and she'll be out of juice for the day. Shit. There's another pay phone by the concession stand, but there's a teenage girl in an unbelievably tiny bikini talking on it and three others who are either waiting or keeping her company. No, here's the signal, she'll try the page operator again. And there's no point yelling at them, she reminds herself, unless you want to get transferred to one of those permanently ringing phone lines.

"Hi, it's Dr. Weiss. I was trying to page Dr. Jack Maddox before, and I stayed on the line, but I got cut off—I'm on a cell phone, so that might be why, but if you wouldn't mind paging him again?"

"You want to stay on the line again, Doctor?"

"Yes, please," she says. "Thank you so much."

And here come the trumpets of *Masterpiece Theatre* again, thank you so much.

And here comes Greg, leading Freddy, who is walking almost on tiptoe, intentionally rubbing his thighs together with the unmistakable gait of a child who waited a little too long to announce that he needed to pee and is now trying to hold it in until he gets to the bathroom. Greg looks at her, as she clasps the cell phone to her ear, afraid to move out of her reception zone; he raises his eyebrows and escorts Freddy up the stairs and into the bathhouse.

And the music plays on. And it's still playing when Greg and Freddy come out and stand looking at her.

"I'm on hold," Lucy says, determinedly meeting Greg's eyes. After all, he sometimes has a work-related call or two to make himself from vacation: are the books he's ordered for the fall semester in stock yet in the bookstore, have they worked out the scheduling problem with the lecture hall assignments, did the proofs for that article come in and could someone check and see when they have to be back by?

"I left Isabel with all our stuff, and she was pissy about having to come out of the water," Greg says. "Are you coming back with us or are you going to stay here?"

And at that instant, of course, the canned music fizzles abruptly and she hears Jack Maddox's voice: "Dr. Maddox answering a page."

Lucy attempts to shrug apologetically at Greg even while she answers, "Hey, Jack, it's Lucy. Sorry to bug you on the weekend."

"'S okay. What's up?"

Greg doesn't move away. He looks like he's issuing a challenge, or maybe like he's putting the pieces together: *she didn't sleep last night, she already disappeared once this morning, she said she was going to the concession stand, and now what do I find—she's getting her vacation craziness, isn't she? I'll end up eating dinner alone with the kids while my wife stands outside and pages doctors to call her on her cell phone, won't I?*

Lucy, who can quite easily read his mind, decides to go for the shock. "Jack, I want to know if you know who those two little kids were who got murdered yesterday. The ones who got their throats cut by their foster mom."

Sure enough, Greg looks immediately shocked and horrified. Then he thinks to look around for Freddy, but Lucy had already placed Freddy, before she said a word; Freddy is over by the concession window, studying the big poster of ice cream novelties, which includes a big blowup, naturally enough, of a Fourth-of-July rocket pop. Freddy would probably like a copy of the poster to take home: how I spent my summer vacation. So Freddy is safely out of earshot.

Greg goes over to him, leaving Lucy alone with her call. Alone with Jack Maddox's voice, confident and seen-it-all, piped directly to her ear. "Yeah, what a bad one. All over the papers. Social Services is going to be in deep shit over this one, and they damn well should be."

"But, Jack, do you know who the kids were? Their names? If they come to my clinic?" *If maybe I might have seen them and missed something, if this is somehow my fault?*

"No, they were new to the system. New to the state. They'd only been in Boston for a week or two—this was a brand-new placement, and that's why there's so much explaining to do. This wasn't some long-term thing where the foster mother used to be okay but then she cracked—they had just set this up."

"God," Lucy says, in heartfelt relief. "How terrible."

"Pretty bad. I did have their names—the kids—but they didn't mean anything to me. I don't think they were plugged in for medical care yet in Boston. Want me to see if I wrote the names down?"

"No, that's okay. They'll be in the paper tomorrow and I can wait," Lucy says, with complete honesty. "I just needed to be sure they weren't mine."

"I know what you mean," Jack says. "You see something like that in the paper and you start going over everyone in your mind—trying to think of a brother and sister ages this and that . . ."

"Right. And it doesn't actually make it any better that they aren't mine, I know."

"They're still dead."

"Jesus, she cut their throats. I can't believe it." Lucy knows that she speaks now with some mix of the requisite general-public horror at a harrowing newspaper story and her own special deep knowledge of the edges that foster children walk, of the weaknesses and the vulnerabilities of the system that is supposed to protect them. She will probably even, Jesus Christ, end up with a slide of this headline in one of her standard lectures, end up using this terrible, awful case to make a point, as she uses so many other terrible, awful cases. But that frantic feeling that it was up to her to have saved these children has receded. She has to remind herself firmly, *It was up to us all to save these children, we all failed.*

"They're still dead," Jack Maddox repeats. "But at least they weren't yours. You didn't meet this foster mother and send her out with a couple of injury prevention advice sheets and a school physical form, if you know what I mean."

"Boy," Lucy says, "do I know what you mean. Boy, do I."

And after she says goodbye to Jack and turns off her rapidly fading cell phone, she goes running down the beach, chasing Greg and Freddy, who have by now bought their own ice creams and headed back. The weight has lifted, the cloud is gone, the shadow has moved and the sun is out—choose any metaphor you like, but Lucy is set free, at least for the moment. She feels the sun on her skin and thinks with joy of pulling off this hot, oversize cotton T-shirt dress, of going in the water, so blue and inviting, with sun sparkles on the rolling waves.

She cannot actually run very far down a crowded beach in the blazing North Carolina sun, and soon enough she slows to a walk, panting, her beach bag sliding down off her shoulder. She can see Greg and Freddy ambling along, way up ahead, almost back at the umbrella. Lucy cannot help the joy that rises in her that on this beach there actually are people who belong to her, who know her, who are waiting for her to return. If you grow up without it, if you spend years looking at the world and wondering, *Why everyone else and why not me?* at least it leaves you with flashes of that particular joy. She will join them, of course, she will explain the story to Greg, now that she has her answer and she no longer needs to call anyone, now that she won't have to sneak away, or suggest that they stop by the room again so she can check the Internet news, or keep an eye out for functional pay phones. No, her heart is so much lighter now, on this beautiful beach, that she knows enough to brace herself, take a deep breath, and look carefully and deliberately around for small children, children the right age to remind her of what has been lost, back in Boston.

7

Disney Assembly

*T*HE SECOND-GRADE *music and movement assembly will be held Friday, October 17, at 9 A.M. Parents are asked to be prompt and to make sure their children are present, with appropriate clothes (see below), by 8:15.*

"You're coming, right, Mom?" Freddy has asked her only maybe seventeen times so far today.

"I'm coming. I wouldn't miss it."

But a few minutes later, he looks worried again. "Don't you have to go to work? Usually on Friday mornings, you go to work." Freddy is good at calendars and has everyone's schedule pretty well memorized. It doesn't mean he can remember to bring his overdue library book in on Tuesday, but he's fairly reliable if you want to know why Isabel is late coming home on Wednesdays (sixth-grade literary magazine) or why Greg has to go in early on alternate Thursdays (TA meetings for his big introductory English Literature course).

"I took the morning off, Freddy. It's okay, I can do that. I wanted to come to the assembly." *So give me my fucking good-mommy medal, willya please?*

Lucy bitched and moaned a certain amount about taking off

the Friday morning, about Greg being in England, the lucky dog, so guess who has to go to the music and movement assembly. But the truth is, she feels kind of happy and excited about the assembly, just because Freddy is so focused on it, so preoccupied with it, so glad she's coming.

"What's this?" Lucy asks with deep and profound suspicion as Isabel drops a crumpled yellow flier onto her lap.

"He left it in the back seat," Isabel says, with her standard infinite contempt.

Warily, Lucy smoothes out the sheet; Isabel is watching her with a calculating look that lets Lucy know that her daughter has already read the notice, digested the information, and suspects that there is something on this sheet that will hit Lucy like a kick in the pants.

"Freddy!"

He looks up, mildly, from the corner of the dining room table where he is laying out some of his baseball cards in neat rows.

"Freddy, it says here you're supposed to have special clothes. For tomorrow, for the assembly!"

Freddy, to whom all clothes are as uninteresting as so many paper towels, does not respond noticeably; he is preoccupied with lining up the edges of the card rows with the edges of the table.

"What special clothes is he supposed to have?" Isabel, however, is hovering, sniffing disaster. Lucy knows, wearily enough, that if *Isabel* had a special assembly coming up, the need to buy a white blouse (Holiday Sing, last year, fifth grade), or oppress her mother into sewing some ungodly costume (Bird Pageant, sacred school tradition, second grade) would have dominated family conversation for weeks in advance and thus justified all tactics by actually getting Greg or Lucy into grumbling action. Isabel, after all, would truly, honestly, literally rather slit her intestines with a curved Japanese knife than appear at a ceremonial school function in the wrong clothing. Lucy, driving the car and therefore blessed by that special chauffeur invisibility, was once treated to an excruciatingly tedious exegesis in which Isabel and Abby, in the back seat, spent a good thirty minutes listing which girls in their class had worn the correct, specified black ballet slippers for the Immigration Unit Celebration Folk Dance; Lucy, who had been grimly dragged to three different shoe stores before Isabel was satisfied, wanted only to demand the names of the parents who had refused to cooperate so she could get them inscribed on a marble monument as heroes of the resistance.

Isabel takes back the yellow flier and scans it quickly, though Lucy is sure she has already read it. She pronounces the words in tones of intense doubt and contempt, shocked that anyone would suggest such stupid clothing, perhaps, or in doubt that her incompetent mother has any single hope in hell of coming through.

The prediction is for warm weather and the children need to wear comfortable clothing for dancing. Boys should wear light-colored shorts with belts and pockets and non-T-shirt shirts with no writing on them.

"Shorts in October?" Isabel asks. "That movement teacher is so spacy. And does Freddy *have* any shirts except T-shirts with writing on them?"

Well, of course he doesn't. Back in first grade that awful Mrs. Gallow made a big deal about Freddy's clothes and they bought him two button-down shirts, but he couldn't do the buttons and he wouldn't wear the shirts. Freddy has a large drawer full of T-shirts, and Lucy tries to get him into a clean one every day, thank you very much, and most of them have some kind of sign or slogan or drawing on them, though some, the ones left over from Isabel, are pretty faded. By the end of the week, the particular shirts that Lucy and Greg tend to reach for (since Freddy has no opinion at all, once he has worn his two Red Sox shirts and they are in the laundry) are gone, so you do the wash and stuff a bunch of clean T-shirts back in the drawer, and every day you put him in a T-shirt and clean underpants and sweatpants and you call that clothed. After all, he's seven years old. And, to tell the truth, not so good with his hands; zippers and buttons can still be problematic.

Ah well, Lucy thinks, it's been a long day and I was looking forward to a quiet evening at home, just me and the kids and some macaroni and cheese and a glass of wine, but spare us the working mother's lament, okay, honey?

"Come on, Freddy" is all she says. "We have to go to the store."

"Can I stay here?" Isabel asks.

"Sure—I'll make dinner when I get back. Is that okay?"

"Are you going to get him light-colored shorts with a belt and pockets?"

"Or die in the attempt," Lucy says, and Isabel shrugs, as if either were equally likely. "You know," Lucy comments, "there's a reason why most people don't buy light-colored shorts—or pants—for small children." And she thinks about the four identical pairs of dark blue sweatpants that constituted Freddy's back-to-school shopping. " 'What an excellent example of the power of dress, young Oliver Twist was!' " Lucy quotes quietly to herself.

At the sprawling discount-clothing store, Lucy paws through racks and racks of children's shorts, most of which, sensibly enough, are not light-colored. Dark blue, olive green, black. Some soccer shorts, thin and shiny and elastic-waisted—no belt, no pockets. She wishes Greg were here; this would be much more fun to do while groaning together, and maybe adding in an errand at the hardware store and then taking everyone out for Korean food. And Greg would enjoy the whole idea of light-colored shorts with a belt and pockets; their fucking WASP yachting fantasy, he would say.

Well, here are khaki shorts, and they do have pockets and belt loops, but they look awfully big for Freddy. She locates a size 6–8, but it's for some kid twice Freddy's girth. Eventually, by moving out of the boys' section and back into the small children's section, she finds waist sizes that look right. Freddy is much better off in the largest sizes of the toddler clothes than in the smaller end of boys'—he's just so skinny. But over here in the small children zone, the shorts are once again mostly elastic-waisted—sensibly enough—and some of them have cartoon characters printed on them. Great. But the thing about this store, with its crowded racks of irregulars and cut-price clothing, is that usually if you hunt long enough, it turns out that someone or other has discounted and discontinued a pile of whatever it is you're looking for, and eventually Lucy comes to a circular rack with stupid-looking little fancy shorts, pale gray and khaki and even white, each with its own little web belt, hanging primly on plastic hangers. A discount-clothing store is a great equalizer, Lucy reflects; here we can find our yachting fantasy costume or stretch our public assistance dollars—or both at the same time.

It's never a short process to get Freddy in and out of clothing, especially when you add in belts, but they eventually get out of the dressing room with a pair of shorts in a color labeled "stone"—she just cannot bring herself to buy white—and her best guess at a shirt, a yellow polo shirt, one of those knit things with the little collars and the double buttons that to Lucy will always say *preppie, preppie, preppie*. But hey, it's only $7.99, and it doesn't have any writing on it, and surely if the school had wanted a button-down they would have specified a button-down, and buttons can be a real problem for Freddy, and anyway, Lucy is hungry.

"Can I have some cards?" Freddy asks, as they head for their car.

"Where do they have cards here?"

He points to the drugstore, so she allows one more stop, and he chooses—surprise—a pack of baseball cards, and they drive home, Lucy bracing herself for whatever Isabel's comments will be on their purchases.

"Dad called," Isabel says. "He said not to call back, it was twelve-thirty there and he was going to sleep. He said to tell you everything's fine."

Five-hour time difference, sure. He was figuring they'd all be there eating supper at seven-thirty. Oh, well, she would have liked a little dose of Greg.

Lucy smiles at her daughter. "'What an excellent example of the power of dress, young Oliver Twist was!'" she recites. "'Wrapped in the blanket which had hitherto formed his only covering, he might have been the child of a nobleman or a beggar; it would have been hard for the haughtiest stranger to have assigned him his proper station in society. But now that he was enveloped in the old calico robes which had grown yellow in the same service, he was badged and ticketed, and fell into his place at once—a parish child—the orphan of a workhouse—the humble, half-starved drudge—to be cuffed and buffeted through the world—despised by all, and pitied by none. Oliver cried lustily. If he could have known that he was an orphan, left to the tender mercies of church-wardens and over-seers, perhaps he would have cried the louder.'"

"Is Greg coming?" asks Beverly Lieberman the next morning, as they file into the assembly.

"No, he's in England, doing research. I'm single-parenting it for three more days," Lucy says, trying for the right poor-virtuous-me, successful-achieving-him tone. She's actually feeling royally pissed off, since she obediently delivered Freddy at 8:15 and then found herself faced with a forty-five-minute void—there was no place at the school to wait, or to sit, or to have a fucking cup of coffee, and she ended up sitting in her car for forty-five minutes and mak-ing phone calls. And this afternoon in clinic they're bringing in a family of four siblings who all need a full evaluation for physical abuse and sexual abuse and it's not clear they've ever had primary care, and it's going to be your standard three-ring circus. So now she has work very much on her mind, and she's kind of slipping into that don't-they-know-we-have-jobs-how-can-they-just-expect-us-to-come-to-an-assembly-at-9-A.M.-on-a-Friday spirit. *I mean, haven't these people ever heard of nine to five, Monday through Friday?*

Well, no, of course, if you look around at them, many of them haven't. Take Beverly Lieberman, or, as Greg calls her, "the Di-vine Bev Lieberman." Bev identifies herself strongly as a working mother and a feminist, and you can tell that because she has been pestering Lucy to come speak at the eighth-grade Career Fair Day and be a role model for the girls, just as she, Bev, is going to do. Lucy, who does in fact have a real job and is less than eager to take the day off to come to an event that does not even concern one of her children, has also been told by Isabel in no uncertain terms that she is *not* to participate in Career Fair Day, and that everyone knows Career Fair Day is totally retarded. So she was happy to decline, on the grounds of her very busy schedule, which no doubt is exactly what would have made her such a role model. Of course, as Greg pointed out, if she had gone, she might have been able to determine exactly what it is that Bev does that keeps her so publicly stressed, yet leaves her free enough, at all times, to organize various dread events and shanghai other parents into participating.

"Doing research! That's great!" Bev is definitely one of the dressed-for-work mothers. Snappy little gray silk suit, something under it that looks a little like a leotard made of lavender lace, just peeking out at the collar. And the kind of pumps that Lucy cannot wear for five minutes. It would be an odd way to dress up if you actually spend your day, as Greg has suggested Bev does, calling up utility companies and lying in wait, naked, for the repairmen.

Then there are all these ridiculously tiny, ridiculously young specimens in the world's most expensive size 2 blue jeans and stretchy sweaters, and those are presumably the full-time moms, though what the fuck they are going to do with the rest of the day, when the assembly is over, Lucy has never been able to quite figure out. And Greg always swears that the Griffiths send their au pair to school events, but there are the Griffiths, both of them, somewhat older than the other parents, resplendent in Old Money New England tat, his blue blazer over plaid pants, her twin set and khaki skirt, as they position themselves smack in the front row and look about them benignly.

But Bev has hold of Lucy's arm, like the ancient mariner. Bev has something sincere to say, and then, if Lucy knows her Bev, some hideous request.

"I think that is just so great, that you and Greg can work things out so that he gets to do this kind of traveling, even though you're both so busy. You really support each other, and that's a very important thing for a couple to do."

"Well, you know, we do our best—you guys do it, too," Lucy

mutters, meaninglessly, since no one has ever seen the mysterious *Mr.* Lieberman, except at one evening potluck, organized by Bev back at the beginning of the year, where he talked on his cell phone in a corner for the first hour and then left, just as Bev was really heating up on the subject of the parent raffle to benefit the new music studio.

"Oh, you know how it is with Steve," says Bev brightly. "He's just so busy—they just work them so hard. It's crazy, there's no sense of balance at all."

Lucy, who was under the impression that Steve is the director, president, and absolute dictator of his own personal hedge fund, whatever that is, clucks sympathetically.

"So I wanted to ask you something," Bev continues, with a slightly lowered voice.

As Greg would say, *You got me dead in your sight, shoot me now and get it right.* Lucy nods.

Bev's voice drops even further. "Would you talk to Tanya Danvers?"

"Talk to Tanya?"

"Yes, after the assembly. Would you have a minute to spare to talk to her?"

"Sure—but why?"

"I can't tell you here." Well, thinks Lucy, in that tone of voice you could, no one could possibly overhear, you're practically lip-synching.

Bev is shaking her well-groomed head. "It's just awful," she whispers. "And Tanya is so nice."

Lucy nods emphatically, though she doesn't actually know Tanya from a hole in the wall; Tanya is a mother of a second-grade girl, some second-grade girl or other, they all look alike to Freddy, and they mostly go to their own birthday parties, so Lucy has not felt obligated to learn the mommies. *Come on, Bev, give me a little more to go on.*

"And I think Elissa is just the nicest little girl," Bev goes on, so Lucy can at least store that for future reference.

"Where is Tanya?" Lucy asks, going right for the practical issue: *I have no chance in hell of ever recognizing Tanya Danvers, so you better point her out to me.*

"Here," Bev hisses, "I'll just take you over and you can sit with her, and that way you'll be right there to talk to her after the assembly." She starts purposefully through the crowd, and as Lucy follows her, turns quickly to fling over her shoulder an emphatic whispered "Lucy, thanks so much for this!"

Freddy's class takes the stage to loud applause. They stand in a neat row, boy girl boy girl, facing their parents and grinning. Lucy sees with absolute unadulterated triumph that two of the boys are wearing T-shirts, one with something written on it (admittedly, "Hilton Head"). Freddy is perfectly dressed and even still relatively neat. Not that any of the second-grade boys can touch the second-grade girls when it comes to clothes and neatness, of course, but that's just the way of the world. Look how they stand there, the boys with their shirts pulling out of their shorts, or that one over there with his button-down shirt buttoned all wrong, with their hair mussed and their hands jammed in those compulsory pockets. Lucy loves the boys, all of them, even the ones she doesn't even like.

The girls, on the other hand—socks that match their blouses, hair ties that match their socks, perky ponytails and French braids. Lucy has been there and done that, though it will be a cold day in hell before Isabel allows her mother to touch her hair nowadays. But look at all these little incipient Isabels, standing at attention, waving at their mommies, and now, in their sweet little piping voices, starting to sing. And the boys are singing, too, in *their* sweet little piping voices, even Freddy, looking blissfully happy to know the words, to sing them right on time together.

"Chim chim cher-ee!"

Oh, yes, Greg would appreciate this, all these milky, scrubbed little muffins warbling a song written for a dancing Edwardian chimney sweep. *But fuck you, Greg, it's pretty damn cute, and I know this will shock you, but I actually remembered to bring a camera. A* disposable drugstore camera, true, but a camera. And Lucy takes it out and leans slightly to the left to take her picture between the two steadily aimed video cameras of the parents in front of her.

Tanya Danvers smiled at her very slightly when she sat down, but she didn't say a word in response to Lucy's "Hi," and she's staring straight ahead. Lucy had thought of asking her to point out which one is Elissa, but what the hell, she doesn't know what all this is about, and she's here for *Freddy*, not for Bev or Tanya or any of their other little friends.

Brianna Poaster, who is supposed to be some kind of an artist, is taking movies of the children with the single biggest video camera anyone has ever seen, and she has her husband, a rather vestigial appendage who is not actually named Pecker Peter Poaster, whatever Greg may say, following her around with a special floodlight. Now that the children have started dancing around ("Pink Elephants on Parade"), Brianna is getting in the way of some of the other parents, and the magisterial Pauline Griffith goes over and squashes her. Not an easy thing to do, since Brianna Poaster's devotion to her art is so extreme that she once turned up as a special speaker at one of Isabel's assemblies, during the course of which she produced some impressionistic portraits of several of the girls and boys in her audience, which Isabel reported looked exactly like splatter-painting. But Pauline Griffith is equal to the task, and a chastened Brianna, trailed by Poor Pecker Peter, goes to stand and film on the sidelines, as the children wave the flags of many nations that they have crayoned and sing, God help us, "It's a Small World After All."

But I am here for Freddy, Lucy thinks. And look how much fun Freddy is having, bless his heart. Oh, bless his heart. Freddy is capering around on the stage now with a silly hat on his head, singing, "Heigh-ho!"

And the truth is, like any mother of a weird and who-knows-just-how-marginal kid, Lucy's pleasure in this performance, and even the slightly twitchy boredom that has begun to settle on her by the fourth or fifth number, is colored by an intense gratitude that there is Freddy, up there with all the rest, doing exactly what they are doing, and enjoying himself. One of the group. He and another little boy, Colin, she thinks, are now dancing wildly together as the music plays "The Bare Necessities." In fact, they are the wildest pair of dancers on the stage, bouncing higher and higher, flinging out their arms and their elbows, while all around them more orderly pairs of boys or girls do a kind of lumbering-bear version of the hokey-pokey.

Lucy tenses, waiting for the crash, the disaster, the injury—but all that happens is that the song ends and the children bow and the parents clap and Tanya Danvers turns to her and says, very intensely, "Your son is a wonderful dancer! He and Colin were just the best!"

"Thank you," says Lucy, wondering how these other mothers always know exactly which kid is which. *I couldn't pick your daughter out of a police lineup on my best day, and you know which one is mine, which one is Colin—is it some kind of girl gene that you have and Isabel has and I just missed? Is it in the same place on the chromosome as the ability to French braid and wear real pumps?*

Well, actually, Tanya Danvers is not wearing real pumps. Tanya Danvers, in fact, looks a little bit scruffy for a mommy in this particular gathering, but she is, Lucy realizes with a kind of a shock, genuinely beautiful. Not mommy well-groomed beautiful, but beautiful like a woman you might look at in a restaurant and wonder, *What must it be like to go through life as beautiful as that?*

Tanya Danvers has thick golden hair bound into a fat braid down her back and a pale, northern European face, thin and fine, with a high forehead and intense, very dark eyes. But she wears no makeup and she has holes in her ears but no earrings, and she is dressed in a rather strange and shapeless flowered jumper, almost a housedress, like one of Lucy's very own foster mothers used to wear long ago, and just like her, Tanya Danvers is wearing white tennis shoes with those tiny little socklets that have pompoms at the back.

Lucy turns away from Tanya Danvers and fixes her attention

quite determinedly on the stage action, where the whole troupe is now singing "Zip-a-dee-doo-dah."

"I wonder whether they had to get official permission," she says sociably to Tanya Danvers. "I understand Disney is pretty strict about all this."

"Well, frankly," says Tanya Danvers, "I really have to ask myself, Are we paying all this money for the kids to come to school and learn *Disney* songs? I mean, really!"

Lucy is more than mildly surprised to hear such seditious talk from someone she hardly knows, and she is even more surprised to hear money mentioned; Greg has a whole theory about the school and the ethics of never mentioning how many dollars a minute it costs, and a monologue, which for some reason he delivers in his Colonel Klink German accent, about "You chust haf to pay vot it costs but ve vill not discuss it."

She is about to agree, assuring Tanya that she herself has wondered about that very thing, when the kids take their places for the finale and the lights go out. The music starts, and the children click on the little flashlights they are holding, illuminating their own faces, and they sing.

"When you wish upon a star . . ."

And then of course, Lucy tears up. She just can't help it. They get to her, the piping little voices, the lights shining on their proud, beautiful, well-cared-for, safe faces. She is not, in fact, remembering herself on a school stage at the age of ten, in a sixth-grade production of *Oliver!*, the true orphan in a group of well-fed suburban children pretending to be starving orphans, Lucy stepping forward to recite her chunks of narrative prose between the musical numbers. There is no reason to cry for that long-ago girl, confidently reciting her lines. But there is Freddy's face, lit by his light, his eyes wide with the thrill of this final special effect, and Lucy digs blindly in her bag for a tissue.

Here's the thing with Tanya Danvers: her au pair has reported her to the state emergency hotline for child abuse, and she's being investigated. And you could just about knock Lucy over with a two-inch flashlight; whatever she was imagining (free pediatric advice, another assault about the Career Fair Day, a fateful invitation to head up some committee for the fall welcome-new-students dinner) she was not imagining that Bev Lieberman was peddling her name around as an expert on the Department of Social Services, or that school mommies were getting turned in by their ever-loving au pairs.

Greg is going to love this one, she thinks, and then, naturally enough, she imagines the scenario: someone has it in for you, someone calls up and says you're abusing your kids. In their house, because of what Lucy does for a living, that scene is actually a kind of standing joke—Freddy's up at midnight because the Red Sox are playing out on the West Coast—quick, call DSS. It's what Greg says to Isabel when she complains too bitterly about some parental cruelty: *Okay, go ahead, report us for child abuse because we won't let you watch MTV.* Lucy's family lives in full awareness of the reporting system, as do all the families of her patients, but she would have said that the parents in her children's school went through their days without ever giving it a thought.

And now someone has actually gone and reported Tanya Danvers. They are off in a corner at the parent reception following the assembly; Lucy has hugged and congratulated Freddy and told him how good it was, and taken the opportunity to wipe his nose and send him to the bathroom so she could help him adjust his shorts and belt afterward, and she has noted Tanya Danvers embracing a stunner of a blond princess, complete with French braid and silver barrettes that coordinate with sparkly silver shoes. Elissa.

And now the children have gone back to their classroom, and the parents are dissipating slowly, and Tanya Danvers and Lucy are over in a corner near the display of authentic Javanese batik made by the fourth grade.

"Do you understand why she did this?" Lucy asks. Sure, she's curious, but she knows she's not the person Tanya Danvers needs, regardless of what Bev Lieberman may think—*I mean, come on, Bev, call in one of the lawyer daddies or the lawyer mommies! The school is full of lawyers—better yet, Tanya, bypass old Bev and hire a lawyer yourself!*

Tanya Danvers gazes straight at her with those unexpectedly dark, compelling eyes. "I would guess because she's in love with my husband and she's trying to get rid of me because she thinks if she can get me put away, he'll go back to screwing her, which she doesn't know that I know he was doing in the first place, and which he's not going to go back to because usually he screws his CFO."

"Oh, okay," Lucy says. She rather prides herself, as many doctors do, on being hard to shock, and she is damn well at least going to seem unshocked.

"I'm probably being unfair," says Tanya, rather flatly.

"How so?"

"I mean, I'm sure she has absolutely convinced herself that I really *am* an evil monster and a child abuser and that she owes it to Elissa and Byron to turn me in. I think she probably does think that she's protecting them. She's very good with them," Tanya adds, dispassionately, as if providing a reference.

With a brief nod to Greg's shadow (*Byron? Give me a fucking break!*), Lucy launches into the required speech: "First of all, understand that I am probably not the person you need to be talking to. I'm a pediatrician, I do general health care for kids, and because my special interest is foster children, I do talk to the folks at DSS a lot. But I don't really have any special pull there"—this is a lie; she has often comforted herself, when the joke hits too close to home, that in a pinch she might be able to pull some strings for herself if anyone ever really does turn her in—"What you probably need is a lawyer—a good family lawyer."

Tanya Danvers nods. Her expression is still calm and untroubled.

"If you want," Lucy offers, "I can just go over the whole process for you—I mean, what happens when a complaint like this gets filed. Because of what I do, I mean, I am pretty familiar with it." Tanya nods again. "Well, when someone calls in a complaint, and you know, it can be anyone—doctors like me and teachers and social workers are what are called 'mandated reporters,' meaning that if we suspect abuse or neglect we have to report it, but it can be anyone, a neighbor, a babysitter—well, as you know. And then the Department of Social Services has twenty-four hours to look into it."

"I know this," Tanya Danvers says.

"Okay—but I'm afraid I don't see exactly what I can tell you beyond this—beyond the protocol. Is there some way I can help you?"

"DSS ruled it in. They—what do you call it?"

"Substantiated it. The allegation."

"Right. They substantiated it."

Well, that's kind of interesting. Lucy allows herself to turn the whole thing inside out for a split second: any chance that the au pair is right and Tanya Danvers is a pathological liar and a child abuser? Well, yes, there's always a chance. Hedge-fund husband and fancy private school and beautifully dressed princess daughter—it could be the kind of textbook case you use to teach residents not to make easy assumptions. Child abuse occurs in all social classes, all races, all ethnicities, yada yada yada.

"Um, Tanya, do you have a sense of why they ruled it in? What they heard or what they saw?"

Tanya grabs her fat blond braid and tugs it forward, over her shoulder. She squeezes it, hard, with her hand. In her deep dark eyes, Lucy sees complete comprehension of all possible doubts and accusations.

"The au pair said I hit my children. She said she saw me hit them, all the time. Sometimes with a stick, sometimes with a belt. The social workers took them to the doctor and they found two bruises on Elissa's back and five or six bruises and scrapes all over Byron's body. The doctor who examined them was quote unable to determine the causes of these bruises and—what did he call them?"

"Lacerations? Abrasions?"

"Abrasions, I think. Unable to determine the causes of these bruises and abrasions, but quote, could not rule out the possibility that they had been caused by physical abuse."

"But for heaven's sake, Tanya, didn't they ask the children where they got those bruises? Didn't they ask Elissa and—how old is Byron?"

Beverly Lieberman is hovering just a few feet away from them and takes this question as an opportunity to join the conversation. "Byron is almost three, Lucy, and he's just the cutest little fellow. We're really hoping to have him in the pre-K next year!"

Now for the first time, Tanya looks visibly upset by the conversation. But she answers in the same quiet, competent voice. "Byron is really too young to tell them much, that's part of the problem. But Elissa—when they asked her, she just broke down. She cried and she cried, and she wouldn't answer them."

And after all, Lucy notes, a child's back is a relatively unusual place to find bruises.

"Does Elissa take gymnastics? Any activity where she might have had a fall?"

"She plays soccer." Of course. All seven-year-old girls play soccer on Saturday. It's a local ordinance. If Elissa *didn't* play soccer, that would probably be grounds all by itself for reporting Tanya to the authorities. "She's on Jade. But as far as I know, she hasn't gotten hurt."

"Well, obviously the au pair is beating her and then blaming you!" says Bev, solving the dilemma, assigning blame, and saving the day.

"I thought of that," says Tanya, and then begins to cry. Bev bustles importantly around with tissues and there-there's (a Greg headline: BIG BEV BUSTLES, BUSILY BRANDISHING BOX). Other parents are looking over at them, and Lucy feels a certain embarrassment, a certain desire to get to work, which she really needs to do, and extricate herself from all this mess. She looks down quickly at the time on her beeper, wishing it would beep and call her away.

"You poor poor baby," says Bev (BEV BABIES BAWLING BLOND).

"What on earth is your husband doing while you're going through all this?"

Screwing his CFO, thinks Lucy, but says nothing.

"Oh, he doesn't know what to make of it all. He feels terrible for me, but he's also worried about the children—he thinks they're going to be very upset about losing another au pair."

"Tanya, tell me this woman isn't still in your house after all this," says Bev, and Lucy has to nod agreement.

"No," Tanya agrees. "She isn't. I told her she had to leave. But then I didn't have a sitter for Byron for today for the assembly—and then my husband said it might look bad that we fired her after she made this accusation . . ."

"Look," Lucy says, "if your response to the accusation is that she's a liar and she obviously hates you, how can you possibly leave her with your children?"

"I know," Tanya says. "You're right."

"So where's Byron?" Bev asks, as if that's bothering her (BYRON BABYSITTING BATTLE BOTHERS BEV BADLY . . . no, I have to stop this, Lucy thinks. Bev is trying to help, and Tanya needs help, and something weird is going on. Enough with the stupid jokes).

"I left him with my neighbor—she said it would be okay, but I should really get back there."

"So, Lucy, what's going to happen next with Tanya and the social workers? Isn't this a terrible business?" Oh, it is impossible not to suspect that the Divine Bev is having a wonderful time.

"Well, I take it there's an ongoing investigation—you're an open case."

Tanya nods.

"So they'll probably assign you a worker—if they haven't already—and they'll try to figure out whether there's really any problem in your home . . ."

"Which there obviously isn't," puts in Bev.

Oh, I don't know, Lucy thinks, husband screwing the au pair, and the CFO, and anything else that moves except maybe his wife, au pair calling in to report the wife for abuse, seven-year-old who gets hysterical when someone asks her how she got those bruises, husband thinks they should keep the au pair anyway so the kids don't get too traumatized . . .

"If they decide—if you convince them—that there isn't a problem in the home, then they may just close the case. In fact, that's probably the likeliest thing."

"You would certainly think so!" *Thank you, Bev.*

Lucy has had enough. "I really have to get to work. Tanya, would you like me to drop you somewhere?"

"Oh, thank you so much, but I have my car."

"Want to walk out with me?" Lucy stands, slings her bag over her shoulder.

"Sure." Tanya is on her feet as well. "And thanks, Bev. I'll be in touch."

"Call me tonight!" Bev instructs, and Tanya nods.

Lucy, as she and Tanya leave the room and cross the insanely manicured, ludicrously lush front lawn of the school, has a sudden and slightly hurtful sense of all the connections and contacts linking all the other second-grade mothers, their phone calls and meetings for coffee, their knowledge of one another's lives, and of one another's children, and of what goes on in the second grade or in the school. On the rare occasions that she gets such a phone call, it's Bev or someone like her recruiting volunteers to bake muffins for the teacher appreciation breakfast, or signing people up for slots to supervise the moonwalk at the school Spring Fair. But Lucy feels a tiny pang for all the little easy friendships she can suddenly imagine going on all around her, the same way she feels a pang for Freddy whenever she hears of group excursions or weekend sleepovers among the other second-grade boys. There must be a casual, easy friendship gene, a being-included gene, and maybe it's located not too far from the wearing-pumps and French-braiding loci, that's all, and she doesn't have it, any more than Freddy does.

They get to Tanya's car, a snappy black Mercedes-Benz, first.

"Look," Lucy says, "is there anything I can do? This sounds really shitty—sorry, I mean really hard, what you're going through."

"Shitty is about right," says Tanya, standing there in the sun in her flowered housedress and sneakers, a drop-dead beautiful woman in a weird housewife muumuu, caught in a weirder story. "Shitty goddamn motherfucking jerk-off pisspot crazy!"

"Is there anything I can do?" Lucy asks again, wondering, *What are the odds that it is this woman who is out-and-out jerk-off pisspot crazy?* Lucy is a mandated reporter, after all, as she just explained to Tanya and Bev—what if she gets to know Tanya a little and concludes that in fact Tanya *is* a danger to her children—does she have to file another report? And what will Bev do then?

"Will you get in the car with me for a minute?" Tanya asks. "I'd like to talk to you."

Lucy gets in the car. What else can she do? She's worried about being late to work, but she's also decidedly curious. Nice beige leather seats, what looks like tortoiseshell inlay on the dashboard.

Tanya pulls her own door closed. "I'm afraid of him," she says, but with no emotion in her voice whatsoever.

"Of your husband."

"I don't believe he'll ever let the kids go. I believe he will destroy me—believe me, he has the connections—he will have people in court testifying that I'm crazy, that I'm brutal to the children—he will have me followed. He will have me beaten up. He will bring in people who will swear that I'm unfaithful to him and that I'm schizophrenic. He will have them institutionalize me before he lets me go. You don't know what he's like. They will lock me up somewhere and throw away the key."

"Does he hit you?" Lucy asks, somewhat automatically, back on her professional ground.

Tanya pauses, hands on her gleaming steering wheel. Outside, through the window, Lucy can see the other mothers dispersing, going off in ones and twos toward their mysterious days.

"Yes, he does," Tanya says. "Sometimes he does."

And here is the awful thing: Lucy just doesn't believe her. She just doesn't quite believe the whole thing. She feels suddenly that she is part of a game and a game she doesn't understand. She doesn't believe that Tanya's husband will have her beaten up by professional goons, or have her locked away in some mysterious shadowy institution for the inconvenient wives of the brutally rich. It's all too much the stuff of sensational bestsellers, and somehow, she doesn't think there is any real conviction in Tanya's voice. Tanya is a bad actress, playing a part off a bad TV show. Something else is going on here, and it is probably about money.

But that is ridiculous. When a woman tells you that she is a victim of domestic violence, you are supposed to take it seriously. Lucy has sat through dozens of presentations on this subject. Probably, Lucy tells herself, I am just thinking in stereotypes; I am doubting the story because everyone is rich and white and the kids go to school with my own kids.

"You need to get help," Lucy says. "You need a lawyer of your own. And there are places you can go if you don't feel safe in your own house—I can give you a number to call."

"I'm not leaving the house," Tanya says. "I'm not leaving my kids."

"They'll take your kids, too, at one of these shelters," Lucy says, then stops to wonder how the DSS case complicates things. No, probably Tanya shouldn't take the kids and run off to a shelter —probably she has to go through her social worker.

"We're not leaving the house," Tanya says, flatly. And again Lucy thinks, Somehow this is all about money. Tanya turns the ignition key. "Do you mind if I drive?" she asks. "I don't want to just sit here. I'll drive you to your car."

And she is driving down the street, decorously below the speed limit.

"Actually, that's my car," Lucy points out, as they crawl past, but Tanya doesn't even look. She is staring straight ahead, and Lucy can admire her lovely face in profile. This is what I get, Lucy thinks, for imagining the pleasures of going off with another mommy for a cup of coffee. I am being driven away from my own car, away from where I need to be, on a weird errand to nowhere.

"You need to talk to a lawyer," Lucy says again. "And if you don't think that it's safe for you at home, then you need to get out of there. You need protection for yourself, and you need to protect your kids."

"Isn't that what the social worker is for?" Tanya's voice is now sarcastic. She is still driving at her funereal pace, carefully signaling a right turn halfway before they get to the corner. "You know," she goes on, "a week ago, everything was normal—or pretty normal. Now I have this social worker and you're telling me to go to some kind of shelter and I'm an open case. That's what I am, an open case."

"It doesn't sound like things were so normal a week ago, from what you've said," Lucy says. "Not if he hits you. Not if anyone is hitting the kids." Not to mention if he's sleeping with the au pair, but never mind that now.

"I'm starting to feel like maybe I shouldn't even have told Bev—I guess I shouldn't want this getting around too much," Tanya says.

Actually, Lucy agrees. But all she says is "Look, you aren't ashamed of anything, right? So you have to act like you're not ashamed of anything. So if you want to tell your close friends, go right ahead." And Lucy looks out the window and notes with panic that they are now moving rapidly enough through town, heading, apparently, for the western suburbs.

"Oh, she's not a close friend," Tanya says. "She just called me last night to try and get me to come staff the ice cream table at the year-end picnic, and somehow I found myself telling her all this, I don't even know why. And then she said that today she would arrange for me to talk to you."

"Tanya, I really need to get back to my car. I need to get to work. I'm parked right near the school, right where we started. Could you please take us back in that direction?"

Tanya signals another of her careful turns.

"Do you want the number—the domestic violence hotline?" Lucy tries once more, relieved to be heading back in the general direction of her own car and her own life.

"I'm not leaving the house." Tanya brakes rather abruptly at a stop sign. She turns her head to look directly at Lucy. "Would you testify?"

"What do you mean?"

"If I do go to a lawyer. You're a doctor—Bev said you could be an expert witness."

Lucy, in fact, has been an expert witness many many times in her life. "No," she says, "I couldn't testify. Everything I know is from you—it's all hearsay. I'm not in any kind of official capacity here—I haven't examined your kids, I'm not their doctor. If you go to a lawyer, you'll need real experts."

As they drive back to Lucy's car, what she is thinking is that it is possible that tomorrow, or next week, Tanya will mysteriously disappear—that her evil, shadowy husband will do away with her, that his dangerous goon associates will dispose of the body. But it also seems possible that she will murder him in his sleep and claim self-defense. *I don't quite believe her,* Lucy thinks again. *I don't know why, but I don't quite believe her.*

Tanya doesn't seem to want to talk anymore. And she's driving at a more normal speed, so they're back at the school very quickly, and Lucy, with great relief, points out her car.

"Thank you," Tanya says. "For talking to me. I appreciate it."

"If there's anything I can do," Lucy starts, then thinks about the expert witness request and changes gears. "If you decide you do want information about people who work with domestic violence," she says, "I can give you some good numbers. I can get you hooked up with people who will protect you."

Tanya doesn't answer; if she said anything, Lucy believes, it would be *I'm not leaving the house.*

"I have to go now," Lucy says. "I need to get to work. I hope things get better for you."

"We'll see," Tanya says, and Lucy wonders whether she is plotting murder.

"Talk to the DSS worker," Lucy advises, opening her door. "Make sure they know your side of the story. Get it on the record."

"Thank you," Tanya says again. "I appreciate it."

"Goodbye," Lucy says, and she closes the door of the Mercedes and heads for her own car.

And for work, and the real start of her day, and for a crazy afternoon in which four children from this one crazy family will each sit in an exam room, tying up the clinic for half the afternoon, as social workers, counselors, and Lucy herself make their way from room to room, examining, asking questions, trying to figure out what the hell has been going on. The oldest of the children is eight, one year older than Elissa—or Freddy—three years younger than Isabel. The youngest is just about Byron's age. Lucy thinks about Byron and Elissa and their au pair and their mother and their father from time to time all afternoon, as she does her usual meticulous exams, as she spends time talking to each of the children. This is in many ways a pretty clear-cut case of neglect, she knows; the four children were found in an otherwise empty but filthy apartment, huddled together on a bare king-size mattress with a hole burned in it. Some neighbor had heard crying and called the police. The apartment contained a few items of what the newspaper calls "drug paraphernalia," which probably means needles, and no food. The children were taken into police custody, handed over to the Department of Social Services, and the parents, who returned at dawn, eight or nine hours later, were arrested, apparently much to their surprise.

So here she is back in the familiar territory of child abuse and foster care, poor people, dirty, bare apartments, drugs, neglected children. No au pair, no philandering husband, no perfect prince and princess with a few mysterious bruises. Lucy has plenty to do, and she is by no means prone to reflecting at any length on the essential unknowability of families, and the dark, strange secrets that lie at the heart of every house—that's not her kind of thing at all. She believes in good sense and practical protocols; in asking questions and noting evidence and removing children into safe environments. She resents it, with all the anger of a child who grew up without parents, when privileged, educated parents who should know better devote themselves to making misery for their children. It's not an enlightened response, especially to domestic violence, but there it is. Lucy tries, as she works, to think of some way to frame questions for Tanya, for Elissa, for the husband, for the au pair. *Is* someone actually hitting those children? Is the au pair crazy? Is Tanya Danvers herself crazy? Are we left, in fact, with the essential unknowability of families, with the terrible vulnerability of children?

Lucy leans against a wall in the clinic, writing up some quick notes on sibling number three before moving on to sibling number four, and what she is remembering is the second-grade class singing about how dreams come true, their flashlights shining on their faces.

8

The Beloved Object

THREE YEARS AGO, when Lucy's son, Freddy, was four years old, he fell madly and passionately in love. The object of his devotion, as pure and wholehearted as a boy can know, was a fellow named Stafford, who worked behind the counter of the coffee shop three blocks from Freddy's house. Freddy got to know Stafford because Freddy's father was a coffee shop regular, known to all the guys who worked behind that particular counter. Greg would bring Freddy in with him for a treat sometimes, and everyone would make a fuss: so cute, father and son out for a walk, one mocha latte, one chocolate chip cookie.

Stafford was the tallest guy who worked at the coffee shop, and he wore a big gold hoop in his ear. His hair was gold as well, lavishly, improbably gold, sometimes falling softly across his forehead and down to his shoulders, other times pulled back in a ponytail that looked good and right and graceful on him, not silly in the least. And once in a while, which may have had something to do with Freddy's initial moment of truth, Stafford wore a red bandanna tied around his golden head, and at those moments he did look like some Hollywood pirate, the guy who leaps onto the boat, brandishing his sword, and you look at him and hope he's come for you.

Freddy had been particularly interested in pirates for a while. All little boys are interested in pirates, probably, but not all after the manner of Freddy, who even at four had already made it clear that he was going to do things his way. Freddy, of course, memorized true facts and figures, and could tell you that Barbary pirates used galleys up until the 1600s, when they switched to sailing ships, and that buccaneers were French and Dutch and English, but they attacked Spanish ships. So he knew his stuff, all right, but he also seemed to be tolerant of little boy pirate paraphernalia; he enjoyed the various pirate toy sets his parents brought home, hung the skull and crossbones flag over his bed, wore the Jolly Roger vest, and for several months wore a particular gray plastic sword around his waist all day, every day at home. He couldn't wear it to preschool, since weapons of all types were strictly prohibited, but Freddy has always liked rules and regulations, so that was okay, too.

Lucy looks back now, three years later, on the pirate obsession, and she misses it. It seems in retrospect so colorful, so boylike, so full of song and story. Freddy right now cares only about baseball and baseball cards—which again is perfectly classic and all-American, but there is something painful and precise about watching him tend his cards. His cards, Lucy thinks, are no longer just a passion; they are also now a protection against the whole world. Yes, the real flesh and blood Red Sox may lose—in fact, the real flesh and blood Red Sox have just lost spectacularly, and Freddy stayed up late and cried when the Yankees won and the season was over—but then he retreated to his boxes of cards, where he is in complete control. He hides behind his perfectly arranged formations of first basemen and shortstops. It's not like it was with the pirates, when every book, every poster, even every swashbuckling gesture with his sword, was a brave and even romantic foray out into the bright, fascinating world.

And then there was Stafford, also back in those piratical days. Freddy talked about Stafford all the time. "Can we go see Stafford today?" Lucy would hear Freddy asking his father on Saturday morning, as Isabel got ready for soccer. If it was a beautiful spring evening and Lucy suggested a walk, Freddy would announce whether this was Stafford's shift. And as they drove past the coffee shop on the way to preschool every morning, Freddy would say happily, "That's where Stafford works."

If Isabel was in the car, she would say, "Duh," or "Tell us something we don't know," but Freddy didn't care. The coffee shop was a light unto his soul, and he didn't care who knew it. Lucy liked to think that he did in fact imagine Stafford as a gloriously daring pirate captain, and she hoped Freddy saw himself, plastic sword and Jolly Roger vest and all, standing close behind him on the deck, the salt breeze blowing in his hair.

Isabel does not mention boys. Not ever. Isabel's world is a world of girls who get good grades and wash their hair every night and think that girls who wear makeup to school are sluts. Which, Lucy thinks, has a certain validity to it, but surely in the sixth grade, the best they can be is aspiring sluts. "Can you tell Daddy to get off the Internet, please?" Isabel says, one night in November. "I have to call someone to check on the homework." This is not news, and Lucy gets up from supervising Freddy's stupid, meaningless, busywork second-grade homework to go negotiate her husband off his e-mail for a fifteen-minute interval, part of which he will spend explaining to her that it's really time to get a second phone line, which he will then not do. What is news, however, is when Lucy asks, rather idly, "Who are you going to call?" and Isabel, not looking at her mother, says, "This kid in my class named Andy Constantine."

Greg comes to consult his wife. "There's something going on with one of my students," he says. "There's something I'd like you to look at."

Students do get these crushes on Greg. Intellectual crushes, sure, but sometimes more. Lucy is sitting at her desk, working on a PowerPoint presentation that Isabel has fancied up for her with moving text, dancing letters, arrows that dart around the screen. Isabel thinks that PowerPoint presentations that don't take advantage of all possible fancy extras are dorky. Unfortunately, Isabel has gone up to bed, since she regulates her own bedtime schedule with the same fierceness that she brings to conditioning her hair, and now Lucy can't improve or correct the text in her presentation because it all keeps dancing around.

Lucy's study at home is very small and very messy. Isabel has been known to pause in the doorway and shudder demonstratively, before coming in to lend a hand with the PowerPoint. Greg has a much bigger study, because he spends his most important days and months at home with his research and writing; his study is also not terribly neat, but because it is bigger, and because he uses it so much, it has a rather agreeable, intellectually cluttered air about it. There is, for example, a large armchair, so though you might have to move a pile of books, you could sit down and be comfortable. In Lucy's study, on the other hand, Greg can barely find a place to stand, awkwardly, on the small patch of floor, among the newspapers and the books and the photocopied journal articles.

"Look," Greg says. He leans over her shoulder and puts down on her desk—on top of something else, of course—a note written on yellow, lined paper.

> Dear Professor, this is by way of thanking you even yet again for all that you have done for me. It must be a tremendous satisfaction to you in your life that you have been able to do so much goodness and kindness, not to mention offer so much inspiration, for so many students. For this reason, however, I hesitate to ask you for yet another favor, and I fear that you must have many many demands made upon you. But I think that the favor I am asking will not in fact inconvenience you or deprive you of any of your time or your energy.

Lucy looks up at her husband. "Who's this from?"

"One of my students."

"Well, yes, I had gathered that."

She looks down again at the note; the handwriting is not beautiful, but it is profoundly regular and readable, the handwriting of a good student who practiced all the letters over and over.

I am hoping to stay in the area over winter break, for personal reasons and also because I am hoping to do a certain amount of my research for my senior thesis, which, as I have previously explained, I am hoping that you will advise next year, though I know there are many demands on you. But since the dormitories will be closed and I do not have the funds to pay for a hotel room, I am hoping that you would be willing to allow me to sleep on your glassed-in sun porch. I would come and go extremely quietly, so as not to disturb your wonderful family; I would come in the evening after they were all asleep, and depart in the morning before they waken. Do not be perturbed that it will be cold on some nights, since I am an experienced hiker and winter camper, and possess a sleeping bag that is guaranteed to sub-zero temperatures, which of course I would use.

Another paragraph of gratitude to Greg—*for all you have given me as a teacher and an intellectual role model*—and thanks in anticipation for use of the sun porch—and a wish for wonderful holidays for Greg and his entire family.

"Anthony Dexter Jackson Davenport." Lucy reads the signature aloud.

"He goes by Dexter," Greg says, rather helplessly.

"So what's with him? I take it you know him?"

"Oh, I know him. He's taken my classes the last three semesters. He's told me before how much he likes them, he says he's changed his major to English lit because of me. He's always seemed like a nice kid—I did tell him I would do a senior thesis with him next year."

"Well, do a senior thesis with him, if you want. Just don't let him sleep on our porch."

"Yes, I understand that," Greg says. "But what am I supposed to say to a student who asks for something like that? This is a pretty weird request. Do you think he needs some kind of professional help?"

Lucy considers, flattered to be asked. She is the expert on children, but Greg is obviously and properly the expert on privileged college students. "I don't know," she says. "College students can live in pretty casual ways. You know, they visit friends in groups of ten, they sleep in sleeping bags, probably they sleep on the sun porch. I think you could just say to him that this isn't a good idea, and see how he reacts." She pauses and looks at her husband. "You think it's more than that, don't you? You think he's got a thing for you."

"I think he's got a major thing for me. I thought it was more an intellectual crush—he's a good student, it's been good having him in class—but it's not just an intellectual crush. I should have seen it coming."

"So where does he live?" Lucy asks.

"Colorado. I think his parents are very very rich. I sort of had the impression that his great dilemma was that he had decided he wanted to study English literature and they were upset because he was supposed to go to law school. I had told him to tell them he still could—and the truth is, he probably will, though I didn't say that to him—but his idea is that my classes changed his life and now he wants to devote himself completely to the writings of Oscar Wilde."

"Oops."

"I mean, he had already dedicated his life to me and to art back in the introductory course. But then he did the Gender and Society in Nineteenth-Century British Literature course—which I shouldn't even have let him into, he was only a sophomore, but you know, it's kind of flattering to have a student who acts like you've saved him from Mammon and delivered him up to art and beauty and literature—guys like me, we fall for that every time—and anyway, he did his paper on *De Profundis*, and it was all over."

"It's a little spooky," Lucy says, "that he knows we have a glassed-in sun porch."

"I know. He's obviously cased the joint. So what do I do?"

"Tell him to go home and see his parents and promise them that law school is still a possibility. Ask him if he's doing okay, passing his courses, getting by. Then take a deep breath and tell him you're a little concerned about him. You don't even have to say why. Everybody always thinks they're stressed out, so if you say you worry he's been under a lot of stress, he'll probably just nod, yeah, of course, you're right. And then you ask him if he's considered talking to someone."

"And I keep the door to my office wide open the whole time."

"I guess," says Lucy, who in fact shuts the door to *her* office when she speaks to the troubled. But she knows the rules that Greg and his colleagues live by, and she knows how careful they have to be when a student is becoming "inappropriately attached," as the expression goes.

Stafford, Freddy's love object from three years ago, was not just a coffee shop worker. Stafford had a dream. To be specific, Stafford was an actor. He played in all sorts of community theater, and for almost a year, Greg loyally dragged Freddy around to productions in churches, school auditoriums, the bandstand in a suburban park. They saw Stafford play Katherine and Bianca's father in *The Taming of the Shrew*, and the drunken butler in *The Tempest*, and a very tall Biff in *Death of a Salesman*, and Public Enemy Number One in *Anything Goes*, and they saw him in the chorus of *Guys and Dolls*, which remains Freddy's favorite musical ever; he has memorized the whole CD and often, on long trips, croons to himself his favorite song, "Luck Be a Lady."

But back when he was four, Freddy did not care what the play was, or even whether he had any understanding of what the play was. Greg described the experience for Lucy: Freddy would sit quiet and well-behaved while the action went on, and then Stafford would appear, swashing his buckles or doing his best to shrink down inside his suit, or tapping into his opening buck and wing, and Freddy would come to life. Would stand up and point to him, so that Greg had to be ready to sit him back down. Would get a grin across his face so wide that Greg got nervous, expecting him to burst into laughter from the sheer excitement of it. Would fix his eyes on Stafford and stare and stare at his hero, properly raised up on a dais, properly spotlighted, dressed and anointed and painted to perfection for Freddy's contemplation and Freddy's worship.

"You got a phone call." Lucy keeps her voice very casual and informational. "Andy Constantine. I wrote down the number on the pad."

Isabel is already standing over by the pad, looking down at the message in her mother's handwriting. Then she is gone, with pad and phone. Lucy can hear her daughter's feet going upstairs, can hear the distinct *click* of her door shutting, fully closed, latch engaged. If Isabel had a padlock and a police lock and a chain—and if Isabel had her way, she would—they would all be locked. And for the first time ever, Lucy feels a treacherous impulse; she thinks of lifting the extension and listening. But of course she doesn't do it, nor does she even invent an excuse to pass casually by her daughter's door and try to catch a word or two. All she does is save it up to tell Greg, who will understand that this is one place, absolutely and completely, where teasing would be inappropriate, who will watch with her and wait with her in silent curiosity.

People do get these crushes on Greg. It does happen. And usually he brings the news home and tells Lucy. It's an occupational hazard for those who teach the young, Lucy supposes, though not, as far as she can tell, for those who provide medical care for the even younger. You wouldn't necessarily look at Greg and think, *Oh sure, him,* but people do get these crushes. And Greg is not particularly susceptible to the young, as far as Lucy knows; the one time that she knows, at least in recent history, that he strayed, it wasn't anyone even marginally studentlike. It was that woman in London and he confessed and he felt lousy and Lucy felt lousy, but the sneaky truth is that it probably altered the balance of power more in her favor than anything else. A crush is all potential and power—as long as you don't act on it, Lucy thinks.

Or maybe that's not what Lucy thinks, or not all the time. Maybe some of the time she thinks, *I'll get you for that some day, wait and see.*

It's all kind of complicated, isn't it? Lucy doesn't have a crush on anyone, ever.

"Who is Andrew Constantine?" Lucy tries asking one day at a carefully chosen casual moment, driving Isabel in the car, after they have just dropped off Isabel's friend Abby at her house. *See, Isabel, I'm a good mom, I drive your friends around, you can tell me.*

"*Andy* Constantine. He's a kid in my grade."

"Is he nice?" Neutral voice, a parental request for factual information. That's all.

"Yeah, he's okay." A pause. "Except he got suspended and now he can't come to school for two days."

"Why is that?"

"He's in my math group? So you know it's the top math group —and he's the best one in it—in the whole class? So the teacher left a copy of the test on her desk—I mean, before she was going to give it—and Andy found it, and he wrote out all the problems on the blackboard, so when we came in to take the test, there were all the answers."

Isabel does not sound shocked. Isabel, who has been known, together with Abby, to be prissily appalled at someone's incomplete homework assignment, does not sound at all shocked or disapproving.

"I guess he shouldn't have done that," Lucy says, seeking confirmation.

"Well, she shouldn't have left the test on her desk. And she shouldn't have been giving a test that someone could do from beginning to end in just five minutes. I mean, it isn't like he cheated or anything."

Freddy's passion for Stafford continued unabated for a good six months. Once there was a picture of Stafford in the local paper —that was when he was in *Fiddler on the Roof*—and Freddy made them cut out the picture and frame it. Under the picture he would set up his little exact arrangements, pirate figurines lined up in ranks, every red Lego in the house snapped together into a series of rectangular blocks, a set of zoologically correct replicas of the poisonous snakes of the world that Freddy had received for his fourth birthday and that had immediately and completely entered into many of his special, complex observances.

This period, this Stafford phase, was right about when they were first talking about getting Freddy tested. Right after the first fiasco with the neuropsychiatrist who wore those long, stringy earrings that Freddy found so scary, he wouldn't say a word to her, and she diagnosed him with at least three devastating conditions, in addition to selective mutism.

They have taken Freddy to exactly three specialists; she was the first and the worst. In reaction to the neuropsychiatrist, they took him to an old-fashioned child analyst, someone a lovable, aging actor would play in a heartwarming movie—a fat, untidy guy who lowered himself down onto the floor with a grunt to connect with Freddy. No selective mutism here—Freddy talked on and on about his interests and obsessions, and the guy told Lucy and Greg that he was a very smart and very eccentric child, but in his opinion, that was enough for now. Take good care of him, he said, and make sure the world is kind to him. And then when they were applying to kindergarten, Lucy decided they should have a little more testing done, but that was mostly IQ stuff, and Freddy scored off the charts—which was maybe more reassuring than it should have been.

And sooner or later, some teacher will want him tested again, and someone will formulate Freddy. He will have a diagnosis; Lucy doesn't believe that he will make it through school without one. And she can't even quite explain why she wants to hold out as long as possible in this complicated world where as far as Freddy knows, he defines the boundaries of normal, and everyone else is off kilter.

Lucy wonders, looking back, whether one reason she and Greg threw themselves into the Stafford mania with such enthusiasm was that deep in their souls, they hoped that it meant that Freddy wanted to grow into a dashing, egocentric, normal kind of guy.

Tossing together someone's double iced skim cappuccino, flirting and chatting and raking in the tips. Out there on the stage, singing and dancing and waiting for fame. What could have seemed further away from Freddy and his eccentric, constricted possibilities? Could they have been that naive though, that willing to believe that you can become the thing you love, or that you even want to? Freddy didn't want to *be* Stafford; he probably wanted to own Stafford, keep him arranged in his proper place among Freddy's other important fetishes, totems, and essential objects.

9

Hotel Secrets

THE ROOMS IN THE HOTEL in Mexico are very big. The floors are made of red tile, and the ceilings are amazingly high, and somehow the rooms look very foreign to Isabel. They're kind of—undecorated—just these very plain, white, high walls, these red floors. The room that she and Freddy will share this week has two perfectly comfortable twin beds—each with a plain white spread, each with a small night table—and one wooden desk, a single chair to match, and a mirror on the wall. No pictures, no armchairs, no mini bar. Not even a closet. There's a little bathroom with a toilet and a shower. There's a television set way up high near the ceiling. It's kind of a quiet room, a room that could swallow you up, like a foreign country.

Actually, it's a room that feels so foreign that you could be kind of grateful to have your little brother sharing it with you, just so it *can't* swallow you up. Isabel appropriates the little desk and the chair. Freddy will just dump his stuff on the floor—his baseball cards, his books, his clothes. Isabel herself will keep her clothing packed in her suitcase, will keep a neat stack of books on her night table.

Isabel's mother knocks on the door, sticks her head in, reminds them once again not to drink the tap water, not even to brush their teeth with it. This is only maybe the two-hundred-and-fourth time she's said it, but okay. Then she asks Isabel to be sure to remind Freddy, and Isabel says she will.

Their parents' room is right next door. Isabel looked in when they opened their door; it's almost identical except it has one big bed instead of two small ones. Both of their parents seem just plain foolishly delighted to be here—they have been to this town before, they keep explaining, years and years ago, before they had children, and they are so happy to be back. Actually, Isabel has to admit, there is something quite remarkably strange and even exciting about the whole thing—changing planes in Mexico City, which is supposed to be the most polluted place on the planet, but what are you supposed to do, stop breathing?—and flying to this tiny little airport set among the mountains, just sitting here and baking in the sun—and then there is her mother speaking in Spanish, and there they are crowded into a cab, and here they are in two rooms in a hotel—and everyone speaks another language, and her parents look so happy to be here. And when you think about it, could anyone even find them? Could anyone actually trace them through that crazy Mexico City Airport—and all those guards who check your passports, and those airline people who check your ticket and your ID—do they actually know where everyone is, all the time?

Isabel unlaces her sneakers, takes them off, lines them up against the wall near her bed, peels off her socks, rolls them neatly, and tucks one into each sneaker. She presses her bare feet against these strange, cool, red tiles. Liking the feeling against her feet, she crosses the room, crosses back, turns to go into the bathroom.

"Remember," Freddy says, without looking up from his baseball cards, and Isabel chimes in and they say together, "Don't drink the water."

Isabel knows that her brother is kind of weird and kind of gross and very immature, even for a second-grader, but she also knows that Freddy needs to count everything and set things in orderly categories, and even though she makes an automatic face of disgust when he does it, she kind of respects it, she really does. Well, she understands him better than she admits; certainly better than either of their two sloppy parents, she thinks. In the taxi, coming from the airport, he said he had stayed at eight different hotels, and then he named them. This hotel will make nine, he said, contentedly. Isabel, drawn into the conversation and the count, automatically corrected him, said he had left out at least two different cabins they had stayed at on summer trips to North Carolina, when they went to the beach, and Freddy said no, he was only counting hotels. Isabel thought of arguing it, but then she let it go. Freddy just wanted to check, he said, whether he had ever stayed at any other hotels when he was a baby, and he was relieved when his parents couldn't think of any, not back before the trip to Florida when he was two, which he had already counted.

"How many hotels did you ever stay at?" he asked.

"Oh, honey, I don't know," their mother said. "I never stayed at a hotel when I was a child—never—but as an adult, there are all these trips to all these places—they don't really stand out, you know. It feels like hundreds—but I don't keep track." Typical.

But Isabel's father surprised her. "It would be an interesting list, if you kept it," he said. "It would be, like, the story of your life. The story of our family. The history of the world. Probably all kinds of hotel secrets, all kinds of things nobody knows."

"What do you mean, 'the history of the world'?" Freddy wanted to know.

"I asked your mother to marry me in a hotel room right here in Oaxaca," their father said. "That's the history of the world."

Five years ago—the Fontainebleau, Miami.

Lucy and Greg are locked in the bathroom, giggling so much they can hardly fuck. It's one of those moments that comes partway through a four-person family vacation: both kids are desperate to watch the Saturday morning cartoons, which are not allowed at home, and they don't want to go out to the beach or down to the pool or anywhere anywhere anywhere except to sit zombie-eyed on Isabel's double bed—she gets one all to herself because Freddy sleeps in the Portacrib—and watch the cartoons. And their parents, who have been sleeping chastely in the other double bed on these public nights (with just a two-year-old in a Portacrib you might take the chance, since after all if he woke up, he'd let you know it, but not with the world's most suspicious six-year-old sleeping just a few feet away, only too ready to be awakened by mysterious noises and lie still and silent, collecting information).

But what the hell, as they say to each other in the bathroom, it's our vacation, too, isn't it?

The funny thing is, in years to come they will remember locking themselves in that Fontainebleau bathroom to have sex while their children watched cartoons, but will not quite be able to keep straight which of them had the conference, the speech, the presentation that brought them to this massive hotel, bringing the kids on cheap airfares for a long weekend in Florida.

And perhaps this in-joke inability to remember that it was in fact Greg's conference, Greg's panel, Greg's luncheon address, this insistence back and forth that it could just as well have been Lucy's, is just their little way of celebrating their lives and their balance and where they have come to. And a way of remembering Isabel's heady delight in that endless stretch of Miami beach, how she ran as far from them as they would let her, and then came charging back, a laughing, sturdy girl in a silver bathing suit that caught the light and sent off sparks, while her brother, two-year-old terrified Freddy, clung to their legs and watched his sister as she ran, kicking up sand in all directions.

The hotel bathroom, needless to say, is bigger than many people's bedrooms—bigger than Freddy's small room at home, certainly, and it was probably this that gave Greg the idea in the first place. Last night they were all four in the bathroom at once: Greg washing Freddy off in the tub, which Freddy hates, while Lucy tried to distract him with a book, and Isabel, unwilling to be left out, disgruntled because everyone was paying attention to Freddy, sorted through the little bottles of shampoo and mouthwash and body lotion with a critical eye. They were all in the bathroom and it wasn't even crowded; at home, if two people are in the bathroom, they are in close physical contact.

As are Greg and Lucy right now, on the bathroom floor, on the big, clean, white bathmat and two of the bath towels, unfolded and spread out on the floor to cushion Lucy, who is on bottom. But truly, they are both so entertained in a sick, mutual-joke, parental way by the idea of this—leaving the kids out there to watch cartoons and getting it on in the Fontainebleau hotel bathroom—that they keep cracking up and losing their rhythm.

(Isabel doesn't know this story—and neither, of course, does Freddy, but he probably wouldn't be interested.)

At a restaurant in Oaxaca, Isabel's mother ordered a sandwich made with the spicy pork she likes, the *cecina,* and the waiter said "*Grande o pequeño?*," which Isabel understood, and her mother grinned and said enthusiastically, "Oh, *grande, por favor! Grande* by all means!" And then the world's largest sandwich came to their little table under an umbrella on the main square, the *zocalo,* with the park in the middle and the balloon sellers and the musicians and all the tourists in the world passing by. It seems to Isabel that she has never seen her best friend Abby's mother eat anything but a salad, though she knows what her own mother would say about the dangers of eating salads here in Mexico.

Isabel knows there is something that she has to figure out about being embarrassed. About people seeing you and knowing things about you. And she knows that her mother and father think it's funny about Isabel checking them over if they're going to come to her school, which they don't do very often, thank goodness. Her rule for her mother is to wear all black, and that's not that hard to get her to do—her mother wears a lot of black anyway. But what about those embroidered dresses her mother keeps fingering in the market stalls—all this bright cotton with big embroidered flowers, which her mother sighs over and says she guesses she wouldn't wear, but plainly *regrets.*

Her mother thinks that Isabel should be loading up on flowered dresses and lacy shirts with bright birds on the yoke—her mother thinks those would be perfect for a young girl, her mother thinks they're pretty and bright and beautiful examples, probably, of native crafts. Lucy strokes the embroidery and tells the peddlers, in Spanish, that their things are beautiful, which only encourages them and makes them try harder to sell. Her mother would be so happy if Isabel said she wanted to bring a pile of these clothes home and wear them—and some part of Isabel would like to make her mother so happy, and some part of her is angry at her mother for setting it up so that to make her happy, Isabel would have to want things that she so much doesn't want. That she could never wear, not anywhere. Now her mother has come up with this line about finding something Isabel could buy that wouldn't be for school—something that could be worn as a "bathing suit cover-up"—as if a person would be *less* careful about what she wore at the beach. In fact, Isabel can hardly bear to think about the whole subject of bathing suits, bathing suits and bodies. Oh, and body hair—what is she supposed to do about wearing a bathing suit if she is going to get body hair?

Four years ago—the Conference Center Hilton, Baltimore.

Lucy is trying to talk a very depressed fellow named Zachary Winkler into ironing his shirt and going out to face the world. They are in his hotel room in Baltimore, where they are both attending a large medical meeting. They are old friends from residency, Lucy and Zach, and at first she was glad enough to run into him and play medical catch-up for a while. He was getting ready to go for what was essentially a job interview, he told her, and he needed the job badly. Lucy walked with him through the streets around the Inner Harbor while he told her his personal sad story: a divorce, a child he doesn't get to see enough, now a job disappearing. If he doesn't get this job today, he will have to either give up his academic ambitions and take a regular patient-care job, or else move to a new city and see his son only who knows how often. By the time they got to Zach's hotel, he was moving slowly, head down.

Lucy took over, the determined mom. You need a clean shirt and a nicer jacket, she told him, and he said yes, he knew, he had them upstairs. So she bustled him on up to his room, set up the ironing board out of the closet, told him to get busy. She could have ironed the shirt for him, she supposes, but the point of the exercise is that old Zach himself is supposed to get a move on. Not to mention that she doesn't know what shirt and she doesn't want the responsibility; left to herself, Lucy does not iron very much. And for crying out loud, she's just as much a doctor as he is; why should she iron his shirt? She wouldn't iron her own husband's shirts, would she? Anyway, Greg operates on a strict no-iron policy, so she really has no experience with men's dress shirts. *Iron your own shirt, Zach my boy. Put yourself together. Walk like a winner.*

Oh, boy, have you ever seen someone who walks less like a winner than poor old Zach Winkler. "It's no use, anyway," he says sadly. "They aren't going to hire me. No one is going to hire me. Everything I touch turns sour."

Lucy finds she is furious with him—disproportionately furious. He's a friend, but not such a close friend, after all; she's just tagging along with him because they happened to run across each other, here in this city where neither belongs. But now she's having a bad reaction, she's having a you're-so-fucking-privileged-and-entitled moment, because here he is, this guy who can be anything he wants, and he sounds like the number-one victim of the world. Poor put-upon fellow, he couldn't keep his marriage together, he can't hold on to his job, he can't even get out there and fight for a new one. She would like to wipe that self-involved whine right out of his voice. If the hotel window opened, she would like to throw his suitcase out: okay, don't iron your shirt! She imagines stripping off her own clothes: *In that case, Zach, why don't we just have sex? Isn't that what out-of-town colleagues are supposed to do at conferences?* That would probably get him into his nice jacket fast enough.

She flips open the room service menu. "How about two bottles of single-malt scotch. Hell, make it three. Some premium rum. A bottle of bourbon. Some Bombay Sapphire. Think I should get any mixers?" Her voice is shaking, she's so furious at him. It's very unfair; she is suddenly eager to unload on poor dishrag Zach Winkler all this pent-up anger that she didn't even know was there. All about people who are free to invent their own lives and don't, and people who have nothing to work with but still manage, and let me tell you a few things about what it really means when things turn sour.

"Come on," Zach says. "My department is paying for this room."

"Iron your shirt, Zach. Otherwise, I say, Fuck your department. Your department doesn't appreciate you—that's why you're in this mess. Either you take action or I take action, that's the way it is. No more whining. You are going to iron your shirt and change your jacket and then we are going down in the elevator and you are going to go in there and get that job!"

She is not screaming at him, really she isn't. She is trying to keep her voice light, in fact, as if the whole thing were kind of fun. But Zach can definitely hear something else, because the something else is definitely there, and he looks at her nervously the whole time he is ironing, and he disappears into the bathroom to change clothes as if he is glad to get away. And even though she does walk him to the interview, and he does subsequently get the job, Lucy hears about it only through the grapevine; he never e-mails her or calls her or sends her a card.

(Lucy told a version of this story to Greg, who thought it was funny; Isabel was only seven at the time, so it seems unlikely that she registered it, though you never know with Isabel.)

There are these moments when Isabel's mother, Lucy, is more on top of things than anyone, these times when her mother notices things. Like when they were sitting at breakfast at those nice outdoor tables in the *zocalo*, which is, Isabel has to admit, really pleasant in the mornings, before it gets too hot. So they're sitting there—her father was having the tamales stuffed with mole, her brother was having scrambled eggs, which he wasn't eating, big surprise, and her mother was having these tortilla chips in green sauce with fried eggs on top, which she has every morning here in Mexico, like she wasn't a doctor and didn't know about cholesterol, which you learn about in fifth-grade health class, for God's sake (cholesterol is just one among all these bad things that Isabel worries will happen to her parents).

Isabel was having the fruit plate. The musicians were already making the rounds, so some musicians came and played at the next restaurant over, not the one mariachi guy that Isabel's father has this joke going about—this fat guy in a black tuxedo jacket who always sings the same song, "*Oaxaca, Oaxaca, Oaxaca! Oaxaco en mi corazon!*" It means "Oaxaca in my heart," and her father sings it in Isabel's ear all the time, threatening to start singing it loudly, to make her pass the hat among the other tourists. Anyway, the musicians at the next restaurant over were just two guys with guitars, ordinary clothes, not mariachis, but then while they were playing, along came someone to play right in front of the restaurant where Isabel and her family were eating, and it was a blind boy—maybe a teenager—with an odd, innocent expression, tapping along with a white cane. He put the cane down carefully on the sidewalk and took a white wooden recorder out of his backpack and played a slow tune—Isabel didn't recognize it, but her father smiled and said, "I swear, I've heard more Simon and Garfunkel since we've been here!"

Anyway, after he played, he moved clumsily along the tables, collecting tips—and there was this couple one table over who Isabel had been watching—a kind of hippie girl but very pretty with wavy brown hair and a tight, tie-dyed shirt that dipped in a V between her breasts, and a more clean-cut college guy in khakis and a Gap T-shirt—and they had fruit plates, too, which had briefly made Isabel feel good, because she had chosen what college students would choose—beautiful college students with boyfriends. Anyway, as the blind musician groped his way to the next table, still smiling that fixed smile, pocketing the ten-peso coin from Greg, Isabel realized that her mother was watching something. Then she had understood that something worth watching was about to happen.

The college girl has eaten all her fruit except her papaya, which Isabel understands; she doesn't particularly like papaya either. No one in her family does, in fact, except her father, so everyone always leaves him their papaya. As the young blind musician stands smiling by her table, the hippie girl smiles back, the confident, open smile of the beautiful bestowing her beauty—though in this case, of course, the recipient can't see it or appreciate it. She speaks to him in Spanish, quite loudly. "*Quieres a comer?*" she asks, pronouncing each word clearly and separately. "Papaya?"

"She's offering him food," Lucy whispers, whispers so quietly she almost has not made a sound, to Isabel. So quietly that neither Greg nor Freddy, across the table, is even aware that anyone has said anything. Isabel and her mother keep watching. The young man says nothing. He continues to smile, continues to hold out his hand, waiting for a coin. Instead, the girl grabs a piece of bread from the breadbasket on her table and piles it high with papaya slices, saying, as she does so, "*Mis manos son limpios.*"

"She's telling him her hands are clean," Lucy translates for Isabel, who notices that still, neither her father nor her brother knows that anything is going on. Her father is looking around for the waiter, probably to ask for more coffee, and her brother is staring out into space, as usual, over his uneaten eggs. Honestly, he could be a blind boy himself, half the time; he doesn't see a thing. The hippie girl presses the bread and papaya into the blind boy's outstretched hand. Isabel watches his face change: politely puzzled.

"*Pan y papaya,*" says the girl helpfully, closing his fingers around it. The boy stands there a moment longer, and Isabel wonders if he continues to hope for money. She understands absolutely what her mother is pointing out, that the blind boy is not in any way a beggar, that he is a performer like the other musicians who play in the *zocalo*, that he is collecting his fee as the others do after playing—the "*Oaxaca Oaxaca Oaxaca*" man, the other mariachis in their black suits with the silver buttons down the sides of their pants, the marimba band—and now this hippie girl has transformed him into a beggar. A hungry, blind beggar. Isabel also understands, and can almost hear her mother's voice explaining, that the boy is not hungry, or searching for food, and that papaya, if he wants it, is cheap and plentiful—for the pesos that Isabel's father gave him, he could probably buy a whole pile of papayas in the market, where Isabel has seen them, heaped high in giant mounds among the mangoes and melons and chilies, some of them cut open to reveal their vivid orange-red flesh, their black seeds. And most of all, Isabel knows, and knows her mother knows, no one in all Oaxaca, maybe in all Mexico, would eat an open-faced bread and papaya sandwich.

Isabel and Lucy watch together, in perfect understanding, as the bewildered blind boy, still smiling vaguely, steps away from the table—away from the whole row of tables, since clearly he cannot go on collecting with his hand full of papaya. His hand, Isabel thinks, which he uses for the fingering on his recorder, and which is now completely sticky. He makes his way, slowly and carefully, back to his backpack, he manages to get his recorder back inside it, to pick up one strap and wriggle his shoulder into it, to pick up his cane—all still holding what she gave him. And off he goes, walking slowly around the corner, off the *zocalo* and out of sight, carrying his precarious papaya sandwich. And Isabel and Lucy shift their regard to the hippie girl, now leaning close to her boyfriend and smiling with very particular satisfaction.

Three years ago—the Radisson, Minneapolis.

Lucy was okay when she flew out. Got to town not too late and checked in and walked down the street to a restaurant that the concierge recommended and had a perfectly good dinner and read a mystery novel as she ate. Walking back to the hotel, she remembers, she needed a tissue. Used it and then needed another, and was relieved to get back to her room with its fully catered bathroom-tissue dispenser. Took a nice hot shower, and as she got out, felt distinctly for the first time that something was wrong, that she was getting sick. So she put herself to bed relatively early, looked over her notes for the morning talk quickly, and called Greg and said, "I think I might be coming down with a cold," and he said, "What a bummer," but he wasn't really interested; he needed her to tell him where Isabel's new white gym socks were, which by a piece of great good luck, Lucy was able to do: in that big shopping bag of stuff from the hardware store that was still in the corner of the kitchen because they hadn't unpacked it yet. Another catastrophe averted. And Lucy conked out.

She woke in the morning with her head stuffed full of something thick and terrible. Oh well, she told herself, another long, hot shower, some hydrotherapy, and some ibuprofen, and stop in the little gift shop downstairs and see if they have any decongestants. It is only in the hot shower, which does indeed feel therapeutic in the extreme, that she clears her throat, and realizes that she has no voice. Can't be. She attempts a short musical number: "Luck be a lady tonight!" *Croak croak croak.*

Wonderful. A three-day conference with the proverbial multidisciplinary everyone you ever knew, and I speak this morning. Maybe I should get out of the shower and get back in my bed.

But she doesn't. She is one of the academic troupers, Lucy is, neither rain nor sleet nor gloom of night nor stray rhinovirus caught in flight shall stay this lecturer from the prompt presentation of her PowerPoint slides.

She comes back to the hotel room immediately after her lecture. This is no ordinary cold. All the time she was heroically croaking into the turned-up podium mike, she was gripping the podium itself, feeling unsteady on her feet, feeling that at any given minute the floor and ceiling could switch places. Now she closes the door, puts out the DO NOT DISTURB sign, profoundly grateful that in the hour she's been gone, the maid has come in and done the bed. She will take another long, hot shower then conk out on smooth sheets.

All day long Lucy naps restlessly and by afternoon, she is sure, feverishly. Periodically she gets out of bed and stands in that blessed shower to deplete the water supply of the Twin Cities for half an hour or so. Downstairs in the conference center, everyone she ever knew sits through their panels and symposia and keynote address. By evening, she feels even worse, though perhaps a little less dizzy and shaky. Mostly now it's the congestion, and the increasing cough, and some general aches and pains. She gets onion soup from room service, and when it comes she eats so avidly that she calls and orders another one, and a club sandwich, too, but when these arrive, she only makes it through the first half of the sandwich before she starts to feel woozy, and gets back in the shower.

It's the only time she's ever been to Minneapolis, which she will always remember through sheets of hot water, and a fuzzy, dull thickness in her brain.

(Everyone knows this story because Lucy tells it on herself as a joke—*the time I had to give a talk and I couldn't make a sound, the time I discovered what a perfect place to be sick a luxury hotel can be, next time I get the flu, I'm going to go check in to the Copley Plaza or the Westin, anyplace with good water pressure and onion soup on the room service menu.*)

Another thing that does not seem to embarrass her mother, and Isabel does not understand how that can be—the other night they were strolling around the *zocalo* in the dark, with musicians playing at all the different restaurants, and Isabel went walking ahead to look at one of the jewelry stalls. She is thinking maybe about bringing necklaces home to her friends, and she thought she saw some possible necklaces, leather thongs with semiprecious stone pendants, and she wanted her mother to inquire how much they cost. So she turned back and there was Freddy, following close behind her, looking worried—he worries all the time that they will get separated, or that they will miss their flight home—he keeps going over and over the timing of their trip. Anyway, behind Freddy, their parents had paused and they were clearly French kissing. It is one of those moments when Isabel has to think, however fleetingly, about what it means that her parents have chosen to take the two hotel rooms side by side, and what it means then, in the evening, when they have helped Freddy into his pajamas, and read him his book, which he has to hear over and over every single night, that they say goodnight and go to their own room together. She has tried to tell herself that it's no different really from being at home—but it's different. They are paying money every single night to have this room alone together, like they were announcing—advertising!—what they want to do. Though there is also something very reassuring about this; maybe later we will get to Isabel's list of the things she worries will happen to her mother—to her parents—like when Sarah Bellamy's parents were planning and planning to get a divorce, they never told her, and she never heard them fighting, but Isabel would bet they weren't French kissing each other right out in a public place, even in a foreign country, either.

Six years ago—a London hotel.

Greg is apologizing, a little bit helplessly. The woman lying on the bed, who is most definitely not Lucy, keeps crying and crying and crying. He has already said all the things he can think of, and all of them are true: *I was honest—I never promised—I told you how it was.* What she wants to know, which is not something either of them has ever asked before, is whether he ever loved her—and he cannot decide whether the kinder—but also more expedient —response is to say yes, or to say no. He supposes that yes is the truer answer—he was certainly more than a little infatuated, last year, his last research trip, when this all began—but he would be happy to say yes or no or maybe, whichever was kinder, whichever would help.

He has already taken refuge in the expedient and not strictly true—telling her, "My wife found out," when the truer thing would be to say, *I told my wife, and she didn't even seem very surprised. But I only told her because I knew I didn't want to come back and pick things up with you. And I knew I didn't want to pick things up with you when you sent me that three-page e-mail with all the plans you were making for this week, for our time together.* For crying out loud, he doesn't say, I have two lousy weeks here and so much I have to do. And there's a very complicated balance of power inside a marriage, he absolutely can't say, since her own marriage, which was so weighty and counterbalancing last year, has apparently broken up completely, gone *kerfut*, dissolved, and who knows how much Greg did or didn't have to do with that.

But there is—there is a very complicated balance of power, and Greg cannot possibly explain to this weeping woman, who is not in any way the English fling that Lucy accused him of, who is actually a dark, drop-dead beautiful portrait painter from Chicago, teaching in a London art school—and who, a year ago, was married to someone she described as a very successful British museum curator, and Greg rather had the impression that they were something of a power couple in the art world, a world he knows not at all. And the curator was out of town, and Greg was away from home and in England and all the rest—all the guilty but real pleasures of escaping from your life, and your children, however dearly you love them—and there was a three-day thing. She was sharp-edged and a little mysterious, selfish, absorbed in her own life, talking only about commissions and exhibitions and the intrigues of her world. No interest at all in his. And he then went home and eventually he confessed, and thus, he is here now, again, but he is here in the position of owing his wife, bigtime. Bigtime. It is no fun, as all the poets of the centuries know, to be cheated on, but all things considered, it may be slightly worse to be generously forgiven. True, a three-day thing on another continent is hardly the reason to break up a family—but there is this awkwardness about it: Greg cannot just switch around his research, cannot find himself suddenly with a reason to go somewhere other than England, so here he is again, and under heavy obligation to his patient and forgiving wife. Or, to look at it from a different angle, here he is again, with a convenient excuse for brushing off a distraught lover.

The painter, Susannah, sits up on Greg's bed. When he checked in, he deliberately asked for a room with only a single bed. It's a rambling, studenty hotel in Bloomsbury, and there are plenty of oddly shaped rooms, and this one is particularly dim and dingy. When he put down his luggage, he thought with satisfaction that this was certainly no one's cozy little love nest. Not expecting Susannah to be lying in wait, completely ignoring the terse e-mail he had sent her—*I'll be pretty busy, I have a lot of work to do, let's not make any definite plans.* He was kidding himself, clearly he was kidding himself, if he thought she would interpret that as a brush-off; he should have written her the explicit "it's over" e-mail—but he's a little bit paranoid about whether e-mail is really absolutely private, he takes more seriously than perhaps he should that notice he sees every time he logs on, the one that tells him that all his correspondence is the property of the university.

She had called the hotel, she had tracked him down. It's not the kind of hotel where there are phones in every room, and the man from the front desk had to come bang on his door, a little irritably, and Greg had to take the call in the lounge, with a small troop of Australian high school teachers looking on. *Sure,* he said, *it's my first night here, and I'm very jet-lagged, but why don't we meet for dinner, maybe somewhere not too far from here.* He had met her for a pretty good Indian dinner, made determinedly impersonal conversation about the art scene in London, about which he knew absolutely nothing. He pretended fascination and asked for details. She had told him, in tears, about her marriage falling apart. It might have been partly jet lag, but he experienced a very distinct feeling that is much more rarely the subject of the poets of the centuries, but is quite universal for all that: adultery fatigue. This is why we don't cheat on each other, he imagines saying to Lucy, because we'll end up tangled up with other people we don't even really like. And Lucy would say, no doubt, Serves you right—which it does, no doubt. And he would try to say again, You know, I really never do this, even though I'm sometimes tempted, and she would say, I know, and he would wonder again exactly what she does know. And exactly what she does or does not do, and whether she completely believes him, and whether he completely believes her.

But he is exhausted and all he wants in the world is to be in a hotel room alone. He had flown a long way and he has his right and proper share of emotional entanglements, and this is not supposed to be one of them, and he wants to be alone in his hotel room, taking care of himself. Enough. He was too much of a coward to say it in the Indian restaurant, so she accompanied him back to the little room that was so clearly no one's love nest, and there, in private, he finally said to her, "I have to tell you, it's not going to be like it was—my wife has found out—we can't be involved anymore." At which she flung herself down on the bed and cried and cried.

(Lucy knows this story in its very broad outlines, of course—*My wife has found out*—but she has no clear notion of that long and weird jet-lagged night that Greg spent, sitting in the uncomfortable chair beside the bed, wondering what the hell he was going to do next. He had visions of sneaking out of the hotel, checking out, leaving, disappearing into some other part of London, no forwarding address, while Susannah was sleeping her tearstained sleep in his bed. Instead, he finally fell asleep in the chair and woke to find her gone, out of there, never to be seen again, though he looked around him warily every time he left the hotel, every time he came back in.)

Isabel, to her own great surprise, really likes the ruins. They went to Monte Alban on their first day in Oaxaca, and Isabel votes eagerly to go back again on the last day. They have also been to Mitla, and to Yagul. Best of all is that high, strange plateau at Monte Alban, a place where strange and ancient things happened. Isabel thinks a great deal about the ancient Egyptians, though she would be unlikely to admit it. And of course she knows that this place has nothing to do with the ancient Egyptians; after the fifth-grade unit on ancient Egypt, Isabel is fully capable of drawing a map, labeling all major sites, and explaining to you the difference between lower Egypt and upper Egypt. She knows where she is or is not standing. But there is something about being on a place where strange and ancient people lived and worshipped their gods and played their strange games. When she was little, she had a book on the wonders of the ancient world, and each wonder was illustrated with a photo of the ruins that stand today. And then each had an overlay page, a clear plastic page decorated with colors and details—and you overlaid the page on the ruins, and suddenly the Acropolis was whole, and painted, and tiny figures in togas swarmed up and down its steps—that kind of thing. Isabel stands on this big, flat terrace, under the hot sun, and she lets her mind do that, lay over this place with a little overlay page. It would be going too far to say that she is really conjuring specific figures—priests or ballplayers—but she is imagining this place full of color and noise—the all-purpose color and noise that she uses to imagine ancient Egypt, but so what? The important thing is to make the jump to a time when what was here didn't look old or strange. When all the people hurrying across the square were busy on their errands—*I must pick up some bread for dinner, I must hurry and get my new plates, I must stop in at the temple and sacrifice to the gods, I must hurry, I must get there!* That's the amazing thing about ancient Egypt, after all—the idea that once upon a time it wasn't ancient Egypt. They didn't sit around saying to one another, *Hey, we're in ancient Egypt, isn't that weird?* They did what they needed to do, bought food and cooked it and got their work done. And all the time, they were in ancient Egypt.

Okay, so now she is getting confused. She knows that the gods she is imagining here on this hilltop in Mexico actually belong on the banks of the Nile. And she's certainly not trying to say that there is any magical aura about this place—Isabel doesn't hold with magical auras. There was a woman from Oregon on the bus they took this morning out from Oaxaca, a woman older than Isabel's mother, completely dressed in those embroidered clothes that Isabel has successfully said no to all through this trip, and wearing way way too many necklaces, and she started explaining to a couple of German guys, and then louder, like to the whole bus, about spiritual energy and what she called "wise old places" and about her plans to find a little altar on Monte Alban where she could arrange a certain set of crystals she had brought with her all the way from Portland—and she showed off a small purple velvet bag—and in this way focus the energy of all the wise old souls who had charted the heavens in ages long past. At which point she began telling the German guys, who were totally trapped—even from across the aisle, Isabel could see that clearly—about the amazing astronomical achievements of the ancient Mexicans. And Isabel, checking first in her father's guidebook and then in the thick paperback book that he carries everywhere, was delighted to find that the woman had no idea what she was talking about. Also, as you might expect, she got astronomy confused with astrology.

Isabel's father is still making jokes about that woman, mostly about what the wise ancient Mexicans would do with her and her crystals, and most of these involve the sacred ball court and human sacrifice. Her mother, who was sitting in the seat behind them with Freddy, caught it all, and of course has whispered to Isabel, "Admit it, I'm not the most embarrassing lady on the bus—I left my crystals at home, after all." Neither the German guys nor the Portland lady are anywhere to be seen, but this is a very big place; Greg did an imitation of the two German guys hiding behind a pyramid, asking each other, "Was ist das?"

But her father also helps Isabel, with the aid of the guidebook, and another small booklet he purchased at the gift shop right here, and together they identify every single major building on the plateau at Monte Alban, working their way around the South Platform, though Isabel finds it mildly irritating that the buildings are not labeled consistently; just when you've found Building M and Building J, you have to start looking for Building IV. But this is how her father likes to sightsee, working his way around with a map and two guidebooks, inch by inch—and she understands that there is something a little unusual about it, that her mother teases him because it's just all part of being a professor—in fact, she calls him Professor when he starts worrying over whether that's Tomb 104 off over there on the hillside, when isn't one tomb just the same as another to him? But Isabel gets it, and she doesn't need crystals to imagine the streets full of people, and the dry green lawns, the sun-baked stones all alive with color.

Isabel and her dad join Lucy and Freddy, who fell by the wayside as they pursued their identifications, and are now sitting in a little patch of shade, looking down at the ball court. Greg triumphantly lays out the geography of the grand plaza, as he and Isabel have determined it, and Lucy listens, nods.

"Do you remember being here before—does it seem familiar? Not from earlier this week, I mean, from sixteen years ago?"

"Of course." Lucy smiles at him, and Isabel can see it's kind of private. Then it's almost like he's asking her a question, she's nodding.

"You know, kids," he says, "your mother agreed to marry me right here, at Monte Alban."

"I thought you said in a hotel room," Freddy protests, before Isabel can say it.

"Ah, that was where I asked her. She didn't say yes right away. She said yes at Monte Alban."

Lucy shrugs. "On the sacred ball court, naturally. After consulting my crystals."

Isabel thinks about her parents before they were her parents —not as long ago as ancient history, of course. Still, she can almost imagine the plastic overlay—the painted page that would insert her long-ago not-married parents into Monte Alban, tiny, brightly colored, almost mythological figures among the ruins.

10

Good Judgment

WHEN THE WOMAN at Ruth's Refuge answers the phone, I am already angry. I already sound impatient and harsh, a first-class bitch. An arrogant doctor. And I don't care. "This is *Dr. Weiss*," I tell her, and I give her the name I wrote down on the back of Delia's lab slip. I need to speak with Caroline. Right away. And when I get Caroline, I'm still mad. I want to shake her and scare her and ruin her whole fucking day. And you can quote me on that.

"This is Dr. Weiss. I'm calling in regard to Delia Devereaux. I understand that you are her official prenatal care provider of record, and I have some very important questions."

There. If by any chance this woman is some remote kind of medical professional, she will know I am talking nonsense—there is no such thing as an "official prenatal care provider of record." There is no reason for me to be calling.

But she doesn't know anything. She has a voice I don't like, a voice with a slight bray to it, a voice that I could easily imagine sounding officious and pushy, but she doesn't sound like that now.

She sounds nervous and concerned. And she's giving me information without asking me any questions at all, a sure sign that she is not part of any real medical establishment.

"It's true that Delia has come here for help, Doctor, but I'm not in any way doing her prenatal care," she says.

"You're *not?*" I try to make it as accusing as I can. "Then I don't understand. Delia herself identified you as her provider of prenatal care—and of counseling, I might add. It was my understanding that you and your agency—and I have to admit I'm not familiar with your agency—but it was my understanding that you were fully responsible."

"We aren't—we can't be medically responsible at all," says Caroline. "We don't provide medical services. The mothers have to get medical services elsewhere."

As I suspected. You are a right-wing, born-again, fundamentalist, right-to-life front organization that lures in fucked-up young women with your warm and fuzzy billboards, and then you show them nasty pictures of dismembered fetuses and promise them a pair of booties, is that it? Well, honey, let me tell you, you have won the jackpot now! Delia Devereaux is quite possibly the most fucked-up young woman in all Boston this week.

"I just saw Delia this morning," I say, severely. "I am the physician of record for her children. You know her children? All three of them?" You know, I think but do not say, the ones named for *The Sound of Music?*

"Well, I've met them, when she's been in for help—"

"Right, so you know them. So when she brought them in today, she happened to mention this new pregnancy, and I have some very serious medical concerns about her, and I need to be absolutely sure she's getting the care she needs, and the counseling she needs—for her sake, for the sake of those three kids." I stop, I take a deep breath. My voice is too loud and too angry. I am too close to saying, *Listen, you turnip-brained earthworm, don't you see that this poor pathetic woman's one and only slender, tiny chance of hanging on to those three little kids is if she* doesn't *have another baby? Don't you understand that she's going to lose everything? Don't you understand that I'm the one who will have to take it all away?*

"Doctor, I told you, we are not a medical agency. I always tell the mothers to get services for that at a medical agency."

"Yes, that's all very well, but when I asked her who was doing her prenatal care, she gave me your name and your number. And when I asked about counseling, she said you were doing that, too. And I better tell you, I think it's pretty close to criminal malpractice if she's not getting the counseling she needs."

"Doctor!" Caroline's voice is louder, a little more desperate, and she cuts me off. "We can't be responsible. We can't—it can't be malpractice when no one here is even a doctor or a nurse. I *tell* them to go get prenatal care, I tell them it's important for their babies. And I know what you mean about Delia, she clearly needs a little extra help, but it's not something we can provide here, it's not our mission."

"So just what *is* your mission?" I can't help it—I should shut up, I have nothing to gain and nothing to prove—but I can't shut up. "You do no medical care, you provide no counseling—what exactly is it that you do?"

"We provide resources and support to pregnant women," Caroline says, clearly back on familiar ground and happy to be there. "Especially to women with unintended pregnancies who lack other networks of support."

"And what exactly does that mean you're going to do for Delia?"

"I'm on the track of a crib for her," Caroline says proudly. "Brand-new."

Delia, when she told me about the pregnancy, asked me to keep it a dead secret. We were in the tiny and crowded exam room: me and Delia and her three kids, the four-month-old in her car seat, the two-year-old sitting quietly on the floor in the corner, sucking on a bottle, the three-year-old stripped down to her underpants on the exam table so I could look carefully at her rash.

The rash was actually kind of dramatic. Lizelle's whole stomach and chest were a bright, angry red with blotches and bumps and even a few concentric pale rings. I had just pointed one of those out to Delia, and said to her, "We call those target lesions—see how they look a little like targets?" And was getting ready to go on about how they probably meant Lizelle was having a bad allergic reaction to something—and then I would have to grill Delia some more about what medications she might have given the kid—she had already denied giving her any, but it would turn out that Lizelle had had a fever and she had found some old not-quite-used-up bottle of antibiotics left over from Curt's last ear infection, and then it would turn out that Lizelle was seriously allergic to amoxicillin and I would have to update her chart and give Delia yet another lecture on how dangerous it was to give a child medicine from someone else's prescription—and I could see it all scrolling out in front of me, predictable and irritating and here-we-go-again, when Delia leaned forward across her daughter's hot red body and whispered to me, "Hey, Dr. Lucy, guess what?"

Delia has no boundaries. That is what we say about her. One of the things we say about her. She tells everything to everyone, she asks everything of everyone. *Can I use the phone here to make a long-distance call, can you let me take a bunch of those lollipops for later, and maybe a big box of those Band-Aids, and those cute little alcohol wipes, you know I use them for taking off my eye makeup, or is that bad, do you think that will dry out my skin and make me look old, can you hold the baby while I go and wash off in your bathroom 'cause I'm really sweaty, do you think I should get my nose pierced, should I marry Andrew now that he's asking me or do you think it's a bad idea, should I go out with this new guy even though Andrew says he'll kill me, do you think I look like Jennifer Lopez when I wear my hair like this?* So it's no surprise that she asks me, clear and straight, "Do you think I should have the new baby or do you think I should get rid of it?" Then she interrupts herself, looking at me earnestly, and she answers for me: "You think I should get rid of it, Dr. Lucy, don't you? That's what you think, I know it is."

What surprises me is that I answer her. "Yes, Delia, that's what

I think." I take a deep breath. I have never never never in my life said such a thing to a patient before. I have presented the options, I have voiced my concerns, I have probably made it clear many times what I secretly believe would be best, but I have never told a patient—or a patient's mother—to end a pregnancy. "You've already got more than you can handle. I worry a lot that if you add in another baby, while these three are still so young and you don't have good housing and you're all on your own—well, it's just going to be too much." Plus you're crazy and your boyfriend is a bastard and a thug—but I don't say that, of course. I still have a boundary or two. But there is something about Delia—sometimes she makes me think of my child self, lost in the world and waiting to be saved, and sometimes it is her children who remind me of that self, and all in all, it makes me crazy that I am going to be the one to do what I am going to have to do: report her for neglect, for incompetence, for being Delia.

She grabs Lizelle up off the examining table and clutches her dramatically. Delia is pretty. She looks younger than she really is—I suppose because she doesn't think too long or too hard about any of the things that ought to worry her and age her. She has smooth, pale skin and long, heavy hair, brown and rich and highlighted with honey, full breasts and a little potbelly. Inevitably, after three kids in three years, and with another one on the way.

Lizelle, bright red with rash and reaction, screams as her mother holds her a little too tight. "You think they're going to take my kids away?"

Delia, I think *I'm* going to take your kids away, goddamn it. But I don't say that. I am calculating—how many damn kids are there in that movie, anyway? Six? Seven? Is it possible that Delia is determined to go on until she has an exact matching family, all named with her best approximation of the von Trapps? *Do re mi fa so la ti do*—don't tell me there were eight kids!

"Delia, I know you're doing your best, but there's just no way you can manage another child. It's too much. No money, no job, no family support, no help from the father . . ."

"He gave me a necklace, you wanna see, Dr. Lucy? It's a real pretty one!" She is fumbling with the buttons of her shirt.

"But he doesn't help you with the kids. You're on your own, with a lousy housing situation, with three kids under four already—and frankly, I think your best chance for holding on to your kids and keeping things together is if you *don't* have another baby right now. It's just going to be too much." I pause, knowing she doesn't like this question. "Are you seeing a counselor?"

"You think I'm crazy! You're saying you think I'm crazy!"

I swing into my little speech about how much stress she's under—how hard she's working—and, so help me, what a great job she's doing, what a great mother she is to her children. I just want her to get support, I say. And that's when she tells me about Ruth's Refuge, assuring me that she gets her care and counseling there, and I become suspicious. "No, really, Dr. Lucy," she says. "I have a great counselor there—her name is Caroline. She's really really nice to me." And I ask her whether they're doing her prenatal care there as well, and Delia nods. Oh, yes, she says, they're doing everything. Oh Delia, I think, they will talk salvation, but they will not save you. And I think about her children let loose into the foster care system, and then about children for whom that system is no refuge—the children who died last summer, whose school pictures looked out for days from the front page. *Oh Delia, why won't you let someone really save you?*

And meanwhile, there is this miserable-looking kid, naked between us, red with this awful rash. I start to ask her about what medicines Lizelle has been exposed to—I start to explain that I cannot be absolutely sure why her skin looks like this, and it may be a drug reaction, but it may also be a strep infection. I switch over to kindly doctor mode, and I tell her that reaction or infection, this could be a dangerous rash, that we have to watch Lizelle carefully, make sure she keeps drinking, that I need to see her back tomorrow morning to check her. Delia is nodding and nodding and not listening at all. She hears something to react to: tomorrow morning.

"Tomorrow morning I might go to a studio that someone told me about and do a video of myself," she tells me, happily, while she buttons Lizelle back into her blue and white striped dress. Delia's children are always beautifully dressed. "Like a screen test!" Delia's own special brand of magical thinking.

"Delia, did you hear what I said? Tomorrow morning you need to bring Lizelle back here to see me so I can check on her rash. If it gets worse, if it spreads, it could be dangerous to her—it could mean we have to put her in the hospital!"

Delia's excited smile crumbles. Instantly, she is in tears. "I don't want my baby in the hospital, Dr. Lucy! She can't stand to be away from her mom! You know, she still sleeps with me—they all sleep with me."

"Just bring her in tomorrow, that's all. She'll probably be fine." I pause. I choose not to pursue the question of their sleeping arrangements. "Is it okay with you if I call your counselor at that place—" I look down at my notes. "Caroline. At Ruth's Refuge? I'd just like to check in with her about whether you're getting all the services you need."

"You think I'm making it all up, Dr. Lucy? You don't think I'm really going there? You think I'm crazy, don't you? You know, I might be getting a car! I know this guy who said he could help me get one, and if I had a car, I could come to all those appointments right on time. I have to call this guy back, because I need to get that car."

"Delia, I want to check in with your counselor. I'm worried about you. I want to make sure you're getting all the care and all the help you need." I fall back on a line I often use, probably not exactly applicable here, but handy all the same. "I just worry that you're so busy taking care of everybody else that you don't always get taken care of yourself, you know what I mean?"

Delia nods, her glowing cascade of hair swinging gracefully around her face. She lowers her voice. "Dr. Lucy, just don't tell anyone else here about, you know—about me being pregnant? 'Cause if I do decide to get rid of the baby—"

"You don't want anyone knowing," I say, reassuringly, buoyed up by the thought that maybe, despite whatever they have told her at Ruth's Refuge, there is some small chance that Delia is going to think this through and save herself. "Don't worry, I won't tell anyone. We can discuss this again tomorrow, when you come in. You know I only want to help you—and the kids."

"I know that, Dr. Lucy." Disconcertingly, Delia gives me a big, affectionate hug. I pat her back, slightly awkward. They don't teach you this one in medical school: how to react to the hug from the patient with the borderline personality disorder whose children, you see more and more clearly, you will have to take away from her before something terrible happens to them. So I pat her back. Then, still smiling beatifically, she slings her big tote bag over her shoulder, picks up baby Louisa in her car seat carrier, grabs Curt's hand and pulls him to a standing position, and gestures to Lizelle to take Curt's hand. And out the door they go. And I am left wondering whether I am identifying with Delia or with her children, when really I represent some completely different authority. I am power, I am separation, I am the world and its standards—but I don't think I can save anyone right now.

And back they come the next day, with Lizelle's rash no better, though I am very discouraged when Mary Ann, the head nurse, suggests to me that I check out what is going on in the waiting room, and I poke my head out to find Delia over at the reception desk, proudly showing all three receptionists—and an interested random mother and someone I think is a social worker from the hematology clinic down the hall—some early ultrasound pictures of her new baby, the one inside her belly. The one she's going to name Gretel, if it's a girl.

When the head of the middle school answered the phone, I played it very carefully. I hadn't had a great deal to do with her since Isabel started sixth grade and moved into the middle school in September, but I had heard she was okay. Reasonable. Nobody's fool. Genuinely liked middle-school-age kids. Ran a pretty tight ship. And this was an unfamiliar position for me to be in, in so many ways. Calling up the school on an Isabel-related subject, instead of one of my perennial Freddy-has-a-problem calls. Calling up the school under so many strictures and prohibitions set by my daughter. Calling up to turn someone in. It did occur to me, as I waited on musical hold for the secretary to connect me with the middle school director, that it was not in every way an unfamiliar *kind* of call for me— I mean, I'm always calling up somewhere to report someone. Kid at risk, parent decompensating, school not delivering services. Well, especially the first; I spend my life judging who's at risk, and when someone is, I have to call.

I said that to the head of the middle school. "My daughter really didn't want me to call," I said, "and I have to ask you to keep this absolutely confidential. But I am worried about the physical safety of one of the girls in the sixth grade. I am worried that her anorexia is out of control, and I am a physician, and I had to explain to my daughter that girls with out-of-control anorexia can have arrhythmias and fall down dead, and that I have no choice." I took a deep breath and gave her the name. "My daughter says that this girl's parents have no idea that this is going on," I continued, "and of course I don't know whether or not that's really true. But I had to call and tell you. I don't have any choice."

That was actually my argument to Isabel, who believes strenuously in following all rules. I had taken her out to the coffee shop on the corner over the weekend. I had a precious little china pot of their fancy tea, which they make by filling a little gauze bag to order with tea leaves, basically creating a six-dollar tea bag. And I insisted on ordering Isabel a cup of hot chocolate, which she has loved since she was small, and she sat there looking at it and sniffing it, and finally condescending to sip it. I said to her, "I brought you here so we could talk in private—I know you worry at home, and I know you want this kept secret." She nodded, and she took another infinitesimal sip. I said to her, "Do you know what a 'mandated reporter' is?" She shook her head. "Try and guess," I said, knowing that Isabel, no matter what, always wants to be the one with the right answer.

"It means you have to report things," Isabel said. "I guess." She didn't want to look at me. I wanted to hug her—as I often do these days, and, as I often do these days, I refrained. In my imaginings, she relaxes into my embrace, she slumps slightly against me, she lets go of some number of her grudges and her worries and her careful, secret scorekeeping. But those are my imaginings; in reality, I think, she would hold herself more tightly, at most, she would perhaps pat me gently, as I patted Delia. And anyway, as I tell myself, and as I truly do believe, Isabel is entitled to build and hold her defenses. Why am I so intent on getting her to relax them? She is a very smart eleven-year-old girl, struggling with puberty and pressure and all the rest of it; let her hold herself as carefully as she wants.

"What kind of things do you think I have to report?" I said. *Come on, Isabel, go for the perfect test paper and the extra-credit points! And for heaven's sake, take another sip of your hot chocolate!*

She does take a sip. Then another. "Like if people get infections? Like measles or something?"

"Well, yes," I said, "I do have to report certain contagious diseases. That's certainly true. The Department of Public Health makes you report them and provide all kinds of information—though, to be honest, measles would be a really really big deal, since kids are supposed to be immunized against measles nowadays. That would probably make the newspapers." I can't help it, I'm starting to lecture. Sometimes it seems as if all conversations with Isabel carry this risk—I can't quite connect with her, so I try to inform her, almost as if I'm trying to establish my credentials: *Listen to me, I'm an expert.* I swallow. Okay, no more questions. Test's over.

I got up and went to the counter. The young woman had four or five piercings in each ear, one through her left eyebrow, one in her nose. I didn't want to know about her tongue; for whatever reason, rational or not, I object to food service workers with pierced tongues. I gestured at the big chocolate chip cookies, hoping she wouldn't speak. "One?" she asked. Her tongue was intact. I asked for two cookies, paid for them, and brought them back to our table. Yes, I know. I don't need the cookie. Isabel regards my weight as clear evidence of my lack of self-discipline—and you know what? She's right. She also struggles hard to regulate her own appetites, and that should be respected. On the other hand, she has an endearingly childish sweet tooth, and she and her friends will surgically push every tiny bit of mashed potato aside on their dinner plates, then order brownie sundaes, and I wanted something sweet between us. I tried not to watch her as she broke off teeny-tiny pieces of cookie and nibbled them, one by one.

"'Mandated reporter' actually means something else," I say. "It's the legal term for people who are absolutely required by law to report any kind of child abuse or neglect, if they suspect it. Pediatricians. Teachers. Daycare workers. If you're Joe Schmoe, and you sometimes wonder whether your neighbor is abusing his kids, well, you can report it or not. I mean, if you seriously think something bad is going on, of course you should report it, but the point is, you aren't breaking any law if you wonder about it but you decide not to report it. I am—I'm breaking the law, because I'm a mandated reporter. It's part of my professional responsibility—if I think a child may be at risk, I have to call it in. I have to."

Isabel looked at least interested, thank the Lord. Interested enough to ask a question. So I wasn't boring her, and she hadn't shut me out, and I hadn't embarrassed her by talking too vehemently in the coffee shop or by eating a cookie in public. "Well, why wouldn't you?" she asked. "I mean, why wouldn't you report it?"

"Good question," I said, and she actually smiled. Bonus points. "You might be worried that the investigation would do more harm than good—you might think that this particular mother was really doing her best, and you might like her, and you might be afraid that by reporting her, you would undermine your own relationship with her, and you would undermine her confidence as a mother—"

"But if she's doing her best, why is she abusing her kid?"

"Well, the thing is, Isabel, child abuse can be hard to define. If she tells you that last night she lost her temper and really let the kid have it—even used a belt on him—is that always child abuse?"

Isabel, who likes rules, nodded.

"What if last night the baby had a fever, and she called the emergency line, just like she's supposed to, and I called in a prescription for baby Motrin, because that way the Medicaid will pay for it, and she went out to get it right away, just like she was supposed to, but the baby had fallen asleep and she didn't want to wake her, so she left the baby alone in the apartment in her crib—was that child abuse?"

Isabel considered, judged, and issued her opinion: No. I didn't complicate the issue by telling her that actually, technically, that is child neglect—and probably grounds for removing the child from the home. I nodded and watched her break off another piece of her cookie. I thought she was interested, I thought she was ready for the next question.

"What about if she ran into someone she knows in the drugstore and went to get a beer with him, and meanwhile the baby woke up and started screaming and her landlord was waiting for her outside the apartment door when she got back, an hour later, and he told her if she can't keep that kid quiet, he's going to kick them both out?"

Now my daughter looked shocked. Something bad and scary had come into the coffee shop, and my daughter's judgment had changed. Whether it was the male friend, the beer, the screaming baby—now she was ready to prosecute that mother and take the baby away for good. And rightly so. Except, of course, that I knew the mother who actually told me this story, through her tears the next day, when she had brought the baby in, perfectly appropriately, so I could examine her and figure out what was causing that high fever. And the mother was Delia, back three years ago, when Lizelle was her only child. And the story was so much more complicated than that—she left the baby sleeping because she'd been crying so much and feeling so hot and Delia couldn't bear to wake her, and then when she got to the pharmacy, it turned out the baby's Medicaid card wasn't any good so they wanted her to pay for the prescription, and she only had two dollars, one a bill and one in change, because she thought all she would have to pay was the

Medicaid co-pay, and so she got really upset and she told the pharmacist all about Lizelle being sick and the doctor calling in the medicine, and the pharmacist was really really mean and rude, and he said, "Lady, this isn't even a prescription drug, you're wasting your doctor's time and my time when you should be just buying it over the counter anyway"—or at least, she thinks that's what he was saying because he was Chinese or something and she could hardly understand him, and she doesn't think they should let people be pharmacists if they can't speak English, and anyway she was crying and she went out of that place and first thing, she ran into this guy she used to know and she asked him if he had any cash and he said he didn't but he was just going to meet a friend in a bar and the friend should have money so she went with him and it turned out the bar was really a long way away and he got them lost getting there and then when they did get there, his friend wasn't even there yet so he said they should have a beer, and she asked him how come if he didn't have money for the medicine, he had money for beers, and he said he had like a tab at this place, you know? And finally his friend did come and then, can you believe it, his friend didn't even want to give her the money, but he finally did and she went back to the drugstore and told that stupid rude Chinese or maybe he was Vietnamese guy to give her the Motrin and she went home . . . and on and on and on. I didn't say any of this to Isabel, and not the long part about what an evil guy the landlord was and how he was always coming on to Delia, either.

I hadn't known Delia very long at that time—her child was only six months old. I knew that she was already an open DSS case—her first 51a had been filed in the nursery when Lizelle was born, because of things she told the obstetrician, because of her lack of prenatal care, because of her somewhat menacing boyfriend who had threatened one of the nurses. I should have filed again after that story about leaving the baby alone in the apartment, but I didn't. I still had some hope, at that point—still believed in Delia's ability to remake herself and get some help and parlay her true strengths—her engaging, likable energy, her beauty, her desire to please—into some kind of successful childhood for Lizelle. I imagined her in therapy, on medication. Maybe even back in school. What I didn't realize yet was that by the time Lizelle was six months old, Delia was already pregnant again. Curt was on the way, and Delia was on her way exactly nowhere.

Isabel was studying me closely. Her hot chocolate was drunk, her cookie was half-eaten, and she was waiting for me to speak, but I had gotten off the subject, in my roundabout way of explaining to her something completely different. And I had gotten myself off the subject as well; I was deep in memories of my early days with Delia, before it was clear to me—as it is now clear to me—that Delia is going to lose all her children, and that I am destined to be the agent of that loss. It came crashing down on me as I finished my own cookie.

"Isabel, after what you told me, I have to call your school. I have to. I don't have any choice. That's what I'm trying to tell you here. I'm sorry, I'm making things more complicated than they need to be. I don't have any choice—I'm a doctor, I take care of kids, and after what you said, I have to do one of two things—I either call the school or I call Emma's parents. And I take it you'd rather have me call the school. And I think you knew that when you told me—I think, whether you know it or not, that's *why* you told me."

And across the little teetery table, my daughter nodded, just once, and took a normal bite of her cookie.

Here is how I imagine it looking in the report that Delia's social worker writes up. Well, why borrow someone else's jargon? Here is how it looks in the note that I type into Lizelle's chart: *Patient was brought in by mother today for follow-up on rash; mother informed medical assistant that child had been afebrile and drinking well yesterday but felt very warm and seemed less hungry this morning, but that she felt the rash looked just as bad. Patient's mother then asked the medical assistant if she would keep an eye on the patient and her two siblings while she, mother, ran down to the lobby and got something for the children and herself to eat; none of them had had any food this morn-*

ing because she had no food in the house. The medical assistant agreed, but told her to hurry, and told her how to get to the cafeteria . . . When the mother had been gone for fifteen minutes, the medical assistant informed me of the situation. When the mother had been gone for a full half-hour, and after another of the medical assistants had gone to check in the cafeteria, without being able to find the patient's mother, a call was placed to the mother's regular DSS worker, Michael Harmon. After hearing the story, he suggested that I file a 51a reporting the mother. I pointed out that multiple 51a's have already been filed, by me twice and by several other people, and that they have all been substantiated after investigation by DSS, and that the result of this process was his involvement in this family's life. He suggested again that I file a new one so it could be investigated . . .

"You don't need to investigate it," I had said. "There's nothing to investigate. It's not like there's any conceivable reason it could show *good* judgment to hand your kids over to the medical assistant and disappear. It's just more of the same typical behavior here, and all the concerns are still the same. I'll fill out the form one more time, if you like, but meantime, you're the person who knows this family, and I need to know what you're going to do. If she shows up here, are we giving her the kids back? And how long are we waiting for her to show up, how long do you want to give her?"

And at that point, of course, he decided to go talk to his supervisor.

The MAs had set the three kids up in an empty exam room. The baby, Louisa, was asleep in her car seat. Curt was playing with a toy farm that someone had donated to the waiting room—all the colorful plastic animals had long since disappeared, but he was rolling a little car into the barn and back out, again and again, and he seemed happy. The MAs had brought in a pile of hospital-issue graham crackers and a container of apple juice. The one who was watching over the kids was a Haitian woman about my age, Monique, a churchgoing mother of three. She was gentle with the kids, but she had very little patience with the moms, and she often thought that I was ridiculously soft. Sometimes I found myself wanting to tell her the story of how I grew up—of the people in the clinic, only Mary Ann, the head nurse, knows that I did time as a foster child, and she only knows the little bit I say in my standard lecture.

But what would I be proving to Monique by letting her know I haven't always been comfortable and privileged and loved? I can't imagine she would be impressed; Monique, I suppose, is in that category of people who have struggled themselves—she'd emigrated, she'd lived poor, she'd worked hard to keep her kids clean and respectable and God-fearing and doing well in their parochial schools. It took plenty of hours worked on a medical assistant's salary to pay for those schools. *No one said it was supposed to be easy* is more or less engraved on her heart, embroidered on her banner. She looked at me as I stood in the doorway, watching Curt play with his car, wondering if this was his first ever moment with a toy.

"What are you going to do, Doctor?" she asked me. "You're not going to let that woman come back here and take these babies, are you?"

"I've already talked to her DSS worker," I said. I lifted Lizelle up to the exam table, where her rash looked even more disturbingly red against the stark white paper. "I need to get a look in her mouth."

Monique chuckled softly. "So of course she'll never cry."

"Never." I reached over and snagged a tongue depressor. I didn't like the look of Lizelle's lips, and I didn't like the look of the inside of her mouth, when I got her to open it at last. I straightened up, still holding the little girl down on the exam table, where she cried, lips together, silently, unwilling to give me any other chances at her open mouth.

"Anyway," I said, "I'm going to admit Lizelle to the hospital. Her mucous membranes are slightly dry, this damn rash gets worse and worse—and she just doesn't look good. She needs IV fluids; she needs bloodwork. Let me go call the ward team and let them know. And then I'll call the DSS guy back and tell him, if he hasn't figured it out yet, that he needs to take emergency custody. I'm sorry you're stuck with the kids, Monique—I don't know how long it will take them to get here."

Monique shook her head and smiled. Somehow, while I was torturing Lizelle, she had enticed shy little Curt onto her lap, and he sat cuddled against her, chewing on a graham cracker, scattering crumbs all over her colorful scrub jacket, printed with rainbows and ice cream cones.

"You have to see it the way she did," Monique said, surprising me. "That mother, she must think, 'What a safe, clean place this is! All these nice, helpful ladies who tell you your baby is so cute. All those staff people in that clinic, what do all those people have to do anyway? There's so many of them, and there's so much stuff there for the kids.' All those medicines, even. She probably thought, 'Why can't they just watch my kids for a little while, they got nothing better to do and my kids will be so safe.' That's what she probably thought."

"You're right," I said. "In a way it shows really good judgment, leaving her kids with us instead of with some sleazy friends who don't know anything about kids, or with some other incompetent mother who's already totally overwhelmed." Both things that Delia had done, in her time. Things she had gotten into trouble for doing. Apparently, she had learned her lesson. She was now leaving her children in the care of trained professionals. "You're right, Monique," I said again. "I mean, she's right if she thinks the kids will be safe here. They will."

Monique smiled at me, a little bit sadly, and she stroked Curt's smooth head. He went right on eating graham crackers. I let Lizelle sit up on the exam table, then looked at Monique again and took Lizelle in my arms. I wiped the snot off her face, which was covered in the red rash.

"I don't know where that lady has gone," Monique said. "I don't know what she is thinking, if she is thinking anything at all."

"I'll go and call," I said. I was thinking about all the times over the past three years that I had called on Delia—or thought about calling and then not called. I was wondering where the hell she'd gone—had she wandered into some other part of the hospital complex and was she now playing video games on the adolescent ward, or stealing little packaged pudding cups, or telling some bewildered maintenance man somewhere about her screen test? Or God forbid, had she actually left the hospital and gone off chasing that screen test, figuring, as Monique said, that the children were safe and well cared for?

Either way, what would she say when she came back to find her children gone, removed from her custody, one of them hospitalized, two of them taken away by DSS? I can't exactly explain why I flinched from the thought, why it seemed to me that it would be up to me to face her with explanations. Monique would be able to stare her down, I thought, Monique would be outraged by the way that Delia had gone off and left her kids behind, and she would face Delia with certainty, with severity, with well-warranted moral righteousness. The DSS workers would feel completely entitled to do what they did. The ward team would pass along the story of maternal neglect and cluck and cluck, like the fresh-faced twenty-seven-year-olds they were. Only I, for some reason, was compelled to stand here, holding her abandoned, feverish, rash-covered daughter, and quail inside at the thought of what we were doing. Only I kept thinking of the moments—and they have never been infrequent—when Delia brings all her energy and attention to bear on her children, loving them and hugging them and tickling them and kissing them, and they respond with joy. When Delia is thinking of her children, she is all they could want. No one else—no foster parent—will ever match the sheer delight of those moments, I suspect. On the other hand, no foster parent, we hope, will ever wander into a department store, sit down at a cosmetic counter for a makeover, and end up spending every single penny of her recently cashed monthly check on a big bag of fancy makeup—and then try to trade in two of the fifteen-dollar eye shadows for diapers at her local CVS. (I have a terrible confession to make about that particular episode: I not only gave Delia three packs of clinic diapers, when she turned up, in tears, in my exam room later that day, to tell me that the kids were hungry and she was all out of money, and the guy in the drugstore was so crazy he didn't understand what a good deal she was offering him—she had paid thirty dollars for those eye shadows, and she was offering to trade them for maybe nineteen dollars' worth of diapers, and she hadn't even touched the eye shadows, not once—as I say, I not only passed her some diapers, but I also bought the two goddamn eye shadows, handed her a twenty and a ten, not the first time I've slipped some cash across the desk to Delia, and not the last. And then, after she was gone, I called her DSS worker and told the whole story.)

No, it's clear enough what has to happen. I'm not arguing. The truth is, for some time, I've been waiting for DSS to step in and take custody of these kids. Hoping, maybe, that they weren't going to leave it up to me, but knowing that in the end, it would be my job to do.

I carried Lizelle with me into my office, sat at my desk with the little girl on my lap. She had stopped crying. I gave her a lollipop, then called out to another of the medical assistants to bring me a Popsicle, since after all she needed her fluids. When the Popsicle came and Lizelle began sucking on it, she relaxed against me, just a little tiny bit, and I thought, fleetingly, of Isabel, and of what on earth my daughter would make of this whole situation—the mother gone off again somewhere, the child so strangely sick-looking, the Popsicle dripping on my shirt, the call that I had tried to explain in the coffee shop that I was required to make. I thought about the machinery I had put into play by calling the head of my daughter's middle school: the school nurses and school psychologists, the parents and the doctors and the counselors. I wondered whether anyone would ever find out who had told, whose mother had called—the middle school director had assured me that she would keep it absolutely confidential; in fact, she said, she always found it more useful in these cases to tell the parents that the information was based on direct teacher observation. "Do you have many of these cases?" I had asked, and she had said, "Oh yes, what

with the eating disorders and the cutting and the occasional suicide threat, there's never a dull moment—but you probably know
all about that, Doctor."

Lizelle dripped more liquid Popsicle onto my shirt. I dialed the
number and listened to the phone ringing. It seemed to me that I
had spent my life like this, on the end of a useless phone. I paged
the admitting intern and hung up the phone, waiting for her to
call me back. I would tell her what she needed to know, I would
tell her that no, Lizelle could not be admitted through the emergency room because there were social service issues, there was no
accompanying parent. Come over to clinic and admit her, I would
say, severely, and they would grumble, because it was a little irreg-
ular, but they would do it. And while we were waiting for them, I
would make the other call and set things in motion, so that Delia's
children would be removed from her care. She would come back
for them later in the day, I was sure. Personally, I thought she had
probably gone to make that video—and as it turned out later, I was
right. But she would come back to claim her children, certain that
we would have taken good care of them—and they would not be
here anymore, they would not be hers anymore. I would have done
it. She would have done it. They would be gone.

11

Social Baseball

T HERE IS ONLY ONE billionaire kid in the second grade, and he is not doing a very good job in left field for the Braves. Half the time, in fact, Thomas is looking away from the game, scanning the street behind the ball field for something — for the ice cream truck, maybe, or for one of his billionaire parents, who are late to the game. The Braves coach repeatedly calls to him to turn around and pay attention, but Lucy also notices him quietly reminding the third baseman, Amir Patel, to keep an eye out if anything goes back into left field toward Thomas. Amir, a fourth-grader at the public school, is one of the few reliable fielders, capable of stopping the occasional ground ball, catching a weak pop fly, and even catching a ball thrown his way by one of the few other reliable fielders, one of whom, to Lucy's great astonishment, is her own son, Freddy. Who is standing now at second base, pounding his glove, skinny and shrimpy in his uniform, positively swallowed up in his Braves T-shirt, face obscured by new and unfairly thick glasses, looking like everybody's easy strikeout, like the kid who doesn't belong in the game, the error-maker, the boy who will go home in tears. But appearances can be deceiving. Freddy, at least, is watching the game.

The Braves pitcher struck out the first batter of the inning, then walked the next two batters, tiny tiny boys on the Twins who had obviously been instructed by their coach not to swing at anything; it's highly unlikely any pitcher can throw three strikes into their two-inch strike zones before accumulating four balls. But this new batter will swing at anything, even with the Twins coach going nuts on the sidelines, yelling to him, "Hey, Tim, gotta watch the ball, gotta make him give you a good one, gotta stay in there!" *Whoosh, whoosh, whoosh,* Tim is gone on three pitches, and the Braves parents dutifully applaud their pitcher and cheer on their fielders. *Two outs, way to go, Joey! All you need is one more, Joey! Guys, you got a play at any base!*

Pitching is all, in these games. More kids get on base by walking than by hitting, though anyone who connects has a high probability of getting on base, due to the deficiencies of the fielding. It's not unusual to see a softly hit infield ground ball turn into an inside-the-park home run, as it dribbles past the pitcher only to be bobbled by the second baseman, and finally picked up by the shortstop, who then lobs it randomly into the outfield. Freddy hit one of those in his very first game, with Lucy and Greg both standing there worrying over whether he ought to be playing at all— but that home run sealed everything forever. Freddy cleaned the bases (there were two runners on base, from walks, of course) and triumphantly circled home himself, while the other team chased the ball, which by that point had been thrown into the far corner of left field.

A three-run home run. Freddy couldn't eat anything at all that night for dinner; he sat in his chair staring off into baseball glory and rhythmically chewing the same mouthful of rice over and over and over. "Leave him alone," Greg said, quietly, "he's in Cooperstown right now. It's a baseball fugue state."

The new batter is neither incredibly tiny nor obviously big and powerful. He's just one of those all-purpose, regular kids, holds the bat like he knows how, swings with a certain confidence. The Twins coach is not yelling at him to square off, or to keep the swing level, or even to make him give you a good one, all the things he calls rather hopelessly at the boys who clearly don't belong in the batter's box; instead, he's yelling, "Okay, Bobby, get a hit. Hit the ball, Bobby!"

Is there any chance, ever, that on the baseball field, Freddy could turn into one of those all-purpose, regular kids? Not a superstar, just a kid, a player, no one you'd especially notice?

At the crack of the bat, the runners go. The ball bounces up the middle, and the Braves pitcher, Joey, who is of course one of the best all-around players on the team, manages to stop it. And then, for whatever reason, he throws to second instead of first, and there is Freddy, thick glasses and all, catching the ball neatly and immediately stepping on the base, and there is the umpire calling the runner out, and the Braves running in triumphantly to take their next at-bat. *Good fielding, boys. Freddy, nice play.*

The billionaire father told Greg last week that Thomas had not particularly wanted to play baseball this summer. Especially when he realized there wouldn't be any kids he knows on the team— except your son, of course, he added, clearly unable to remember Freddy's name. It's true—Little League is mostly kids from the public school and the Catholic school; Thomas and Freddy are the only second-graders from Country Day on the Braves. "But we have a deal," the billionaire father went on, in tones suggesting that a deal was always a good thing to have. "The deal is, Thomas plays one year of Little League, then he gets to decide. I mean, at the very least, one season of Little League will leave him able to play social baseball for the rest of his life, don't you think?"

"Oh, sure," Greg said. "Absolutely." Then he came home to ask Lucy, in genuine bewilderment, what the hell she thought the guy was getting at. Maybe that when Shearson-Lehman Brothers plays Goldman, Sachs, no one will ever say that Thomas throws like a girl?

And now here comes the billionaire father. Usually it's the billionaire mother who comes to the games, and she makes a real pest of herself in the bleachers, too. She does not seem to be able to understand the difference between a ball and a strike, or which one you cheer for in a given situation—like when your son is at bat. And she worries nonstop about her son's self-esteem and how it will be affected by this baseball nonsense, which she blames completely on her husband and his crazy ideas. She has told everyone several times how Frank insisted that Thomas play a season of Little League, and he said he, Frank, would be involved and would come to every game, and she agreed in part because she thought it would be good for Thomas to have more time with Frank, and more of Frank's attention, and if this was what it took, well then. And now, wouldn't you know, Frank doesn't come to the games half the time and guess whose job it is to get Thomas here and watch him play. And so on and on and on.

Freddy is on triple deck right now. *Hi, billionaire father Frank. Yes, we're having a great game. Why yes, that is your son up at bat right there. Why, you got here right at the very perfect moment. That must be why you're a billionaire and we're not.*

Lucy is pacing angrily around her own living room, holding the phone. To be fair, Greg told her not to call Bradley's mother. "You can if you want to, but I sure wouldn't," he said. But Lucy does call. "I'm Freddy's mother," she says. "From the second grade." And she could swear she hears the other mother suck in her breath. Lucy spares a moment for chitchat—*Of course we've met, and I know you have a daughter in the sixth grade as well, don't you? Yes, so do I.* "Oh, yes, of course," says Bradley's mother. "You have Isabel, she's a delightful girl."

Lucy sucks it up. No way is this going to be easy. Well, maybe it could be easy, maybe it's all a mistake, or maybe at least Bradley's mother will lie and say it's all a mistake. "I'm calling you about Bradley's birthday party," she says firmly. "About the Red Sox game."

At first Bradley's mother does in fact try to lie. "It's not that kind of a birthday party," she says flatly. "We aren't inviting the whole class—actually, we wanted to, but we couldn't get enough tickets, even this early in the season. So we're just taking a smaller group."

But Lucy knows better. "Actually, Freddy seems to think that every other boy in the class is invited," she says, trying to keep her voice light. "And I did tell him I thought that was unlikely, because the school does have a rule about it, but he seems quite convinced." *And he's miserable about it, I've never seen him quite so unhappy about anything,* Lucy wants to shout at the telephone—but she doesn't. *Never let them see they've hurt you, Freddy. Never let the sons-of-bitches get you down. Let them think I'm just an entitled, demanding mother, sure, but I'm not going to tell them you cry about this every night.*

"I'm so sorry if Freddy has it wrong," Lucy adds, when Bradley's mother says nothing. "I guess I could have just checked with the other mothers, but I thought it might be simpler to ask you directly." *Listen, you stupid, cruel bitch from hell, may your gums rot and your teeth fall out, there is a goddamn rule in the school about not excluding children. We had your loathsome little snot-nosed Bradley at our bowling party last year, didn't we?—or if we didn't, it wasn't because we didn't invite the little fuck.*

"Look," says Bradley's mother, "I guess I just have to tell you that Bradley isn't *comfortable* with Freddy. He's just—he just isn't comfortable. I guess he just doesn't think they have much in common. He finds Freddy a little—kind of odd, I guess. And after all, it *is* Bradley's party. And we *did* have trouble getting enough tickets."

Lucy knows she must just say one thing and hang up. She would like it to be caustic and unforgettable. But she would not like her voice to shake, and she cannot let Bradley's mother hear her cry, any more than she can tell her about Freddy crying. So she pitches her voice low and reproachful. "Think about the lesson you are teaching your children," Lucy says. "Think about this when it comes back to haunt you—you have taught them cruelty and exclusion, and you are bringing them up to be bad people. I feel sorry for your whole family." And her voice is starting to shake, and she hangs up.

Okay, so maybe that was a little over the top. But not nearly so over the top as what takes over Lucy afterward. Lucy is obsessed.

Yes, Freddy is upset, but Lucy is obsessed. Freddy may be tearful at bedtime, but then he goes to sleep, and who is this highly educated, adult woman in her forties lying awake in her bed?

Hello, this is Freddy's mother, you remember Freddy, the kind-of-odd one? I just wanted to give you a weather report. The day of Bradley's party will be overcast and chilly with on and off showers—the whole gang of you will shiver through a forty-five-minute rain delay, and then watch the Red Sox lose miserably; miserable will also be the word for all those cold, wet, crying little boys you'll be escorting home—oh, and did I mention, that nasty Jason Mancini will slip and fall on those wet cement stairs and slice his chin open, nothing serious, but he will definitely need sutures, and his father, the personal injury lawyer, will sue you for damages, and you'll lose that fucking mansion in Weston.

Hello, is this Bradley's mother? I just wanted to tell you that you are a terrible person—you have crushed and hurt a sweet, loving seven-year-old out of your Nuremberg Laws desire to eliminate all taints of weirdness, of anything different.

Hello, Cathy Cooper, I just wanted to tell you that I have a sense that there is a cancer growing deep inside you, that I am willing your cells to divide crazily, that all of the oddness and irregularity that you fear is being expressed in a yet-to-be-named organ courtesy of your oncogenes; I am a doctor and I know it! Your cells are going nuts, Cathy, and when the doctors finally detect it and it's too late, think of me!

Lucy knows that *crazy* is the word, *nuts* is the word—all over a child's birthday party, all over an April Red Sox game! But she also knows that this is about something else; this is the first official exclusion, after God knows how many unofficial ones—the first that Freddy has noticed and cared about. This is perhaps the forward shadow of a lifetime of never fitting in, of making the Bradleys of this world not feel *comfortable*—and how dare his fucking bitch of a mother teach him that that's okay. This is about watching Freddy always outside the circle and not being able to help him—and knowing that the children in the circle, as they turn their carefree, confident backs on Freddy, have the full silent support of all those righteous mommies and teachers and school psychologists who are so determined to provide them with the perfect, flawless, weirdness-free, picture-book childhoods they deserve, from their sealant-protected white teeth to their arch-supported athletic feet. Fuck them all. Oh, fuck them all.

It is not fun to be the team that has to invoke the Mercy Rule, and God knows Lucy and Greg have been there and done that; two weeks ago the Braves lost 19–4 to the Astros. But it is a dirty, sneaky, evil kind of fun to be the team that causes the other team to invoke the Mercy Rule, and for one of those unexplainable Little League reasons, on this particular overcast afternoon, the Braves are destroying the Mets. The Mets pulled their starting pitcher after one interminable can't-get-an-out-no-matter-what-we-do inning, and then the poor boy they put in to pitch couldn't throw a single strike, walked seven straight batters before they pulled him—you get the general idea. The third inning will be the last, and thank God for that, Lucy thinks, sitting in the bleachers. She and the other Braves parents have subdued their applause, clapping only modestly for each successive hit. Freddy has already come up to bat three times, walked twice, and gotten a hit; he has scored every time. It's that kind of game. But you have to think about the Mets parents, over there behind the other dugout, gamely cheering every strike that gets them a little closer to the end of this saga.

Mr. and Mrs. Billionaire arrive with the final strike—a boy named Christopher, batting for the fourth time in three innings, swinging wildly at a pitch that is almost over his head, as if he is also finally bored and just wants it over. The Braves take the field as Frank settles into a seat on the bleachers next to Lucy and begins to check his BlackBerry. "Come on there, Thomas!" he yells, without looking up. "It's really a little chilly for them to be playing, isn't it?" asks his wife, leaning across him to talk to Lucy.

"They won't be playing much longer," Lucy says. "Just this one half-inning to see if the Mets can get some runs back—but then I think they'll call it. Mercy Rule."

Frank looks up. "But Thomas was on deck," he says. "Thomas should lead off the next inning."

"They probably won't have a next inning, unless the Mets catch up," Lucy says.

Frank looks perplexed. In his world, Lucy supposes, there is no Mercy Rule; how many times has she heard a parent, usually a father, make that joke. *We have no Mercy Rule in the law, no Mercy Rule in the stock market.* She watches as Frank gets to his feet, a rather tall, rather graceful guy, and goes stepping carefully back down the bleachers to talk to Joe Shilts, the coach of the Braves, who is hanging out near the Braves bench, clutching his clipboard, and conferring with Amir Patel's father, the unofficial assistant coach. "Okay, Braves, tighten up, play good defense," Joe calls, but he leaves it at that.

Lucy shoots a glance over at the other bleachers, the poor beleaguered Mets parents. Been there, done that. The game will end, probably, with boys in tears, and Lucy is quite experienced at the look-right-past-them technique of not noticing crying boys at the end of a game, as their parents, smiling the brave, accepting smiles of good sportsmanship, guide them toward their cars and their suppers and their showers and their homework. *You played a good game, some days are like that, better luck next time, you did your best and that's what matters.* Some of the fathers will meet one another's eyes and shrug and say, "Tough game."

The first Mets batter actually connects, and the parents go wild, screaming, jumping, clapping. But it's a slow dribbler right up the first base line, and the first baseman scoops it up and steps on the base, almost before the batter, who probably thought it was going foul, has made up his mind to start running. Oh, for heaven's sake, Lucy thinks, let them get a base runner. Even a run or two. But of course, she knows she wouldn't be thinking that if she were the pitcher's mother.

The next Mets batter is a kid who swings at everything. Lucy can't watch him strike out one more time, so she looks over at Frank the Billionaire, now huddled with the coach, and tries to follow their conversation. Frank is gesturing, explaining, expostulating. Joe Shilts, who doesn't talk much to parents, stands there, nodding slowly. Then, when Frank stops talking, the coach changes his

245

head motion; instead of nodding, he slowly shakes his big and balding head from side to side. *Nope. No can do.*

Strike one. Strike two. Dog on the field—big black dog, running fast—and everyone is probably a little bit relieved to stop play for a minute and laugh as a blond woman in spandex runs him down. The dog is clearly having fun, running from fielder to fielder, and she finally gets to him and clips the leash on when he stops to investigate Thomas, standing out there in left field.

"And that's another thing," comes the voice of Frank, Thomas's father, loud and getting louder. "Why is he always stuck in left field? Left field is for losers—there's never any action in left field! I want him to get some experience in the infield! I want him to play some real defense!"

Joe Shilts doesn't raise his voice, but very clearly, Lucy can see, he tells Frank to go sit down. The dog is dragged off the field, and the game continues. The boy who swings at everything actually manages to hit the ball on his next swing, and the shortstop charges it, overruns it, trips, and bumps into the pitcher, so the kid makes it to first. The Mets parents are standing and cheering. And then the next batter gets a real and true hit—sends the ball out into the outfield. In fact, he sends it out toward Thomas, who is standing out there and still, apparently, watching the black dog—or maybe the woman in spandex—as they jog together around the perimeter of the field, ignores it completely, until he hears both his father and his coach, standing together, yelling his name. Joe Shilts yells, "Look alive, Thomas, throw it in," and Frank yells, "Come on, Thomas, make the play, for Christ's sake!"

Thomas runs over to the ball, picks it up, and throws it in the general direction of the infield, where the two runners are by now bearing down on second and third. In any case, Thomas's throw falls way short of any of the infielders, and three of them run to pick it up. Freddy should probably stay on his base in case there's a play there, but the truth is, as so often in Little League, there's no play anywhere; by the time someone comes up with the ball and throws it to someone else, both runs have scored and there is jubilation over by the Mets bench, boys pounding one another on the back and parents screaming.

And Joe Shilts turns to Frank, who is still breathing down his neck, and tells him, loud enough for everyone on the Braves' side to hear, to go sit down! Frank retreats back to right behind the fence and stands there, hands on hips, glowering, as the next Mets batter strikes out and the one after that pops to the pitcher. His wife slides over to sit closer to Lucy. "I wish Frank wouldn't get so worked up about this," she confides. "I know he doesn't really think the coach is very good."

"He's actually one of the best coaches," Lucy says loyally. Freddy likes to repeat the things that Coach Shilts tells them at practice —"Always charge the ball," he will say, seriously. *Coach Shilts says always charge the ball. Coach Shilts says make the pitcher throw you strikes. Coach Shilts says always run out a grounder.*

Game called. Mercy Rule. The two teams huddle and give their cheers, then line up and slap hands ritually—*good game, good game, good game.* The parents stand and make their way down the bleachers to claim their players and congratulate them or console them and rush them home to dinner. It's almost dark. And just as you expertly avert your eyes from a boy in tears, you also avert your eyes from a billionaire father as he comes stomping back up the bleachers.

"What total crap!" he says to his wife, who nods gamely. "Thomas was supposed to lead off the next inning, they've played three lousy innings, and now they're calling the game?"

He's going to say it, Lucy thinks, with a low-down dirty thrill.

"In life," Frank pronounces, loudly enough that people turn their heads, "there is no Mercy Rule."

Freddy, of course, does not have the subtle social sense that would tell him to avert his eyes. He is staring at Frank with intense interest, and Lucy collars him and wraps an arm around his sharp, skinny shoulders and starts to walk him away. "Good game," she says to him, loudly. "Great hit you got." She does not turn to Frank the Billionaire, does not demand, *Why shouldn't there be a Mercy*

Rule in life? or even announce, *Hey there, life is full of Mercy Rules, and I follow them as much as I can.*

"Come on, Thomas," says Frank. "Grab a bat. Let's hit a few balls around. I'll pitch. Your mother will field. You never got your chance to bat."

Freddy stops walking, turns to watch what's going on. Lucy turns with him, ready to pull him away toward home, but curious as well. Joe Shilts and Amir Patel's father stand side by side. The two of them are short, both balding. Joe, Lucy knows, has two daughters, one of whom is now in college on a full softball scholarship. He's been coaching the Braves ever since she played Little League, fourteen years ago. And here come the coach and the assistant coach from the Mets, walking over to shake hands.

And there goes Frank, heading for the pitcher's mound.

"Dad, let's go home." Lucy can hear Thomas's voice, even though he doesn't speak very loudly. "Dad, the game's over."

"Don't you want to hit a few grounders?" Frank calls. "There's still plenty of light. I'll pitch to you."

Suddenly Thomas takes off, running as fast as he can. He's rounding first almost before anyone can react, and for a second Lucy thinks he's just going to circle the bases while everyone stands there watching. But just as his mother calls his name, just as she starts after him, he changes direction, and he sets out running across the outfield, heading for the busy street on the far side of the field.

"Thomas! Thomas, come back here!" yells his father. And then both his parents are running after him, his father gaining on his mother, but Thomas, moving fast, still well ahead of them both.

The four coaches, from the Braves and the Mets, watch them go. And there is also a more scattered audience, Lucy and Freddy and other parents and other kids, standing where they've been awkwardly watching and listening.

Joe Shilts turns to the Mets coach and sticks out his hand. "Tough game," he says, and the other man nods. "There are days like that," he says, and they shake. Out at the edge of the outfield, in the gloom, it looks like Thomas's father has caught up to him. "The kid can run," the Mets coach says.

"I know," Joe says. "I had no idea he could move like that."

Lucy comes up with the admittedly forced and ridiculous idea of buying two very expensive tickets to Fenway Park for the very same game where Bradley is celebrating his birthday. So Greg could take Freddy and indulge his every whim, buy him ten-dollar programs and hot dogs and team paraphernalia. And maybe they'll run into Bradley's group, and they'll have much better seats—and Greg has no desire at all to do this, of course, and probably even Freddy has no desire to do this, and it's a bad idea all around. It's just that it drives Lucy crazy that there is no way to hit back.

"So this is Laurel Cooper's little brother?" Isabel asks. Lucy and Greg are having yet another go-round about Bradley's party, and Isabel, it turns out, has been listening from the living room. Freddy is up in his room, doing his homework.

"Yes," Lucy says. "She isn't one of your friends or anything, is she?" A quick, crazy, come-and-gone idea of asking her to intercede. But Isabel's friends are on a closed short list, and Lucy has never heard her mention Laurel Cooper.

"She's sort of silly," Isabel says dismissively.

"Every other boy," Lucy says. "They're taking every single other boy. The ones who don't even care about baseball, they're taking. Horrible Thomas, with his horrible parents, they're taking. And there's Freddy, who asks me every single night at bedtime if I think maybe this year the Red Sox can win the World Series, who has more baseball cards than—than I don't know what. And he doesn't get to go."

"Let it go," Greg says, not for the first time. "Sometimes you have to let things go. He's on a team, he's playing baseball, I'll take him to a game later on this summer. You have to let this go."

"Greg, I think he thinks about this every time he mentions Fenway Park. He thinks about all the other boys in his class being there together for a party and not him and it makes him sad—so they've poisoned the thing he cared about most, the thing that gave him so much pleasure—and here we are, we're helpless! They can just hurt your child and hurt your child and you're just helpless!"

"Let it go," Greg says again.

At that point, there is a loud and familiar crash from upstairs —Freddy has unbalanced his rickety table. He will not let them replace it and he will not stop tilting it. Greg goes running up the stairs to put Freddy and his homework back together again, and Lucy sits down at the kitchen table and folds her arms across her chest. Isabel is regarding her closely. "I'm not going to cry," Lucy says. "And I know he's right. I have to let it go." But her eyes are brimming, and she jumps up again to start cooking, so her daughter won't see.

Greg comes back into the kitchen, leading Freddy. "Time for dinner," he announces. "Freddy has most of his homework done. Let's all take a break and eat." On cue, Lucy takes the pot of spaghetti off the stove and carries it to the sink, as the steam mists her glasses. She pours the water and the spaghetti into the colander, puts the pot back on the edge of the stove, wipes her glasses on her shirt, and puts them on again to see Isabel looking closely at Freddy, who is sitting in his place at the table and carefully tearing his paper napkin into strips and then tearing each strip into confetti. Lost in space as usual.

But Isabel, it turns out, is not helpless at all. Isabel is quick and ruthless.

Lucy has had so many conversations in her mind with Cathy Cooper, mother of Bradley and Laurel Cooper, that she almost cannot believe it when the woman actually calls her up. Actually calls her up in tears to beg for mercy.

"Isabel, I have to ask you something. I got a call today at work from Laurel Cooper's mom. She says—well, she says every girl in the sixth grade has stopped talking to Laurel. That she's totally excluded. That no one will even eat lunch with her."

"She's not really one of my friends. I told you that." Isabel is sitting, upright, at her desk, working away with a glue stick. Her poster on cell division is not actually due until next week, but it's almost done. Lucy stands in the doorway, feeling like she is block-ing out the light.

"Isabel, this is serious. Laurel's mom says that Laurel comes home from school every day and sits in her room and cries." Isabel keeps gluing.

"Isabel, did you do this? Because of the birthday party?"

Isabel looks up, though she keeps her finger on her mitochon-dria diagram. "Maybe sort of. I told some people that her brother was being really mean to my brother, so I didn't really want to have much to do with her. That's all."

"But it isn't—I mean, of all the people whose fault this is, Laurel Cooper doesn't have anything to do with it."

"Sure, Mom, I know that. I just don't want to hang out with her because it makes me think about how bad you're feeling and how bad Freddy is feeling. That's all. And anyway, she's not really one of my friends. She never was." Isabel nails the mitochondrial dia-gram, then regards her poster closely. "You know what I think is cool? Reverse transcriptase. That's my favorite illustration."

"Yes," Lucy agrees, "it's a very cool enzyme. And I like what you did with the glitter." And she squeezes her daughter's shoulder.

What if I told you that CATHY COOPER CAPITULATES COM-PLETELY, as Greg would say, and somehow finds Freddy a ticket to the ballgame, and calls Lucy again and again, begging her tear-fully to have Isabel make things all right with the sixth-grade girls? Would you say that virtue has triumphed and the evil have been punished and the good rewarded for maybe the first time in ele-mentary school history? Greg wants to tell Cathy Cooper to take her ticket and shove it where the sun doesn't shine, but Lucy says, and she's right, that Freddy will be happy. And so Freddy *does* get to go to the famous baseball birthday party, but unfortunately, the Red Sox *do* lose, and the group doesn't even stay till the end of the game, which Freddy finds astonishing and somewhat troubling; all the way home, strapped securely into one of the two Cooper family minivans, he keeps demanding that everyone be quiet so they can listen to the radio and hear every pitch of the last depressing inning.

What if I told you that it is the spring of 2004, and Freddy is about to live through the most magical season in the history of Boston baseball? Of course, if you know anything about baseball (or Boston), you already know what will happen down the road in October, and you've been suspecting it ever since Freddy's heart was broken last October—but what if I told you that the Boston Red Sox will win the World Series, ending an eighty-six-year wait, long before Bradley's sister, Laurel Cooper, is ever again invited to a sleepover party—or any other significant party—by a girl in her grade? What if that should turn out to be true, not just Lucy's frightened fantasy, what then? But surely that is highly unlikely. And the most important lessons of this baseball season, which is just getting under way on that chilly birthday-party day at Fenway Park, are that luck can change, that happy endings can appear where you didn't expect them to, and that the season is long and full of surprises.

12

Mandated Reporter

I NEED TO BE GOING somewhere," Lucy says. "I need to be in motion." She regards her daughter, Isabel. The bedroom, the desk, the bookcase in perfect order—Lucy, standing in the doorway, feels like mess and disorder incarnate. All she would have to do is step through the doorway, onto the floor, onto the small floral rug that Greg's mother hooked for Isabel, which is of course meticulously centered, and something terrible would happen. The books would get out of alphabetical order, or the paper clips would come flying out of their dispenser, or the ornamental pillow would slip sideways on the bed. *Oh, Isabel,* she wants to say, *don't you ever get tired? It makes me tired just to look at you sometimes.* And of course, she doesn't say it. "Isabel, come for a drive," she says, instead. "Let's go somewhere, it's such a beautiful day."

Isabel looks at her, more than a little bit dubiously. This is not Isabel's style—but to be fair, it isn't really Lucy's style either. Isabel considers the prospect. "Where?" she asks.

"Anywhere you want," Lucy offers. *The mall. The Staples Superstore. Just keep me company so I don't have to drive alone, just come with me so I don't have to stay here in the house.*

• • •

Here is the weird thing about cell phones: if you think about it carefully, they change everything. History, literature. Crime narratives, love stories. If wherever you are, out of all other context, your phone can ring, if you can look at the tiny window and know who is calling, if your phone can store the numbers of other phones that have tried to call—think of all the plots that change. All the stage moments when a phone rings mysteriously, and the character either answers and has to deal with whatever voice is manifested, or else lets it ring and ring and ring, holding its secret. Very different if the character has the option of picking up a cell phone, squinting at it in concentration for a minute, and then announcing, "It's just my mother, I'll call her later."

I'm serious. This entire story now revolves around cell phones and caller ID, and I can't think of a way to make it seem more, oh, I don't know, more dignified, I guess. Lucy is worrying and worrying about two of her patients, two little kids, ages four months and two years, whose mother, Delia, has grabbed them out of the temporary foster home in which DSS placed them and disappeared. Leaving a third child, the three-year-old, hospitalized, with no one to visit her except the security guard now stationed outside her room in case her mother shows up to try to kidnap her as well. Lucy, like the DSS workers, like the foster mother, has tried calling the mother's cell phone, and there is no answer and no recording. Which is not so surprising; she's probably had her service cut off for nonpayment, just as she has with every other cell phone she's owned—and for that matter, with the phone service in every apartment she's rented, with her gas, her electricity . . . But the truth is, if Delia still does have that phone tucked away in one of the assorted bags she's taken on her flight from justice, then eventually she will pull it out and it will offer her back the full list of phone numbers of everyone who's called. And she can recognize the DSS exchange, of course; she's spent the last three years of her life calling those numbers, and taking their calls, as the social workers have hovered over her and her children. But if Lucy happened to call her from Lucy's own cell phone, as she did, over and over, while she was driving home after spending an hour meeting with the cop and the social worker about the Delia emergency, well, then Lucy's phone number will pop up on Delia's phone, and Delia may be just curious enough to call it back. And then, who knows what may happen?

Delia is gone. A week ago Lucy admitted her three-year-old to the hospital, and the Department of Social Services took emergency temporary custody of all three kids, and put the other two in an emergency foster home. And the three-year-old seemed to be getting a little bit better, and she got out of the hospital, and then yesterday she developed a high fever and a new rash, and her foster mother trusted Delia to take the other two kids to the playground while she took Lizelle back to the emergency room and waited through the blood draws and the exams and the slow progress back to a bed on the pediatric floor. And now Delia has taken the two younger children and, as they say, absconded. Lizelle she has left alone, in her hospital bed, but the other two are gone. Delia was careful and slick, cooperating with the police and the court and the DSS workers, all with that same apparent bewildered desire to please. Oh, Delia had laid her plans carefully; she fooled them all. Except that probably she hadn't laid any plans; probably when the foster mother trusted her to take the two little kids to the park, some guy she knew happened to come by in a car and he said, "Hey, Delia, how about a road trip?" and off she went. It could be that. It could be anything. Lucy tells herself, it could be that Delia has gone to make another video, another screen test, and she'll turn up in a couple of hours to return the children, and when she finds the police waiting at the foster mother's house, she'll just say that, bewildered: "But I went to make a video." As if to say, *How could I not? Wouldn't anyone?*

And speaking of videos, Lucy has to hope that nobody focuses too closely on what these videos are. Some sleazebag or other convincing Delia to take her clothes off, no doubt, leading her on and on with promises of stardom. That would look great in court someday. Another of the many things that Lucy has never asked about, because Delia would tell her, proudly, happily, eagerly—and then Lucy would know. And then she would have to tell.

Maybe it's this, Lucy thinks. Maybe I think I understand why

Delia is so determined to become a star. Maybe I look at her and I see the kid who didn't get recognized and rescued. I starred in a sixth-grade show and I turned into myself; the right people noticed me and I found my place in the world. Maybe Delia needs to be noticed in the right way. But then there's the little problem that Delia is unbalanced and kind of nuts. But maybe I would be, too, if no one had called my name at the right time. And Lucy wants fiercely, for a moment, to be able to show herself to the woman who saved her. *To Miss Weiss, to Ina, to Mom. Look what I am, look what I became. Look at your granddaughter.*

She is driving, a little too fast, out the Massachusetts Turnpike. Isabel is in the seat beside her and in control of the radio; recently, she has started listening to a very particular radio station, KISS 108. Lucy has asked her once or twice if she really likes the music, and Isabel just shrugs; Lucy has the sense that Isabel is treating pop music as yet another assignment to be aced: in the sixth grade, this is the music you should listen to, these are the songs you should like and recognize and prefer.

What Lucy wants to say to her daughter is this: *I get so tired of telling all the time. Of turning people in.*

But frankly, it does not seem to Lucy that there is any part of the Delia story that Isabel should really hear. Or any part of the Athena story, or any part of so many stories. She is suspicious of herself, Lucy is. She knows how doctors tend to play the I-do-life-and-death card, she worries that she is always trying to educate and impress her daughter, always waiting for Isabel to say, *Boy, Mom, you do a really important job.* Or would Isabel just grimace at the idea of a job so shaded with gray from front to back, from side to side?

"You need gas soon," says Isabel, who worries when she sees the gauge get anywhere near empty. Usually, Lucy laughs her off; she has driven this car for years and she has an excellent sense of how much farther she can go even when the needle is exactly on the E, even when the yellow warning light is on—and they are nowhere near there yet. But here comes a rest area, on the right, and what is the point of teasing Isabel? Don't we want to encourage the people who plan and budget and think things through and keep order in their parts of the universe? The children who will grow up to pay their bills?

"You're right," she says, switching on her signal. "We'll stop here."

Think about the phone thing a little. The astute among you will have already asked, *Shouldn't Lucy have caller protection on her cell phone? Doesn't she take a risk if her number is indeed available to Delia's phone—or to the phone of any other patient she calls? Don't doctors keep their phone numbers secret?* You say that because you have never been on call, never spent a weekend—or even an evening—returning the calls of worried mothers all over the city. See, it works like this: they call in after hours or on the weekend, and they get switched to the answering service—you've probably been switched to an answering service or two a few times yourself. Then the answering service pages Lucy—or calls her directly—or puts the information through to some fancy electronic beeper. Whatever. The thing is, she then has to call the mother back. And at least 80 percent of her patients' phones will not accept calls if the number is blocked. Lucy, whose home phone happily accepts all incoming calls, most of which seem to be from fundraisers, has wondered about the complexities of her patients' lives—why do they universally want this feature, why do they want to shut out all shielded numbers? From whom are they hiding, of whom are they afraid? None of her own friends have this thing on their phones, do they? So yes, the mechanics of her life are governed a little bit by phone features, and so is her story: Lucy's family home phone has a block on it for outgoing calls, so its number won't show up on your caller ID, but not her cell phone. She uses that to return calls, and she is philosophically resigned to the fact that that number is all over town.

So if Lucy's phone rings in a little while, and she lets her daughter answer, Isabel will say hello, and then hear a very wary question—*Who's this?* And she'll explain, already aware that this must be a voice out of her mother's work life—"I'm Dr. Weiss's daughter," she'll say. "Would you like to speak with her?" And then, safety-minded, Isabel will carefully hook up her mother's phone to the hands-free earpiece and will listen with unabashed interest to Lucy's side of the conversation, which will begin with Lucy explaining Isabel's existence: "Yes, Delia, that was my daughter. Yes, I have a daughter. She's eleven. Yes, it's very nice. Yes, thank you, she is a very nice girl, just like she sounds. Where are you, Delia? Do you have the children with you, Delia? Are they okay? Are you okay? Delia, tell me where you are."

They are going to Cape Cod for the day. That's Isabel's choice—well, it's Isabel's choice after Lucy encourages her a little—*Sure, I'll take you to the Chestnut Hill Mall if you really want me to, but would you rather do something—anything—a little bit more adventurous?*—and when Isabel didn't shut her out and shut her off right away, didn't say, "I thought you told me, *anywhere I liked,*" just looked wary but interested, and said, a little tentatively, "Like what would be a little bit more adventurous?"—emphasis on the *little bit*—and so Lucy thought of Cape Cod. Maybe because she was still thinking of Delia—one of the places Delia disappeared to, a year ago or so, leaving her kids in that crazy apartment with those sleazy guys, was somewhere on Cape Cod where she supposedly has a sour, difficult old great-aunt. Whom she hoped would give her money, but who didn't, and she had to hitchhike back and this guy was totally weird so she had to get out of the car and that's why she was so late getting back, and why couldn't the social workers understand a simple thing like that?

Maybe that's even where Delia has absconded to, with baby Louisa and two-year-old Curt. It's on the list of places that Lucy gave to the Department of Social Services yesterday: *She's got a great-aunt out on the Cape somewhere, I'm not sure where exactly, and I think she has some relatives in Maine, but I don't think she likes them, and once she and her no-good boyfriend took the kids out to Ayer and he got into some trouble there with the police, and I'm pretty sure he comes from somewhere farther west but still in Massachusetts—maybe Fitchburg?* In theory, DSS has some or all of this information in Delia's file, though Lucy's faith is limited. Delia has never been lucky in her DSS workers—or, to put it another way, she's been insanely lucky. She's had a succession of very young, very new social workers, and each one has earnestly and idealistically decided to really *help* this charming, well-meaning, enthusiastic young mother. Lucy has been cast in the role of Scrooge at least three times with three different workers, explaining sourly and cynically that Delia is crazy, is not to be taken at her word, is completely disorganized, is completely impulsive, needs very strict rules and agreements and guidelines and penalties if there is to be any hope of her keeping her kids. "Get her a full psychiatric eval," Lucy says. "She needs to be on some kind of psychotropic meds. Get her GYN care, for God's sake, and see if they can talk her into Depo-Provera shots so she won't get pregnant again. Put all the kids in therapeutic daycare, and tell her she'll lose them if she misses a single day without calling in. Or if she doesn't take her meds. Ride on her back, make her budget her money so the rent gets paid and they don't get kicked out again and the gas doesn't get turned off and there's a little food in the house. Make her keep her WIC appointments. Ask her if her shithead boyfriend is bothering her, and if he is, get a restraining order, and see if the cops will lean on him a little bit. You're the only ones with real power in this situation, because you can threaten to take the kids. And if you don't do this, you will end up taking the kids, I promise."

So much for Lucy's song, which she has sung over and over. Which she was still singing yesterday, this time to a DSS supervisor and a police officer, now that Delia has snatched her two younger children out of foster care and disappeared with them. All these times, over the past three years, she has said this and said this, with increasing force and conviction, to those sweet young social workers, who hear her and wonder at her negativity, at her cynicism, at her inability to understand all the pressures and traumas and stresses weighing on poor, young, overwhelmed Delia, who loves her children so. Lucy imagines them listening to her in horror—*I hope I die before I get that old*, they are thinking.

And the truth is, Delia and the two little kids could be on their way to Hollywood, California, in the back of someone's car, so Delia can finally meet J. Lo and get into the movies. On their way to Orlando, Florida, to go to Disney World in the back of someone else's car, hoping they can get a picture with Minnie Mouse. They could be going anywhere, and if they cross state lines, it is very unlikely that anyone will find them or bring them back. The policeman yesterday even looked bored: "She doesn't hit the kids, she doesn't hurt the kids, you're basically saying she's a little irresponsible, right?" He didn't say it, but Lucy knows you don't spend a lot of time and energy on interstate pursuit for "a little irresponsible."

Lucy and her family don't go to Cape Cod very often. They have had bad luck, now and then in the summer, with the traffic south out of Boston and over the bridges. Many years ago they spent a summer weekend in a cottage somewhere, and Greg decided that the water was too cold. And mostly they go south in the summer, at least as far as the New Jersey shore, sometimes all the way down to the Outer Banks. Lucy knows that they have lived in Boston all these years without quite understanding about Cape Cod, without falling in love with it or dreaming of owning property there.

Holiday houses, second homes. Lucy thinks about the folded clipping in her purse. All day yesterday, she had it in her pocket and she found herself unfolding the clipping again and again and staring at it: Tanya and William Danvers and their children, Byron and Elissa, posed on the deck of the massive new house they have just built on Nantucket. The article, from the Home section of the paper, is illustrated with photos of the two-story fireplace in the great room and the children's themed bedrooms (sailors for the boy, mermaids for the girl, bless their gender-clichéd hearts), though the subtext of the article, Lucy thinks, is clearly that this family is part of the new wave of super-rich building their too-giant mansions and destroying the character of the island. Still, she wondered about a more sinister subtext as she stared into the beautiful and unknowable face of Tanya Danvers, kneeling between her lovely children, arms around their shoulders, as her husband perches casually on a teak table behind them.

So the rich and unknowable families can take their secrets off to an island. Probably they go by private jet; they don't fight traffic like the rest of us.

But there is no traffic toward the Cape today. It's too early in the year, too cold for the beach. The gas gauge is now optimistically upright, the tank as full as it can be, and Lucy is driving happily in the middle lane.

"How's Emma doing?" Lucy asks.

"She's in a program," Isabel says. "She has to eat certain things for lunch every day or they make her go eat with the school nurse. Who is a total retard, of course. But after Emma eats lunch, she's not allowed to go into the bathroom for an hour and a half. I mean, she had to sign a paper that she wouldn't."

"And does she keep the agreement?"

"Sure she keeps it," says Isabel, and Lucy is immediately grateful—even if Isabel is lying and Emma is lying. Just please, Lucy thinks, don't tell me anything I have to *tell*.

"Does she look any better?"

"Maybe. I don't know. She never looked all that bad when she was dressed, you know. It was just that time we saw her getting changed for gym and she looked so weird."

"Awful, they look awful," Lucy says, getting right in there with her propaganda, her reality testing for this daughter of hers who eats exactly half of everything on her plate and leaves the rest to show she can do it. "You know what we say about them, they look like concentration camp victims—they look terrible. It breaks your heart. Isn't that what you and your friends felt when you looked at her?"

"She looked weird. And the really weird thing was what I told you, when she showed us in the mirror how she had all this cellulite on her thighs."

"Isabel, they're sick, they're crazy. They have something called a body image disorder, it's a psychiatric diagnosis. They look at themselves and they don't see what's really there, they don't say, 'Oh my God, I am destroying my beautiful strong body, I am chewing it up'—they look at themselves in the mirror and instead of a concentration camp victim with ribs sticking out, they see fat everywhere—because they are crazy, they are out of their minds!"

"It's okay, Mom," Isabel says gently. "I understand what you mean. I get it."

Would Lucy believe that on any level she has planned this—that she knows she is heading straight for Delia? She drives happily through the spring sunshine, talking to her smart and sensible and sane daughter, who will surely grow up to strike a better balance of organization and planning in the world than Lucy does herself—Isabel, who will, please heaven, have all the good sense and control and willpower that Lucy herself lacks, who will be functional in every sense, who will never tip over into any of the crazy detours out there—not into Delia's border zone, but not into Lucy's swamps of self-doubt and chaos either, and not into the rich-girl cliché neuroses that will claim some of her classmates. Lucy can crack the window open a little every now and then, and let the car fill with the smell of this good warm air and the promise of warmer days to come and the whistle of movement—and then close the window again and shut herself in with Isabel.

When the call comes from Delia, Lucy slows up. She has to be especially careful driving when she is having a conversation like this; what if her right foot decided to add all the emphasis and urgency that she is carefully keeping out of her voice when she says, "Delia, they're looking for you, the police are looking for you, and the very best thing you can do right now is go and turn yourself in, so that way it's not like they caught you, it's like you were responsible and you brought the kids back yourself—that will look really good for you, that will help you so much!"

Isabel will be fascinated, listening to her mother. Maybe she will even be able to hear some of what Delia is saying, coming through the earpiece, as Delia's voice gets louder.

"Delia, it's okay if you don't have a way to get back to Boston with the kids. We can get you some help. Delia, it's okay if you don't have any money. It's not a problem. Delia, tell me where you are —you and the kids—and tell me if it's safe there."

Because another thing about cell phones, of course: the number that registers on Lucy's own caller ID is just Delia's old familiar number, Boston area code and all. She could be calling from Hollywood, or from Orlando, or from somewhere in between. There are no clues in the complicated electronic communications between the cell phones; they recognize and identify each other, they connect and communicate and store information, but it is as if they are floating in a void, no fixed points at all. And from my floating point I connect to your floating point, and we are linked, but there is no location, no certainty, no clear coordinates. We are phone voices in cellular space, we are numbers that identify us on one another's tiny screens, and that is all we are.

Lucy takes her right hand off the steering wheel and makes a writing gesture to her daughter, the kind you make in a restaurant when you want your check. *Write this down, Isabel!* Isabel yanks open the glove compartment, searching for a pen, afraid she won't find one in time—and a pile of neatly folded maps comes cascading down onto her feet. Isabel piles up the maps, stuffs them back in, retrieves a felt-tip pen, and grabs an old parking-lot tag off the dashboard. She writes it down.

"Dennis," Lucy is repeating slowly into the phone. "You're in Dennis. You're not at your great-aunt's house, you're at a motel. Delia, what's the name of the motel?"

Isabel waits, pen poised. "Delia, you know I have to let them know where you are. You know that. You know that if they don't get the kids back soon, you'll be in terrible trouble. Delia, of course you can make them give you back your kids, but not if you just take them and run—you know what DSS will say about that. Just tell me the name of the motel. Just tell me."

Isabel is turned in her seat, watching her mother's face. Lucy is driving steadily, keeping a nice long distance from the navy blue minivan up ahead.

"Okay, Delia, if you tell me where you are, I won't tell anyone till you say I can. I just need to know you're okay. I need to know you're safe. Okay. Yes, I know what a good mother you are. I know how much you love those kids. Yes, I remember when you got Lizelle all the Disney videos, the whole set. Yes, I know. The Sea Breeze Motel?" She gestures violently to Isabel, who writes it down. "Great, yes, the Sea Breeze Motel. So now you'll think it over and decide when it's okay for me to let DSS know? Well, yes, of course. Yes, they'll come there and the first thing they'll do is return the kids to the foster care situation—but that's just till they get everything sorted out. And they'll make sure you get prenatal care, too, and that you take care of yourself. And meantime, you can let the foster mom watch the little ones, and you can go visit Lizelle in the hospital—I know she wants to see you. Won't that work well—you can use the foster mother as a babysitter, Delia, do you see what I'm telling you!"

"She didn't give you permission to tell, did she?" asks Isabel.

"No, she didn't. But she must know that I'm going to—that I have to." Lucy, by this time, is approaching the bridge to Cape Cod, the high arch over the canal. "Let me just get across the bridge and I'll call."

Lucy finds bridges a little frightening, to tell the truth—driving over bridges, that is. She is glad to have both hands on the steering wheel and no crazy voice in her ear. *Like I had to tell about Emma, honey.* But she doesn't say it. Lucy believes that if she leaves her daughter alone, Isabel will come to understand and agree: sometimes you have to tell. And on the other side of the bridge, after she makes the call to DSS, she can figure out how to break the news to Isabel that their frivolous adventure together on the Cape will now start with a quick visit to the Sea Breeze Motel. It's only fair, after all, she thinks, but will not say to her daughter, it's only fair because I've had Delia on my mind, I probably only thought of the Cape because it was on my list of places she's been known to go to ground. And she also doesn't quite say, because it would seem silly to say it, *Let's just make sure that Delia's kids are safely in custody, and then we'll go in search of something good for lunch. You like lobster rolls, don't you?*

Lucy drives her car. This is Lucy's car. It isn't very new or very expensive, but it's new enough and comfortable enough. It's the car you get if you were a good girl and you went to medical school, and Lucy keeps it relatively clean and neat. The windows roll up and down automatically when you press the buttons, and the air conditioner keeps you cool in the summer. Lucy likes the little temperature-controlled kingdom of her car. This is her daughter, sitting beside her, both of them obediently belted in. Both of them with their good straight teeth, chewing the air that the blowers blow as Lucy drives around the rotary, steering carefully, and heads for the town of Dennis.

What is in Isabel's mind? Is she resentful to see her day with her mother, her day on Cape Cod, hijacked and pushed aside? Lucy doesn't know—she hopes that Isabel is interested. She hopes that she and Isabel will soon be on their way, knowing that Delia's children are safe and sound and in protective custody, she and Isabel will go on and find their treat, whatever it may be. She has called the highest-up person she can reach on a weekend at the Department of Social Services, she has told all she knows. "Don't scare her," she said. "She's not a danger to those children, she's not a danger to herself. She's just seriously, majorly flaky, that's all. Treat her gently. Tell the cops to treat her gently."

Isabel asked her, actually, was she going to call Delia now and tell her the cops were coming, and Lucy said no. "I don't want her to flee," Lucy said. "I don't want her to do something crazy and stupid—I don't want her out on the highway with two tiny little kids trying to hitch a ride. I don't want her stealing someone's boat when she doesn't know how to sail and she doesn't know how to swim. But you know, honey, deep inside she knows perfectly well that I must have called someone. She wouldn't have called me on my cell phone, she wouldn't have told me where she was, if she didn't sort of want me to call. She knows I have to call."

"Why would she want you to call?"

"Because she knows she's getting into deep, deep trouble. Because she can't buy food for the kids, or pay her motel bill, for all I know. Because she never really planned to take the kids and run away with them and now she's sorry—because she's someone who never thinks a step ahead, and then she finds herself in these messes and she looks for someone—anyone—to get her out."

"She's pregnant?" Isabel asks.

"She's pregnant and she's mixed up with some very dubious outfit that pretends to do pregnancy counseling but really it's a right-to-life front, their only goal is to prevent women from getting abortions."

Isabel considers. "Do you think it would be better if she did get an abortion?" she asks.

"Yes," Lucy says. "Yes, I do. Even so, though, I don't think she'll get to keep these kids. And that's too bad, because she really does love them." She has a sudden overwhelming memory of coming into the exam room, back when Louisa was a newborn. Outside in the corridor, everyone could hear that Delia was singing, and when Lucy opened the door, she saw Delia sitting in the plastic chair, nursing the baby, and singing. She was singing "Eleanor Rigby," and the older two children sat on the exam table and stared at her as she sang, and the baby nursed. And never mind that it was bad judgment to put little kids on the exam table and then sit across the room, Lucy can't help hoping that those children, wherever they go in their lives, will remember what it sounded like when Delia sang, and the song echoed off the walls of the little clinic exam room.

Isabel calls the Sea Breeze Motel in Dennis and gets driving directions, which are easy to follow. Lucy is expecting a welfare-motel-type dump, but actually it's a rather pretty little place. Freshly painted, with a little logo of whitecaps against a blue background. Cable TV, queen-size beds, free breakfast, VACANCY, says the sign out front, and the motel is a long, low, light blue building. As she pulls into the parking lot, Lucy can see through an open door right into the tiny office, which is dominated by a gigantic tropical fish tank, almost empty. A counter, a rack of tourist information pamphlets. But the owner is out front, in the parking lot, dealing with the mess.

Two local police cars. And that must be the motel lady, a little elderly, a little dumpy, standing out there and talking to the policeman. The policeman himself, Lucy sees with gratitude, is no kid. Tall and thin, very upright in his uniform, but old enough to be sensible. The other cop is still in his car, and Lucy can barely see him through the tinted windows.

"Stay in the car, honey," Lucy says to Isabel.

She herself gets out, and sees the policeman and the motel lady turn to look at her. She crosses the parking lot to talk to them, lowers her voice. Introduces herself, tells them, "I'm the one who called DSS. Delia called me and I called DSS. Which room is she in?"

The motel lady looks a little bit annoyed. Lucy supposes that from her point of view, this must look like all Lucy's fault—this mess, this trouble, these police cars in her lot. She's in room two, the motel lady says. In there with those kids. She doesn't want to come out.

Lucy looks at the policeman. "Is it okay if I go knock?" she asks. "I bet I can get her to open up."

The policeman nods. "If you can," he says, "that would save a lot of trouble. You say you don't think she's any danger?"

"She won't have a weapon or anything like that," Lucy says. "Not unless she's got someone else in there—she doesn't have a guy with her or anything?"

"No," the motel lady says, "just the mom and those two little kids."

"Why don't you get back in your car," Lucy says to the policeman, "and why don't you go back in your office? She knows me pretty well, and I know her pretty well."

As she marches over to the room with the metal number two on the door, Lucy thinks of all of them watching her: the two policemen in their separate cars, the motel lady in her office, Isabel in Lucy's own car. Her body feels light and firm and unfamiliar to her. What is she doing here? She is finishing the story, that's what. She started this back in the hospital, back in the clinic, back in the exam room. She has been thinking about it ever since. She has been mysteriously drawn here by some seed Delia planted, by cell phone calls. Sometimes you have to try and save someone. Sometimes it's up to you. It is up to me, Lucy thinks, and she knocks firmly on the motel room door.

"Delia, it's me!" she calls. "It's Dr. Lucy. Open the door, there's no one out here but me!"

A pause, during which Lucy imagines Delia, on the other side of the door, listening and wondering. "Delia, open the door. Open it right now and let me in! This is Dr. Lucy, do you hear me?"

A click, a pull against the slightly swollen wood, probably a little out of shape now at the beginning of the season, a tug, and the door is open, just enough for Lucy to see Delia standing there. Delia all dressed up in a slinky scarlet dress that cups her breasts, that ties behind her neck, that sweeps down, filmy and slightly transparent, almost to the floor. She is holding Curt in her arms, and even though he is eating orange chips out of a plastic bag, still, beautiful Delia in her sweeping gown looks, no question, like a Madonna.

Lucy moves in through the open door, and Delia lets her. Yes, there is Louisa, awake and alert in her car seat carrier. The television is on, a cartoon show, and both children seem to be watching. Delia swirls around and her dress flares out and Curt, in her arms, gives a crow of delight. Delia collapses onto the bed with him and begins to tickle him, and both of them are giggling, and Lucy smiles, too, because she can't help it. She even gives a tiny chuckle, but at the sound of her laugh, Delia sits up straight and stares at her.

"Dr. Lucy, you called the police!"

Lucy doesn't say, *Of course I called the police, what did you expect?* She doesn't waste any time on any of that. Instead she says, "Delia, you look so beautiful!"

And Delia stops worrying about the police and preens. She swans up off the bed and looks at herself in the large mirror that hangs over the low motel chest of drawers, she admires herself in the mirror in her lovely dress. Lucy, oddly, wants to turn off the television and call the children to attention: *Curt, Louisa, pay attention, and always remember your mother like this, all dressed up in red!*

"Dr. Lucy," Delia says, "are you any good at fixing hair?"

She was really beautiful, Isabel will not say to her friends. Isabel will not say anything, in the end, to her friends, not for some years to come, though she will start to tell the story later on, in high school, and she will go on telling it, now and then, right through college, as she becomes steadily less and less afraid, Isabel does, that any one thing will make her true friends change the way they look at her and stop being her true friends. High school will turn out to be good like that, college even better.

She sat there, staring into this mirror, this big mirror, that took up, like, half the wall, Isabel will not tell her friends. She stared and stared at herself. She had a little box full of earrings—a beautiful little box, made out of silver and lined with red velvet, that stood up on four skinny little silver legs. She opened it and she looked through the earrings, and then she took out earrings and held them up to her ears to see how they looked, one pair after another. And my mother said later that they were probably fakes, but one pair looked like big diamonds, and one looked like rubies, and they went exactly with her dress.

"I paid for her hotel room," Lucy does say to the policeman. "And the lady's going to let her stay overnight—and I gave her bus fare to get home to Boston tomorrow. So she has enough money to get home if she doesn't spend it—if nobody takes it away from her." The policeman nodded. He had the baby seat securely strapped into the back of his police car, with Louisa, still wide awake and not crying, snugly belted into it. Curt had been a problem—too small to wear a regular seat belt—but the other cop had driven off somewhere and come back with a child safety seat, and also with a cheerful young policewoman, who was waiting in the front seat, already hanging over the back and singing to Curt, doing the hand gestures for the "Itsy Bitsy Spider." Lucy was filled with a strong sense of gratitude to this resourceful, good-natured police department; it was so easy to imagine what might have been. Screams, pleas, a baby tugged by force out of its mother's arms, a crying child, a woman coming apart before them, falling to her knees . . .

"So, what's this place like, where she says she has a job tonight singing?" Lucy asks.

"The Windmill Lounge?" The policeman shrugs. "A little seedy. You know. This time of the year, mostly locals. She's not very likely to be *discovered* singing in the Windmill Lounge, off-season. Let's just say that."

He doesn't ask, and Lucy is deeply grateful to him for not asking, what Delia would have done with her four-month-old and her two-year-old tonight, if Lucy hadn't conveniently knocked on her door, if he and his colleague hadn't conveniently strapped the children into his squad car to drive them back to Boston. He doesn't ask, presumably, because he knows, and Lucy knows, too.

I did her hair all different ways, Isabel will not say to her father. She doesn't ask her mother, *Is it okay for me to tell him about this?* She knows that her mother would on principle not want to collude with her in keeping secrets from her father—but she also knows she won't tell. Dad would never be able to understand—just like none of her friends would understand. You had to be there, to see the policeman talking to Delia, so kind and gentle, watch him strapping those car seats into the car, just like Dad and Mom used to do for Freddy, Isabel's own younger brother. You had to see Delia, so pretty in her red dress, staring into the motel mirror while the male cop and the female cop started on the drive to Boston with her two little kids.

I did her hair all up in a kind of twist, with just a little curl pulled out on each side, Isabel will not say to her friends, who would know what she meant. *Then I did it down and combed forward over her shoulders, with just a little of it in a French braid. Then I pinned it back on the sides and tried some of this mousse she had so it would get a little bit more wavy. Then I tried brushing it straight back and putting on this kind of tiara thing she had, but she didn't like that. Finally, she decided she wanted the twist back, but softer in the front, so I did that. And then she took out this whole enormous bag of makeup—I mean, she must have had a hundred different things. And she did her eyes with two different colors of eyeliner, and a whole set of shadow, and mascara—oh, and she curled her lashes.*

She has my cell phone number, Lucy will not say that night to Greg, as they go out to dinner together, just the two of them, leaving the children with a familiar sitter. An occasional Saturday evening treat, by no means a weekly event. They will go to an expensive Japanese restaurant in Brookline and eat somewhat rococo sushi and more substantial buckwheat noodles, and Lucy, as she always does, will push the wasabi envelope until her sinuses expand and open out with pain and pleasure. Lucy will, in fact, give Greg a very brief outline of her day with Isabel, the drive to the Cape, and she will manage to fit in a light account of Delia—that she knew Delia was there, that they stopped off at the motel to make sure everything was okay, because her kids had to go back to the foster mother in Boston, and everything *was* okay, and then they went in search of lobster rolls, and walked along this beautiful beach, and had ice cream at this totally adorable place, and drove back to Boston without ever seeing any traffic, and Isabel was great all day.

What will Lucy do tomorrow, if Delia calls? Calls to say God only knows what—*This guy took all my money and all my stuff, what should I do, Dr. Lucy?* Or maybe, *This guy says he knows someone who owns a recording studio in New York and so I'm going there with him, Dr. Lucy.* Or maybe just, *Dr. Lucy, I want my babies back, why did they take them away?* What will Lucy do? She could turn off her cell phone, of course, but she won't. She could tell herself, which is probably true, that Delia has a variety of other people she could just as well call, that Delia is most likely to call whichever numbers are showing up on her cell phone's recent memory, whoever called her last, which may well, by tomorrow, no longer be Lucy at all. In fact, Lucy thinks, recovering enough to go for yet a little more wasabi, it all may in fact depend on what kind of memory function Delia's cell phone has, on how many incoming calls it can record.

As I said, this whole story depends on cell phone technology—why shouldn't that continue to drive it? Why shouldn't it be a question of what your cell phone can remember and what is beyond its ability? Why shouldn't it be up to Delia's cell phone, not up to Delia, whether tomorrow, after the adventures of tonight, she will call for help to Lucy again, or to someone else? If her rotten boyfriend has been calling her and calling her, maybe that will be the number she dials. Maybe the new investigating social worker assigned to her case has a cell phone of his own, and maybe he's calling her to try to set up a time to meet. Maybe her great-aunt has begun to wonder what the hell is going on, ever since she told Delia to get the hell away from her house and never to come around any more begging for money. Or maybe there's someone new, or maybe there's someone old—Delia has a mother somewhere, in another state, and two half-sisters and a bunch of shadowy friends, and that counselor from Ruth's Refuge, and all the other counselors she's seen along the way. All sorts of people could call in to Delia's phone, good news, bad news, and in between.

"Will she be okay?" Isabel does ask her mother, as they wait for their lobster rolls. They are in a stand by the side of the road somewhere near Dennis—maybe the next town over. The seafood stand is quiet—it's a little late in the day for lunch, it's a little early in the season for tourists. The counter is run by a tall, thin teenage boy, with bad skin and a remarkably sweet smile; he smiled at Isabel, when they came in, and she found herself smiling back. Lucy embarrassed her daughter—of course—by asking whether the lobster rolls were good—just like her parents, always treating every side-of-the-road opportunity like some kind of gourmet adventure, asking advice on lobster rolls, for heaven's sake. What's the guy supposed to say—no, they're lousy? But he smiled again—right at Isabel, even though Lucy had asked the question, and he said, "The lobster rolls are fantastic. We make them fresh, we use the best lobsters we can get, we toast the rolls perfectly—it will be the best lobster roll you've ever had, I promise." Like he was promising it to Isabel, directly, and so even though when her mother first asked that stupid question, Isabel was thinking she would order a hamburger, or a grilled cheese sandwich, of course she didn't. She smiled back at the boy and she said she would have a lobster roll.

And then she found herself sitting at one of the four picnic tables with her mom, the two of them waiting while the boy toasted their rolls, while he opened a refrigerator and took out a square metal tub of lobster meat, and a smaller tub of butter, while he arranged two paper plates, two plastic forks carefully rolled in napkins. And Isabel, her voice soft, asked her mother, "Will she be okay?"

Lucy looked at her across the picnic table, and Isabel could see that her mother was trying to decide whether to lie to her. Or maybe how much to lie. Or maybe which particular lie to tell.

"I don't know, honey," Lucy said finally. "In lots of ways, of course she won't—she's just had her three children taken into a foster home, one of them is in the hospital, she's pregnant again—I mean, how could she be less okay? She doesn't have any money and she doesn't have any sense. She could go sing in this place tonight and she could go home with anyone—anyone at all. Someone who would hurt her or someone who would take her money or—"

Lucy stops. Isabel knows there are some possibilities that she isn't getting to hear, and she's grateful. Lucy takes a deep breath.

"Two lobster rolls!" the boy calls out, and Lucy swings around on her picnic table bench and goes to get them, leaving Isabel both a little bit disappointed—because she would have liked to go get them—and a little bit glad—because she doesn't have to go get them.

Isabel can hear her mother thanking the boy, telling him the lobster rolls look beautiful. She would never have been able to do that, she knows, she would have probably not been able to look at him, even, she would have mumbled thanks and worried she would drop something as she gathered up two plates and two rolled napkins. Her mother, as usual, is cheerfully willing to go back and ask for a Diet Coke and a bottle of water.

"And yet," Lucy says finally, holding her lobster roll up and admiring it before she takes a bite, "I have to say that in other ways, Delia usually does seem to be all right. I mean, she'll keep on thinking that any day now, she's going to become a movie star, you know? She doesn't get up sad in the morning, whatever else you want to say about her—I mean, something seems to protect her. She kind of keeps rolling. And maybe, you never know, maybe she'll come back to Boston to be near her kids, and this time she'll have a social worker who knows how to make things happen, and she'll put her life together." Lucy takes a big bite of the lobster roll. "God, that's good," she says, softly.

And Isabel, as she takes a more delicate, careful bite of her own buttery lobster, does actually understand that if her mother is lying, is making things up, it is not purely for Isabel's benefit. Isabel looks past her mother's shoulder, at the boy behind the counter, who is wiping off the soda machines with a cloth. He meets her gaze and smiles at her, as if he is asking a question, and Isabel nods emphatically. She points to her lobster roll and smiles and nods again, and the boy's smile broadens.

Or someone who would pimp her, or someone who would infect her with HIV, Lucy manages not to say to her daughter. Not in the seafood stand, and not as they walk along the beach, bent slightly into the wind. The ocean sparkles, and Lucy thinks of the whitecaps on the sign at the Sea Breeze Motel, thinks of that motel lady —or her husband—carefully refreshing their sign for the new season with blue and white paint. She puts an arm around her daughter, as they trudge along the sand, and Isabel doesn't pull away. *Call me,* Lucy wants to say, *if you're ever in any kind of trouble. Any kind at all. Call me and I'll come.* Instead she says, trying to keep it light, "Isabel, you know you're named for the woman who adopted me?"

"Your sixth-grade teacher," Isabel says.

"Her name was Ina, but she wished it was Isabel. She thought it was a beautiful and dramatic name."

"I like it, too," Isabel says.

"The air tastes so good here," Lucy says. And everything else, too—the light is so beautiful as the sky changes, as late afternoon begins to look a little bit golden, a little bit like evening. Could it be that Delia is safer here than she would be in the city? "Want to hear a few lines of *Oliver Twist,* Isabel? About the city at night?"

"This is from when you were in that play? When you were my age?"

"And I was the narrator," Lucy says, "because I was the only one who could memorize long speeches. Listen: 'Midnight had come upon the crowded city. The palace, the night-cellar, the jail, the madhouse: the chambers of birth and death, of health and sickness, the rigid face of the corpse and the calm sleep of the child: midnight was upon them all.'"

Well, not midnight yet, but time to go back soon, Lucy thinks; she and Greg have a babysitter coming; they're going out to dinner. What will she tell Greg about this afternoon, she wonders—or will Isabel fill him in? Will he think she was crazy, dragging their daughter along into something like this?

The ocean is full of tiny whitecaps, sunlit and bright, and the breeze is indeed full of salt. And whatever else, Delia's children are safe for the evening and the night and for tomorrow. Not permanently rescued, never that, but pulled from danger for the moment. You do what you can. And maybe tonight Delia in her red dress and her hair done up by Isabel will sing at the Windmill Lounge and people will clap for her and she will go to sleep, alone and safe and happy in the Sea Breeze Motel. Maybe. And Isabel doesn't pull away as they walk down the beach together.

If you are ever in any kind of trouble, call me. Find a way to call me. Call me from anywhere. I want to see your number flashing on my phone, I want to know we are connected. I will always answer, I will always hear, I will always come. Look what the phones can do, nowadays. Look how that can change the story. And the right connection at the right moment is all it takes.